the Forbidden Wish

Jessica Khoury

the Forbidden Wish

razor
bill

An Imprint of Penguin Random House

Khoury

razOr
bill

An Imprint of Penguin Random House
Penguin.com

ISBN: 978-1-59514-767-7

Printed in the United States of America

1 3 5 7 9 10 8 6 4 2

Interior design: Eric Ford

114164000

For Papa

الافضل في العالم

مع كل حبي

Chapter One

I SENSE THE BOY the moment he sets foot in the cave.

For the first time in centuries, I stir.

I am smoke in the lamp, and I curl and stretch, shaking off the lethargy of five hundred years. I feel I have half turned to stone. The sound of his footstep rattles me like a clap of thunder, and I bolt fully awake.

I push against the sides of the lamp, calling out to him, but of course he cannot hear. He is just a common human boy. He cannot hear the cry of a jinni, a lamp spirit, a granter of wishes.

The boy is alone, and I sense his cautious footsteps as he crosses the threshold of the hidden cavern. I reach out with my sixth sense, following him as he steps down the narrow stair cut into the sandstone, his fingers trailing along an ancient wall carved with symbols, their meanings lost to time. How strange it is, Habiba, after my long solitude, to feel his presence here: like a light at the bottom of the dark, dark sea.

I reach as far as I can, sensing his quiet breath, his hammering heart. Who is he? How did he find this place? He is just a boy, a moment in time that will soon pass. I have known a thousand and one like him. I will know a thousand and one more. He is nothing. I tell myself this, so that I will not hope for him. I am not allowed to hope. I am forbidden a wish of my own. And so I will not think of the world above, of the open sky, of the fresh air and the light of day. I will not show how madly, deeply, desperately I want the boy to carry my lamp out of this accursed darkness. Instead, I fold and unfold, I swirl and I curl, waiting with bated breath. My sixth sense is blurred, like watching fish swim in a rippling pool, and I must concentrate very hard to see him at all.

He carries a small torch, which he holds up as he stares into the great cavern, truly no cave at all but a vast, echoing hall, once part of a great palace lost long ago to war and time. Now it lies deep, deep in the desert, one ruin among many, buried beneath layers of sand and memories.

Columns tower over my intrepid visitor, holding up a ceiling lost in shadow. Carvings wind up the pillars: gaping lions, winged horses, dragons spitting fire. Jewels embedded in their eyes glow softly, as if watching the boy with silent malice, just as they once watched the bright and colorful people who lived here centuries ago, before their city sank into the sand. This place is haunted by ghosts, and I am one of them.

"By all the gods," the boy murmurs, his quiet words drifting through the enormous vault. He holds up his torch, and light spreads from him in a golden pool.

He is right to be awestruck. This is no ordinary hall but was once a sanctum deep inside the royal Nerubyan palace, where long ago, a beautiful young queen wished for a garden that had no equal, where she could rest and meditate.

It was one of the better wishes I've granted.

The floor is carpeted in delicate blades of grass, each carved from purest emerald. Low, spreading trees with leaves of jade glitter beneath a high domed ceiling studded with glowing diamonds, like stars in a night sky. From the trees hang fruit: ruby apples, golden lemons, amethyst plums, sapphire berries. They glint and gleam, millions of jewels cut with a precision no mortal art could match. Below in the grass glitter delicate blossoms of topaz and lapis lazuli. You must look closely to realize they are not real trees or real flowers but priceless stones all.

The boy walks as one in a dream, not blinking, not breathing. Not a single living plant is to be seen, and yet it seems more alive than any garden in the world above. For the last few centuries, these jeweled fruits have been my constant and sole companions. The greatest treasure in all the world, as comfortless as light to the blind.

The boy lingers too long.

The air is thick with old jinn magic, a vestige of the great war fought here many centuries ago. It clings to the walls, drips from the ceiling, puddles between the golden roots of the jewel trees. It fills the empty ruins already half sunk into the desert, the long crumbling corridors that branch like roots, linking the towers and halls and storehouses. The city is a breath away from collapsing entirely. For five hundred years this magic has churned and coiled in its chambers, building up like gas beneath the earth, waiting for a spark to set it on fire.

This boy is that spark. He will trip a trap set long, long ago, triggering an explosion of pent-up magic, and the desert will bury us both. I will be lost, a myth, a dream. Trapped forever with myself in this prison of sand and magic. I cannot imagine a more terrifying doom. I thought I had resigned myself to this fate long ago, when it seemed no one would ever find me. Now I know this to be untrue, and that hope has pulsed deep within me like a dormant seed, waiting to flourish at the first sign of escape.

But then the enchantments twang like the strings of a lute, and my fragile hope grows cold. A wind rises from the darkness, rustles through the stone leaves, until the entire cavern echoes with their clatter. The trap has been sprung.

As if sensing this, the boy hastens onward, past the beautiful trees and flowers, leaping over a stream in which lumps of gold and silver sparkle. The chamber grows lighter as the diamonds above swell with light. It is blinding, harsh. The jeweled garden glitters with razor-sharp edges and points, beautiful but deadly. The boy dodges leaves that cut the air like knives, hissing when one slices the back of his hand.

And at last he arrives at the hill at the back of the enchanted garden, and there he stops beneath the tossing branches of a willow tree hewn from copper, dripping with leaves of emerald. He twists a ring on his finger, his eyes widening as they settle on the lamp.

It sits on a throne-like chair wrought from iron and rubies, the metal twisted to resemble rose vines. Once, the queen of this city would sit here for hours, reading and meditating, but that was a very long time ago. Now there is only the lamp, gleaming in the diamond light. Inside, I expand, filling every inch of the small space with my glittering smoke, urging him to hurry. I pulse with nervous impatience that this chance at escape will slip through my fingers. Never has my lamp felt smaller.

The boy climbs the hill, panting for breath, sighing a little when he reaches the throne. For a moment he stands there, brushing the dust from his hands, his eyes fixed on the lamp.

The cave shudders. Sand trickles down the walls, tinkles across the piles of golden coin. The enchantments hum, and the jewels on the trees begin to rattle. The boy doesn't seem to notice. He is transfixed by the lamp.

"So this is it," he breathes.

He reaches out, and I shift from smoke to fire with excitement. When his fingers touch the bronze sides of the lamp, a crackle of energy pulses through me. I can feel his heartbeat through his fingertips, wild and strong.

"What are you?" he whispers. "Why have you been calling to me?"

As if dazed, he runs his fingers along the bronze, his palm tracing the curve of the spout, and at his touch, his human heat courses through the walls.

I simmer and expand. I gather and bunch and ready myself, red smoke turning gold.

The boy rubs the lamp.

And I answer.

I pour upward through the long dark tunnel of the spout. I am a funnel of smoke, a whirlwind of fire. I open myself and multiply, swelling into a great cloud over the boy's head. I press a thousand smoky hands against the stone ceiling of the cave. I roll a thousand fiery eyes and stretch a thousand glittering legs. I unfold and unfold and unfold. How *good* it feels to be out! I crackle with energy and excitement, my blood lightning and my breath thunder.

I could stretch for hours, relishing the space around me. But because time is short, I shrink and harden, assembling my wayward tendrils. For the first time in five hundred years, I assume the form I love most.

The form of you, Roshana, my Habiba. Sister of my heart. You of the pure heart and the merry laugh, who taught me joy and called me friend. A princess among men, and a queen among her people.

I dress myself with your shape. I take your hair, long and black as the river of night. I take your eyes, large and sharp and glittering. I take your face, slender and strong. Your beautiful body is mine. Your hands, swift and nimble, and your feet, graceful and quick. I wear your face and pretend your heart is mine as well.

And at last, the smoke clears away, and I stand in the garden I created for you. Human to the eye, inside I'm nothing but smoke and power. I stretch and sigh, and slowly, slowly smile at the boy.

He is lying on his back, eyes wide, mouth gaping. Once, twice, thrice his mouth opens and shuts, before he finally chokes out, "Bloody gods!"

This Amulen is young, perhaps seventeen or eighteen summers. His poor thin robes betray a body that carries not an ounce of fat. He is bone and blood and smooth, hard muscle, a boy who has stolen for survival, no doubt, from the fruit vendors and camel drovers and the gutters. Who knows that each day is not a gift but a prize that is to be seized. "You're a—you're a—"

Say it, boy. Demon of fire. Monster of smoke. Devil of sand and ash. Servant of Nardukha, Daughter of Ambadya, the Nameless, the Faceless, the Limitless. Slave of the Lamp. *Jinni.*

"... a *girl!*" he finishes.

For a second, I can only blink at him, but I recover quickly.

"Tremble, mortal!" I declare, letting my voice echo through the cavern. "I am the Slave of the Lamp, the mighty Jinni of Ambadya. I hold the power to grant your desires thrice. Command, and I your slave shall answer, son of man, for such is Nardukha's law."

Ah, Nardukha, mighty King of the Jinn. My Master of Masters. Damn *his* smoke-and-fire bones.

"A jinni," the boy murmurs. "It all makes sense now."

He pauses as a string of sand trickles onto his shoulder from above. He brushes it away and steps aside, but it begins to fall all around him. The floor slides, jewels rattling and rolling. He stumbles.

"What's happening?" he asks breathlessly as he climbs to his feet.

"These ruins are old. The magic that fills them is older still, and it will kill you very soon." No point in blunting the truth. "But if you wish for your life, I will save you."

He grins, cheeky as a crow. "Why wish for it when I can run? Can you keep up with me, jinni girl?"

At that, I can only laugh, and in an instant bind myself into the form of a hawk and begin winging across the treetops. The branches sway and crack in the gale that sweeps around the room. Jeweled fruit crashes to the ground. The air is filled with the sound of breaking glass and roaring wind.

The boy slides down the hill and sprints through the grass. Branches reach for him, trying to ensnare his arms and neck, but I pull them away with my talons. Shadowy hands reach from the stream and grab his ankles. I beat them away with my wings.

The boy is fast, but is he fast enough? I lead him over and around the piles of treasure, through arches made of glittering, buckling sand. I will credit my young master this: He is quick, and he does not surrender easily.

The exit is not far now. Sand falls in sheets, so thick it beats the boy down and drives him to his knees. He chokes and coughs, his mouth filling with sand. Still he fights forward, his legs straining to bear him up again. He presses on with his eyes shut, hands groping like a blind man's.

With a swirl of smoke, I shift from hawk to girl, dropping to the ground beside him. I take his hand and pull him along, trying to ignore the warmth of his touch. I have not touched a human in . . . oh, so very long, Habiba. His fingers tighten around mine, his palm dry and gritty with sand, his veins pulsing with life. As always happens when I touch a human, his heartbeat overwhelms me. It pounds at my ears and echoes mockingly in the emptiness of my chest, where there is only smoke instead of a heart.

There! A gaping doorway, half sunk in sand, which once led to your throne room, Habiba, but that now leads to a dark desert sky bright with stars. The teak door that hung there has long since rotted away, and the stones are chipped and dull, but after five hundred years of lonely darkness, it is the most beautiful thing I have ever seen.

The magic makes one last effort to stop us, and this trap is the most dangerous of all. Sand turns to flame, and the flames rush to us hungrily from the belly of the great chamber. But I can taste the sweet night air, and I redouble my efforts to get the boy out alive. If I fail, I know I will never have another chance to escape.

"Faster!" I urge, and the boy glances back at the fire, then scrambles madly on. He moves so quickly he passes me, and now I am the one being tugged forward. The fire licks my heels. I turn to smoke, and the boy's fingers close in on the space where my hand was.

"What are you doing?" he yells.

"Go!" I expand and shift again, becoming a rippling wall of water, pressing against the rush of the flames, holding them at bay. Wind and fire and water and sand—and sky sky sky!

The boy is first to emerge. He leaps out of the door and rolls, clutching my lamp to his stomach. I turn to smoke the moment I am in the clear, a great billow of glittering violet. Flames spew across the sand, like a thousand demon hands rending the earth, grasping for a handhold in the world. Fiery claws rake the desert and scratch the sky all around us.

The boy winces and holds up a hand as a blast of heat blows over him. Tendrils of smoke curl from the tips of his hair where the fire singes it. For a terrible moment, we are entirely encased by flames, and I surround the boy, choking him with my smoke but saving his body from the fire.

And then the magic finally collapses, a blaze that has run out of fuel. Fire turns into the sand it came from and falls in a sparkling white mist around us. The desert swirls around the door and sinks into it, until at last the opening is drowned by sand.

All around us rise the ruins of Neruby, once a vast, sparkling city. Over the centuries it has fallen apart, looking like the skeletal remains of a long-dead beast. Now, those ruins begin to rumble and shake. Massive stones fall from crumbling towers, and walls shatter into pieces. The desert heaves like the sea, swallowing the ruins stone by stone, dunes tossing this way and that. Slowly, loudly, the city sinks beneath the desert, crackling as the last of the old jinn magic burns away.

The last time I saw the city from above ground, it stood proud beneath a sky filled with black smoke, its air clanging with the sound of fighting and the cries of the dying, both human and jinn. Many died that final day. I should have been one of them.

Now the city sinks once and for all, taking the dead with it.

On his knees, the boy watches with wide eyes, and I swirl above him. Soon the last tip of the last tower is swallowed by the earth, and the city—once the greatest in the world, the city of kings and conquerors—is gone.

The desert ripples, throwing the boy onto his back. I shift to human form and stand beside him, staring at the ground that held me captive for centuries. When the dust clears, there is nothing but a glinting blue stretch of sand, pure and virgin, coursed with wind ripples. The only evidence that there ever was a garden of wonders, the only testimony to the great city lost beneath the sand, is a single pale coin that lies on the surface, winking at the moon.

And, of course, there is me.

One: The Thief

After the battle, the Queen and her warriors entered the throne hall of the vanquished Akbanids, where they found displayed on pedestals of marble all the great treasures of that kingdom. And the Queen, having little interest in the jewels and gold, passed all these by, until she came at last to the center of the room. And there, on a sheet of silk, sat a Lamp of humble aspect, wrought in bronze, and without a drop of oil inside.

With great reverence, the Queen took up the Lamp, and at her touch, from it rose with a glittering cloud of smoke a terrible Jinni. And all who looked upon her quailed and trembled, but the Queen stood tall and trembled not. Yet in her eyes was a look of wonder.

"I am the Jinni of the Lamp," pronounced the Jinni. "Three wishes shall ye have. Speak them, and they shall be granted, yea, even the deepest desires of thine heart. Wilt thou have treasure? It is thine."

And the Queen replied, "Silver and gold I have."

"Wilt thou have kingdoms and men to rule over?" asked the Jinni. "Ask, and it is thine."

And the Queen replied, "These I have also."

"Wilt thou have youth everlasting, never to age, never to sicken?" asked the Jinni. "Ask, and it is thine."

"Does not the poet say that hairs of gray are more precious than silver, and that in youth lies folly?"

The Jinni bowed low before the Queen. "I see you are wise, O Queen, and not easily fooled. So what would you ask of me, for I am thy slave."

"Give me thy hand," said the Queen, "and let us be friends. For does not the poet say, one true-hearted friend is worth ten thousand camels laden with gold?"

This the Jinni pondered, before replying, "The poet also says, woe to the man who befriends the jinn, for he shakes hands with death."

—From the *Song of the Fall of Roshana,*
Last Queen of Neruby
by Parys zai Moura,
Watchmaiden and Scribe to Queen Roshana

Chapter Two

WE ARE ADRIFT ON A SEA of moonlit sand, the silence as infinite as the space between the stars. The night is calm and deceptively peaceful, the city that stood here just moments ago nothing more than a memory.

Inside, I am roiling with apprehension and dread. Will the jinn know I have escaped? How long until they come running? Their fiery hands could close on me at any moment, their eyes red with fury. I wait for them to drag me down and chain me in the darkness once more, but they do not come.

I lift my head and let out a slow breath.

No jinn are racing through the sky. No alarm bells clang across the desert. And at that moment, it strikes me fully: *I have escaped. I have well and truly escaped.*

We are surrounded by the sand of the great Mahali Desert, endless sand, sand in hills and heaps and valleys, stained pale blue by the moon. The sheer immensity of empty space staggers me after my long confinement. As the boy catches his breath, I turn a full circle and breathe in the desert night. I had long ago given up hoping that I would ever see the sky again. And such a sky! Stars like dust, stars of every color—blue, white, red—the jewels of the gods displayed across black silk.

I long to stretch myself out, to crawl smokily across that glorious moon-blue sand, spread myself like water, a hand on each horizon. And then up, up, up to the stars, to press my face against the sky and feel the cool kiss of the moon.

I feel the boy's gaze on me, and I turn to him. He is still lying on the sand, propped on one arm, staring at me like a fisherman who has unexpectedly caught a shark in his nets.

I return his gaze with equal candor, adding him up. His stubbled jaw is strong and just slightly crooked, his copper eyes large and expressive, his lips full. A small, cheap earring hangs from his left earlobe. A handsome boy growing into a man's body, already powerfully built. Were he a prince or a renowned warrior, he would have entire harems vying for his attention. As it is, his rough beauty is hidden in his poorly cut clothing. I pick out the scars on his hands and his legs. The gods have been negligent with this one.

With a sigh, I say, "You look like you've been kicked by a horse. Here, get up."

I offer my hand, but he scrambles away, his eyes wild and wary.

For a moment, he and I regard one another silently beneath the pulsing stars. His ragged breathing is laced with fatigue, but he is as tense as a cornered cat, ready to flee, waiting to see what I will do. My head is still spinning from the suddenness of what's happened: the first human I've seen in five hundred years, the mad race to escape the collapsing ruins, the vastness of the desert after so many centuries confined to my lamp. I sway a little, taking a moment to sort out earth from sky.

"I cannot hurt you," I say. My hands clench at my sides, and I force my fingers to open disarmingly. "The same magic that binds us together prevents me from harming you. Don't be afraid."

"I'm not afraid."

"Have you never seen a jinni before?"

The boy clears his throat, his eyes fixed on mine. "No, but I've heard stories of them."

Turning my back to him, I look up at the stars. "Of course you have. Tales of ghuls, I'm sure, who devour souls and wear the skins of their prey. Of ifreet, all fire and flame and no brains at all. Or perhaps you mean the maarids, small and sweet, until they drown you in their pools."

He nods slowly and climbs to his feet, brushing sand from his palms. "And the Shaitan, most powerful of all."

A chill runs down my spine. "Ah, of course."

"So are they true? All these stories?"

Turning to face him, I pause before replying. "As the poets say, stories are truth told through lies."

"So are you going to devour my soul?" he asks, as if it is a challenge. "Or drown me? What sort of jinni are you?"

With a curl of smoke, I shift into a white tiger and crouch before him, my tail flicking back and forth. He watches in amazement, recoiling a bit at the sight of my golden eyes and extended claws.

"What are you?" he whispers.

Should I tell him what—*who*—I really am? That even now, legions of angry jinn—ghuls, maarids, a dozen other horrors—could be racing toward us? If he has any wits about him, he'll abandon my lamp and put as many leagues between us as he can . . . which would leave me completely helpless. At least while he holds the lamp, I have a fighting chance.

"How did you find me?" I ask. So many centuries, and this hapless young man is the only one to have found my prison. After that final battle, after you fell, Habiba, my kin threw me into the garden I had created for you. *Sit in the dark and rot, traitor*, they said. And for so many years, I was certain that would be my fate. But then, surpassing all hope, the boy appeared.

"I'm from Parthenia." At my blank expression, he adds, "Two weeks by horseback, to the west. On the coast. As for how I found you . . . I was led here. By this."

He pulls from his finger the ring he'd been twisting earlier. He holds it out on his palm, and after a slight hesitation, I pick it up. A tingle in my fingers tells me the ring was forged in magic. There is something familiar about it, but I am certain I have never seen it before. The band is plain gold but for the symbols carved into the inside, symbols that have been blurred by time and fire.

"And you say it led you to me?" I straighten and stare hard at him.

He takes the ring from my palm. "When I . . . um, *found* it, it began whispering to me. I know it sounds insane, but I couldn't get it to stop. Even when I took it off and tried to throw it away, I kept hearing it. So I thought, why not see what it wanted?"

"What did it say?"

"It wasn't so much words . . ." He closes his hand around the ring, looking haunted. "I just knew it wanted me to follow it, that it would lead me to something important. I didn't know what. Only that I *had* to find out, like it'd put a spell on me or something.

When I found your lamp, it went silent for the first time in weeks, so I guess . . . it was leading me to you."

I wonder if he is truly as naïve as he seems. Perhaps he is a simple pauper who stumbled across an ancient and powerful talisman without understanding its true worth. The ring is enchanted, meant to lead the bearer to me. But who created it? It is very old, likely made around the time I was abandoned by my kin in the jeweled garden five hundred years ago. Why hasn't it been used until now, and why by such an unlikely individual?

"So you followed a magic ring all the way to Neruby, just out of curiosity?"

"Well," he says gruffly, glancing aside, "it's not as simple as that. Let's just say I'm not the only one interested in the ring. I knew it would lead to something valuable, and finding valuables happens to be my . . ." His voice fades and his eyes grow wide. "Wait a minute. What did you say?"

I frown. "I said it's strange that mere curiosity—"

"No, not that. You said this city was called Neruby."

"Of course," I reply.

He sucks in a breath, taking a half step backward, and he scans me head to toe as if just seeing me for the first time. When he next speaks, his voice is tight, excited, breathless.

"I know who you are," he says.

Something about his tone causes my heart of smoke to flicker in response, and I throw my guard up. "Oh? And who, O boy of Parthenia, am I?"

He nods to himself, his eyes alight. "You're *her*. You're *that* jinni. Oh, gods. Oh, great bleeding gods! You're the one who started the war!"

"Excuse me?"

"You're the jinni who betrayed that famous queen—what was her name? Roshana? She was trying to bring peace between the jinn and the humans, but you turned on her and started the Five Hundred Wars."

I turn cold. I want him to stop, but he doesn't.

"I've heard the stories," he says. "I've heard the songs. They call you the Fair Betrayer, who enchanted humans with your . . ." He pauses to swallow. "Your beauty. You promised them everything, and then you ruined them."

A thousand and one replies vie for my tongue, but I swallow them all, bury them deep, deep in my smoky heart. Was it too much to hope, Habiba, that five hundred years would be enough to bury the past? They sing songs of us, old friend. This *boy*, in his rags and poverty, knows who I am, knows who you were, knows what I did to you. And how can I deny it? Beneath our feet, the ruins of your city lie. He saw them with his own eyes. And why should I hide who I truly am? *The Fair Betrayer.* The name fits. I add it to the long list of other names I have collected over the years like flotsam in my wake, many of them far less flattering.

Letting out a long breath, I shrug one shoulder. "So what now? Will you toss me away? Bury me again?"

He laughs, a cold, sharp laugh. "Throw you away? When you can grant me three wishes? Would I throw away a bag of gold just because I found it in a pile of dung?" He winces. "I didn't mean . . . It's just all so . . . I need to think."

I watch as he paces in a tight circle, his hands raking his hair over and over, until it nearly stands on end. When he finally stops, I feel dizzy just from watching him. I'd nearly forgotten how frenzied you humans are, always bouncing here and there, like bees drunk on nectar. And this boy is wilder than most, his energy radiating outward, warming the air around him.

He seems to arrive at some conclusion at last, because he stops his mad pacing and faces me squarely, his jaw hardening in resolution. I have to bend my head back a little to meet his gaze.

"So. Three wishes. Anything I want?"

"Anything in this world, if you're willing to pay the price."

His eyes narrow. "Tell me about this price."

With a sigh, I conjure a small flame in my hand and let it dance across my fingers, like a charlatan's coin. "Every wish has a price, O Master. Seldom do you—or I—know what that price is, until it has already been paid. Perhaps you'll wish for great wealth, only to find it stolen away by thieves. Perhaps you'll wish for a mighty dragon to carry you through the sky, only to be devoured by it when you land. Wishes have a way of twisting themselves, and there is nothing more dangerous than getting your heart's desire. The question is, are you willing to gamble? How much are you willing to lose? What are you willing to risk everything for?"

At that, his eyes harden, and I see that he knows exactly what he wants. He turns and begins walking, his steps sliding in the sand. I follow behind, my eyes on his tattered cloak as it snaps in the wind that whips across the dunes. As I wait for him to reply, I pass my little flame from hand to hand.

"You destroyed a monarchy once," he says after a moment, his voice low and dangerous, a dark current beneath a still sea. "I want you to help me do it again."

I close my fingers, my flame disappearing in a puff of smoke. "So. You're some kind of revolutionary, then?"

Again with that short, bitter laugh. He keeps walking, his words carried over his shoulder by the wind. "A revolution of one, that's me."

"Very well." I run ahead of him, turning and walking backward so that I can look him in the eye. "What is your first wish, Master?"

"Well, to begin with, stop calling me *Master*, as if I were some kind of godless slaver. I have a name."

Names are dangerous. They're personal. And the last time I got personal with a human, it ended badly. The evidence is buried just a few spans beneath my feet.

"I don't care to know it." Better that way.

"If I tell you my name," he says, "you must tell me yours."

I stop walking. "I don't have a name."

He stops beside me, watching me with his head cocked a bit, like a chess player waiting for me to make a move. "I don't believe you."

How can one so mortal be so positively infuriating? "Don't your songs mention my name?"

His lips slide into a half grin, and he resumes walking, the wind blowing his hair across his face. "Not any you'd like to hear, I think."

He leads and I follow, a boy and a jinni striding across the moon-blue dunes. Beneath our feet, the sand shifts treacherously. Halfway up a particularly steep hill, it suddenly gives way, and I cry out involuntarily as I slide backward.

But suddenly a hand grasps mine, holding me in place, though I have already half shifted to smoke to catch myself.

"Careful, Smoky," the boy says, pulling me to the top of the dune. "You haven't granted me any wishes yet. I can't have you disappearing on me already."

"My name's not *Smoky.*" I yank my hand away. His touch still burns, leaving me shaken, the echo of his heartbeat resounding through me. Looking away, I shake sand from my robes. I've transformed my clothes from rich silks to sturdy white cotton, so that I blend into the desert.

"It is until you give me something better."

"Where are we going?"

"Why? Bored already? I'd think you'd want to stretch your legs after lying around in that cave for—how long were you in there, anyway?"

"Since the war ended. Five hundred years ago."

With a whistle, he slides down the other side of the dune, and I transform into a small silver cat and spring after him, shifting back into a girl at the bottom.

He stands still for a moment, watching me. He has tied the lamp to his belt, and his hand strokes it absently. It's an affectation common to Lampholders, and he's picked it up already.

"How old are you?" he asks.

A cool wind flows between the dunes, pulling my hair across my face and ruffling his patched cloak.

"Three thousand and one thousand more."

"Great gods," he says softly. "But you look no older than me."

"Looks are deceiving." I don't tell him that the face I wear is stolen, its possessor five hundred years dead. Of course, I have a face of my own, one slightly younger than yours. I was seventeen the day I was first put into the lamp, when I ceased aging and became the timeless slave I am now. I have little desire to wear that face anymore. It is the one that betrayed you to your death, Habiba. The face of a monster.

At times I feel as old as the stars, but mostly I feel just the same as I did that day—lost, small, and afraid. But I keep that to myself. I square my chin and meet his gaze challengingly.

"Strange," he murmurs.

"What's strange?"

"It's just . . ." He pushes his hair back. "You're not like the jinni in the stories and songs. That jinni was a monster. You seem . . . different."

Then he turns and begins trudging up the next dune, wrapping his cloak around him to keep the wind from tearing at it.

I stand still a moment longer, watching him. "Zahra."

He pauses and looks over his shoulder. "What?"

"My name," I stammer. "I mean . . . one of them. You can call me Zahra."

He turns around fully, his grin as wide and as bright as the moon. "I'm Aladdin."

Chapter Three

WE WALK FOR TWO MORE HOURS before Aladdin finally says, "We're here."

He drops to his hands and knees and crawls slowly up the side of a dune, and when we reach the top, Aladdin goes flat and motions for me to do the same. Slowly, cautiously, he peers over the crest of windswept sand, and his expression turns grim.

"There," he murmurs.

I look over and see a small camp tucked in a sandy depression, out of the wind. Several soldiers sit around a small fire of burning horse dung, their mounts hobbled nearby. One finely dressed young man stands alone between two tents, his shoulders hunched as he studies a map by the firelight.

"That's him. Darian rai Aruxa, prince of Parthenia."

"Friend of yours?"

Aladdin snorts and slides down a bit, until the sandy ridge blocks the camp from view. "He's been tracking me for two weeks, ever since I left Parthenia. Not that I can blame him, really. He's after this." Aladdin tosses the ring and catches it with one hand.

I raise a brow. "You stole it from him."

His eyes are hard as diamonds, glittering in the starlight. A change passes over his face, and he suddenly seems older, harder, angrier. Like a cloud crossing the sun, so fleeting I nearly miss it, but it turns me cold.

"Zahra, if I wished for someone to die, could you do it?"

Outwardly, I am stone, but inside I rock like a stormy sea. I loathe this wish more than almost any other. It is cruel and cowardly, and I reevaluate this boy thief. There is a darkness in him I hadn't seen. "I could do it, but the price will be high."

He swallows, his eyes deep and haunted. "What's the price?"

"I don't know. But you'll find out soon enough, I think. Will you wish this Darian dead?"

"He deserves it," Aladdin whispers.

"Then what are you waiting for? Go on, *Master.* Say the words. Wish a man's life away."

He averts his gaze. "You don't have to put it like that."

"Isn't it the truth?" I stand up and walk to the top of the dune, sending a river of sand running down the side. Aladdin, panicking, gestures for me to get down.

So he wants to make a death wish, does he? Wants me to do his dirty work, taking out his enemies while he sits in the shadows? Not if I have anything to say about it. I stand in full view of the camp below and say loudly, "Here we are, Aladdin. Now is your chance. Say the words—it isn't hard. *I wish, I wish . . .*"

"Zahra! Get down!"

But it's too late. I've been seen. The men below start shouting, and their steel sings as they pull it from their sheaths. They call for me to stop.

Aladdin hurries to the top of the dune, bundling his cloak under one arm so that it doesn't tangle his legs. With his other hand he pulls the lamp from his belt.

"You insane creature!" He skids to a halt, cursing at the sight of the men as they hastily mount their horses. "And to think I was starting to *like* you!"

I sweep a hand through the air. "There he is. Your mortal enemy! So go on. Make the wish!"

"I—" He meets my eyes, his face drained of color.

"What are you *waiting* for?"

Below us, the men turn their horses toward us. They're led by the prince, who's wielding a curving scimitar.

"*Aladdin*. They're nearly on us! You'd better make up your mind!"

He looks from the soldiers to me, his mouth open but no wish on his tongue. Ignoring the men galloping toward us, I seize Aladdin's cloak and pull him close. His panicked gaze locks with mine.

"Decide," I say. "Decide *now*. What kind of man are you? Are you really the sort who wishes death on his enemies from the shadows?"

"I wish . . ." He stops, licks his lower lip.

"Zahra, get down!"

Aladdin throws himself across me, and an arrow that had been speeding toward my heart strikes him in the shoulder. With a cry he falls, sliding down the dune, and the lamp tumbles from his grasp.

In an instant, I lose control of my body. My flesh turns to smoke, and I am sucked through the air, pulled into the lamp's spout, and dumped at the bottom. There I swirl around and around, scarlet smoke, throwing my sixth sense as far and wide as I can.

My lamp has rolled to the bottom of the dune, near Aladdin. He scrambles toward me, and I feel the pain of his shoulder radiating from him in hot, angry spikes. But before he can reach me, they are upon us. With a pounding of hooves the riders swarm around us, their camels heaving and blowing foam. They are all indistinct shapes hovering around me, sensed rather than seen, as I push myself to my limits to follow the events as they rapidly unfold.

The riders circle us and shout over one another excitedly, maintaining a small distance from the lamp and herding Aladdin away from it. He curses them, and I sense him swaying with pain from his wounded shoulder.

"Silence!" thunders a voice.

The men halt their camels and fall quiet as one of the riders dismounts. I cannot sense his appearance, but I feel the vibration of his steps. When he speaks, his voice is young and melodic. "I will give you this, scum. You are slippery as a shadow. I might even offer you a job if I weren't about to cut your throat."

"Darian." Aladdin's tone is strained, but mockingly civil. "Took you long enough to catch up."

"That's *Prince* Darian, thief."

"What did your father say when he found out I stole your precious magic ring? Right off your *finger* as you slept! Hey, boys, did you know your prince snores like an old woman?"

Even through my bronze walls I can hear the loud smack as Darian backhands Aladdin, throwing him to the ground. I feel a surge of heat as my lamp is lifted from the sand. Curious fingers explore the bronze surface, tracing the sensual curve of the long tapered spout.

Darian sniffs, and his fingers tighten around the lamp. His pulse hammers at me, echoing through the small space. I huddle against the wall and press my hands over my ears. "For something so powerful and priceless, it's quite an ugly thing, isn't it?"

"It's worthless," says Aladdin. "Just an empty relic."

"For all the good it did you, it might as well be. Let's see . . . The stories always said . . ." He begins to rub the lamp, and as easily as exhaling I shift to smoke and stream out for the second time this night. My new master lets out a long, appreciative sigh as I swirl into the air, a muted display compared to my first one for Aladdin. I am a little disappointed in the boy of the streets for losing me so quickly.

I coalesce into a tiger as white as the moon, crouched on the sand before this Darian. He is not much older than Aladdin, but his face, though handsome, is rounder and softer.

Aladdin is down on one knee before him, his hand pressing his cloak to his shoulder. He has yanked out the arrow, and it lies on the sand beside him. Aladdin's face is pale, but his eyes burn. He watches me silently.

"Tremble, mortal," I say in a gravelly tiger voice, my eyes flickering away from the old master and to the new. "For I am the jinni of the Lamp—"

With a wild cry, Aladdin suddenly lunges up and makes a desperate grab for the lamp. Before he can make it, one of the other riders—the archer—swings his bow and clouts Aladdin on the ear, knocking him down again. Quick as a snake, Darian is on him, kicking him in the stomach and then roughly stepping on his injured shoulder. Aladdin hisses and seems to nearly faint, but hangs ruggedly on, trying to grab Darian's ankle with his other hand. The prince laughs at this feeble effort and kicks him again, this time in the chest. With a grunt, Aladdin curls up and spits blood on the sand.

I watch like a statue, telling myself it doesn't matter, that none of this matters, that I can't do anything anyway. And why should I feel sorry for this boy? I do not know him. I should not care. But I wince as Darian kicks him one last time just for spite.

He didn't make the wish.

They could kill him, but still he didn't make the death wish.

Then the prince stands over Aladdin, breathing heavily, his eyes going from me to the injured boy. He leans over, pulling the ring off Aladdin's finger. He tosses it high before catching it and slipping it into his pocket, and then he spits on Aladdin.

"I'll take that back, you dirty, thieving bastard." He grabs Aladdin by his shirtfront and hauls him to his knees. Aladdin's head lolls on his shoulders, but he manages to glare at the prince.

"Who told you about the ring?" Darian demands. "Why did it work for you and not me?"

Aladdin only laughs, though it sounds strangled. The fire does not fade from his eyes. Darian pulls a curved dagger from his sash and presses the blade against Aladdin's throat.

"Go on, then," Aladdin says through his teeth, his eyes blazing with defiance. "Do it. Get your hands dirty for once. But be careful. Your father's not here to clean up after you."

"You're not worth another minute of my time. Count yourself lucky, bastard. Nobody steals from me and gets off this easy." He digs the blade into Aladdin's neck, drawing blood, and I tense and look away. I have seen thousands of men die, Habiba, but murder always makes me feel cold and hollow. How cruel humans can be.

I am sad for this thief. His spirit is strong and wild, but it seems he is lost.

He doesn't have to be.

The thought comes out of nowhere, sounding so much like you I almost believe your ghost is standing behind me. I look back at the thief, struggling against the prince's blade.

There is something of you in him, Habiba. A certain unyielding steel. He took an *arrow* for me.

And you know I never could resist stirring up trouble.

I rise on all four paws and brace myself, even as my mind revolts. *What are you doing, you stupid, stupid jinni? You've been down this road before—you know this will end in disaster! Remember Roshana? Remember the war?*

But I'm committed now. I roar mightily at the prince, startling him enough that he lets go of Aladdin before he can slice the thief's veins. Quick as lightning, Aladdin throws himself backward, flinging sand into Darian's eyes. The prince cries out and stumbles, flailing blindly with the knife. His men shout and dash forward, but not before Aladdin snatches the lamp from Darian, dodging the prince's swinging blade.

I feel the power of possession shift from prince to thief, and I go dizzy. Changing masters so quickly is disorienting as my alliances reverse and the connection between master and jinni collapses and re-forms, until Aladdin and I are bound once more.

As a half dozen swords come swinging at his head, Aladdin cries out, "I wish to go home *now*!"

Chapter Four

FOR A MOMENT IT ALL FREEZES: The moonlight flashing on the swords swinging at Aladdin's neck. The prince's roar of anger. The wide, reckless hope in Aladdin's eyes.

In that eternity between heartbeats, I think.

I dream.

I create.

Time slips back into motion, and I rise from tiger to girl, dressed in crimson silk, my face veiled. I lift my hands. The blades deflect off thin air, bouncing away and throwing the men off balance. Ignoring them, I slide seamlessly into the next movement. The will of this boy thief flows in golden streams. It is the thread with which I weave, the colors with which I paint, the element with which I create.

Sand begins to rise from the ground. It coils and swirls, making Aladdin's robes flutter. I summon the wind and charm it, sending it spiraling around my astounded master. Into the air I weave the ancient songs of the people of Ghedda, who lie buried now beneath the cold ash of the Mountain of Tongues.

The force of the spiraling wind throws the prince's men wide, and they go sprawling on the ground. Darian falls to his knees and struggles to stay upright, a hand in front of his face as he snarls in rage.

I slip inside the whirlwind and stand facing Aladdin, who stares at me with eyes like twin moons. He is half dazed, the lamp clutched tightly in his hands. Blood runs down his neck and from the corner of his mouth.

Wishes are born in the will of men and women, and it is the true and pure source of power all humans hold. Few realize it is there at all. I remember your will, Habiba: You shone like the moon, a sly gleam in a dark sky, secret and intemperate. Aladdin burns like the sun, driving away every shadow and warming the sands. I draw on his will, holding it up like a torch in the dark, lighting the way. I close my eyes and follow the thread of his thoughts with my mind's eye.

I glimpse a dark street, puddles of moonlight on the cobblestones. The smell of salt and smoke, canvas awnings fluttering softly in the midnight wind. Less a point on a map and more a region of the soul, but it is a path I can follow.

I open my eyes and clap my hands once.

The desert bends away and the horizon draws near, and in a heartbeat, Darian and his soldiers vanish, left behind as Aladdin and I cross through impossible space. I draw the land up like fabric pinched between my fingers, and thread Aladdin and myself through like a sharp needle. Aladdin's eyes stay locked on mine, as his hair and cloak whip in the wind. Tiny grains of sand bead his lashes. He holds his breath, his body rigid, his hands clamped tightly around the lamp.

Without moving, we pass through desert and sky, through sand and stone, through a mountain rising spectrally in the dark. Mount Tissia. When last I saw it, half a millennium ago, it was bathed in the bloodlight of dawn. You and I stood on its summit, Habiba, and faced the vast armies of the jinn as they rushed to destroy us.

Then the mountain shrinks behind us and a city appears ahead, a twinkle of soft light on the edge of the vast Maridion Sea. Aladdin's Parthenia. The city is roughly egg-shaped, divided into districts by high walls and cut through the center by a river running from the northwest, toward the great River Qo and the mountain kingdoms beyond.

With a soft exhalation, I release what little magic is left in me, and the world slows to a halt. The wind and sand fall away, leaving Aladdin and me standing as if we had never moved at all. We have made a journey of weeks in a matter of seconds.

I have brought us to a small rocky slope beside the river, north of the city. From here, we can look down toward Parthenia. The city glitters in the night, and I can make out the bobbing torches carried by the watchmen atop the wall. To the east, across the sea, dawn is beginning to break, the horizon a rose-gold line.

Aladdin starts, sucking in a sharp breath, as if he's just surfaced after being immersed in water.

"That was . . ." he begins, then his voice trails off. He looks down at the lamp, and I see that he has truly realized just how immense its power is.

I point at his wounded shoulder and the cut on his neck. "Wish for it, and I can heal you."

"This scratch?" he scoffs. "It just needs a little cleaning. Now what? Isn't there some kind of price I have to pay?"

"Just wait for it," I say, folding my arms and watching him.

He frowns and starts to reply, only to retch instead, his skin turning ashen.

"And there it is," I sigh. "Moving instantly from one place to another almost always results in losing one's dinner. Not a bad price, compared to most I've seen. It'll pass soon."

"I haven't had any dinner to lose," he groans.

He takes a step toward the river but staggers, and I move quickly to his side and slip an arm around him. He stiffens at my touch, nearly pulling away, but he is too weak. I help him to the water's edge, and with a wince he eases himself down beside it and leans in to drink from his cupped hand. He is shaking too much, and the water spills.

"Damn it," he mutters, then laughs huskily. "This is so embarrassing..."

He faints, his hand falling into the water, his cheek planted on the wet sand. His skin is ashen and hot to the touch.

With a sigh, I look around at the empty landscape. The dunes of the Mahali are far behind us; here the land is rocky and stubbled with wild olive trees and twisting cedars. Somewhere in the underbrush, a jackal barks twice. Moonlight filtering through the trees turns the river into flowing silver.

The lamp is still hanging on his belt—a stroke of luck. If he'd dropped it when he fainted, I'd have been sucked inside until he awoke or someone else picked me up and set me loose again. As long as it remains on Aladdin's person, and as long as he remains alive, I am bound only by the invisible perimeter that surrounds the lamp. One hundred forty-nine paces. I have measured it many, many times.

I turn Aladdin onto his back and tug off his tunic and cloak, until he's wearing only his loose trousers and leather boots. His shoulder is crusted with blood, and the skin around his wound is sticky. I dip his cloak in the water and gently dab at his skin, my eyes wandering over his chest and stomach, looking for any other injuries.

Warmth rushes to my cheeks as my fingers come delicately to rest on his bare skin, and I chide myself for my foolishness. I have seen a thousand and one boys, Habiba, many in less clothing than this, but I have never been so foolish as to *blush*.

Aladdin groans softly, and I snap my eyes back to his face, but he remains unconscious. After cleaning his shoulder, I grimace and plunge my fingers into the wound, locating the arrow tip and drawing it out. Aladdin's eyelashes flutter, but he doesn't wake.

I stanch the wound with a piece of cloth torn from his cloak, then rip off the hem to bind it. The arrow didn't go deep, and if he can keep the area clear of infection, it should heal well. The cut on his neck, though wide, is shallow and already clotting. I wipe it clean and press a cloth to it. He doesn't stir again, and I sit back, my legs folded.

Just as the sun begins to rise, I hear a rustle in the rocks behind us, and a prickle runs up the back of my neck. I stand and turn, staring at the hillside, but see nothing. A wind, sharp with salt off the sea, rattles the branches of the olive trees. I watch for a long moment, fearing wolves or jackals roaming the night. Few are the beasts I have cause to fear, but wolves and all their cousins are no friend to jinn. They hunt us ruthlessly, bearing a hatred we return in equal measure, and they have been known to bring down ghuls in their prime. I hear no feet padding along the ground, no howls cutting the night, and relax a little.

But when I turn around again, I freeze, my stomach clenching. A little girl stands directly in front of me, her hair long and tangled, her eyes milky white. She wears a tattered gray tunic and nothing else. Sores and cuts mar her tiny bare feet. I would feel sorry for her—if she were in fact a little girl. But one look at those sightless eyes, and I know that though she may once have been human, her soul is long gone.

"Ghul," I whisper.

The girl bares her teeth in a smile that comes across as more of a grimace. When she speaks, it is in the tongue of the jinn, which no human can hear: *Jinni.*

The ghul hisses, her breath hot and reeking like decayed flesh. I reach out with my sixth sense and feel her reaching back, her thoughts probing like tentacles. At once I retreat, sealing my mind to it, but that quick mental glance was all I needed to recognize her. We jinn know one another by the patterns of our thoughts, the way humans use facial features. Our names are like the meaning *behind* names, sensations and images rather than words, communicated by thought and not voice. I recognize the ghul as Serpent-Scale, Water-Drips-in-Darkness, Echoes-in-the-Cave. A high-ranking jinni . . . and also one of those present the day you and I fell, Habiba. Before then, she used to haunt the mountains in the north, gobbling up stray children. The northerners called her Shaza—"toothed one."

We see you know who we are, O Curl-of-the-Tiger's-Tail, Smoke-on-the-Wind, Girl-Who-Gives-the-Stars-Away.

"What do you want?" I ask, shivering a little at the feel of my own jinn name.

So this is the fool who found your lamp. The ghul steps aside to peer down at Aladdin, her lip curling. *He looks tasty. I would not mind wearing his form for a time. Tell us, jinni, will you destroy him like you did your last human?*

I turn cold. "You know what really happened that day."

Oh yes, we saw, saw it all. She giggles and bends down to twist a lock of Aladdin's hair around her finger. *Such a pretty human, this one.*

Bristling, I move between her and Aladdin. "Why are you here?"

She bites her nail. *We came to deliver a message from our lord.*

My stomach drops, and I sway on my feet. "And what does Nardukha have to say to me?"

He sends us to tell you that he knows you escaped the ruins where we left you to rot, for it is no coincidence the humans learned of the ring.

Unease ripples through me, like waters stirred by a slinking crocodile. If the Shaitan is behind all of this, it can mean nothing good. Nardukha did not become the King of the Jinn for no reason. I can still recall the days when he hunted down all the other Shaitan, my kindred, slaughtering them one by one to secure his own power. He is ruthless and cunning, older than the earth, stronger than any creature in existence. "But why? I thought he was content to let me rot."

She shuffles, her nose wrinkling. *He offers you a deal.*

"I made a deal with Nardukha once before, and paid a terrible price for it." I narrow my eyes and take a step toward her, my hands curling into fists. "Why should I trust him again?"

Her head whips up, her teeth flashing. *The humans with their cursed charms have trapped and bottled one of our own, holding him deep in their warded city. No jinn may enter, for their protection is strong, and to pass through their gates or fly over their walls is death to us. But not to you—not to Curl-of-the-Tiger's-Tail, Smoke-on-the-Wind, Girl-Who-Gives-the-Stars-Away. As Shaitan, you alone may be able to pass through the wards and get inside the city.*

"So he wants me to rescue this jinni," I say doubtfully. "But I know Nardukha. No jinni is worth that much trouble to him, none but—" I pause and swallow.

The ghul laughs humorlessly. *The jinni they hold is no mere burning ifreet or dripping maarid, but our Lord's own son.*

I can picture him at once, though I have not seen him in more than a thousand years. We last parted with angry words, as we always did. *Sun-Burns-Bright, Scale-of-the-Red-Dragon, He-Who-Makes-the-Earth-to-Shake.* To me, he has always been Zhian, the name given him by the Akbanu people when they worshiped him, thousands of years ago. He always did love parading around like a god, demanding offerings and temples from the humans he terrorized.

"The humans have captured *Zhian?*" I ask, laughing until Aladdin stirs fitfully. "He must be utterly humiliated. The great jinn prince—bottled up like a common maarid. How did the humans do it?"

They are stronger than they were. These Amulens have grown tough and clever, fighting us as they have all these years. And whose fault is that?

For once, I'm happy to take the blame. How proud you would be of your people, Habiba, still carrying on the fight these hundreds of years later! And to think they've even captured the great jinn prince himself.

I cross my arms, smiling a little. "And what do I get in return?"

Shaza pauses a long moment before replying, and when she does, her thoughts drip with disgust. *The Shaitan offers you freedom.*

Chapter Five

I DROP MY ARMS, as smoke turns to flame inside me.

What? I reply. The jinn tongue feels rusted in my thoughts, but I am too stunned for spoken words.

The ghul sniffs. *These are the terms.* Turning away, she points at the silver crescent hanging low in the sky. *The moon will die tomorrow night, and be reborn again. It will grow fat, then it will grow weak, and then it will die once more. On that moon death, if you have not freed the jinn prince, then the Shaitan shall shake the skies, and death will rain upon you and all the humans in that city. But succeed, and he will sever the bond that binds you to the lamp, and you will return to Ambadya a free jinni.*

She gives me a sly smile over her shoulder. *But if you make one mistake,* he *will come, and a deserved traitor's death he will give you. Do you know what that means?*

I do. I have seen jinn executions before. They last for days. When you're practically immortal, there's no end to the torture you can endure, and the jinn are experts at wringing every last drop of pain from their victims. My chest tightens at the thought. I may be one of the strongest jinni alive, but I can feel pain, and I can be killed.

"Yes," I whisper, then I cough a little and repeat in a louder voice, "Yes. I accept Nardukha's deal. Tell him . . . tell him he will see his wretched son within the month."

It shall be so.

And just like that, the ghul is gone, slipping away into the shadows and rock, blending into the earth from which she was made, leaving me trembling. I lift my face and stare wonderingly at the stars above.

Freedom.

It's a dream I never dared to dream. I cannot even imagine what it would be like. Ever since I became jinn, I've been bound to my lamp. The concept is foreign, as distant and untouchable as the new moon behind its black veil. But for the first time, I feel hope. And I know I will do everything in my limited power to seize it.

The sun rises, and the Parthenian gates open. Two roads—one from the east, one from the west—lead to the city, and carts and travelers slowly make their way inside. No one sees us nestled among the rocks upriver. The sun peaks and then begins sinking again, the trees' shadows growing long, and still Aladdin sleeps as if dead.

There is no more sign of Shaza or any other jinni nearby, but I keep careful watch. I turn Nardukha's deal over in my mind, pondering how to accomplish it. It is one thing to say I will do it—another entirely to pull it off. Parthenia is a large city, and there's no telling where Zhian is being kept. It's not as if I am free to wander around looking, either. I'm bound to Aladdin as long as he has the lamp. But I won't let that stop me. I won't let *anything* stop me—not human or jinn. Because for the first time in four thousand years, *I*, Curl-of-the-Tiger's-Tail, Smoke-on-the-Wind, Girl-Who-Gives-the-Stars-Away, have a chance at freedom.

When the sun falls behind the city and the towers deepen into silhouettes, I turn back to my master, beginning to grow concerned.

This time, his eyes are open, and he is staring at me.

"You're very pretty," he murmurs, his voice thick with sleep, "for a jinni."

"Have you met many jinn?"

"No." His lips curl into a dazed grin. "But I've met a lot of pretty girls."

I check his bandage; the bleeding has stopped, but he'll need a fresh dressing soon.

"Why did you help me?" he asks softly. "Back in the desert, you distracted Darian so that I could get the lamp. Why?"

"You took an arrow for me." He couldn't have known it would not harm me. He acted without thinking, from some instinct deep inside himself—the same instinct that prevented him from wishing for Darian's death. "Now we are even, thief."

"We'd better—" He cuts off with a hiss, his hand going to his shoulder. He is silent for a moment, his eyes shut, as if he is trying hard to push down the pain of his injury. Then at last he says in a tight voice, "We'd better get moving. We have to slip into the city before they shut the gates for the night. Once they close, they don't open till dawn. Not for anyone. There are jinn in these hills." He pauses, then gives a little laugh. "Though I guess that doesn't bother you."

The walls of Parthenia rise in the distance, and it will take a hard, fast walk to reach it by sunset. But he sets out gamely, stopping only to strip a small fig tree of its fruit before leaving the riverbank. We follow a dusty track through low hills covered in scrubby bushes and loose stones.

We near the gates just as the guards are preparing to shut them. The doors are massive, heavy slabs of oak, and they must be drawn closed by a pair of elephants. The soldiers are busy tethering the huge animals to the doors. On either side of the gate, enormous stone gryphons glare down on us with blank eyes.

"Hurry," says Aladdin, breaking into a run. "They won't wait for us."

I sprint to catch up, then, just steps from the gate, I stagger as a spasm of pain twists my gut. A shudder passes through me, and I double over, unable to take another step.

Looking up, I spot them immediately: glyphs carved into the stone bases the gryphons stand upon. Symbols of Eskarr, the language of scorsmiths to bind magic to objects. These read *jinn*, *demon*, *repel*, and other similar words. They were put there to turn away any of my kind who might try to enter, and their power rakes over me like claws. It seeps through me like poison, tainting my smoke sickly green.

"Zahra, are you all right?" Aladdin asks, halting beside me.

I shake my head and struggle to stay on my feet as my head reels. It's like being caught in a landslide. Shaza said I was the only one with a chance of getting through these gates—but even I might not be strong enough. I try to force myself into motion with the thought of freedom, but all I can manage is one half step before my stomach twists violently and I drop to one knee. The sea wind batters me, and I wish I could turn to smoke and let it carry me away.

"It's warded," I whisper. "Against the jinn. I can't . . . I can't get through."

The doors suddenly groan, and I look up to see the elephants beginning to move, drawing them shut. Alarmed, Aladdin looks at the gate, then back to me. "Zahra, you *have* to go through. If you don't, the guards will know what you are. They'll kill us both right here. Killing jinn and anyone who sympathizes with them—that's what they *do*. They're *Eristrati*."

He says the word as if I should know what it means, and I study the guards closer. They all carry spears of iron, their shafts carved with more Eskarr glyphs. These are no ordinary soldiers; they are armed to fight jinn, and they know what they're doing. Four thousand years may be quite a long life, but I'm not ready to be done living just yet. Not when I'm this close to breaking free of my cursed lamp.

"I can do it," I murmur.

"Are you sure?" He's studying me as if he's worried I'll pass out. I very well may.

I nod, not entirely certain but willing to try. Not because I'm truly worried the guards will kill us—Aladdin does have two wishes left, and I'm far from unskilled in defending myself. But because I know this is it. This is the last chance I'll ever get. If I fail, I don't even think I'll protest when Nardukha strikes me down. I can't take another *year* in that lamp, much less an eternity, not when a chance at freedom is so close.

"I have an idea," I say. "But I'll need your help."

"Hurry," he says, watching as the doors swing inward. Already they are half closed.

I conjure a small puff of smoke beneath my dress, letting it settle over my stomach, making me round as a melon. Add the pain in my eyes and my tight breathing and I am the perfect image of a woman going into labor. Aladdin looks down, makes a strange noise deep in his throat, then nods.

"Right. We can do this. No problem." His tone is a little high, but he grabs my hand. "Let's go!"

I must lean on Aladdin, and not only for show—the closer we get, the harder it is for me to hold out. The air feels like knives, the ground like burning coals. It seems all the elements bend themselves toward crushing me, repulsing me, grinding me into the earth. Somehow, his heartbeat gives me strength. Perhaps it helps to hide my jinn nature from the wards. Either way, I can feel myself gaining a little more control of my own body. I burst forward, and together we run for the gates. They're seconds away from shutting entirely.

"We won't fit," I say.

"Yes, we *will*," Aladdin replies through clenched teeth, as if he can will them open with sheer stubbornness.

"If you wish for it—*ugh!*" As we pass through the stone gryphons, their stare seems to hone in on me. The Eskarr glyphs seem to glow. The power behind them pushes at me with the force of a hundred horses, seeking to trample me into the earth.

"My wife!" Aladdin cries to the guards. "She's going to give birth! Stop the gates!"

The men exchange looks but remain resolute. The space between the doors shrinks until it seems not even a cat could slip through. But Aladdin remains undeterred. He sprints ahead, gasping, his shoulder crimson with blood. I don't have to fake my own pain, as if I'm being speared from the front and hooked from behind. Everything in me screams, *Turn around! Run away!* But I force myself to keep moving. Spots dance across my eyes. Every thought I have is bent on maintaining human form. I ache to shift into smoke just to stop the pain.

And then we reach the gates. Aladdin stops, pushing me through first. I can hardly see at this point, and I realize I'm sobbing aloud. Ordinarily I'd be mortified at such a display of weakness, but I don't have a thought to spare for my pride. It hurts too much.

All I can do is force myself not to shift, not to give us away. I feel Aladdin's hand in mine, his voice in my ear, but the words make no sense. There's shouting, arguing. Everything swims around me. I am a twig caught in a flood.

With a moan, I collapse, the false pregnant belly dissipating. Instead of hitting the ground, though, I drop into Aladdin's arms. He lifts me and holds me against his chest, then begins running. The scent of him overwhelms me: fresh figs from this morning, goats' milk soap he last washed his cloak with, smoke from the ruins of Neruby, wind, and sea salt. Human smells, rich and heady. I can sense his pain through his pulse, but he doesn't slow or stop. He must be hurting as much as I am. Why doesn't he let me go? Why doesn't he leave the lamp and save himself? Or make a wish— if I could even grant it in this state.

With a shudder, I feel myself slip, as if from a tall tower, and I plummet into darkness with one last thought:

But I was so close...

Chapter Six

WHEN I COME TO, I'm lying beneath stars, my back on a hard, cold surface. I startle awake, all at once, and bolt up into a sitting position.

"Whoa, easy there, Smoky."

I turn and see Aladdin sitting beside me, eating roasted lamb speared on a small stick. We're sitting on top of a building, with an expansive view of the sea beyond the city walls. I turn around and study Parthenia from above. The buildings rise where the land swells to the north, a domed palace sitting at the city's highest point. Even on this nearly moonless night, it glows like a pearl in the darkness. Zhian is somewhere out there, raging unheard in a tiny bottle or jar. The thought, which amused me earlier, now only fills me with grim determination. I stretch out my sixth sense, probing the night, but it doesn't reach far, and I catch not a glimmer of him.

"What happened?" It's rare for me to black out like this, and it frightens me more than I like to admit. I don't know how humans do it every night—falling asleep, letting darkness swallow them.

"You passed out. I had to carry you."

"How is your shoulder?"

He's wearing a fresh bandage, but it's been sloppily applied. "Had to redo it. Tough with just one hand. And I grabbed these." He pulls two little clay pots from his pocket. "There's an herbalist one street over, so I made a run while you were out. I hope they're for wounds and won't, you know, cause warts or something."

I hold out a hand, and he drops the pots into my palm. I open them and sniff. "This one is for soothing women's birthing pains."

Aladdin winces.

"But the other one should do the trick." I hand them back. "It's a cinnamon-and-clove mixture and will stop any disease from spreading in your wound."

He pockets that pot and leaves the other behind as he stands. "You feeling better, then? Or want to take a ride from here?" He pats his cloak, and a dull *ting* tells me the lamp is still tied to his belt.

I try not to sound too desperate when I reply, "I'd rather walk. Where are we going?"

"I've been chased, shot, cut, beaten, and dragged a hundred leagues in the blink of an eye." He shrugs and offers me a hand. "I need a drink."

I stare at him a moment, conflicted. *He carried me. He took an arrow for me.* I've had few kind masters in my long, strange life. Cruelty, I understand. But kindness frightens me, for my defenses are weak against it.

Warily, I take his hand and he helps me up. He leads me down a narrow stair along the outside of the building we're on top of, down to the street.

"Why did you want that prince to die?" I ask.

Aladdin halts, looking back at me with wide eyes. "Not so loud! Gods."

"Well?"

"Are you always this nosy?"

"I am when someone asks me if I'll *kill* for them."

He lets out a short breath. "I changed my mind about that."

"I still want to know."

He rubs his hand across his face. "We're here."

Aladdin steps off the street into one of the many narrow capillaries that lead into the deeper bowels of the city. Walls close in on either side, and lines hung with worn, clean cloth crisscross over our heads. Wind rustles the fabric, so it seems as if the air is filled with whispering ghosts. Through the closed shutters that dot the walls, only the faintest lines of light can be seen.

Aladdin steps behind a stack of rotting crates and holds up a fist to knock on a small wooden door. We wait in the darkness, breathing in the smell of baking bread, and beneath that, the stench of piss, rat, and simmon, a drug made from corris leaf. This last scent wafts out of the door before us, and when it opens suddenly, a wave of the smell washes over us.

The man behind the door is broader than he is tall, but every inch of him is muscle. Leather straps cross over his hairy chest, while his bald head glistens with sweat in the light of the lamp he holds.

"Two coppers," he says in a bored tone, without looking up.

Aladdin clears his throat. The man glances at him, then straightens. "Oh. It's you. Balls, boy, what happened to you? You look terrible."

"Been traveling. What're you doing out of prison, Balak? Thought you got ten years for that pig you stole."

Balak grunts. "That pig they *claimed* I stole. The bastards can't prove nothing. The Phoenix sprang me."

Aladdin tenses slightly. "What, he's still knocking around?"

"He loosed a bunch of us from the prison, those of us he thought were unjustly condemned. Petty thieves, debtors, and the like. Guards have rounded up a few of the fools not smart enough to stay low, but they won't catch up with me again."

"Did you see his face?" asked Aladdin. "Has anyone figured out who he is?"

"Never saw nothing but a shadow slipping by, unlocking the cells. He'd knocked out all the guards, cleared the way out. Nobody knows who he is, but he's got the whole city singing his praises. Look there." Balak points to a wall across the street, where a crude red flame has been recently painted. "Sign of the Phoenix. It's like the whole bloody Tailor's Rebellion all over again." The man's eyes widen, and he drops his gaze. "Sorry, lad."

Aladdin shrugs. "Anyway, he's an idiot. This so-called Phoenix will end up on the gallows before long, like all the other fools who think they can make a difference in this city."

Balak laughs and steps aside to let us pass through the little door, then shuts it behind us.

We descend steep, narrow stairs in the dark, the smell of simmon and sweat growing stronger the deeper we get. The passage grows lighter, and the swell of voices reaches our ears. Aladdin pulls the hood of his cloak low over his face.

We step abruptly into a cavernous room packed wall to wall with sweating bodies. Braziers circling the wooden pillars give off acrid smoke that obscures the ceiling. The air is so thick with simmon that it is impossible to see the other end of the room. Aladdin takes my hand so that the press of bodies doesn't pull us apart, and together we wind our way through the crowd. There are mostly men down here, and a few night women, all of them drunk or clouded by simmon, all of them sweating. With my free hand, I wrap a strip of black silk around my face, covering my mouth and nostrils in an attempt to block out the stench.

"Welcome to the Rings!" Aladdin calls over his shoulder. "Stay close." Though we are inches apart, it is difficult to hear him over the sudden roar of the crowd. A potbellied man jostles me as he lifts his arms to cheer, and the blast of his odor leaves me gagging.

"For once I think I prefer my lamp," I mutter.

A harried serving girl, dressed in little more than scraps of fabric that reveal her lithe figure, steps up to ask us what we want to drink. Then she does a double take and peers closer at Aladdin.

"You!" she hisses. "You were banned for life from this place! Ugh, Balak is the most worthless doorman I ever—"

"Quiet, Dal." He tugs his hood lower. "I'm in disguise. Bring a flagon of the strongest liquid you have, will you?"

She purses her lips. "You have some nerve, thief, asking me for anything."

Aladdin presses a coin into her hand and gives her a cocky grin. "Oh, come on. We had some good times, didn't we?"

"I'd have a good time breaking this flagon over your head. Who is *she*? I've never seen her around before." Dal looks me up and down, and I return her gaze coolly.

"She's with me. New to town. I'm showing her around a bit."

Dal rolls her eyes. "I've heard that line before." She leans closer to me. "Here's some advice, sister: Don't waste your time on this one. He's more trouble than he's worth."

"I think I'm starting to get what you mean," I reply.

"All right, all right," Aladdin interrupts, frowning. "We came

here for drinks, not girl talk. What's this?" He points to a red ribbon tied around her arm. "I've seen a couple of people wearing them
since I got back."

She puts her hand over it, her eyes flashing. "It's a symbol, says
I stand behind the Phoenix, and against injustice. You know they
doubled taxes *again* yesterday? If you don't pay, they either throw
you in prison or take your property, if not both. They're hanging
people just for speaking out against it!"

Aladdin only grunts.

"I'd have thought *you* of all people would want to join up.
Remember the plague in the eastern quarter? The guards quaran-
tined it and were prepared to let all those people die? The Phoenix
snuck in and gave medicine to all the sick. He saved *hundreds* of
people. This is *real*, Aladdin. The Phoenix isn't just another talker,
he's . . . well, he's giving us hope. And it's more than we've had
since . . ." She gives him a long look, as if about to say more, but
then she sighs and just shakes her head.

"Since my parents? You don't have to dance around it, Dal. I
know what you're thinking, what all of you are thinking. I don't
want to talk about the damn Phoenix anymore," Aladdin grumbles.

She snorts and turns away, pocketing the coin, then returns in
moments with a bottle. "Your friend Xaxos was in here looking for
you a few days back. Didn't look too happy."

Aladdin opens the wine. When he offers it to me I shake my
head. "Old Xax?" he says casually. "I've got no business with him."

"He'd disagree, I think. He said he hired you for a job—I didn't
need to ask to know what *that* meant. So you're still up to your old
tricks, then?" She shakes her head. "Anyway, he's pretty angry with
you. Said you pulled the job, then left town. Guards are hunting for

a thief too. Offering a thousand gold crowns for his head." She narrows her eyes. "Did you break into the *palace*, Aladdin?"

"A thousand crowns?" Aladdin gives a low whistle. "Nearly makes a man want to turn him*self* in."

"Of all the stupid things . . ." Her eyes glowering, Dal gives us both a brief, sharp look before going to mop up someone's spilled wine.

Aladdin finds a table near the central ring, where two men the size of bulls are grappling. One, whose neck is easily the size of my waist, is getting the upper hand. He's stripped nearly bare, doused in oil to make him slippery. His head, bald but for a long black tail sprouting from the top, gleams like a boiled egg. His opponent, slightly smaller, is on the defensive, holding up his hands to block the bigger man's blows.

Aladdin watches with disinterest and takes a long swig of wine.

"See that?" He runs his finger over the tabletop, where someone has carved a small symbol.

"It looks like a sewing needle," I say.

He nods and drinks. His eyes are starting to get foggy from the wine. "Not just *a* needle. *The* Needle. The sign of a rebellion that started up years ago. This is where the leaders of the movement met. Here. At this table."

He traces the needle with his thumbnail.

"My father was the Tailor," he tells me. "I mean, he was just *a* tailor at first, but when I was a kid, he started running with these rebels. The king's vizier was press-ganging peasants onto his warships, rowing them to their deaths in a mad attempt to rebuild the Amulen Empire of the past. My father and his friends protested by burning garrisons and guardhouses, stealing weapons, sabotaging ships." Aladdin's face darkens. He leans back and pulls the coin from Neruby from his pocket. I hadn't even noticed him pick it up. He flips it idly; on it flashes the face of a king who died so long ago, no one in this world would even know his name. "Eventually he got my mother to join in. Soon people were calling him *the* Tailor, and a reward was offered for his head. His needle became the rebellion's symbol."

I listen in silence, watching his hands. They're clever hands, his nails neat, his fingers long and nimble. He spins the coin and catches it, over and over, as he talks.

"When I was twelve they caught him. Remember that prince in the desert, Darian? His father, our *exalted* Vizier Sulifer, held me and forced me to watch as my parents' heads were cut from their shoulders. Darian was there. He laughed at me when I began to cry." Aladdin makes the coin disappear up his sleeve, then takes a long drink of wine. "Afterward, Sulifer made me pick up their heads and hold them so he could drive stakes in them. He let them stand there in the city square for weeks."

I lean back, my hands in my lap. "Why are you telling me all this?"

He shrugs and sniffs. "You wanted to know why I . . . almost wished for Darian's death." The wine is nearly gone, as are Aladdin's wits. "Ever since I was young, people thought I'd be the next leader of the rebellion, that I'd rise up and fight. They think *I* should be the one out there breaking people out of prison and stopping bloody plagues. They think I've wasted my life, becoming a thief and a criminal. Well, I've no interest in fighting for lost causes that only get people killed. All I want is to avenge my parents, not start a war we can't win."

I lift my face. He's staring at me with drunken intensity, his lips a thin line. "And now," he goes on, "I find out I don't even have the guts to go through with it. I had Darian right in front of me! And I couldn't even . . . I failed them."

With a sigh, I pull the half-empty flagon from his fingers, drinking simply so that he cannot. The wine is cheap but strong, burning my throat, though it will have no effect on my senses.

A roar from the ring next to us draws Aladdin's attention. The fight has ended, and the smaller of the two men lies unconscious on the floor in a puddle of sweat and blood. The victor raises his beefy arms and bellows in triumph.

"Who will face Ukkad the Bull?" cries a ratty man who climbs into the ring. "Twenty gold pieces to the victor! Five to the loser!"

Aladdin starts to turn away, but then the crowd on the opposite side of the ring parts, and a fighter steps out and nimbly climbs into the small arena. A murmur of laughter ripples through the audience, and Aladdin rises to his feet, his eyes widening.

It's a slender young woman of seventeen or so. She wears a simple top cropped just above her navel and a long linen sarong held up by a leather belt. The skirt exposes one long, athletic leg, and save for a simple gold chain around her ankle, her feet are bare. She sheds her cloak and drapes it neatly over the rope surrounding the ring and then stretches her arms in front of her and tips her head to each shoulder, cracking her neck. She is pretty, her thick dark hair tied back in a simple braid and her eyes entirely smeared with kohl so it looks as if she's wearing a mask. She smiles at the Bull and bows, spreading her leather-wrapped hands wide.

I glance up at Aladdin and see his eyes alight with interest.

Aladdin waves Dal over. "Who is she?" he asks.

She rolls her eyes. "I don't know. Some East Sider, I'd guess. She's been out here every night for two weeks, brawling and then vanishing. Doesn't even collect her winnings." Her tone turns sour. "I'd keep my distance if I were you. That one's likely to break your arm if you anger her."

The tendons in the Bull's neck bulge as he turns red and roars, "Who makes a mockery of me? I came here to fight men, not little girls!"

The girl spits at the ground between them, still smiling. "So did I, but it seems we must both leave disappointed."

The crowd gasps, and the Bull's eyes nearly pop from his skull. Aladdin pushes through to the edge of the ring, and I scramble to keep up, looking wistfully toward the door, but it seems my master is intent on watching these events unfold. Resigned, I lean on one of the wooden posts supporting the rope perimeter and turn my attention back to the girl.

They have begun circling one another, their stances wide and tense, their eyes locked, but the Bull still seems hesitant, as if he thinks this is all a prank.

"You should go back to baking bread," he says. "Or do you make your coin by warming beds? Perhaps once I've broken your pretty nose, I can use my winnings to have you warm mine."

"I don't go in for livestock," she returns.

With a wordless roar, the Bull charges. The audience holds its breath. Aladdin tenses, an enthralled smile tugging at his lips.

For a moment it seems she is finished, but at the last moment the girl smoothly dances aside and drives her elbow into the Bull's temple, knocking him off balance.

The crowd erupts back into life. The fights at the other rings have suspended, and now everyone is focused on the central match. Wagers are drawn—overwhelmingly in the Bull's favor, but a few adventurous spirits bet on the girl. Aladdin's hand goes to his pocket, and he pulls out the Nerubyan coin, thoughtfully considering.

"You wouldn't," I say.

"What? I like her style."

"That coin is quite possibly the last remnant of a once-mighty civilization that existed for hundreds of—"

"A gold on the girl!" Aladdin calls, catching a bookmaker's attention.

I sigh and turn back to the fight.

Around and around they dance. She is a mouse desperate to avoid the stamping feet of an elephant, and the longer she evades, the more tired she gets. The crowd is frantic now as more money is thrown on the Bull. Aladdin leans in and mutters, "Come on, come on . . ."

I notice a few faces across the arena that watch with silent intensity, their eyes filled with worry. All of them are girls the age of the young warrioress in the arena, and they are all dressed similarly.

Then the Bull hesitates, stopping to catch his breath, and the girl takes the chance to rest as well. She is standing directly in front of Aladdin and me, within arm's reach. Bent over, her hands on her thighs, she gasps for air and drips sweat onto the sand.

Aladdin leans over the rope and whispers, "His right leg is slow. There's a hitch every other step. If you're quick . . ."

She looks over her shoulder, through strands of sweaty hair that have escaped her braid. "You betting on me, handsome?"

Aladdin grins. "You busy later?"

She shrugs and pops her knuckles, her eyes traveling over his shoulders and torso. "I think I could spare a minute."

His grin widens, and the girl suddenly springs forward, sprinting toward the post behind the Bull. He snorts and moves to intercept her, but she is too quick for him. With a cry she leaps into the air, plants a foot on the pole, and pushes off, vaulting through the air toward her opponent. Before he can make a move, she connects feet-first with his face, snapping his head around with an audible crunch. As he shakes his head and sways on his feet, she bats away one of his halfhearted punches and throws her bare leg up and around his neck, the other leg following. With her ankles locked behind his head, she arches and twists herself, her momentum bringing the Bull crashing facedown to the ground. Quick as a snake she rolls free and rises, then plants a foot on the back of his meaty neck.

Aladdin nearly falls into the arena as he whistles and cheers, more than a little drunk, and the rest of the crowd descends into chaos as the fight concludes. The gamblers settle their debts, and the few lucky ones who bet on the girl grab their winnings and then wisely disappear before they can be mugged. Aladdin wins back his gold piece and a pile of silver.

"I'm going in! Wish me luck!" he says breathlessly, and he climbs over the rope and joins the small crowd gathered around the girl, cheering her on and offering her drinks. I lean on the post and watch, shaking my head. Aladdin's sorrows seem entirely forgotten.

Dal appears at my side, her hands full of empty cups. She gives me an appraising look with one eyebrow arched. "I know that look."

"What look?"

"Don't sweat it, sister. We've all had it." She sighs. "The girls he loved and left."

Irritably, I look away. "I don't know what you're talking about."

"Sure you don't." Dal smiles sadly. "You can either hate him or accept that that's just who he is. When Aladdin sets his heart on something—or some*one*—nothing can stop him from getting it. And when he does have it, he realizes it's not what he wanted after all, and then something else will catch his eye, and off he goes again. Over and over. And here we are, the casualties."

"I'm nobody's casualty."

Aladdin has made his way to the girl's side and is chatting in her ear, crossing his muscular arms for her benefit. I can't help rolling my eyes.

"She's pretty," says Dal. "And she's tough. But she's not what he wants. Not that he'll believe that until after he's won her."

"And what *does* he want?" I turn and face the serving girl.

"The same thing we all want. He just won't admit it." I see longing in her eyes, and also anger, when she looks at Aladdin. "Freedom from the past."

I watch the thief thoughtfully, my face softening.

The girl in the ring says something, and Aladdin laughs, his smile lighting up his face. He leans over and whispers in her ear, and she nods, then takes his hand and coyly leads him from the ring, dodging admirers.

Dal sighs and shakes her head ruefully. "I give her four, maybe five days—hey! Where are you going? Let him go, sister! It's not worth it!"

I slip under the rope and into the ring, ignoring her. *You don't know anything about it, "sister."* I am the last person in the world who is interested in Aladdin. What I *am* interested in is sticking close enough to him that I won't get inconveniently sucked back into my lamp.

I struggle through the crowd, trying to catch up to him, but a brawl breaks out between two gamblers, and I am knocked to the ground. Instead of trying to get up and fight my way back to Aladdin, I quietly shift into a tawny cat and dart through people's legs until I reach him. If anyone did see me, they'll probably attribute it to too much simmon. I'm sure stranger things have been hallucinated in this den of sweat and barbarism.

Aladdin and the girl have escaped into the blissfully quiet street, where they laugh and walk through the shadows. In one of the buildings nearby, a baby cries and a dog barks in response. The smells of roasting meat and strong spices waft out of a window above us. Though the crowd in the Rings is surely still shouting and cheering, not a sound escapes through the wide stones beneath our feet.

I stalk across the cobblestones, tail high and ears alert to every sound—while trying to block out the sound of Aladdin and his new friend, who are laughing and whispering. Eventually they stop and stare at each other, the girl taking Aladdin's hands and drawing him close.

"What's your name?" he asks her.

"First tell me yours."

"Aladdin."

"I've heard of you." She smiles and runs her hands down his chest.

Aladdin is like one intoxicated, but not only from the wine. He leans forward, until her back is to the wall, and he inhales the scent of her hair. "Oh, really? And what have you heard?"

Her hands move up to trace his jaw and his lips. "That you are bold and that you are the best at what you do. That you"—she plants a light kiss on the corner of his jaw—"even stole something valuable from Prince Darian."

He pauses, his lips brushing her hair. "And where did you hear that?" he murmurs.

"You know how we girls are. Always gossiping."

"About me?" He grins.

She laughs and lifts her face, enticing him with her lips, but when he moves his mouth to hers she turns her face and says in an entirely different tone, "*Finally.* Take him, girls. He's the one."

Before I can make a move, a small knot of girls appears from the alley behind Aladdin, and a black bag is thrown over his head. The girl he'd been so close to kissing knocks him unconscious. I recognize them at once—the silent spectators in the Rings.

"A shame," sighs the leader. "I think he'd have been a good kisser."

Then she and the others drag him down the street and into the dark.

Chapter Seven

By transforming into a sparrow and flying overhead, I am able to follow the girls as they hurry through the streets, carrying Aladdin's unconscious body between them. The girl from the ring takes the lead, and silently they work their way south, sticking to side streets and avoiding lit and populated areas.

For now, I shadow them silently, waiting to see what they will do. To be honest, I am a bit vexed with Aladdin at the moment, and not very inclined to swoop in and save his drunken hide.

See what comes of kissing strange girls in dark alleys? I want to tell him.

The girls stop to rest after several minutes, letting Aladdin drop rather heavily to the ground. I alight on a beam above them and listen.

"How much farther?" one asks. Through her veil, her voice is high and girlish.

"We've barely gotten anywhere," replies another.

"My back is killing me!"

"*I'll* kill you if you don't stop complaining, Ensi."

"No names!" snaps the leader.

"No one's listening!" Ensi protests. "Look around—we're alone!"

"Someone is *always* listening. So be silent, and let's keep moving."

The girls sigh and hoist Aladdin up again, two with his arms, two with his legs. Exposed beams above them provide perches for me to flit to as I shadow them.

"He's heavier than he looks," one complains.

"It's all these muscles," says Ensi, giggling. She's holding one of his arms, and she squeezes his bicep appreciatively. "You didn't tell us he was so *handsome*. What a shame we had to put a bag over his head. And you had him wrapped around your finger!"

"Shush!" Their leader turns and draws a finger forcefully across her lips, signaling for silence.

Suddenly a shadow drops in front of them, and the girls halt. The shadow rises and drops its hood; it's another girl, this one tall and lithe, carrying a supple bow.

"Raz!" Ensi cries. "What is it?"

She reports, "Guards ahead. Too late to run. Act casual."

The girls curse, drop Aladdin roughly, roll him into a gutter, then lean against the wall, hiding him with their cloaks. I land on the edge of the roof above them, the cool night wind ruffling my feathers. From my perch, I can see around the bend in the road, where the guards are walking toward the girls. There are six in all, wearing chain mail and pointed helmets.

When they round the corner, the girls look down at their feet. If *casual* is their intention, they're not doing a very good job. Five girls, dressed head to toe in black, standing silently in the gutter is not exactly a common sight at any hour, much less the middle of the night.

And indeed, the guards stop short when they spot them.

"You there," calls one. "What are you up to? Don't you know there's a curfew?"

"Just heading home," says the girls' leader, keeping her eyes averted.

The guards, instead of walking on, gather around them, grinning and nudging each other.

"And where's home?" asks the first. "Madame Padyme's pleasure house, perhaps?"

His fellows laugh appreciatively, their eyes glowing with interest. The girls group closer together. Their hands move subtly, fingers wrapping around concealed weapons. Behind them, Aladdin groans.

The guard cocks his head. "What've you got there, eh?"

"None of your concern." The girls' leader lifts her chin, stepping forward and staring down the guard.

He only laughs. "Tell you what, ladies. We'll make a deal. We'll give you the chance to *persuade* us not to arrest you for suspicious behavior. What do you say?"

Ensi sidles up to him and runs her finger down his chest. "Well . . . I'd say that's quite generous of you."

His tongue darts across his lips, and he snakes a hand around her waist—only to have her twist out of reach and fling a hand toward him, a burst of blue powder exploding on his face. He drops instantly. Ensi already has another handful of the stuff ready, drawn from a pouch on her belt. The other girls draw daggers, and Raz nocks an arrow onto her bow. They all pull veils across their faces, protecting themselves against the powder Ensi throws.

The guards, startled only for a moment, pull out their swords, but the girls are already attacking. They move with deadly precision. Ensi's poisoned powder takes down another guard, while the leader and a third girl knock another two unconscious with the hilts of their daggers. At first I can't tell how the fourth girl bests her opponent—but then I see it: a yellow-and-white snake coiling up her arm. Its victim foams at the mouth, his eyes rolling backward in his head as he falls, a hand clasped to the bite on his neck.

The last guard backs away, his face white.

"I—I'm new at this. I never meant—please!" He turns and flees.

The leader nods to the archer. "Don't kill him. They *are* just doing their job, however reprehensibly."

Raz nods and draws back her arrow. The man is twenty paces away when she lets fly. The bolt strikes his helmet, knocking him flat before deflecting harmlessly. He strikes his head on the stones and falls still.

The fight is over before it hardly began, without a single guard getting in a blow. The girls clean up quickly, dragging them all behind a stack of barrels between two buildings, where they'll likely lie unnoticed till dawn. Ensi administers a few drops of clear liquid to the one with the snakebite.

"He'll live," she says. "But he won't be visiting his *pleasure* houses any time soon." She spits on him, then giggles.

Their leader sighs and nudges Aladdin with the toe of her boot. "Well, not exactly how I hoped things would go. We'll have to hurry."

Ensi, whose store of potions and powders seems impressively thorough, wakes Aladdin with a small bottle of white liquid that she holds under his nose. He comes to with a gasp and starts coughing. The girls stand in a close circle around him, their expressions grim.

After their brief fight with the guards, they carried Aladdin through the city, to an old storehouse near the south wall. Inside rests the partially constructed hull of a ship, but judging by the cobwebs collecting on it, no one has touched it in a while. It sits upside down, like the rib cage of a whale. The girls dumped Aladdin on his knees on the floor beneath it, his hands bound behind him. I sit nearby, in the form of a black cat with green eyes, watching. The lamp is still concealed, but for who knows how long.

I'm starting to feel a bit exhausted. First the prince in the desert, now these girl assassins or whatever they are—I will grant the thief this: My time with him has been anything but dull.

Aladdin blinks and groans, his head rolling. "Bleeding gods . . . What . . . ?"

He focuses on the faces around him and goes still, confusion crinkling the corners of his eyes. They watch him by the light of torches as he twists his bound hands, his fingers brushing against the hidden lamp. "What the . . . Who in the black skies are you?"

"We'll be the ones asking questions, thief," replies the girls' leader.

His eyes roam the room searchingly, and I pad softly out of the shadows. When he sees me, he lifts a brow, and I blink slowly in response.

"Oh, look!" Ensi cries, following his gaze. "A cat! Here, little sweets!" She leans down and holds out a hand, and I run to her and rub against her ankle, purring when she picks me up and scratches my ears. Aladdin rolls his eyes just slightly. I hiss at him.

The leader removes her hood and pulls her braid over her shoulder. "You *are* Aladdin, son of Mustapha the tailor, are you not?"

"Finish that kiss you were about to give me, and I might tell you." He tilts his head, studying her with fascination.

"I remember hearing of your rebel father," she replies, drawing Aladdin's eyes back to her. "As a child, I admired his courage, though my parents often cursed his name."

He watches her closely, the corners of his lips turning slightly upward, as if amused. "You took down the Bull like he was no bigger than a goat. Who are you? Why haven't I heard of you before?"

The girl drops to a crouch in front of Aladdin, pulling out a dagger and twirling it idly while she locks eyes with him. "A few weeks ago, I hired you to steal something. And now I want it."

"What?" He looks around at the girls, bewildered. "Look, I don't know what you're talking about. I've never met you before. And I certainly didn't steal anything—"

The girl presses the dagger to Aladdin's cheek, and he stiffens.

"The ring," she says softly. "Where is it?"

Aladdin lifts an eyebrow. "Don't tell me you work for *Xaxos*. I'd definitely have heard of you if you do."

"I don't work for Xaxos," she replies, lowering the dagger. "Xaxos works for me."

He digests this in silence, shock turning to skepticism. "Are you saying that *you're* the Phoenix? You're the mysterious rebel who set those prisoners free and stopped a plague?"

"We helped her," says Ensi, pouting a little. "I don't know why they couldn't call us the Phoenix*es*. I'm the one who made all those little bottles of medicine, remember?"

"Hush, Ensi," says the leader. To Aladdin, she replies, "It's complicated, all right? But I *am* the one Xaxos works for, and I *am* the one you have to answer to for not giving me that ring!"

"The Phoenix," Aladdin repeats, shaking his head a little. "*The*

Phoenix. Does Xaxos know you're a girl half his age?" He laughs. "I'd love to see his face—"

"How long is this going to take?" the archer asks suddenly. "They'll notice we're gone."

"There *are* faster ways of interrogating someone," says the one with the snake. She opens her cloak, and the viper coils down her arm, tongue flickering. I stiffen in Ensi's arms, my hackles rising. The snake lifts its head and glares at me; animals are never fooled by jinn disguises.

"Hush, Khavar," the leader is saying. "Raz, go stand outside, in case any guards get curious."

The archer nods and heads to the door, looping her bow over her shoulder. Khavar keeps glaring at Aladdin, her snake coiling around her arm and resting its head on the back of her hand.

Aladdin swallows hard, his eyes fixed on the reptile. "Look, even if what you say is true, I don't have the ring. Maybe Xaxos didn't pass on the message, but I never had it to begin with. Not that I didn't *try*." He laughs and lifts a shoulder. "I *am* the best thief in—"

"You're lying." The leader stands up and crosses her arms. "Two nights after I had Xaxos hire a thief to steal the ring, Darian rode out like a madman in the middle of the night, his best soldiers with him. He hasn't been seen for days. There's only one object he would go to such lengths to recover. You *did* steal that ring, and now you're going to give it to me."

"What do you want with it?" he asks. "Who *are* you? A revolutionary? A thief? What's your name?"

The girl only stares at Aladdin, her brow creasing. She seems to waver for a moment, then she looks up at one of her girls and nods.

"Nessa, tell him."

Nessa, the quietest of the group, steps behind the leader and pronounces in a low voice, "Aladdin rai Mustapha, pay your respects to your king's daughter, your princess, and your sovereign, Caspida nez Anadredca of Parthenia, Heiress to the Throne, Jewel of the Amulens, the Beloved of the Gods, and First Daughter of the Anadredcan Dynasty."

Startled to my core, I stare with new eyes at Caspida. I have known an Anadredca before: Queen Roshana Mithraya nez Anadredca. This girl is *your* descendant, Habiba. Your heir. Could it be, after everything that happened that day, that your bloodline lived on? That your little daughter was saved from the destruction and smuggled out of Neruby and crowned amid the ruins of your empire?

Aladdin goes very still, his eyes unreadable—but I see with more than eyes. My sixth sense picks up waves of shock and anger rolling off him.

"You mean *her*?" he asks slowly. "The girl I kissed?"

"*Almost* kissed," Caspida corrects.

"She is your future *queen*!" Khavar snaps, and with her foot she shoves him forward, sending him sprawling. "Show more deference."

"Khavar! Enough." Caspida holds up a hand. "Step away."

Khavar shoots Aladdin a dark look as she stands aside. He struggles back onto his knees, his face pale. He stares at Caspida with wide eyes. And then he laughs, drawing astonished looks from the girls, his voice echoing through the warehouse. Raz sticks her head through the door and shushes him, and only then does he break off, coughing a little.

"Sorry, *Princess*." He brings his hands forward, and the ropes they'd bound his wrists with fall to the floor. Khavar starts forward threateningly, but Aladdin throws up a hand. "Easy there, snake eyes. I'm not going to run."

Turning to Caspida, he asks, "What's going on here? I'm supposed to believe you're some kind of rebel, only to find out you're a *royal*?" He throws a finger toward the door. "There are people out there who leave offerings at the temples in the name of the Phoenix. They believe you're a guardian, a savior. They sing your praises, wear your symbol—but they have no idea you're one of *them*. One of the same oppressive rulers they think you're protecting them from!"

"I never claimed to be a savior," she returns coldly. "And believe me, I wish I could tell them the truth. But not all battles can be fought in the light. Those *people* out there are *my* people, thief, and I will fight for them. The Phoenix is the only way I have. The moment I step out of the shadows, my uncle will see to it that I never cross him again. Aladdin, I'm on *your* side! Why do you think I asked Xaxos to hire *you* to steal the key? I'd heard you were a great thief, yes, but I thought of all people, you'd understand my cause."

"Well, I guess you don't know me well enough," says Aladdin darkly. "I'm not my father. I'm not some kind of rebel or leader. I took the job from Xaxos for the money, nothing else."

"Enough," sighs Caspida, holding up a hand. "Thief, the ring you stole belongs to me. It's been in my family's possession for hundreds of years, going all the way back to my ancestress Roshana the Wise."

The fur on my back prickles, drawing a concerned pat from Ensi. You had no such ring, Habiba. Surely I would have known if you had such a powerful talisman in your possession—especially one meant to lead the wearer to me. My interest in this ring expands tenfold, and I wish sorely it had not been lost.

"This is taking entirely too long," Khavar says. "Just search him!"

"I'll do it!" Ensi volunteers, her eyes lighting up.

"All right, fine!" Aladdin twists away from her reaching hands. "I stole the ring!"

Ensi withdraws regretfully, and Caspida's eyes sharpen. "Go on."

"I did steal it, and I absolutely *meant* to give it to your man Xaxos. But . . . I lost it in the desert."

She frowns. "What were you doing in the desert?"

He pauses and chews his lip, studying her a moment before replying. "Princess, have you ever *worn* the ring?"

She hesitates. "Once."

"And what did you feel?"

"Feel? Nothing. Why would you ask that?"

"When I put it on, it . . . sort of spoke to me. Not in words, really, but . . . sort of like a rope pulling at a horse. It *led* me into the desert, like it wanted to show me something."

The girls are suitably rapt, leaning closer. Their flickering torches throw dancing shadows over their faces.

"Well?" asks Ensi. "What did you find?"

He shrugs. "Nothing. It just *stopped*. Like it had reached whatever it was pulling me toward. But there was nothing there except some old ruins. Maybe there never *was* anything there. Anyway, Darian caught up to me then, and he took it back."

She wrinkles her brow perplexedly. "You mean the ruins of Neruby, the old Amulen capital. But the place is empty, said to be haunted by the jinn. You're *sure* there was nothing?"

"Just sand and broken towers." He tilts his head, his eyes glittering with torchlight. "What did you *think* it led to?"

She looks around at each of her girls, then back at Aladdin, her eyes full, as if she is weighing whether or not to tell him.

"I don't know," she says at last. She is a good liar, and I nearly miss the elevation in her heartbeat and the slightest pause before she speaks. But I cannot see into her thoughts to tell what she truly does know about the ring and about the lamp. Does she know it leads to me? And does she know who I am, or that she and I are linked through you, Habiba, her mighty ancestress?

Unsettled, I look closer at her and her friends, trying to discern what their goal is. The girls are all Amulen, it seems, except for one—the quiet one who listens and says little. Nessa, with her dark skin and hair, is Tytoshi, judging by her appearance and accent, though by her dress and fluent Amulen, she's been in Parthenia for a while. Her hair is twisted into dreadlocks, each one tipped in hardened silver that tinkles musically when she moves. Only royalty wear silver in their hair; everyone else's locks are tipped in bronze or copper. What is a Tytoshi princess doing this far north?

Then I spot something tucked beneath her black cloak, and my hackles rise. To get a closer look, I jump onto Ensi's shoulder, then leap onto Nessa's. Surprised, she takes me in her arms and strokes my head. I nose under her cloak and sniff the flute she carries on her hip, then back away hissing.

"You're hurting her!" says Ensi, snatching me back. It's all right. I found out what I needed to know.

That's no ordinary flute, and Nessa is no ordinary girl.

She's a jinn charmer, capable of hypnotizing my kind with that flute, inlaid with Eskarr glyphs, and trapping us in bottles. I watch her mistrustfully and know that more than ever, we have to get away, and fast.

Because now I know where Zhian is.

Chapter Eight

TURNING AWAY FROM ALADDIN, Caspida signals to her girls, and they gather close around her, out of Aladdin's earshot.

"Do you believe him?" asks Ensi in a whisper, curling my tail around her finger.

"Of course she doesn't believe him," Khavar interjects. "He's a thief. His very nature is dishonest."

"I'm not sure I *do* believe him," says Caspida slowly, running her finger thoughtfully over her dagger's blade and looking over her shoulder at Aladdin. He stands with his hands in his pockets, trying to look harmless. "After all, where is Darian? How did the thief escape my cousin and his men and manage to make it to the city before them? Has anyone heard from Darian in the past week?"

Ensi shakes her head. "I've been intercepting every message sent by pigeon, and there's been nothing from the prince."

"What of my uncle? Has Sulifer had contact with him?"

"Not that I know of. The vizier rarely leaves the council chambers and keeps his business secret."

"You were right in the beginning, Khavar," sighs the princess. "We should never have hired a third party to steal the ring back. I should have done it myself."

"Sulifer watches you too closely," says Ensi. "You'd have never pulled it off, and if you'd been caught, the consequences would have been too great. Speaking of which, we really should be getting back to the palace."

Khavar's snake pulls back and hisses at me, and I hiss in return. Khavar catches its head and pushes it back into her cloak. "Is it really a bad thing, Darian missing? I'll not shed a tear if he never shows up again. Think of that, Cas. You wouldn't have to marry him."

"I doubt it will be that easy," Caspida replies. "And however much I loathe my cousin, I would not wish death on him." She pauses, then adds, "A cell in the dungeons with rats for company, perhaps. But not death." She sighs and rubs the bridge of her nose. "We should have destroyed the ring long ago."

"We couldn't have known Darian would steal it," replies Ensi. "It's stayed safely in that vault for hundreds of years. This isn't your fault, Cas."

"Roshana's ring was mine to guard," she replies flatly. "I don't want comfort. I want it found and destroyed. I don't know what it does, but I know that it's linked to the jinn, and that's never a good thing."

"We really should get back to the palace," says Nessa. "We've been gone too long already."

"What about the thief?" asks Khavar. "We can't very well drag him along."

"Search him," Caspida says. "Just in case he's lying."

Aladdin, who heard this last pronouncement, throws me a horrified look, but I am already moving. I leap out of Ensi's arms and dash away into the shadows, turning to smoke the moment I am out of sight. I have just seconds before they search Aladdin and find the lamp. I cannot imagine the Amulen princess will be as openminded about my presence as Aladdin has been, not when her own handmaiden is one of the jinn charmers who likely trapped Zhian.

I blow through a crack in the wall and collect outside, then waste no time in raising a terrible racket. I clang against the warehouse and shout out in a deep, male voice: "Who's in there? Show yourself!"

Raz, keeping watch, runs inside to alert the others. I turn to wind and blast open the door to find the girls are gone, startled by the noise and vanished into the dark city with soft, hasty footsteps. Aladdin stands alone, untouched. He pats the lamp.

"Nice work," he says. "I wouldn't mind having you along when I pull jobs."

"If you have me along," I reply dryly, "you won't *need* to pull jobs."

"Fair point."

Aladdin goes to the doorway and stands staring at the night, his frame rigid. He is a dark current beneath a still sea.

I shift back into a girl, dressed in black silk with tiny white moonflowers sprinkled in my hair. As I wait for him to speak, I idly conjure bangles on my wrists, each inscribed with a verse from the "Song of Roshana," the poem written in honor of your nineteenth birthday by twelve of the world's most esteemed poets.

Roshana Mithraya, Warrior Queen,
rode to war on a Jinni's wings,

Roshana Mithraya, fair and bold,
wielded a sword of steel and gold.
Her foes who looked upon her swore
For love or fear, they'd fight no more.

The princess is heavy in my thoughts. After you died, Habiba, someone must have spirited your infant daughter out of Neruby before the jinn destroyed the city. Your line lived on, and your spirit too, it seems; this Caspida is a fiery one, just like you were. What would she think of me if she knew who I was? My old guilt lurks deep within, like a wolf in a cave, and I look up toward the palace in the north district, shining like a pearl beneath the stars.

Now she fights the jinn. She even has her own jinn charmer at her side. I don't know if Nessa is the same charmer who bottled Zhian, but charmers are rare, and there can't be many others in the city. So it seems the best place to start my search is the royal palace. Even if he's not being held there, perhaps I can find a clue there as to his whereabouts.

But first, I need a way into the palace.

I study my master thoughtfully.

Aladdin stirs at last, turning to glance at me over his shoulder, his fingers dancing on the lamp.

"The Phoenix is the princess," he murmurs. "And I'm talking to a jinni. Gods, this night just keeps getting stranger."

He starts forward, walking down the dark street as if in a fog. We pass other storehouses and closed carpentry and shipwrights' shops. A dog scrambles out of Aladdin's way, raising its hackles and growling at me, not fooled by my human disguise. We pass the city gates, shut against the night. They are washed in the orange light of massive braziers suspended from above, and guards stand watch on the wall beside them. Aladdin skirts around them, staying concealed in the shadows.

Eventually we reach the center of the city, where the river runs in a channel of cut stone. The water flows deep and fast and dark, its banks edged with low walls of rectangular bricks. From grates set into the channel, runoff from the gutters and houses pours into the river, joining the mad rush to the sea.

Aladdin stops at the center of an arching bridge, its railings smooth wood supported by statues carved in the likenesses of the undergods. At the foot of each carving, little offerings have been left. Candles, flowers, dolls made of straw, each representing a prayer. At the foot of Nykora are ten times as many offerings as the others, and so many candles are lit before her that she seems to shine. The railing above her flutters with ribbons and strings of beads. Nykora is the undergoddess of the oppressed and poor, and her sigil is the phoenix.

Aladdin pauses before her statue for several long moments, his hands deep in his pockets. His face is softened by the candlelight. His cloak, tattered and patched, rustles in the breeze that sweeps upriver.

"She really is the Phoenix. And they love her." He lifts his face and stares at me. "I can't remember the last time they loved anyone at all. Even my father was hated by many for stirring up trouble."

Along the opposite railing grow vines thick with white moonflowers. I lean over and look down at the river rushing below, hastening on to the cliffs, where it pours into the waiting sea, like a lovelorn bride running to meet her groom. Aladdin turns away from the little shrine and joins me, his shoulders hunched pensively.

"When I was a boy," he says softly, "I used to stand on this bridge with my father. We made little wooden boats, and he sewed sails for them. We dropped them into the water, then raced along the bank to see whose left the city first. Once I slipped and fell in, and my father jumped in to save me. He couldn't even swim. I don't know how he did it. Later he told me that the goddess Nykora must have pulled us out of the river." He turns and looks at the shrine. "We left a little boat right there as an offering of thanks. But I never believed in Nykora. People remember my father as a hero who set fires and led marches. I remembered him as a hero because of that day in the river."

Turning to me, he says, "I'm not a hero, Zahra. I'm not my father." He turns away and pulls something from his sleeve. It is one of the princess's daggers, its hilt carved into delicate lilies. How he managed to steal it off her, I can't imagine. "The night I snuck into the palace to steal the ring, I carried a dagger like this. Much plainer, of course, but the same length and weight." He balances it on his finger. "After stealing the ring, I snuck into Sulifer's rooms. I stood over the vizier as he slept and held that blade, trying to work up the nerve to cut his throat."

Aladdin sighs and drives the dagger into the rail. The hilt quivers. "Maybe I'm a coward. But I couldn't avenge them. When the ring started pulling at me, I knew it must be enchanted. I thought, if it's so valuable to the prince that he would keep it locked in his own room, then perhaps I could get my revenge by stealing whatever it led to. When that turned out to be *you*, I thought, well, here's my chance. I can just wish for revenge. But as it turns out, I'm too cowardly even for that."

"*Coward* is not the word I'd use," I say softly.

He shrugs and pries the dagger out of the rail. "And now there's this princess. All my life, I thought she was like the other royals—selfish and spoiled. She's engaged to Darian, after all, and her father the king is said to be addicted to simmon, wasted away to nothing.

Her uncle executed my parents." He holds up the dagger and stares at his reflection in the blade. "But now she says she's the Phoenix, that she's on *our* side. What am I supposed to do with that?"

"Not everyone is what they seem."

His eyes turn to me. "Like you?"

I raise a brow. "And what do I seem to be?"

Aladdin studies me, and feeling suddenly shy, I turn away. I pluck a moonflower and pull the petals off one by one, letting them fall into the river.

"You seem sad," he says at last. "And lonely."

Letting the flower stem drop, I laugh. "You know nothing about me."

He shrugs, still watching me closely. "I don't think you're the same jinni they sing about at all. I think there's more to your story. Did you really kill that queen? I don't think you did."

A bit startled, I meet his gaze. "I killed her. I am a jinni, Aladdin. Never think I am anything but heartless."

He looks down, one of his hands moving closer, until the back of one finger comes to rest on my wrist. I stare at it, unable to breathe. My skin warms under that gentle contact. "You saved my life twice already. That doesn't sound heartless."

Pulling away quickly, I drop my hands, out of his reach. "You don't have to say that."

He frowns, withdrawing his hand. "Maybe I want to. Even a thief may have honor, and even a jinni may have a heart."

The roaring of the river fills my ears. Avoiding his gaze, I cross to the other side of the bridge, staring north at the dark shadow of Mount Tissia. I struggle to swallow the knot in my throat.

I need a plan. A plan to get inside the palace.

A plan to cool the embers Aladdin's touch stirred to life.

Turning around, I find him watching me, cautious and curious. "You should make a wish."

At once he turns skeptical. "What?"

A part of me hates myself for feeding his obsession. That part wants me to tell him he's haunted by the dead, that I know how that feels, that I've drunk that poison many times. I'm sickened with it even now. But I don't, because I am a selfish spirit, and looking up at the dying moon, I can almost feel the bond between me and the lamp snapping once and for all.

"The princess," I say. "She's the heir to the throne, right? Whoever marries her will be the most powerful man in the kingdom." I turn and gaze at the statue of Nykora. "He could do whatever he wanted. He would command the vizier, the military, the guards here in the city . . ."

I meet his gaze and find him rigid, his body tense as a drawn bow.

"This is it, don't you see? You don't have to kill anyone, but you can still get your revenge. I can help you."

"What are you saying?" he asks.

I smile and lean in to whisper, "I can get you into the palace. I can give you power, wealth, and titles. I can help you win the princess, and in doing so, win your revenge. What would anger Darian more than seeing his enemy take his bride? What would be sweeter than seeing this vizier forced to bow before you, his prince?"

Aladdin holds his breath, and I can see that he's caught my meaning. Not for the first time, I feel truly monstrous. I've always hated the jinn for being cruel and selfish. Do you remember how I once told you that I wasn't like them? But I know in the space where I have no heart that I'm no different at all.

I'm a very good jinni, and that's a very bad thing.

But *freedom*, Habiba . . . For freedom, I might become anything. It terrifies me to think how far I will go for it. But I've never wanted anything so badly before, so I swallow my conscience and nod encouragingly at my master.

"It could work," he says softly. "Zahra, you're *brilliant*."

I straighten, my hands beginning to tingle. "Then say the words."

Aladdin pauses, takes a breath, steeling himself. When he speaks, his voice burns with conviction.

"Zahra, I wish to be made a prince."

Two: The Princess

As they often did in the late afternoon, when the sun was ripe and the day hazy, the Queen and the Jinni walked together in the shade of the Jewel Gardens in the heart of the palace, which the Queen had wished for and the Jinni shaped for her. They spoke of many things, of past wars and rulers, of faraway lands, of gods and jinn. For the Jinni had lived long and seen much, and the Queen, possessing a keen mind, had many questions.

At last the Queen said, "Thou hast become a friend like unto a sister to me. I favor not only thy counsel, but thy company. May I ask thee anything?"

And the Jinni answered, "I have had many masters, but none like you, O Queen. I am honored to be thy friend, and surely I will answer whatever thou ask of me."

"Then what troubles thee?" the Queen replied. "For I know the look in thine eye—thy thoughts are tossed as the storm-driven sea."

"It is true, Ḥabiba," said the Jinni. "For I am afraid."

"What dost thou fear?" cried the Queen. "Name it, and I shall slay it for thee."

Taking the Queen's hands in her own, the Jinni replied, "Long has it been forbidden that a jinni and a human may bear any love for the other, yet you have become sister to my heart."

"Who dares forbid us?" asked the Queen.

"The one they call Nardukha, the Shaitan, who rules the jinn and all of Ambadya. He is as old as the gods, and none may defeat him. If he knew of the love I bear thee, swift would be his wrath. For this is the first rule of the jinn: that no jinni may love a human. For always must our allegiance be to Nardukha, and none else."

"Then let him leave his hall beneath the earth and tell me so himself," said the Queen. "For I do not bow to the laws of fear-mongerers. He forbids this and he forbids that, but he is not all-powerful. Even the Forbidden Wish may be spoken, and there is naught he may do to stop it."

At this the Jinni raised a mournful cry. "What dost thou know of the Forbidden Wish?"

"Thou once told me that none but the Shaitan might free thee from thy lamp, but I know it is not so. For I could wish thee free, and there is naught he could do to stop it."

"It is true," the Jinni replied in distress. "But every wish has its price, and the price of the Forbidden Wish is thy life. Thou must swear upon the souls of thy people that thou wilt never speak those words. If thou shouldst suffer for love of me, I would never forgive myself. We have already transgressed the law that divides man and jinn, and I fear our time together is running out."

"Do not say such things," said the Queen. "We have today and yesterday, and we will seize tomorrow. We will have all the time in the world if we are clever enough to take it."

"What use is time against the might of Ambadya?"

"Dear Jinni." The Queen smiled. "Time is the strongest magic of all."

—From the *Song of the Fall of Roshana,*
Last Queen of Neruby
by Parys zai Moura,
Watchmaiden and Scribe to Queen Roshana

Chapter Nine

THE POWER HITS ME like a strike of lightning to my brain.

It radiates in glowing tentacles from Aladdin and coils up my arms and legs. It sinks through my skin and collects in my chest, a pulsing ball of white-hot energy. The hair on my arms stands on end. This feeling is like swallowing the sun. It has been centuries since I felt this much power at my disposal. Aladdin's first wish was a mere trick, a simple reshuffling of reality. It took just a puddle of magic. This wish calls for an ocean of it.

Aladdin can't see any of this, of course. He sees me draw a deep, gasping breath, sees my eyes grow wide, perhaps. He watches intently, his face flushed with excitement.

I turn my hands over, where the magic curls in gold patterns and sinks into my skin. Making Aladdin a prince will be tricky. No grand display of fire and explosions. No flourish or fanfare. In the old days, I could have put on a spectacle seen for leagues around— but if Aladdin is to be welcomed into the palace instead of beheaded in front of it, this must be done quietly. I sift my thoughts like sand, searching for hidden jewels.

"Take my hand," I say.

He looks down at my open hand and winces. "What are you—"

Impatiently—I must release this magic or I'll burst!—I grab his hand and the world spins and suddenly we are standing on the high cliff overlooking the sea. Far, far below, the waves crash into the rocks, and the moon, suspended over the dark water, seems much larger and nearer than it did in the city.

Aladdin shouts and stumbles backward, away from the edge, his face a bit green.

"What are you doing?" he gasps.

"Thinking." I stare out at the sea, and my vision is tinged with madness. This much power is intoxicating. I can see the possibilities glowing on every surface of the world, the way a sculptor might see forms hidden in a block of stone. I can change it, mold it, melt it in whatever way I need to grant his wish. My hands itch to begin. My body hums with energy.

I extend one hand and point it at the horizon, concentrating with all my might. Far out on the moonlit sea, magic gathers. The water foams and froths. The air sings and burns. I see the threads of reality, and I grab them and twist them and weave them in new patterns. Water becomes wood; air becomes cloth. I draw the elements together and transform them.

"It's a ship," Aladdin breathes. He stands on the edge of the cliff now, enraptured.

"It's *your* ship," I tell him.

In moments, it is finished. The ship is made of red cedar, with three rows of oars and a tall figurehead carved in the form of a roaring lion. The sleek ram beneath it is painted black. A proper warship. A ship fit for a prince.

As the sea around the ship settles, I turn to Aladdin, who is still gaping like an open clam. "Well? Do you want to get a closer look?"

"This," says Aladdin breathlessly, "is *incredible*."

He is standing proudly at the bow, relishing in the beauty of my magic ship.

"I'm glad you like it," I mutter. I lean weakly against the rail, my stomach churning. The moment I transported us onto the deck's ship, I felt a wave of regret.

"Are you *seasick*?" asks Aladdin, his eyes bright with amusement.

"Shut up, human."

After conjuring the ship and transferring the pair of us onto its decks, I enchanted the oars and set them rowing, but the wind is against us, and every wave strikes the hull like the slap of a whale's tail. I've always hated the sea. So dark and deep and wet. It swallows things and never lets them go.

With a shudder, I flick my hand at the oars and speed us up a little.

It must look as though we're coming into port like any other ship, which is why I conjured it at such a distance. The story goes that Prince Rahzad rai Asnam, youngest son of the Shah of Istarya, set out to explore and make his fortune. After a terrible run-in with a tribe of vicious maarids, only he and his servant, the lowly but lovely Zahra, survived. Now we limp into the Parthenian port, seeking refuge at the king's court.

Alas. I gaze about the beautiful ship and try to decide how best to destroy it.

"Aladdin, you may want to stay close to me."

"Why? What are you—no! Not my ship!"

"Duck!" I send a torrent of water blasting over his head to snap the mast and rip the sails. Aladdin looks on with dismay.

A few waves thrown about, some teeth marks in the planks— maarids are particularly nasty biters—and finally a gouge in the hull finish the job. I do the work quickly, fighting nausea all the while. Aladdin looks close to tears as his beautiful vessel is blasted apart.

Suitably beaten and battered, the *Artemisia* now lurches across the water like a drunken duck. Aladdin and I huddle against the mast and do our best to look wretched, which really isn't difficult at all, as the rocking waves make me ill and irritable, while Aladdin is withdrawn and pensive. As the final touch, I change our clothes to expensive but torn and dirty robes of silk and damask.

Aladdin's appearance is a problem; the princess and her hand-maidens have all seen his face, and it's unlikely we'd be able to explain that away. So I let a bit of magic sink into his features, cre-ating a glamoured mask. It isn't a foolproof spell—permanently altering his appearance would call for another wish. But it's enough to discourage recognition. When the princess looks at Aladdin, she will see only a young man who may slightly resemble the thief from the Rings.

As we wait for the tide to carry us to the harbor, I drill Aladdin on his new identity, making him repeat it over and over until he throws his hands in the air.

"I'm not saying it one more bleeding time, jinni!"

Miffed, I cross my arms and look away. "I don't want to end up murdered by one of your jinn-killers."

"Neither do *I*. Look, I've got this all under control."

Unconvinced, I give him a doubtful look, and he grins. "Smoky, if there's one thing I am, it's adaptable."

And so we arrive in Parthenia, the travel-weary but dashing Prince Rahzad rai Asnam of Istarya and his servant girl. Everything happens in a whirl once we are towed into the harbor. Soldiers whisk us through the city, past gaping crowds, to the palace. There we are handed over to a group of bearded ministers, who ply Aladdin with questions while escorting him through the echoing halls. Aladdin, giving them simple one-word responses, bends his head this way and that, taking in the splendor of the Parthenian court. The palace is marble and sandstone, all smooth curves and vast, empty spaces filled with whispers and roaming peacocks. Rich carpets and tapestries add color to the walls and floor, and we pass many courtyards babbling with fountains. Nobles lurk in the corners, watching and whispering, gathering in a train behind us.

Aladdin is pulled aside and dressed in fresh clothes, fine silk and cashmere in tones of rich green and gold. I, for the most part, am forgotten, left to shadow my master in silence. I don't mind a bit. I use this time to scan the palace, searching for some sign of Zhian, but it seems my search will not be that simple. I can sense nothing of him.

"Your Highness," says an approaching minister, his beard long and perfectly combed, his head covered with a tall cylindrical hat of purple and gold. "I am Jalil rai Feruj, the Minister of Diplomacy here in King Malek's court. You're from . . . where did you say? Forgive me. The name was unknown to me."

"Istarya," says Aladdin. "Far to the south."

"Ah, yes, of course." Jalil nods, but his eyes are still clouded with confusion. He beckons to a boy standing nearby with an armful of scrolls, and the boy hastens forward. Jalil selects a scroll and unfurls it, his brow knitting. "Istarya . . . Istarya . . . you must forgive me, Your Highness. My memory is so weak of late."

I step forward and grasp the edge of the map, smiling at the minister. "If I may, my lord?"

While he is distracted, his eyes on me, the last drop of magic from Aladdin's wish leaks from my thumb and trails across the parchment, turning to ink.

"Here it is," I say, pointing.

Jalil looks down and blinks, his gaze settling on the tiny island at the bottom of the map. "Ah! Of course. Well, allow me to escort you to His Majesty's throne, for he is eager to meet you."

"Lead on, old man!" Aladdin slaps the minister on the shoulder, then, noting the stunned faces around him, coughs and attempts a bow. "I mean, um, thank you, my lord."

The hallway to the throne room is tasteful but ornate, sculpted into a series of fantastic arches, each carved with detailed vines and leaves and supported by blood-colored marble columns. Tall windows between the arches let in sunlight that makes the stone bright with colors and patterns, revealing the delicate white veins of the deep red marble, as if the columns are made of exposed muscle.

The king's throne room is set in the center of the palace, like the hub of an enormous wheel. We pause outside tall doors of polished teak wood carved with grapevines. On either side, stone lions as tall as three men stretch their mouths in unending silent roars, their sightless eyes glaring down at us.

The doors are opened by stoic guards with peaked helmets, and we walk into the grandest room I've yet seen in Parthenia. The chamber is enormous, divided into three long, narrow sections by the double rows of stone pillars that march from one end to the other, supporting a roof that vaults upward into three massive domes. Pigeons circle the space above, cutting through beams of light that pour through square holes in the ceiling, filling the air with the sounds of wings beating air, their shadows flickering across the columns. On the walls, enormous carvings depict detailed battle sequences, some of them recalling Amulen history I witnessed myself, such as the sacking of Berus and the surrender of King Madarash of the Baltoshi Islands.

My eyes fall on a bas-relief that chills me: It is of you, Habiba, standing atop Mount Tissia, Neruby burning in the background. You are on your knees, looking pious and tragic, as an ugly jinni with horns, wings, and claws crouches on your back and prepares to tear out your throat. I think that one is supposed to be me. Below the relief are carved the words "The Fall of Roshana the Wise."

I turn my eyes away and do not look at any more of the carvings.

On a throne set on a high dais in the center of the room, flanked by tall stone gryphons painted to look startlingly real, sits the man who inherited your great legacy. Surrounded by the majesty of this grand hall and dwarfed by his stone gryphons, the king of the Amulens is small and sickly, slouched in his throne beneath heavy leopard-skin stoles. His complexion is pale, almost translucent, and his hands tremble. The yellow tinge in his eyes betrays the source of his condition: simmon smoke.

The mighty Amulens are ruled by a drug addict.

Caspida stands to one side of the throne, her hand perched on her father's shoulder, as if she is pouring her own strength into him. She looks quite transformed from the girl who spat and sparred in the Rings the night before, though her eyes are a bit tired. She wears a gown of pale gold, with sheer red silk draped over her shoulders. Tassels hung from the hem of her dress brush the tops of her sandals, which are studded with gemstones. She regards Aladdin's glamoured face without a hint of recognition; her eyes are cool and appraising, and a little suspicious.

I sense a flutter of panic from Aladdin at the sight of Caspida, but he calms when my glamour holds and recognition does not flare in her eyes.

As Jalil and Aladdin approach the throne, I hang back in the shadows of the pillars and watch closely. Guards stand at the base of each column, so still they might be statues themselves, and they don't stop me from walking along the wall beneath the friezes. Other servants move in the shadows, and nobles gather in groups of four and five, talking in hushed whispers while regarding Aladdin with open curiosity. I blend in with them, a shadow myself, within full hearing and view of the dais.

The king makes an effort to sit up straighter as my master bows low before him, but his eyes are dull and uninterested. There is power in this room, but it does not sit on the throne.

The court crier, a barrel-chested man wearing a tall peaked hat, is announcing the king: "... Malek son of Anoushan son of Arhab son of Oshur, King of Kings, King of Parthenia, King of Niroh, of Beddan and of Mon Asur, Chosen by Imohel, Blessed by the Gods, Favored of Amul, King of the Amulens ..." On he drones, listing a seemingly endless litany of titles, until at last he turns to face the king and introduces Aladdin.

"I present to your Exalted Majesty for your pleasure, Rahzad rai Asnam, Prince of Istarya."

The list ends there, almost humorously brief compared to Malek's. Aladdin, throughout the length of the arduous introduction, remained bent at the waist, as he'd been instructed by Jalil. Now he rises, face blank, and waits for Malek to speak.

Except Malek has fallen asleep.

Jalil coughs and looks down at his feet. Aladdin, reddening, starts to say something to him, but the man on the other side of the throne bends and whispers in the king's ear, and Malek blinks furiously and looks down at Aladdin. Then the man straightens and fixes his eyes on my master, and one of his hands lingers on the side of the throne.

While Malek greets Aladdin with a formal rehearsed speech, offering him hospitality and wishing him health, I watch the man who'd awoken the monarch. The similarity between him and the king is apparent, now that I look for it. Vizier Sulifer is the heartier, stronger version of his older brother, his flesh filled out where Malek's caves in. They have the same brow, the same arched nose, and the same round jawline—traits also shared by Sulifer's son, Darian, though of course he is not present. It will take the king's nephew at least a week to make the journey back to the palace. So these are the Anadredcas, the Amulen dynasty who inherited your great legacy, Habiba.

When the exchange of formal greetings ends, Malek slumps in his throne as if fatigued and lets Sulifer take over. The other men seem to accept this with relief, as if they see their king as a figurehead or a puppet. As if they are thinking, *Finally, the fool is finished.* Only Caspida looks concerned for him, and she squeezes his shoulder, her eyes flickering to Sulifer as he steps forward.

Aladdin's eyes are deceptively blank as he regards the man who killed his parents. Sulifer stands in front of the throne and stares back at him. He wears robes cut in precise military fashion, dyed deep blue and hemmed with silver. A ceremonial sword, its sheath inscribed with Amulen script, is tucked into his red sash. His head is bare, his long graying hair sweeping his shoulders, his beard trimmed short and sharp. There is a cunning in his face that makes me uneasy. Perhaps I should have shifted into a spider, to hang in Aladdin's ear and whisper advice.

But no. If he is going to truly pass himself off as a prince, he must learn to *be* a prince. To think like one, to scheme like one, to look wolves like this Sulifer in the eye and be unafraid. This is a crucial moment for us both. I gave him the ship, the clothes, the story he needed to gain entry into this room. But if he is to truly convince these people of his false identity, he must do it here and now—and on his own. I can only stand in the shadows and urge him on silently. *I'm adaptable*, he told me. I hope he wasn't lying. Both our fates depend on it.

Sulifer questions Aladdin about his arrival in Parthenia, and my master repeats the story yet again.

"We have not heard of this Istarya before," says Sulifer.

"I'm not surprised," Aladdin replies, his voice strong and clear. "It is very small, and our people do not often venture this far north."

"But *you* have," states Sulifer.

"We heard of Parthenia's strength in fending off the jinn. Naturally I was intrigued, so I came to learn from you, if I could, how you have withstood these monsters. Your bravery and skill are unparalleled, from what I'm told. Not many cities are willing to anger the jinn, and instead they leave offerings to appease them."

I exhale in relief, feeling a glow of pride. There is not a breath of hesitation in him, not a tremor in his voice. He is as skilled a liar as I have ever known, and I have known a very great many liars, Habiba.

The other men nod and murmur in appreciation of Aladdin's

words, but Sulifer looks him over carefully, his shrewd eyes narrowed. "A pretty speech and a valiant sentiment, young prince. We must speak more of your travels after you have rested. Jalil, show our guest to his rooms, and see that he is given all he requires."

Aladdin bows low. "My thanks to you, my lord, and to your Exalted Majesty. I have heard of the bravery of the Amulens, and to stand here among you is the height of honors."

He backs away, briefly bowing to Caspida, and does not turn his back to the king until he reaches the doors. I slip through the crowd and out of the chamber just before the doors shut.

Chapter Ten

WITH MUCH BOWING and exchanged pleasantries, we are left in a
set of rooms somewhere near the eastern rear of the palace. There
are three chambers—one for lounging and receiving visitors, one
bedchamber for Aladdin, and a small servant's room for me. The
chambers open to a small, grassy courtyard populated with white
lilies and a fig tree heavy with fruit. I pick a few and pop them
in my mouth as I walk around the chambers, taking it all in. The
floor, made of smooth black and white clay tiles, is spread with rich
carpets, and the open arches leading to the courtyard are covered
with gauzy curtains. Aladdin wanders into the bedchamber and
flops onto the bed, letting out a long sigh.

"Oh, gods," he sighs. "They can chop off my head or quarter me
or whatever it is they do to impostors, as long as I get one night to
sleep in this bed. Then it'll all be worth it. I might even thank them."

"Thank *them*?"

He rolls onto his stomach and peers through the doorway at

me, grinning. "Oh, right. It was *me* who made the wish, wasn't it? I guess I get all the credit."

A well-aimed fig hits him square in the forehead and bursts. He splutters and licks the juice that drips down his cheek.

"Point taken. Thank *you*, Zahra." He rises and leans in the doorway, his arms crossed, and watches me as I pace the room. "To be honest, though, it all makes me kind of sick. To think so many of us grow up sleeping in gutters, like rats, when all this space is given to one man just because he has an extra word in front of his name." He pauses, his face darkening. "Did you see him? Standing up there like a king, thinking himself untouchable. The great vizier of Parthenia." A small, dry smile twists his lips. "And here I am, right under his nose."

A knock sounds on the door, and then a pair of servants—a girl and a boy—enters with fresh clothes for us.

"Your Highness, my name is Esam," says the boy, "and this is Chara. We will be at your service for as long as you are here. Please allow me to assist you in dressing for the evening meal."

Aladdin turns a bit red and stammers, "Ah, I don't think—"

"It is customary in our homeland for princes to dress themselves," I insert, a bit hastily. It won't do to have anyone seeing the lamp hidden under Aladdin's clothes. "It is a tradition going back many generations. Here, I'll take those. I'm sure you're needed elsewhere, right?" I crowd them to the door and then shut it, smiling, in their faces.

"So if I meet a noble who is *older* than me, but of lower station . . ." Aladdin stands in the grassy courtyard and scrubs wearily at his hair. "I bow like this?"

He leans over and throws out an arm.

"Gods, no." I'm sitting in front of him, enjoying a fresh pomegranate and attempting to cram as much etiquette into him as I can before dinner. "That one is for a minister who has held his office for more than ten years, or who has a personal fleet of ships."

"Are you sure? I thought that one was like *this*." He attempts another awkward bow. "Why am I listening to you, anyway? You've been living in a lamp for the past five hundred years!"

I flick a seed at him. "I still know my way around a court, which is more than can be said for you! Now try the proper greeting for a man who is related to the king, but with no possible claim to the throne."

He thinks for a moment, then puts his hands together and hesitantly leans forward, before cocking a hopeful eyebrow at me.

"I give up!" I groan, tossing the rind of the pomegranate aside. "You're hopeless. Just stick with a basic bow at the waist, and let them credit your appalling social graces to your foreignness. People are always more lenient with foreigners."

With a sigh, Aladdin collapses into the grass. "This is exhausting. There has got to be an easier way to bring Sulifer down—a way that doesn't involve *bowing* to him."

It has been a week and two days since we arrived at the Parthenian palace, and still I have found no sign of Zhian. I wish I had the power to freeze time, but time is the one element no jinni can control, not even the Shaitan.

At night, when Aladdin sleeps, I slip into the hallway, shift into a cat, and explore the palace. But my invisible chain does not reach far, and though I have covered every inch I can, most of the palace is out of my reach. I hope I didn't make a mistake in bringing us here, only to find that Zhian's somewhere else entirely.

When Aladdin is awake, I drill him on court etiquette, making him a prince in manner as well as in name. Servants bring us meals twice a day, and Aladdin is well supplied with clothing and other necessities, as well as invitations to dine with various curious nobles and merchant lords in the evening, which gives me a little time to search other parts of the palace, still to no avail.

Aladdin is impatient to meet Caspida—as Prince Rahzad this time, instead of as a kidnapped thief—but she is elusive, and no one, not even a prince, may call on a princess uninvited. And so we are both frustrated and edgy, and the lessons aren't helping.

As he states several times, rather strongly, "I can figure it out as I go."

"You're more stubborn than a stinking camel!" I protest.

He only shrugs and grins in that maddening way he has. "I've been called worse."

Sometimes, I think he makes mistakes just to infuriate me. Like today. We've been over these bows a thousand and one times, but he keeps bungling them.

Someone raps on the door just as Aladdin begins to doze off in the grass, ignoring my protests that he'll stain his clothes. He squints at me.

"Get that, will you?"

I glare at him. "I'm not *actually* your servant."

"I know," he says, with a wicked half smile. "I just like it when you get angry with me. Smoke comes out of your ears."

"It certainly does *not*."

I open the door to reveal two young nobles. One I recognize: Raz, the tall archer who was there the night the princess kidnapped Aladdin.

The other noble is a handsome young man with a Tytoshi complexion and dreadlocks tipped with silver. I can tell at once that he is brother, likely even twin to Nessa, the princess's jinn charmer and handmaiden. Does he too carry a jinn-charming flute?

I bow to Raz and greet the Tytoshi in his native fashion: by pulling my hair over my shoulder and tugging the ends, displaying my untipped locks and thus my inferior status. A look of surprise and then appreciation flits across his features. Then he turns and bows to Aladdin, and I step aside.

"Greetings, Prince Rahzad, and welcome to Parthenia. I am Vigo, son of Vigor. This is Lady Razpur nez Miran. We've come to escort you to dinner."

Aladdin bows stiffly—unfortunately, it is the one that ought to be used only for naval officers—and steps through the door. Raz and Vigo flank him, trying to look indifferent but exchanging looks of curiosity behind his back. I trail behind, head bowed demurely, eyes and senses straining to pick up every detail.

"We heard about your journey here," says Raz. "You must tell us more sometime. To survive an attack by maarids on the open sea—that's remarkable!"

"Yes," adds Vigo. "It's remarkable, isn't it? Almost *too* remarkable."

Raz shoots him a cross look, and the Tytoshi shrugs.

We are led through a tiled courtyard and then down a long walkway framed by a series of elegant white arches, through which the sky can be seen deepening into twilight. A servant girl in a gray robe flits from arch to arch, lighting cleverly concealed candles that, when lit, make the arches seem to glow as if enchanted. On either side of us, cypress trees pruned into perfect spheres give off an earthy, rich scent.

Raz shoos away a white peacock that lands on the walk in front of us, then extends an arm toward a low building with a graceful minaret roof. Though covered, the walls are open to the outside, and I can spy the court seated on cushions within.

"This way, Your Highness. Your servant, of course, may join the others in the kitchens." Though this last remark is directed at me, Raz does not make eye contact. She waves dismissively in the other direction, at a plainer stone building with several smoking chimneys.

I nod and walk toward it, but once I am out of sight, I duck behind the cypresses and shift into a peacock. Not my favorite form. My legs are spindly, and bobbing my head will leave my neck sore later, but it is the safest way to get into the dining hall. Several other peacocks wander in and out of the building freely. No one will notice one more.

Thus disguised, I strut into the open, my long tail feathers dragging behind me, and boldly enter the dining hall.

The court dines in two groups: men and women. They are separated by lattice screens, symbolically more than anything else, for it is easy to spy one another through the screens, which many of the young men and women do. Their flirtation is ignored by the older nobles. In the back of the room, a musician strums a gentle melody on a tall harp, and I recognize in the tune hints of the songs once sung in your court, Habiba. The men are seated in a large circle around an array of dishes that are continually replenished by gray-robed servants. They carry in bowls of rice, steaming flatbread, kebabs of lamb, beef, and chicken. Even to my peacock form, the smells of cinnamon and saffron are delicious.

I find Aladdin seated between Vigo and an old, hairy nobleman who reeks of garlic. My master nods eagerly as Vigo points out which dishes he should try. I note with chagrin that he's already drunk half a glass of wine. Not a good sign, with the evening still young and the Amulens watching him like hungry leopards looking for a sign of weakness. Not openly, of course. Their glances are sly, but the suspicion is there, burning behind their pleasant expressions.

I scan the room for any sign of the king or his brother, but neither seems to be present. We haven't seen either since our first day in the palace.

Tonight's dinner features nobles of middling to high rank, judging by their clothes and manners. But on the women's side of the room, I spot Caspida surrounded by her handmaidens. They whisper and laugh and sip wine, casting curious looks through the screen. To see them now, they look innocent and harmless as doves, nothing like the little fighting unit that kidnapped Aladdin.

I strut around the perimeter of the room, listening in on conversations, hoping for mention of any jinn prisoners. But the talk is disappointingly mundane. I edge in to Vigo and peck at his coat, searching for a hidden flute, until he swats at me and I am forced to flee.

Suddenly the room falls silent and everyone stands. Aladdin scrambles to imitate them, bowing low as a small group enters from the courtyard. When I see who it is, I ruffle my feathers.

It is Darian and three of his friends. The prince is wearing a tight-fitting black kurta hemmed with elaborate embroidery over black trousers and a gold sash. He nods to the room, and everyone sits again, with several nobles shifting aside to give him room.

"Prince Darian!" A nobleman raises his wine cup. "Good to see you back! How was your hunt?"

"Rotten," says Darian. "There's not an antelope left for a

hundred leagues around that isn't smaller than a dog. The damn ghuls have eaten all the good game."

The others greet him warmly, drinking to his health. Darian greets them all by name, but his eyes keep flickering to Aladdin. He gestures for the others to sit, then nods to my master.

"I do not believe we have met," he murmurs.

Aladdin bows, remarkably composed. "I'm Prince Rahzad rai Asnam of Istarya."

"I know your name. I would be a poor host if I did not know everything about my guests, don't you agree? Though apparently on the topic of Rahzad of Istarya, there is remarkably little to know. It almost makes one wonder if he wasn't conjured from a story." Darian flicks his wrists and holds his hands out for two servants to quickly wipe them with warm, moist cloths. Then he sits, and Aladdin mirrors him. The prince breaks off a piece of bread and dips it in oil and spices. "I hear you ran into trouble with the jinn."

"Just some maarids," Aladdin replies. "But they put up a nasty fight. My crew was lost, and me nearly with them."

"And yet here you are. Imohel favors you." Darian takes a cup of a tea from a servant.

"Imohel, destiny, dumb luck . . . Something's looking out for me, I suppose," Aladdin returns coolly.

Darian's eyes glitter over the rim of his cup. "How fortunate you should find our port just when your ship was on the verge of sinking entirely. The timing can be nothing but divine, wouldn't you say?"

"I'll leave the divine to the priests." Aladdin laughs. "Give me solid ground beneath my feet and a cup of this wine and I'll pray to a fig on a stick if you like."

"Hear, hear!" says a young nobleman, lifting his glass. The others join in the toast, and Aladdin grins.

Darian glances around at the men, drinks deeply, then sets his cup down with a loud clink.

"You must be quite the voyager, Prince Rahzad, to survive an attack by the maarids. Well . . . if you can count it *survival* when your entire crew is killed. Tell us, how did you manage to stay alive? You must have killed dozens of the creatures."

The men fall quiet, looking expectantly to Aladdin. The thief holds Darian's gaze, a taut smile at his lips.

"Not all my men were lost," Aladdin says softly.

"Ah, yes. There was a girl, wasn't there? A servant? Pretty too, from what I hear." Suddenly Darian gives a little gasp and snaps his fingers. "Ah . . . so that's it." He leans forward, grinning. "Don't worry—I completely understand. I've known a few girls who could make *me* miss an entire battle too. I'm sure your men didn't blame you for staying belowdecks." He winks conspiratorially and holds up his cup for a servant to refill.

Aladdin's hand clenches his wine cup, his face paling dangerously.

Don't speak, I beg him silently. *Don't let him bait you.*

The other men, sensing the spiking tension between the two princes, suddenly seem extremely interested in the food on their plates, but their eyes dart up furtively from Aladdin to Darian.

"Dear cousin, back at last?" says a voice, neatly severing the tension between the two boys.

The men all turn to Caspida, who steps around the screen dividing the room. Darian rises to meet her, taking her hand and bowing over it.

"Prince Rahzad, have you met my betrothed?" Darian pulls her close, his fingers playing with the ends of her hair.

Aladdin rises and bows. "Princess. I am honored."

"She's the most beautiful woman in the city," says Darian. "Perhaps even the world. When we're married, maybe I'll take her on a grand tour of the nations, to compare her to their beauties. What do you say, my love?"

Caspida's face is serene as porcelain, but her eyes glitter when she smiles at Darian. "Alas, the last time we went sailing, my dear cousin was overcome with seasickness and stayed below deck."

Darian's face goes still. "You forget yourself, my love. Go back to the women. It's not proper for you to share bread with the men."

She holds his gaze for a moment, and I wonder if her composure will break and she will strike him. But instead she turns and nods to Aladdin, then bids the others good evening and glides back to the women's side, where her handmaidens are watching silently through the screen.

With a laugh, Darian sits and holds up his cup for more tea. "Women! They think it so romantic to break the rules. But what are we if we don't hold to tradition, am I right?"

The men laugh and nod in agreement, but Aladdin stares hard at the prince.

"I've heard of the wonders of this city all my life," Aladdin says. "I read about your kings and queens and generals. Can't recall hearing of you, though. What did you say your name was?"

Darian frowns. "Darian. Son of Sulifer."

"Oh, right. And who's he again?"

"The vizier of all Parthenia, the commander of the Amulen military, *and* brother of the king." Darian's fingers tighten around his teacup. When he sets it down, it clinks loudly. "Perhaps you Istaryans need to update your histories."

Aladdin shrugs. "Oh, right. Him. Yes, I do remember reading something about your vizier. Of course, after meeting him, I'm sure our historians must have been mistaken."

Silence falls. Darian, cold as winter, says through his teeth, "Oh, do explain."

"It's nothing, really. Just something about how he's been trying to rebuild the Amulen Empire. Sends grandfathers and children out to row his warships, but that he's lost every battle he's attempted." Aladdin smiles. "I'm sure it's all a misunderstanding. Surely he's not *that* stupid."

Oh, gods save us.

"*What* did you say?" Darian rises quickly to his feet.

Everyone is staring openly in astonishment, and on the other side of the screen, Caspida presses a fist to her lips, her eyes creasing in a wince. I sense Aladdin's muscles tensing, his anger spiking, his thoughts moving from anger to violence—time to break this party up.

With a wild honk, I launch myself upward, my large wings ponderously belaboring the air, and burst into the circle. My tail and feet overturn dishes and wine goblets, sending men yelling and cursing. I land in front of Aladdin and spread my tail feathers in a marvelous display—really, I've outdone myself with this form— and hop this way and that, wings flapping, avian throat screeching and honking. Caspida, laughing, disappears with her handmaidens, and a host of servants appear from the shadows where they have been lurking. They wave their arms and try to drive me out, and out I go, folding my wings and tail and honking at them as if *they're* the ones interrupting. Out of the hall and into the courtyard they chase me, while others remain to help clean off the astonished and irate noblemen, including Aladdin. I lose them in the darkness and double back, shifting into a black cat to blend silently into the shadows.

The dinner is over. Darian is fussing at the servants, the nobles are dispersing, and Aladdin is lingering by a column, looking sullen. I run to him and bat his foot.

"Get away, cat," he says. I hiss in reply and arch my back, and he does a double take. "Oh. It's you."

He follows me into the courtyard and around a small pavilion, where we are alone. There, I transform into a human, once again in plain servants' clothing.

"Hungry?" he asks. "I got something . . . hang on." From his pocket he pulls out a wadded napkin full of dates, bread, and meat, all mashed into one indiscernible mound. He holds it out.

"Thanks, but . . . that's disgusting."

He sighs and returns the mush of food back to his pocket. "Old habit, I guess. When you grow up never knowing where your next meal will come from . . . Did you see him? That bastard Darian was there. I could have throttled him, but there was this bird. Went crazy, smashed right into our dinner."

"Brainless creatures," I mutter.

"The men or the peacocks?" says a voice. "It would be a close bet."

Aladdin and I turn to see Caspida approaching, her face flickering with orange light from the brazier blazing above. Her handmaidens are nowhere to be seen, but when I stretch out with my sixth sense, I feel them lurking in the shadows, watchful and silent.

"Princess," Aladdin says breathlessly, his eyes clearing a little.

"Prince," she replies smoothly. "Walk with me?"

He steps forward eagerly, leaving me to trail behind. With his hands clasped behind his back, his pace a bit unsteady, Aladdin allows the princess to lead him up a stair and onto a north-facing portico that looks out to the hills above Parthenia. With the city behind us, the stars are brilliant as diamonds strewn on black silk. A few lights burn in the cedars that grow below them, signs of farms and outposts scattered across the hinterlands.

"Your arrival has caused a stir among my people," Caspida says at last. Her gown, cut from glittering teal silk, drags behind her, and the light of the lanterns hung from the portico's arches glints off the elaborate jeweled necklace resting on her collarbone. She is every bit the princess, and beside her Aladdin is . . . every bit the prince. Taller than Caspida by several inches, he walks with his head tilted, so he can look in her eyes while she speaks. "It has been some time since anyone of importance has visited Parthenia. We are not quite the great influence we once were in this world, and I'm afraid many of the larger southern cities find us odd and backward. You might find yourself something of a curiosity to my court."

"Like a trained monkey," says Aladdin.

Her lips curl at the corners in amusement. "Once, we received princes and kings and queens from all across the world. Parthenia was a center of learning and art, renowned for its open doors and tolerant court. But our feud with the jinn has weakened us, and it is all we can do to maintain our own borders. Being shut off for so long has made my people suspicious and prejudiced. We fear those we once welcomed, and see jinn lurking in every shadow."

She pauses and leans over the railing, staring out at the horizon. "I don't mean to sound pessimistic. I just want you to understand the mood in my court."

Aladdin, his back to the view, watches Caspida instead. "Why are you telling me this?"

She smiles humorlessly. "So you don't think us all backward and prejudiced. There are some in this court who would have us reach out, to rekindle our old alliances and rally support against Ambadya. If we all stood against the jinn together, we might succeed. Too long have the nations of our world cowered before these monsters and their whims."

"Some . . . meaning you?"

Caspida looks down at her hands, idly fingering the bangles around her wrist. "The eastern kingdoms don't think women are fit to rule, did you know that? There are even those in Parthenia who think I should be set aside in favor of my uncle or my cousin Darian. They think our enemies will not take us seriously if a woman is on the throne."

"Let them. And while they're busy laughing, you'll be busy ruling. Being underestimated isn't flattering—but it's an advantage." He shrugs. "I've been underestimated all my life and have found it a cloak as useful as invisibility."

Caspida turns her face toward him, her eyes probing his. "You are cunning, Rahzad rai Asnam. Are you a student of war?"

Aladdin laughs. "I take it you didn't get a look at my ship, or you wouldn't ask."

"So what are you then?" She takes a step toward him, lifting her face to study him closely. "A scholar? An artist?"

"More like a dreamer."

"It must be nice, to afford dreams."

"Don't you dream?"

"Dreams won't protect the city from jinn. Dreams won't feed my people. Dreams won't . . ." She presses her lips together.

Aladdin, in a gentler voice, asks, "Princess, if you could wish for anything in the world, what would you wish for?"

She studies him for a long moment, as if unsure whether he is teasing or serious. Then she gives a little sigh and says, "You shouldn't picks fights with Darian. He's more dangerous than he looks."

"Do you love him?"

She draws back, startled at the frank question and the directness of Aladdin's gaze. For a moment, she only stares at him in evaluation, her cheeks flushing. Then she turns away, her chin lifting. "Good evening, Prince Rahzad. I hope you find your stay here most comfortable."

With that, she disappears inside, leaving him to beat his head against a stone pillar.

"Smoky," he groans, "this isn't going to be easy, is it?"

Amusement tugs at my lips. "Not a chance, thief."

Chapter Eleven

As soon as Aladdin is asleep, I slip out the door and shift into a cat, then run through the halls, ears perked and whiskers twitching. The palace is quiet at night, the corridors dark except for the moonlight that pours through the tall arched windows. Crickets chirp in the many courtyards, and I pass the peacocks roosting in a small grove of lemon trees. I listen at every door, and move on when I don't find what I'm looking for.

I'm almost at the edge of the lamp's magical perimeter when I finally hear Darian's voice.

The door to his room is shut, but that doesn't deter me. I shift into a spider and crawl beneath it, then scurry up the wall, staying in the shadows. Taking the form of a spider is difficult—so many legs to manage, and staring through all those eyes makes me dizzy. So when I reach the ceiling, I transform into a bat and hang upside down, my toes clinging to a groove in the wall.

Darian and Sulifer are in the midst of a heated argument.

They're both breathing heavily, and a bowl lies shattered on the floor. The rooms are larger and more resplendent than Aladdin's, and save for the broken pottery, immaculately tidy.

". . . and by a *common thief*, no less!" Sulifer is saying. His voice is low and dangerous, his eyes slits. Gone is the formal, composed vizier we met in the throne room nearly ten days ago.

"He must have had help from the inside," Darian replies in a muffled tone. He's leaning against a table, his shoulders hunched and his face hidden from my view. "And once he had the lamp, how was I to stop him? He had the jinni at his side, and he made a wish! I could have *died*. All I got was this."

Darian digs into a pocket, producing the ring Aladdin had been wearing when he found me. Sulifer takes it and grasps it tight.

"Why did it speak to the thief and not to me or to you?"

Darian's retort is bitter. "I don't know, Father. I'm not an expert on these things. I never wanted any part in it at all!"

Sulifer raises a hand, and the prince flinches, but then the vizier pauses. "You said you heard him make a wish. *What*, exactly, did he say?"

"He wished to go home."

"He's here. In the city," Sulifer muses. "Why didn't you say that first, you idiot? All we have to do is send the Tytoshi charmers out with their flutes. That should enchant the creature out of hiding, and it will lead us to the boy."

"Do you really think it's *the* jinni?" asks Darian. "The same one who betrayed Queen Roshana and started this war?"

"The maarid we captured told us the lamp contained the most powerful jinni of all. What other monster could it be?" Sulifer's eyes turn distant and greedy. "They say it created a garden for Roshana made entirely of jewels, a wealth greater than any in the world." He scowls at his son. "I don't suppose you found any sign of *that* on your misbegotten foray into the desert?"

"As soon as the thief escaped I turned around and rode straight back here, as you well know," Darian snaps. "I didn't have time to dig around old ruins. Anyway, I don't know why you're so obsessed with this one jinni. We have a hundred others bottled up below, waiting to be used."

I tense, my bat ears stretched wide.

"Those jinn are feral and uncontrollable." Sulifer rolls the ring between his fingers, his lip curled in disgust. "The minute you let one out, it will turn on you. They have no compulsion on them to grant wishes, no loyalty to their masters. Only one of the old lamp jinn will do, and there are very few of those left. No, I *will* get my hands on this one, and when I do, our people will finally retake their place in this world. No more cowering behind these walls. We will undo the curse Roshana's foolishness left on us and extend our empire once more. First thing tomorrow, have Vigo begin playing his flute throughout the city."

Darian just looks up at his father with burning eyes before turning away. "I've been riding for days. I'm exhausted."

But Sulifer goes on as if Darian had never spoken. "If the thief is still here, he's probably lying low, waiting to see what we will do. I'll smoke him out and put his head on a pike, just like his rabble-rousing parents. Report to me after you've dispatched the charmer. I won't tolerate any more incompetence from you."

Without another word, Sulifer storms from the room, slamming the door behind him.

Darian leans against the wall, then slides down to the floor, his eyes shutting. He lets out a long sigh before dropping his face into his hands.

I shift quietly to gray smoke and curl across the ceiling, down the wall, and under the door before he can look up again.

Sulifer's footsteps are still echoing in the hallway, and I shift to cat form and dart after him, but I get only ten steps before the lamp jerks me backward, dissolving me into smoke, and I can only rage in silence as I rush through the hallway, beneath Aladdin's door, and down the spout.

Zhian is here, somewhere. *Below*, Darian said. I've seen staircases leading down to lower levels of the palace, but have been unable to follow them. I have to find a way to draw Aladdin down there, giving me a chance to find where Sulifer keeps the bottled jinn.

I don't have much time left. A week and more has already passed, and the moon is a quarter full.

I swirl around in the lamp, thinking hard. Everything's falling into place now. Nardukha sent a maarid to the city to be captured, so it could tell Sulifer about the ring to lead him to me. But the ring didn't seem to work for Sulifer or Darian. Why, then, did it speak to Aladdin? Who created it, and why? Again and again I find myself back at the same questions.

I curl and think in my lamp, slow, lazy smoke, waiting for morning so that Aladdin can let me out again.

"Where do you go at night?"

Startled, I blink at Aladdin. "What?"

"Every night you slip out. You think I don't notice. You're gone for hours, and sometimes you come rushing back, all smoke, into your lamp."

We're sitting beneath a small canvas shade at the edge of a chaugan field. Horses gallop about on the grass, their riders leaning down with their mallets to whack a small ball from one end of the pitch to the other. Nobles look on from their shade along the sides, like we do, spending more time gossiping and drinking than watching the game. It's been a long time since I last saw chougan played, and that was the day it was invented by the Blood King of Danien. The rules seem much the same all these centuries later, except that original match was played not with wooden balls but the severed heads of the king's enemies.

I much prefer the modern version.

Aladdin and I are temporarily alone. Visitors come and go, mostly curious nobles—and a good many of them young, female, and coy. Aladdin lounges like a king, a tray of fruit at one hand, a flagon of expensive wine at the other. I stand behind him, ready to wait on his every whim, though so far I've met all his requests with scowls.

Aladdin twists around in his seat to stare at me, clearly not letting me get out of answering.

"I like to roam," I say with a shrug. "My kind are more active at night, you know."

He raises his eyebrows as if he hasn't considered that, then turns back around to watch the game.

"The Rings are so much more exciting than this," he says, yawning. "I ought to take a few of these rich boys down to town one of these nights, show them some real entertainment."

"That would be a bad idea. Spending too much time around those familiar with you will weaken the glamour hiding your true identity."

He sighs and pulls a few grapes from the tray beside him, but instead of eating them, he just rolls them in his hand. His eyes are locked not on the game but on the pavilion erected on the other side of the field. Darian sits here, with his friends, Caspida at his side. The prince and princess don't talk or even look at each other; he chats with his boys, and she sits stiffly, her eyes roaming the crowd.

Sulifer appears at the far end of the field, surrounded by ministers and military officers who vie for his attention. Aladdin's eyes follow the vizier, and one by one, he squeezes the grapes in his hand until they pop. Shadows haunt his eyes, and he grinds his jaw so hard I fear he will break a tooth.

"Why do you not hate the jinn?" I ask, diverting his attention.

Aladdin turns, the anger in his face dissipating. "Hate the jinn?"

"Every other person here would just as soon strike off my head as say hello if they knew what I was."

He runs a hand through his hair. "I don't know. Didn't really have to deal with jinn, staying inside the city all my life. And anyway, how could I hate you? Without you, I wouldn't be here."

He might hate me if he knew I'm using him, manipulating him, leading him into danger and worse, all for my own selfish reasons. What would he say if he knew the truth? Perhaps I should tell it to him. Perhaps I need to see the hate in his eyes, to stifle the lightness in my stomach whenever I look at him. But the truth turns to smoke in my throat, and I choke it down.

"Prince Rahzad!" a sunny voice calls out, and Vigo saunters over, twirling something in his hand. My teeth clench when I realize what it is—a jinn-charming flute, identical to Nessa's. "Enjoying the game?"

Aladdin grins and stands up, shaking hands with the Tytoshi. "It's a damn bore."

Vigo's head tips back, and he lets out a booming laugh. "I

THE FORBIDDEN WISH 115

couldn't agree more, friend! These Amulens will watch it for hours a day! What about in Istarya? What do you do for sport in this fabled island kingdom we hear so little about?"

Aladdin waves a hand. "Oh, you know. Lots of water stuff. Wrestling sharks and things. And in Tytos?"

"Wouldn't know. Haven't been there since I was a boy. I'm heading down to the city to do some work." He taps his flute to his forehead. "Want to come along? Playing this thing all day gets damn tedious, but afterward, there are some fun girls I could introduce you to. That is, if, uh . . ." He glances at me.

Aladdin does too, and he catches the look in my eyes. He turns back to Vigo. "Thanks, man, but I've already promised to play dice later."

"Right, sure." Vigo grins and raises his eyebrows at me, then slaps Aladdin on the shoulder. "Enjoy yourself, man!"

He heads off, and I let out the long breath I'd been holding.

"Well?" Aladdin turns to me. "What's wrong? Why didn't you want to go?"

"I—" Taken aback, I flounder a bit. "You told him no, just because I didn't want to go?"

"We're in this together, aren't we, Smoky?" He gives me a crooked, bemused smile.

"But . . . you're the Lampholder. Whatever you say goes. I don't have a choice."

He laughs, and I frown at him in surprise. "You think it's funny?" I ask.

"No! Sorry. I should probably say how awful it is you have to go wherever I want, but . . . When I look at you, I see a jinni who's not afraid to tell me what she thinks. Who isn't afraid to disagree with me. If I make a wish, you could use it to crush me. You've done it before, haven't you? Ruined your masters with their own wishes?"

I lift a shoulder in begrudging agreement.

"I don't think you're as helpless as you want people to think."

"What does that mean?"

Aladdin stares at me for a long moment, then says softly, "When I was little, and the guards would come around and beat my father until he paid them off, my grandmother used to take me onto the roof of our house so I didn't have to watch. I asked her why my father resisted the guards when they always won in the end. Why didn't he just save himself the pain and pay them what they wanted? She told me that sometimes, you can't choose what happens to you, but you can choose who you become because of it. That's why my father fought back. He knew in the end, it wouldn't change anything. But he wouldn't let the circumstances control who he was." His eyes turn stormy. "I always thought there's no freedom in fighting back—just death. What's the point of fighting for a lost cause? You're like my father. You fight back."

"And you think I'm a fool for it?"

"No. I think . . . you're brave."

"Brave?" I choke out a laugh. "Are you forgetting who I am? Or why your people hide inside these walls, fearing the jinn? I am the—what do your songs say?—the Fair Betrayer. Tell me, O Master, what is brave about betraying someone you love?"

"Love?"

I freeze, wondering how I could have been so foolish as to let the word slip. But it's too late now. I glare at Aladdin, as if it were his fault, as if he'd tricked me into unveiling my secret.

"Forget about it," I mutter.

"What happened that day? Did you really betray that queen and start this war?"

"Yes, I did." Though not in the way he imagines. I loved you, Habiba, and in doing so, I betrayed you. The rules were clear, the cost inevitable. Even so, I was arrogant, thinking myself so clever to befriend a human and dream of peace between our races. I thought I was above the law that held all jinn captive, imagined I could bridge the chasm that had separated man and jinn since the dawn of this world. But I learned my lesson, at the cost of you, your people, your city. And the consequences of my foolishness are still echoing through the centuries.

I slip behind Aladdin, retreating from any further prying on his part. Soon, I will have rescued Zhian, and Nardukha will grant me my freedom.

And once I am free to run, not even the shadows of the past will be able to catch me.

Chapter Twelve

ANOTHER WEEK PASSES. The moon is nearly full. I have yet to find any sign of Zhian.

I am growing desperate.

Aladdin is passed around the court like an exotic pet, from this clique to that, invited to games of cards and camel races. I trail after him, feeding him bits of etiquette when I can, but soon find he doesn't need it. He told me he was adaptable, but I underestimated him. He blends in perfectly, his manners charming, his conversation fascinating.

"Shall I tell you the story of how I and my two brothers stole a roc's egg?" he tells a group of young noblewomen one night over a game of dice and tiles. They giggle eagerly, and he launches into a ridiculous story. I stand behind Aladdin, as usual, ready to fetch him wine or whatever else he fancies. As his tale grows wilder and wilder, I watch the faces of his listeners as they move from wonder to shock to horror.

"Higher and higher we climbed, with the Great Falls of Oznar thundering around us, and the rocs screaming as they dove at us." Aladdin leans in, and his wide-eyed audience holds its breath. "But don't forget! We carried with us arrows made of ivory, which is of course the only thing known to kill a roc. We fired as we climbed, holding them at bay, until at last we reached the summit, where the mother roc waited on her nest. A nest as vast as this palace!" He spreads his hands.

Gasps rise all around, and I blink, catching myself wrapped up in his story. Aladdin is silver-tongued indeed, and though his stories grow more improbable each night, he never fails to draw a crowd. Where he draws these fantasies from, I cannot say. I may have invented Istarya, but Aladdin brings it to life. There is so much more to this thief than I had imagined, and the nobles are not the only ones who begin to fall under his spell.

Too often I find myself listening raptly to his tales when I should be on the watch for Zhian, a realization that fills me with alarm and confusion. I remind myself why I am here, what I am seeking.

I remind myself of the cost of failure.

"Are you completely shameless?" I ask Aladdin later that evening, after the gaming and drinking and storytelling finally end, somewhere well north of midnight. Vigo walks with us, he and Aladdin both tipsy and leaning on each other. The Tytoshi boy has grown accustomed to Aladdin and me chatting as equals, and asks no questions, but his assumptions are plain in the way he looks at us and smirks.

"What?" asks Aladdin, eyes wide with innocence.

"She was twice your age, and you had her blushing like a virgin."

He shrugs, throwing an arm around Vigo's shoulders. "I liked her necklace. It was a fine necklace, wasn't it, Vigo?"

"Very fine. So fine," slurs Vigo.

"See? Vigo liked her necklace too. Why, I liked it so much . . ." With a wink, Aladdin pulls down the sash around his waist just enough to reveal a flash of ruby.

"You *stole* it." I run a hand over my face.

"You have *got* to teach me how to do that," says Vigo.

"Here," says Aladdin. "Let's practice with Zahra. Zahra, put on this necklace."

"Oh, look!" I cry, stopping and opening a door. "Vigo's room."

"Mmhm." Vigo groggily claps Aladdin on the shoulder. "Horse racing tomorrow—you going to come, Rahzad?"

"Definitely."

I place a hand against the small of Vigo's back and propel him to his door. "Good *night*, Vigo."

The Tytoshi stumbles inside, and I shut the door, wincing a little when a loud thump sounds inside.

"I'm sure he's fine," I say. "Come on. Let's get you to bed."

I slip an arm around Aladdin and support him the rest of the way. He coils a strand of my hair around his finger and murmurs, "Where would I be without you, Zahra?"

He is so close that his breath warms my neck. "You'd be in the desert, a pile of bleached bones, that's where."

"Mm. Right. Have I ever told you thanks, by the way? I don't thank you enough. Vigo thinks you're my concubine. Did you know that?"

"Here we are!" I say, a bit too loudly, as I shoulder open the door and pull him into our chambers.

He chuckles and drops onto the divan. "Your face is red."

"It's not!" I turn away, hiding my flushed cheeks, but then he grabs my hand.

"Don't go."

Startled, I tense and nearly shift into smoke. He watches me, his gaze steady—if a bit glazed—and his grip on my hand warm. Hesitantly I sit beside him, pulling my hand away. He leans back with a sigh.

"Storm's about to break," says Aladdin.

I look out to the courtyard, where a strip of the dark sky is visible. Swelling clouds obscure the stars, and wind bends the fig trees before rushing into the chamber. The flames in the lanterns flicker out, leaving us in darkness. A moment later, lightning pulses in the belly of a cloud, illuminating Aladdin's face for a heartbeat. His eyes are on me.

As thunder breaks, low and angry, I open my hand and conjure a flame over my palm. Yellow light flickers over Aladdin's features as his gaze lowers, and his lips part slightly.

"I'll get some candles," he says.

"Don't." I pass the flame back and forth between my hands. "It wouldn't work. The fire isn't real. It's just a part of me—shapeshifting magic. It won't set anything ablaze."

The flame reflects in his eyes, while outside, the storm rolls in from the sea, filling the air with the smell of salt. The sheer curtains hanging in the arches billow and snap. Lightning flashes in rapid succession, white-hot sparks thrown from the anvil of the gods.

Aladdin lifts a hand and passes it slowly over my palm, through the slender flame playing across my skin. The fire dances at his touch, and a shiver runs through me, making the hair on my neck stand on end, as if he'd run his fingers through my hair.

I meet his eyes, feeling the vibrations of the thunder outside echoing in my chest.

The way he looks at me—steady and silent, bold and

bright—makes me feel as if the storm outside were trapped inside me, thunder and rain and light, rolling and crashing.

"You're beautiful," he murmurs. "How could anyone believe you were just a servant?"

I close my hand, the flame vanishing, and wrench my gaze from his.

"You're drunk," I say.

He laughs low in his throat, then nods. Leaning back, he rubs his face wearily. "It must be nearly dawn."

Already the storm begins to dissipate, its fury spent. Light rain falls on the courtyard, soft and pattering, darkening the stones. I rise and search for flint to light the lanterns, but before I find it, Aladdin falls asleep on the divan, still sitting upright, his head dropping toward his chest.

Gently I ease him onto his side, pushing away pillows and drawing a cashmere blanket over him. He sighs, shifting slightly, and I wait until he falls still again before sitting across from him. For several long minutes I watch him sleep, my chest aching strangely. I should go and search for Zhian in the few hours before dawn, but I can't pull myself away.

I reach out and brush Aladdin's hair back, my fingers lingering in his black curls. I can feel his life force crackling like sparks on my skin. So bright, so brilliant this mortal boy, here and gone so quickly, a strike of lightning.

"What am I doing?" I whisper. I know where this road leads, for I have traveled it before. I don't dare follow it again, no matter how tempting it is. If only it were as easy to smother the fire leaping inside me as the one in my palm.

Finally, my stomach twisting, I rise and go to the door, face flushed and hands trembling. I gather myself and shift into smoke.

I spend the rest of the night prowling the halls, and once, briefly, I almost think I can feel the faintest wisp of . . . *something*. A force, writhing below. Not human. But then it is gone, and when I try to pursue it, I nearly go too far from the lamp. I stop, frozen at the edge of my unseen leash, and stand for several long minutes, unable to go forward, afraid to go back.

The next morning, I am lounging in the courtyard in the form of a tiger, swatting lazily at flies, when a knock sounds on the door. Instantly I re-form into a girl and run to open it.

It is Khavar, her snake coiled like a living necklace across her collarbone.

"My mistress Princess Caspida requests your presence in her chambers," says the girl in a bored tone. "Immediately. If convenient."

"I'll have to wake him," I reply. "He's—"

"Not him. *You*."

I stare at her for a moment, then slam the door. As an afterthought, I open it again and say, "Just a minute," before shutting it again in her face.

I go into Aladdin's room, where he dragged himself into bed at some point during the night, and whip aside the heavy damask curtain, letting the sunlight pour in. Aladdin, throwing a hand over his eyes, cries out and falls off the bed.

"What are you—why—!?"

"I've been summoned to see Caspida."

He groans and massages his head. "It hurts. Everything hurts. Light. Sounds. Ugh . . ."

"Next time," I say cheerfully, "maybe you'll think before letting the jackals get you stinking drunk. If you're going to throw up, do it outside. I'm not cleaning up after you."

"Gunhhh . . ."

"I'm going to see Caspida. Don't go out if you can help it. Don't do anything stupid. And *don't* let go of my lamp. Your ill manners we can explain away. My evaporating in front of Caspida's eyes we can't. *Aladdin*." I pull his hands from his face to be sure he understands. He squints and moans pathetically. "Do you hear me or not?"

"Right. Now go away. Leave me 'lone." He pulls the blanket off the bed and covers himself, curling up on the floor.

Leaving him, I open the door and smile at Khavar. "I'm ready."

Caspida will want to interrogate me about Aladdin, I am certain. It is easier to invite me, his only female household member, unless she wants to ignite scandalous gossip. Good. I had been hoping for this. Perhaps I can finally get a clue to finding Zhian.

Khavar leads me through the palace, through arches and doorways and stone courtyards. We pass many servants but few nobles; I suspect Aladdin is not the only one waking to a headache this morning. The palace is built to allow as much light and fresh air as possible inside, with many open arches and windows. The cool morning air is filled with birdsong and the sound of running water from the many fountains in the courtyards, and we pass the flock of peacocks I'd taken up with at dinner a week ago. Several run up to me and peck curiously at my shoes. Khavar hisses at them, and they scatter.

"In here," sighs Khavar, swinging open a narrow cedar door. The rooms inside are wide and open, connected by arched doorways hung with sheer silk curtains. Similarly to Aladdin's chambers, they open to a courtyard, as well as a wide, shallow pool. The room Khavar leads me into is lush with carpets and cushions, silk and embroidery.

Caspida's handmaidens are all here, and there is one other

presence: An elephant calf stands in the center of the room. The girls are idly painting designs onto its skin, and they give me curious looks before turning back to their work. Raz is halfheartedly firing arrows at a pillow across the room, her shots flying dangerously close to Nessa's head but finding their target every time. Nessa seems hardly to notice.

Caspida lounges on a long cushion in front of the elephant and offers up handfuls of apple slices, which the calf picks up with its trunk and tucks into its mouth. She giggles when it tugs her hair, asking for more, and for a moment I see her for the girl she is and not the queen-to-be she presents to her court.

The princess glances up when I enter, her hand pausing above the bowl of apples. The calf nudges her with its trunk.

Caspida wears only a white kurta and skirt, her feet bare, but the fabric is encrusted with delicate embroidered flowers that must have taken a very skilled seamstress several months to create. A simple gold stud is pressed into her nostril, and a delicate chain hangs from it to her earlobe, brushing her smooth cheek.

"You must be Zahra."

I bow low. "Your Highness."

"Hungry?" She lifts the bowl of apples and pushes aside the elephant's trunk when it tries to grab the fruit.

I look at the bowl, then at Caspida, reading the unspoken words in her eyes. This is an ancient game that I have seen played, won, and lost many times over. Take the fruit, and I am demonstrating that my loyalties to my master can be tested, perhaps broken. Decline, and she will know that I am his to my last breath.

"You do me honor," I say, and I take an apple slice.

She smiles slowly, her eyes narrowing with interest. "Walk with me."

Without lifting her skirt, she steps into the shallow pool outside the arches, leaving the bowl in Khavar's hands. I follow, wading into the water. It comes only to my ankles, but it is cool and refreshing, the black and white tiles at the bottom free of slime or sand. Lotus blossoms float placidly on the surface and swirl aside when we walk through them.

Caspida steps onto a grassy space beyond the reflecting pool. The palace encloses us on all sides, and the shadow of a tall minaret darkens the water, yet this small garden is framed with trellises and trees so that it feels as if we are the center of a distant oasis. Set in the middle of the grassy plot is a weathered statue of a winged woman holding a lamp in one hand, a sword in the other. I cannot help but catch my breath when I behold her.

The elephant plods after us, and the girls cry out in dismay as their paintings are smudged. The calf prances in the water and sprays itself happily while the girls, giving up on their artwork, begin splashing each other.

The princess sits on the grass and folds her legs beneath her, her skirt spreading around her in a pool of silk. I kneel beside her and wait for her to speak first. Her silence is filled with birdsong, splashing, and the girls' soft laughter. She watches the elephant and her handmaidens for a few moments before beginning, eschewing pleasantries and cutting straight to the point.

"Tell me about your master."

I nod. "He is eighth in line to the throne, the son of—"

"No, no," Caspida interrupts irritably. "Tell me what he is *like*."

"He is a gambler," I say. There is no point in lying about these things. "He is bold, but reckless. Brave, but impetuous. A man who . . . holds grudges." Pausing, I finish in a whisper, "He would risk his life to save someone else, without even thinking twice."

Caspida turns her head a bit, interest growing in her eyes. "And he sets out on a mad voyage and sails straight into a nest of jinn."

"My master is noble," I say with a smile, "but I made no suggestions as to his intelligence."

"I have never heard of Istarya, so I did some research. You know, none of the scrolls or histories in our library mention it?"

"We're a small nation, Your Highness, and we keep to ourselves."

She stares at me with shrewd eyes, but doesn't reply.

The elephant calf has discovered it can suck up water and spray it on the girls, and seems to find this vastly amusing. The girls shriek and try to hide, but the calf merrily lumbers after them, shooting water in glittering sprays. Caspida watches it, but does not smile.

"The calf's name is Shasi. Her mother died giving birth to her, and my uncle was going to have her killed because she was born small and sickly. But we took her and made her well again, and she would rather play with my maidens than with her own kind." She absently runs her thumb and forefinger up the chain on her cheek, making it tinkle softly. "My great-grandmother Fahruaz was part Tytoshi. It was she who imported the first of our war elephants. She was a great strategist and commanded our army for more than thirty years. It is said that her enemies laid many traps for her but that she was too cunning for them, for she always saw the truth behind their lies. Some believe that I am very much like my grandmother."

Caspida turns to me. "You are no servant, Zahra. You hide it well from the others, but your eyes are too proud, your glances too defiant. But if you are not a servant, what are you? Royal? Noble? A soldier in disguise, sworn to protect your master?"

Now I am the one who stares. "You do have a keen eye."

"I grew up in court," she replies. "Everyone I've ever known is an expert liar. I learned long ago to see the intent behind the masks. So tell me, Zahra, what are you to this Rahzad? Are you his lover?"

"No!"

She gives me a sly look. "Do you wish that you were?"

"No." Perhaps I say the word with too much emphasis, because she smiles a little.

"It was an honest question. He is handsome, and you speak highly of him."

"We are friends." My thoughts are treasonous, insensibly conjuring up the image of Aladdin on the rooftop, his eyes deep with concern as he watches me wake after the wards knocked me out.

Caspida's full attention is now trained on me, and her eyes cut deep. "I will have to be careful with you, I think. Your lies are smooth, your tongue quick. I brought you here to learn more about your prince, but perhaps I should be paying more attention to *you.*"

Time to steer this conversation into safer waters. As much as I would love to tell her the truth—after all, she is *your* own blood, Habiba, and your spirit is strong in her—I know I can't trust her, not when she has a jinn charmer at her side. The thought refocuses me on my mission.

I stand up and walk to the statue of the winged woman and place a hand reverently on her foot. The pedestal she stands on is tall, and her knees are on a level with the top of my head.

"This is remarkable," I comment. Caspida is watching me with interest as I circle the statue, inspecting it from all sides. "How old is it?"

"It was made for my mother, when she married my father."

I turn to Caspida and ask in a tone deceptively neutral, "Is she an ancestress of yours?"

"Very distantly, yes." Caspida rises and joins me in gazing up at the stone face, which isn't a very good likeness, truth be told. Time has weathered the memory of you, or else I wouldn't be able to walk freely here, wearing your face. "This is Roshana, the last queen of the Amulen Empire, back when my people ruled all the lands from the east to the west. She is something of a legend among us. Every queen aspires to learn from her mistakes."

"Her mistakes? Surely you mean her victories."

"What?"

I frown at her. "Roshana was one of the greatest queens in the world. She ended the Mountain Wars, she routed Sanhezriyah the Mad, she—"

"For a foreign serving girl, you are strangely well versed in Amulen history."

"I spent a lot of time in libraries as a girl."

"Were you there to dust the scrolls or read them?"

"Surely Roshana's victories outweigh her errors."

"The higher you rise, the farther you fall. For all her wisdom, Roshana was fooled by the jinni, believing it was her friend, and then it destroyed her. Ever since that day, my people have hunted the jinn. There is no creature more vicious and untrustworthy."

"This is not the story I heard," I say softly. "My people tell it differently. That the jinni truly was a friend to Roshana but was forced to turn against her. That she had no choice."

"Surely I know how my own ancestress died," returns the princess, a bit hotly. "Anyway, it was a long time ago, but we Amulens do not forget."

"No," I murmur. "I suppose you don't. And you've grown into strong and clever fighters, from what I hear. That you even have those among you who can trap jinn."

Caspida watches me closely, a small, curious smile on her lips.

"Jinn charmers have been around for centuries. We did not invent the art. Do you not have them in Istarya?"

"I'm afraid we're among those who would rather bow to the jinn than fight them."

"But not your master," Caspida notes. "Isn't he here to study our methods?"

"What do you do with a trapped jinni? It sounds dangerous. Surely you dispose of them."

She watches me for a moment, then says, "Perhaps one day I will tell you. Forgive me, but my people's secrets are not mine to give."

She is a princess apologizing to a servant. Speaking to me as if we are equals. And it strikes me then, as it had not before, that she truly is your descendant, that some part of your spirit has passed to her. I feel I know her far more intimately than the space of a few minutes of conversation would make possible. I see you in her, and for that, I cannot be angry with her.

"No," I say softly. "Forgive me. I didn't mean to pry. Into that or . . . or Roshana. I'm sure your version is the true one."

"Well, it *was* a long time ago," she says graciously. "A different world altogether. And anyway, you're also right. Roshana defeated Sanhezriyah the Mad, and she stood against the armies of the jinn even when all her allies deserted her. She was a heroine, one of the greatest queens to have lived, in a time when women stood equal to men. But the world moved on, and other lands preferred kings over queens. Their ways of thinking have poisoned our own, and now when they speak of Roshana, they whisper it as if it were a joke. That foolish, capricious woman who trusted her heart, and her kingdom paid the price. They would use her example against me, forgetting all the great things she accomplished." Caspida sighs and kneels at the edge of the pool. Her reflection shimmers back at her. "But if I could be even half so great as she was, I would count myself fortunate."

"In that, we agree," I whisper.

Suddenly my stomach wrenches violently, a feeling I know all too well. *Damn it, Aladdin, what are you doing?* The lamp is moving farther away, and I am standing at the very edge of my invisible boundary. My stomach tugs again, and I gasp a little.

"Are you all right?" Caspida asks, her eyebrows lowering in concern.

"Just . . . not feeling too well," I groan. I sidestep toward the pool, trying to alleviate the pain. The longer I resist, the more it hurts, as if someone has reached inside me and is twisting my gut. I can feel my skin getting lighter, preparing to dissolve into smoke, but I strain with everything in me not to turn.

"Zahra!" Caspida stands and puts her hand on my arm. "You're cold as ice!"

"Ah!" Doubling over, arms crossed over my stomach, I gasp out, "I should go. Something I ate, probably!"

"Of course. I will have Nessa take you to the physician."

"No—I'll be all right. Thank you."

I bow painfully and walk quickly across the pool, Caspida beside me. The girls have managed to calm the elephant calf by bribing it with fruit. They glance at me curiously as I rush for the door. After bidding me a brief farewell, Caspida lets me out.

A few steps, and the pain vanishes. I lean against the wall for a moment and simply breathe, stilling myself. Deep in my chest, I sense the lamp's movement. Aladdin is somewhere at the other end of the palace, and now he's standing still, thank the gods. After another moment of rest, I resume walking, wondering what Caspida and her handmaidens must think of me.

I am not far down the hall when I sense I am being followed. The passage has no windows or skylights and is quite dark save for a few smoldering braziers. I turn a corner, as if heading back to Aladdin's chambers. But then I stop and shift to smoke, rising upward.

When Ensi and Khavar creep around the corner, I shift back into a human, drop from the ceiling, and land in a crouch behind them. Ensi shrieks and Khavar whirls, batting my arm aside, her hand sliding around my throat, her other hand producing a knife. She slams me hard against the wall. Ensi, her eyes wide, holds a handful of red powder that she'd been about to throw in my face. Khavar's snake rises on her shoulder, hissing.

"Well, well." I can't help grinning. "Caspida has a little coterie of girl assassins, just like Roshana did. Do you call yourselves the Watchmaidens too?"

Ensi, looking sheepish, pockets her poisonous powder in a concealed satchel beneath her thin silk coat. "Let her go, Khavar."

"No," the other girl snarls. "I don't trust her. She asks too many questions." She presses her forearm against my throat, and I wince and suck in a thin breath. "I thought you were sick?"

"I'd listen to your friend, if I were you," I croak, smiling still.

"How'd you get up there?" Ensi asks, studying the ceiling curiously. "You must be very nimble."

"Who are you really?" Khavar demands. "Speak, or I'll strangle you."

I shrug. "I gave you a fair chance." With a twist, a spin, and a grunt, I reverse our positions, pressing Khavar's face into the wall and wrenching her arm behind her. She bares her teeth at me angrily, while Ensi gasps and covers her mouth.

"Let me make one thing clear," I say softly into Khavar's ear.

"There will be no spying or shadowing my master and me. We mean you no ill will, I swear, but I will not tolerate being watched all the time. It's exhausting and pointless for you and me both. Khavar, I'm going to let you go now. Let's agree to talk like civilized people."

When I release her, Khavar turns and throws up her hands defensively, but I am already standing several paces back, hands spread amenably. Ensi, her eyes darting nervously from me to her friend, steps between us.

"So. You *are* Watchmaidens, then?" I ask.

Ensi sighs and twists her hair in her hands. "We're descended from the original Watchmaidens created by Queen Roshana."

"Your order has survived all these centuries?" I ask.

Ensi smiles proudly. "Our knowledge was passed down, mother to daughter, for generations. We've been protecting the Amulen queens and princesses for hundreds of years. Khavar here can even trace her ancestry directly to Parys zai Moura, Roshana's personal scribe."

I glance at Khavar's sour face. *I bet she can.* Parys had never liked me, and I can see the same mistrust in Khavar's eyes. "Go back to your princess," I tell them. "Please pass along my regards, and tell her Prince Rahzad will *not* be spied upon."

They nod and back away, watching me warily until the corner comes between us. I stand for a minute and listen until I am certain they've gone, then let out a long sigh and run to see what my master has got himself into this time.

Chapter Thirteen

I find Aladdin in, of all places, the library.

For a moment I pause behind a tall case of scrolls and watch him. He stands in a beam of sunlight that pours from a high window, dust motes swirling around him, staring at an open scroll. Shelves around him overflow with parchment and papyrus, in sheets and rolls and bound stacks. Aladdin is dressed in a knee-length red waistcoat, his head bare and his hair tousled. His lips move as he reads, though I don't think he realizes it. As I watch him, I feel a subtle stirring inside, a swirling in my heart of smoke, a warming of embers. I know what it means, and I know how wrong, how dangerous it is. I almost cannot bear to smother it, it is so small and fragile and hopeful.

"What happened?" I ask, stepping from behind the case.

Aladdin starts, and his hands clamp the scroll shut. He blinks at me for a moment, until his eyes focus and his mind leaves whatever world it had been lost in.

"Zahra! Um, I thought—" His hand goes to the lamp, and his eyes dart to his right. I follow his gaze and see Jalil sitting at a low desk a short distance away, painstakingly inking a sheet of parchment with a long peacock quill. He seems lost in his work, but still, we must be careful what we say.

I walk to Aladdin and take the scroll he is holding, pretending to scan its contents.

"I nearly shifted," I whisper. "Right in front of her. What happened? Why did you leave your rooms?"

"I'm sorry," he whispers back. "He insisted on showing me the library and said if I was determined to learn about Parthenia this was the place to start. I couldn't think of a way out of it."

I look back at his scroll and raise an eyebrow. "A treatise on the jinn, hmm? Very historical."

He snatches the scroll back. "I was just—"

"Looking for information on me. Or my kind, anyway." I frown and fold my arms. "You can read? A boy from the slums?"

"Don't look so surprised. My mother was a scribe once, and she taught me letters. And anyway, we weren't *that* bad off, not at first." His eyes turn distant. "My father had a good business, tailoring, and my mother penned letters and ledgers for people. We did all right, until . . ." He shakes his head and furls the scroll. "What did Caspida want?"

"To talk about elephants and dead queens."

"What? Really?"

"Oh, stop frowning. She asked about you too—what you're like, what kind of person you are. Don't worry." I pat his hand conspiratorially and smile. "I lied."

"Well?" Aladdin waves the scroll impatiently. "Did she seem, I don't know, interested?"

"Interested? She's barely spoken a dozen words to you. Give it time."

He nods distractedly and scratches his ear; his earring still hangs there, a simple gold ring. I'd wanted him to take it off on the ship—any part of his old life would make it easier for someone to see through his glamoured appearance—but he'd insisted on keeping it.

"We've been here more than two weeks," he says. "And I only see her at dinners, and we can't talk there. How am I supposed to win her over if I can't even talk to her?"

On a table nearby, someone has left out a map of the world, its corners held down by stone gryphons. I run a hand across the parchment, tracing the coastlines. Around the edge of the map, the dates of the year have been inked in tiny letters. I eye them thoughtfully, then tap one of the numbers.

"Fahradan."

"What?" Aladdin comes to stand behind me, looking over my shoulder.

"In two weeks, the Amulens will celebrate the feast of Fahradan, in honor of the god Hamor." The god of lovers and fools—how appropriate. "Unless the traditions have changed drastically since I last celebrated, it's the perfect time to get Caspida's attention."

"Why?"

I turn and frown at him. "Haven't you ever celebrated Fahradan?"

"If by *celebrate* you mean pick people's pockets while they're dancing..."

I roll my eyes. "I should have guessed. Look, during the night of Fahradan, anyone can ask anyone to dance, and nobody's allowed to refuse."

A slow grin dawns on his face. "I see. But . . . two weeks? That's an eternity!"

It's also one night before the moon dies and my time runs out.

"Trust me," I say dryly, "it's hardly that. Did you think you'd walk into the palace, ask for her hand, and marry her within the week?"

"I don't know." He picks up one of the stone gryphons and tosses it from hand to hand. "I didn't really think at all, I guess. And don't forget, this was all *your* idea." He looks down at me, his eyes troubled. "It's killing me, Zahra. Seeing the vizier every day, passing him in the hall, pretending to bow and grovel. I hate it."

I glance over at Jalil, who is lost in his work, then back at Aladdin. "Come on."

"What?"

"Let's get out of here. There's too much dust. Too much . . . history." I take the scroll of jinn lore from his hand and set it on a shelf. "I want to sit in the sun and feel the sea breeze on my face."

"All right," he says, a bit amused. "And you can tell me more about the jinn."

We climb the tallest tower in the palace and find ourselves at last standing upon the rooftop, beneath a striped canvas awning, looking down on the city. From this height, it looks flawless, like a city in a story, stained with the golden light of midmorning. White rooftops bake in the sun, colorful awnings stretching between them, the crowns of the palms and other trees casting spiky patches of shade on the streets. And beyond the south wall, the cliffs overlook the turquoise sea. Not a cloud is to be seen, and the sun blazes like the eye of a beneficent god. Seabirds ride the warm air, drifting in the sky and turning lazy circles around the glittering minarets of the palace.

"Look at it," breathes Aladdin, leaning over the parapet. His elbows brush the leaves of a potted lemon tree, its branches budding with tiny fruits. "Not a bad view. I could get used to this."

"So. Becoming a prince isn't *entirely* about revenge, is it?"

He grins at me. "There are definitely other attractions."

"Can you really see this through? Marrying the princess, banishing or imprisoning the vizier, and then ruling this city? Guiding its people? Watching your children navigate the treacherous waters of court?"

With a shrug, he lifts his face to the sun, shutting his eyes and basking in its heat. "With a view like this? I could get used to anything. Of course, it all depends on winning the princess. She might hate me."

"She might."

He rolls his eyes. "Not helping, Smoky."

"My name isn't . . ." But I sigh and let it go. The nickname doesn't rankle me like it did a few weeks ago. I'm growing too used to it. Too used to *him*.

He lowers his face. "Is it true all jinn were once human?"

Caught off guard, I look up at him sharply. "Why do you want to know about that?"

"The scroll I was reading talked about it. I wondered if it was true." He turns around, leaning against the parapet, his arms folded.

I sigh and sit on the warm stone floor, my back against the potted lemon tree. I pull a fruit that dangles at my elbow and turn it over in my hands.

"Not all of them. The oldest ones were born jinn, but most of us were . . . adopted. Long ago, there were only two realms: that of the gods—the godlands, as you call them—and that of the jinn:

Ambadya. The jinn were the gods' first creation, and they made them powerful and proud and magnificent."

A yellow butterfly lands on my knee, and I pause a moment, watching it as it rubs its legs over its face before flitting off again.

"And?" Aladdin prods.

"For many ages the jinn lived in peace. There were the maarids, of the water, small, lovely, petty things. There were the ifreets, creatures of fire, who were few in number but great in power. There were the ghuls, creatures of earth, who even in those days were the most despised of the jinn. They lived in caves and holes, like rats, but were mostly harmless as they could never work together. There were the sila, jinn of the air, rarely seen by the others because they spent most of their lives drifting in the sky, invisible and secretive. And most powerful of all, there were the shaitan, masters of all elements, lords of all the jinn. In those days, Ambadya was much like your world: rich with color and life, beautiful and vast and wild."

Aladdin sits beside me, his shoulder against mine. "Everything I've heard describes the jinn world as dark and wretched."

"It is now. They ruined their world when they began warring with each other. They burned it, twisted it into a ruin. That is why the gods created men. They wanted to start over. And it is why the jinn and the humans have never got along since. The jinn were jealous, their place of privilege usurped. Many times they have tried to take over this world, and every time, the gods interceded."

He is sitting very close. My throat goes dry, and I stop to swallow, overly conscious of his warmth and the minty smell of the soap he used to wash his face this morning.

"Finally, the gods struck them with infertility—no new jinn could be born. But Havok, the god of rebirth, took pity on the jinn and allowed them to replenish their ranks only with humans who were given over to them. These sacrifices were meant to appease the jinn, and they were taken and turned into ifreets and sila, maarids and ghuls. A few were even made shaitan."

"Human sacrifices?" Aladdin's voice is thick with disgust. "I'd heard that in other parts of the world, they still leave children and girls and warriors for the jinn, but I didn't want to believe it."

"You should. It is the easiest way to ensure that the jinn won't burn your crops or sicken your livestock. After the gods abandoned the world, temples called alombs became shrines to the jinn, places where people could leave their sacrifices and buy another year of protection."

"Zahra . . . were *you* sacrificed?"

I haven't thought about that day in a long, long time. It was a thousand and one lifetimes ago. Ignoring the question, I point to the north, to the mountain sitting in the distance behind a screen of haze. "There is one such alomb on the summit of that mountain."

He watches me, fully aware of my evasion, but he doesn't press me further. His gaze turns north. "We don't use it. It's forbidden. That's why our city is starving. Few cities will trade with us, because they think we should make offerings to the jinn as they do."

I nod. "Roshana was the first Amulen queen to outlaw sacrifices. It was a bold move, but it infuriated the jinn."

He leans into me, nudging me softly with his shoulder. "So? What about *you*? What's it like being a shaitan?"

I stare at him. "What makes you think I am a shaitan?"

"I've seen you grant wishes, and the way you change your form . . . Well? You are, aren't you?"

"Yes," I admit. I am part of a dying breed, one of only three left in existence. Of the other two, one resides in Ambadya, ruling the jinn, and the second is likely somewhere beneath my feet, trapped in a bottle.

"Were you in Ambadya before it was destroyed?" Aladdin asks.

"Of course not. I've been a jinni for four thousand years. Ambadya was razed long, long before that."

"Who were you? Where did you live?"

"It doesn't matter anymore." I stand up, dropping the lemon, and turn to look down on the city. "It's too hot out here. Let's go inside. I'll teach you how to properly enter a room based on who is already there, and whether they are sitting, standing, or eating."

Aladdin groans. "I'm sick of playing prince. Let's pick pockets."

"No."

"Wait a minute, Smoky . . ." He leans in close to study me, mimicking Jalil's habit of raising one eyebrow ridiculously high when suspicious. I can't help it—his expression makes me giggle—actually *giggle*, like a little girl. "Do you even know *how* to pick pockets?"

"Of course I do," I lie. "I've picked a thousand and one—"

"Yes, yes, you've done it all a thousand times, I get it." He raises a doubtful brow. "So prove it."

"Him," Aladdin murmurs. "The one with the feather on his hat. He's got a pipe in his left pocket."

We're in the palace gardens, pretending to admire a massive statue of King Malek. Many nobles are out today, lounging around the pools and fountains, strolling beneath the shade of the trees. Nearly as vast as the palace itself, the gardens spread in a luxurious carpet of green, organized in perfect symmetry. One could walk for hours out here and never find the end of them.

Our target is a man a bit older than Aladdin, walking in our direction. We stand in a more secluded spot. Our back is to him, and when he passes behind us, Aladdin coughs.

I turn and run straight into the man and quickly slip my hand into his pocket, but the pipe is too deep to reach.

"You clumsy wench—Gods above! Are you trying to *rob* me, girl?" The nobleman seizes my wrist and yanks it from his pocket. My hand comes up with the pipe clenched in it. I stare at him, horrified.

"I . . ."

We're standing by a tall, neatly trimmed hedge, and without another word I grab the nobleman and drag him into the bushes with me; we burst through the other side into a private clearing populated with small, half-tame deer, which startle and flee. Surrounded by tall shrubs and trees, we're hidden from view of anyone else walking by.

"I'll have your head for this!" the man rages. "I'll have you whipped!"

Aladdin climbs through the hedge after us. I'm gripping the man by his coat, while he spits curses at me, his face turning bright red and his beard flecked with spittle.

"What are you doing?" hisses Aladdin.

"I don't know!" I stare at him helplessly. "I panicked!"

Rolling his eyes, Aladdin turns to the man. "Shut it, will you?"

"I've never been so—mph!"

Aladdin clasps a hand over his mouth, holding him in a headlock. "Easy, old man. Gods, we're not going to murder you."

I let go of him and let out a long breath. The man ceases struggling and glares hard at me.

"All right, listen up," Aladdin says. "See, this is all part of a game.

A sort of treasure hunt. It was all Prince Darian's idea, I might add. Between you and me"—he drops his voice to a whisper—"I think he's a bit insane. But if you want to complain, talk to him. I'm sure he'd be reasonable about it. I'm going to let you go now. Don't yell, or I might have to gag you and let you sit here till dark."

Slowly he releases the man, who whirls angrily but doesn't shout out. He straightens his hat and coat, looking from Aladdin to me.

"I never . . . Young people these days!"

"Yes, we're a rotten lot," agrees Aladdin. "Go on, now. If you run into Darian, be sure to give him a piece of your mind."

The man hurries off with many backward glances, his face still red. Then Aladdin lets out a heavy sigh and rubs his face.

"I got the pipe," I say, holding it up.

He stares for a minute, blinking, and then bursts into laughter. A few curious deer stick their heads through the shrubs to see what the racket is. Aladdin doubles over, laughing loud enough to startle birds from the trees overhead, and after a moment, I start laughing too. I haven't laughed this hard in a long, long while, and it feels wonderful. We sit on the grass and laugh until our faces are red and we're out of breath.

"You are the *worst* thief I have ever seen," declares Aladdin.

"I don't know what you're talking about. I got it, didn't I?"

"My grandmother could pick pockets better than that! Though that's not quite fair; my grandmother was the best pickpocket in Parthenia. She taught me all her tricks. Drove my mother crazy."

Taking advantage of the private spot, I shift into a tiger and roll on the grass, groaning with pleasure. The few deer remaining panic at the sight and dash off.

Aladdin lies beside me, his hands flung wide, eyes closed, and face turned to the sun. The sky is brilliantly blue, and the grass lush and deep. I stretch out, relishing the cool dirt under my claws. Then, with a sigh, I shift back into a girl and sink into the grass.

"If you had a wish to spend," says Aladdin suddenly, "what would you do with it?"

My eyes are half shut, my thoughts slow and lazy. "Spend a day in Ashori, eating grapes." I don't add that I'd also be free, without a lamp or a master in sight, staying as long as I pleased and answering to no one.

He rolls on his side, head propped on his hand. "Really? *Grapes?* You could wish for anything—but you'd wish for *grapes?*"

"I take it you've never had an Ashori grape." I shut my eyes and imagine it. "They're sweet and plump and perfectly crisp . . . the last Lampholder used to order them by the shipload."

"Huh." He pulls up a small white daisy that's sprouted in the grass. "I must have one of these grapes."

I open one eye. "Is that a wish?"

He makes a face and tosses the flower at me. It lands on my cheek, and I pick it up and twirl it between my fingers. I could lie out here all day, not moving an inch, feeling the sun above and the grass below. With a contented sigh, I stretch my arms wide, raking the grass with my fingers—and find myself brushing Aladdin's hand with my own. I pull it away quickly, my cheeks warming. He laughs a little.

"Sometimes," he says, "I forget you're supposed to be four thousand years old. You act as shy as a girl of sixteen."

"I do not!" I sit up and glare at him.

He grins and shrugs, sliding his hands under his head. There are bits of grass stuck in his hair, and after a moment's hesitation, I reach over and flick them away.

Aladdin watches me silently, his throat bobbing as he swallows. I drop my gaze.

He pulls out the pipe I stole and sticks it between his teeth.

"What do you think?" he asks around the stem. "Do I look noble?"

I snatch it away, and his teeth close with a clack. "Don't you know that will kill you?"

He stares at me a minute, a mischievous light coming into his eyes. Then suddenly he lunges at me.

"Give it back!"

"It's mine! I stole it!"

"I saved you from getting flogged!"

He makes a grab for the pipe, and I roll aside, holding it out of his reach. With a wicked laugh, he tickles my side, and I drop the pipe as I hasten to shove him away.

Aladdin picks up the pipe and brandishes it triumphantly, while I lie in the grass and laugh.

"Who knew jinn were ticklish?" He sits cross-legged and taps the pipe on his knee. "I should tell Caspida. I've discovered the jinn's greatest weakness! Sure, they hate iron, but wave a feather on a stick and they'll run to the other side of the world!"

"That was a dishonorable move, thief."

"As if I had any honor to begin to with."

I lift my eyes skyward and start to lean away, but then Aladdin reaches out and grabs my wrist, stopping me. I look up at him questioningly, and freeze.

His eyes are staring deep into mine, suddenly curious and thoughtful, and a strange wind rustles through my body. I go very still, not even breathing, as his hand lifts and he runs his finger so gently, so softly, along my jaw. He gazes at me as if seeing me for the first time, his lips just slightly parted.

For a moment I'm certain he'll say something he will regret, and apprehension wells up in me.

But then he draws back with a husky laugh, his eyes slipping away. *"Grapes."*

Chapter Fourteen

THE TWO WEEKS PASS SLOWLY, until at last we arrive at the day of Fahradan. Darkness falls, but the festival will not commence until midnight. After a stiff, long dinner with the nobles—Darian failing to make an appearance—Aladdin returns to our rooms to find a new set of clothes has been laid out. They are resplendent, showy garments, scarlet and gold, complete with cape and feathered turban. Aladdin regards them with dismay, then goes to his room to put them on.

When he emerges, dressed in all but the turban, I catch my breath, caught off guard. The tight-fitting cut of the long coat accentuates his taut abdomen and broad shoulders and is drawn in around his waist with a thin black belt. The scarlet fabric with its exquisite gold-and-black embroidery brings out the copper streaks in his eyes, and the high collar stops halfway up his neck, brushing his stubbled jaw when he looks down to survey himself. The cloak, which is scarlet on the outside and lined with pale gold fabric, crosses from his left shoulder to drape over his right arm.

"Well?" he says gruffly. "How do I look?"

"Um." I swallow hastily and look away. "You might catch the princess's eye, I suppose."

"I itch all over. If I'd known being a prince mostly consisted of wearing damned uncomfortable costumes like this, I'd never have made that wish."

"You itch because you need to shave," I note. "Sit."

I retrieve a shaving knife and creamy goats'-milk soap and throw a wool blanket over Aladdin to spare his fine clothes. He grumbles but goes along as I order him to sit on a stool in the grass, in the light of a strong lantern.

Aladdin tilts his head back and swallows as I soap my hands and then run them over his cheeks and jaw, leaving a thick lather.

"Don't move," I say softly. His eyes follow mine as I press the edge of the blade to his cheek and gently scrape away the short, coarse hairs. His irises are golden in the candlelight, and his long, dark lashes almost make him look as if he's lined his eyes with kohl.

"Where did you learn to do this?" he asks.

"Don't talk unless you want your throat cut," I warn. "I've been around a long time. You tend to pick things up."

"How long have you been in the lamp?"

"What did I say about talking?" I sigh.

"Well? How long?"

I bend over him, running the blade along the angle of his jaw. "For as long as I have been jinn."

"Who put you there?"

"Why do you care?"

THE FORBIDDEN WISH 149

His brow wrinkles slightly. "Because it seems wrong to keep someone locked away, just sitting around waiting to make other people's lives better."

"Who said I made their lives better? Will you *please* keep still?"

"Was it Nardukha?"

I pause, the blade resting on his cheek. "Where'd you get that idea?"

"Well, isn't he the king of the jinn or something?"

I grip his chin lightly with my free hand, forcing him to keep his mouth shut while I scrape beneath his nose. Gods, how did he come by such perfect lips? And why do I feel warm as a fire? "He is. And yes, he's the only jinni left with enough power to bind us to lamps and bottles and other such prisons."

"Like the jinn charmers?"

I pull the blade away sharply. "What do you know of the jinn charmers?"

"Just that they play sometimes in the streets, or outside the city walls. People say their music can charm jinn right into bottles."

"Kind of like that," I reply. "But Nardukha's magic is much stronger. It not only binds us to our vessels, it strips us of our magic and compels us to grant wishes."

"Why does he do it?" he asks, when I pause to wipe the blade clean.

"Because he can," I reply flatly. "It's one of the ways he keeps us under control. If we disobey or threaten him, he enslaves us to humans until we repent and beg for his forgiveness. Even then, he might not relent."

"Which did you do? Threaten him or disobey him?"

I scrape beneath his chin, then down the skin of his neck, taking particular care around his delicate veins, before replying. "Both."

"That's all you're going to say, isn't it? No matter how much I ask?"

With a tight smile, I shave the last of his stubble away. "You know me so well already."

I drop a plush cloth over his head and tell him to clean himself up.

He stands wiping his face while I flit about the room, lighting lamps and opening the silk curtains to let in the cool night air. I can still feel his neck's pulse in my fingertips. What would Nardukha do if he saw me running my fingers along Aladdin's jaw? I shudder to think of the answer.

"We should go soon," I say. "The dancing will begin in an hour."

"Dancing. Wonderful." His tone is deflated.

With a sigh, I shut the glass door on the last lamp. The flame burns steady and bright, casting flickering lace patterns through the metalwork encasing it. "Don't tell me you don't know how."

"Oh, sure, because I've had so *much* time for dancing, in between not starving to death and not getting thrown in prison." He tosses his facecloth aside. "I know plenty of dances. My favorite is called Not Getting Your Legs Broken for Stealing Figs from That Baker on Pearl Lane."

"That's sure to charm the princess right into a wedding pact."

Grinning mischievously, he crosses to me and takes my hands, trying to draw me onto the open floor. "*You* can teach me how to dance."

"No." I wrench my hands away and turn my back to him.

"I thought the whole point of Fahradan was that everyone *has* to dance."

"Wish for it, and I could make you such a dancer you would charm the fish out of the sea."

"*Zahra*. Are you angry with me?" He walks around to face me. "Is this because I beat you at dice the other day?" His eyes going wide, he drops to his knees in front of me. "I apologize from the bottom of my soul, O great and powerful jinni of the lamp."

"You didn't beat me. I let you win."

"Zahra." Aladdin shuffles closer and takes my hands. "I *need* your help."

With a soft groan, I pull my hands from his and throw them in the air. "Fine! Just stop groveling! You're supposed to be a *prince*, you idiot. Anyway, you'll get your fancy clothes dirty."

His face blossoming with delight, he lifts me by my waist and spins me around before I have a chance to dodge him.

"Put me down!" I shift, and his hands close around white smoke. I reappear behind him, barefoot on the smooth tiled courtyard, dressed in a Fahradan gown of red and gold to match Aladdin's coat, a turquoise comb set in my hair that drops a tear-shaped ruby over the center of my forehead.

Aladdin turns and stops dead with a soft "Oh." His eyes scan me from head to toe, his mouth slightly ajar.

I wave a hand. "Come here."

He hurries to me, stopping a pace away. The lamps that hang from the pillars around us cast delicate patterns of light across the white walls and floor, painting glitter like trapped stars. But for the clicking song of a nightjar in the trees behind us and babble of the wall fountain, all is silent.

"The dance of Fahradan," I begin, "is a dance of paradoxes. It is restraint versus passion. It is desire versus purity. It is push versus pull."

I lift my arms, which are bare of jewelry. "This dance is born in the wrists. They are the points upon which the rest of the body hangs."

Demonstrating, I begin rotating my hands, shifting foot to foot, my hips swaying to unheard music. My gown whispers against the tile, my bare feet lifting only at the heel.

"It is one of the few dances shared by a man and a woman," I go on. "Step closer."

He does, swallowing, and he holds up his wrists at shoulder height. Without pausing, I step to him and press the inside of my left wrist lightly against his right.

"Nothing touches," I whisper in his ear, "except the wrists."

I can feel his pulse beating through the delicate skin of his wrist, warm and strong and vibrant. The power of his energy pours through me like a rush of wind.

"When you dance with the princess, you must resist her and at the same time let her entice you. You are stone, and she is water. You are the earth, and she is the sky." With a swift spin, I reverse directions, locking my other wrist to his. "See? Push and pull. Restraint and passion."

He nods and licks his lips, his eyes locked with mine.

"Now," I say, "when I step forward, you step back. When I turn to the left, you go right. We are mirrors of one another, do you see? But always we come back, wrist to wrist. Imagine an invisible ribbon tying us together, always bringing us back to where we began. This dance, like time, is a circle."

He begins to dance with me, mirroring my movements, until we are circling one another, turning, twirling, and always returning to the starting position, opposite wrists pressed together, vein to vein, pulse to pulse.

"The woman leads, and the man resists. The woman invites, and the man follows. Your part is easy—let Caspida lead. Mirror her movements, and you will fall into synthesis. Your bodies will read each other's heartbeats through the wrists, and your pulses will become one rhythm."

"I think I understand," he says hoarsely.

"Then prove it."

I twirl away, then back to him, staying on my toes, my hips always lightly rotating. He reacts clumsily at first, but soon the awkwardness fades away and he begins matching my movements, reflecting them in reverse. We dance like this, wrist to wrist, twirl and turn, step for step, for several more minutes. He holds my gaze, our eyes connecting at every turn, anticipating one another's movements.

His pulse is so strong against my wrist that it echoes through me, almost like a heartbeat of my own. My skin warms; my breath catches in my throat. I know how closely I dance along the line of destruction, but I cannot pull myself away. He is intoxicating, his force of life an addiction I cannot refuse. I have not felt this alive in centuries, not since you, Habiba, when you taught me the dance of Fahradan. Ours was a dance of giddy laughter, a dance of friends, sisters, a dance of life and youth and hope.

But this dance is different.

It is not I but he who entices, reversing the ancient roles of the dance. And I resist because I must, because if I don't, because if I give in to the all-too-human desires racing through me—then it is Aladdin who will pay the terrible price.

"Stop." I drop my wrists and step away, and he does the same, still caught up in mirroring me. Except that he is breathing heavily, his chest rising and falling with exertion, his eyes filled with a strange, wondrous, curious look as he stares at me. He moves closer, his eyes fixed on mine, and despite myself I cannot look away.

Aladdin raises a tentative hand to my cheek. Immobile with

both dread and longing, I can only stare up at him, flushing with warmth when he gently runs his hand down the side of my face. I shut my eyes, leaning into his touch just slightly, my stomach leaping. Longing. Wishing.

I feel him leaning closer, bending down, his face drawing nearer to mine.

"No," I whisper. "I can't."

"Zahra—"

I pull away, averting my gaze. "You are ready for her."

With that, I turn and run back into the palace.

Chapter Fifteen

It is a custom of Fahradan that for the evening, the lines between the classes are temporarily erased, and a servant may dance with a prince, and a cook may break bread with a king. And so when Aladdin enters the great throne room of King Malek, I am standing at his side, equal for this night. I wear my conjured gown of red and gold silk, a ruby perched on my brow.

I still feel Aladdin's touch burning on my cheek, the weight of him leaning toward me. My skin courses with rippling heat, and never have I felt so out of control of my own form. I cannot shift away the tingles in my stomach or the image of his eyes locking on mine as we spun around one another.

It was a fluke, an accident, I tell myself. It won't happen again. Still, I feel every inch of space between us as we walk, and I wonder if he feels it too. I don't dare glance at him to find out, because I fear meeting his eyes and seeing the truth in them—that what happened *wasn't* an accident.

That it might be real.

And worse, that I might want it to happen again.

This isn't what I came here for, I remind myself. I need to focus, need to find Zhian, need to do it *fast*. I have two more days before I lose my chance at freedom and Nardukha unleashes his fury on Parthenia. This isn't just about me anymore. This is about the people dancing around me, unwitting of the destruction waiting to fall on them. This is about saving Aladdin. And what I felt in our rooms minutes ago—that cannot happen again.

There is far too much to lose.

Our entrance is not grand—we slip in with the crowd, and with everyone dressed in red and gold, it's easy to blend in. But Aladdin begins to gather looks of appreciation and of envy, of desire and of open hostility—this last from the various men whose female companions cast admiring looks my master's way. And Aladdin does cut a breathtaking figure, moving through the crowd with the grace and carriage of a born prince. Where did he learn that? Where did he learn to hold his head so high, to carry his shoulders so squarely, to look every person he passes in the eye and to give them a small, knowing smile as if they are old friends? He has a bearing to him that no degree of my magic could impart, some deep inner strength that is entirely of his own making. Watching him makes me ache inside.

"They're staring at me," he whispers. "Gods, Zahra, is this thing on backward or something?" He tugs at his coat.

"Stop it," I hiss, swatting his hand. "You look fine. You look . . . damn princely."

He smiles brightly, and the pleasure in his eyes is too bright to bear. I look away, scanning the room for familiar faces. Though the custom is that servants may mingle freely with their lords, it is easy to see that most of the people here are nobility. The servants must be having their own Fahradan in some other part of the palace. But not all—a few unlucky ones wind through the crowd, bearing flagons of wine or trays of pastries.

The empty throne is cordoned off with silk rope, awaiting the king. A temporary dais has been set up against one wall, and on it a group of musicians play a lilting, fast-paced tune to which a few couples are already dancing wrist to wrist, as I taught Aladdin. Braziers twice as high as a man and propped up by massive tripods cast light that reaches even the tops of the mighty domes overhead. I don't see the pigeons that had populated the ceiling the day we met the king, and I wonder what poor fool's job it was to clear them out. Here and there, the crowd opens to give space for fire-breathers, acrobats, snake charmers, and sword swallowers.

"I don't see her," says Aladdin. "Is she coming? What if she—"

"Sh. Look."

At the far end of the throne room, atop a high double stair carved with winged men and horses, is a tall door of rich teak. It opens slowly, drawn by four servants, to reveal Caspida and her girls, who float into the hall. The princess wears a gown of pure, pale gold lined with crimson. Her hair, bound up in an elaborate swirl, is encased in a fine net of delicate gold chains, each dripping with tiny diamonds. Her hair is the night speckled with stars, but none brighter than her eyes, which sweep across the room. Across the backs of her hands, delicate red patterns worked in henna swirl and curl like smoke.

The court lets out an appreciative sigh, pausing to bow toward her. She descends the stair smoothly, her girls flanking her. Above them, Darian appears in the doorway, dressed in a tight red coat, topped with a gold turban. He waves regally before descending, his head high and his lips peeled back in a smile.

I lean over and nudge a poleaxed Aladdin, whose eyes are trained on the princess. "Hurry. Go ask her to dance before anyone else does!"

He nods dazedly and steps forward. I release a short breath, forcing myself to let him go alone. He is on his own now, and I can only hope he won't make an utter fool of himself. Now if I can make my way to an exit, I can get back to searching for Zhian. The seconds slip away faster than ever, and my stomach twists with worry.

I turn around and nearly smack into a skinny noble with a thin mustache and bad breath.

"Will you dance with me, lady?" he asks. Then, leaning in, he whispers, "You can't say no! Not tonight."

I am trapped between him and one of the tall pillars, and I wince as his breath assaults me. He grabs my wrist tightly and tries to pull me toward the dance floor, when suddenly a hand closes on his arm and wrenches it away.

"The lady already promised me the next round," says a voice.

I turn to see who has come thinking to rescue me—and freeze.

Darian's smile is small and tight. He bows, but the gesture is mocking, his eyes brazenly studying my form through the gown.

"We haven't met," he says. "I am Prince Darian."

The skinny man mumbles an apology and disappears. I start to turn away, but Darian smoothly steps in front of me, putting his wrist to mine and turning me into the dance. The crowd around us parts, giving us space to turn. I flush with annoyance. The gods are conspiring against me tonight.

"Your Highness, I am—"

"I know who you are," says Darian. "You're Zahra, Rahzad's

girl." He turns sharply, and I mirror him, watching him from the corner of my eye.

"You're very bold for a prince," I tell him, whirling and meeting his wrist.

"You're very pretty for a serving girl."

I spot Aladdin then, not far away, settling into a dance with Caspida. He's babbling at her, smiling too widely, and she's more interested in watching Darian and me. Our gazes cross, and in her eyes is burning curiosity, but then we both turn away.

"What's your master's game, then?" Darian asks in a low tone.

We circle one another, wrists pressed together, his pulse racing with anger. He has seen Aladdin and Caspida dancing, and rage burns beneath his cool exterior.

"I'm sure I don't know what you mean, my lord. I am just a servant."

"Liar. You're more than that. Caspida's taken an interest in you, and you meet my eye without looking down. Frankly I don't care who or what you really are—what I want to know is where your master gets off thinking he can cross me."

I suppress a wince. I always was bad at passing myself off as a servant. *Too impressed with yourself for your own good* is what you often said, Habiba.

"How could he possibly threaten you?" I ask Darian.

"He doesn't. He annoys me."

"It's a particular habit of his." The music quickens and our steps match it, until we are whirling and turning at a dizzying speed.

Darian ceases talking to concentrate on the dance, but when the music slows again he says, "Caspida and I have been betrothed since birth. She loves me."

"How could she not?" I drift closer to him, my skirts brushing his legs as we circle one another, then switch wrists. "You're handsome and powerful. You're what every little princess dreams of."

His hand traces my waist and hip, hovering but not touching. "And what do little serving girls dream of?" he whispers.

With a smile I spin away from him, arms held in front of me, giving my skirts room to flare as I twirl. Then, before he can catch me, I slip into the crowd and leave him standing alone.

Caspida and Aladdin are still dancing, their steps stiff and formal, and Aladdin's attempts to get her to laugh seem to be in vain. When he spies me watching, his eyebrows raise in a plea for help. I shrug and smile. *Wish for it, thief, and I could make her beg for your love.*

The diamonds in her hair reflect tiny pinpoints of light across his face, making him look bewitched. They are a beautiful pair, like lovers out of a story, brought together by destiny. I sigh and start to move away, but a voice stops me.

"You look like you swallowed a lemon."

I turn to see Nessa at my side. She's dressed in a two-piece gown of crimson that exposes her muscular stomach and the small gold ring piercing her navel. Her dreadlocks are worked into a braided knot on top of her head, their silver tips fanning out like a crown. I prickle with wariness at the sight of her, but she doesn't seem to have brought her flute. A book of bound parchment is tucked under her arm.

Noticing my stare, she laughs and taps the book. "I always get bored at these things. So I brought a friend." Drawing it out, she flips through the pages. "A history of the greatest queens of the eastern sea kingdoms, going all the way back to the Shepherdess

Queen of Ghedda, who offered herself as sacrifice to save her city from sinking into the sea."

My skin prickles, and I turn and look at her fully, my eagerness to find Zhian temporarily forgotten. "An ancient story," I say slowly. "Few people know it."

"I know a lot of old stories most people forget," she says, running her finger down the spine. "And the Parthenian library is a marvel. One could spend a lifetime exploring it and never even count all the scrolls and books tucked away in there."

"May I ask, Highness, how a Tytoshi princess finds herself in an Amulen court?"

"I suppose you may, since it's Fahradan, after all." She looks across the crowd, her eyes briefly lingering on Aladdin and Caspida. "When a Tytoshi king dies, his successor often cleanses the royal household, murdering his siblings and their children in order to protect his throne—and not without reason. Few Tytoshi rulers die of natural deaths, you know." She turns back to me, her tone matter-of-fact. "When my grandfather died, my eldest uncle became king. Instead of letting my brother Vigo and me be strangled in our sleep, our mother smuggled us here. We were only babies at the time."

"And was it your mother who taught you the art of jinn charming?"

The only indication Nessa gives of her alarm at this question is a slight flaring of her nostrils. "I beg your pardon?"

"Forgive me. I noticed your flute the other day. It is carved with Eskarr symbols—not an instrument for idle melodies."

She studies me for a long moment, her jaw tensing, before replying shortly, "My twin and I earn our keep." She nods at Aladdin and Caspida. "Your prince and my princess are stirring up quite the gossip."

I glance around at the watching nobles, who all have eyes for Caspida and her companion. They whisper behind their spiced wine, and not all their expressions are benevolent.

"I'd tell your master to watch out," Nessa continues. "Darian's probably in some corner plotting murder." She looks away, her face impassive, and I sigh. I'm likely to get no help from her in finding Zhian. The crowd presses in on me, until it seems I can hardly breathe. I must get out, must continue searching. I've wasted too much time already.

But before I can make a move, a peal of trumpets and a crier announce the king's arrival. The crowd goes still and silent, watching with bowed heads, and I suppress a groan. Running out now would only draw unwanted attention.

The door atop the stair opens, and Malek leads in a small procession, Sulifer at his right shoulder. The king is hunched and pale, and the bright festival garb he wears looks more comical than regal on his wasted frame. He stumbles down the stairs, nearly toppling altogether before accepting an arm from his brother. Leaning on Sulifer, Malek makes his way to the floor and there pauses to catch his breath. His glazed eyes rove disinterestedly about.

A few snickers bubble out of the crowd, unnoticed by the king. I spot one young nobleman in a far corner—one of Darian's boys—mimicking the king, tottering around and miming holding a simmon pipe to his lips while smiling vacuously. Darian himself is expressionless, but I have lived long enough to learn to read the emotions beneath the surface. He masks disgust and satisfaction when he looks at the king.

Caspida's face is as still as the moon. Without a word to Aladdin, she pushes through the crowd and reaches Malek's side. With a wave she dismisses Sulifer and takes her father's arm. He seems to rouse from his stupor at her touch, and smiles and pats her hand. She leads him to the throne, helping him sit and arranging cushions behind his back. The crowd begins to lose interest and goes back to their dancing and talking.

"How long has he been like this?" I ask Nessa.

She sighs and watches Caspida and the king with sorrowful eyes. "Ever since the queen died, ten years ago. He was once bright and strong and adored Caspida completely."

"How did the queen die?"

Nessa's gaze darkens. "A jinn attack, long ago. They ambushed the queen and all her Watchmaidens while they were on a journey to seek an alliance with Ursha. Our mothers. All gone in a single day."

Ah. Small wonder then that the princess hates the jinn so deeply. Uneasily, my thoughts wander down paths I've tried very hard to avoid: What will happen to Aladdin once I've won my freedom? What will Caspida do when she learns he tricked his way into the palace with jinn magic?

Vigo appears suddenly at his sister's side, grinning wickedly. His dreadlocks are in a thick braid down his back, their silver-tipped ends tinkling. "Come on, Ness! Let's show them how the Tytoshi dance."

"All right, ugly, but don't cry when you can't keep up." Nessa smiles and hands me her book. "Hold on to this for me, Zahra."

They slide onto the open floor and throw themselves into a lively dance composed of jumping, whooping, and twirling, which looks altogether exhausting. The crowd around them cheers and claps along. I watch, smiling a little, recalling entire fields filled with dancing Tytoshi back when I belonged to one of their kings. After a while, I look down at Nessa's book and open it to the first page. It bears an illustration of the Shepherdess Queen of Ghedda looking down on her city as waves rose to devour it.

With a shudder, I slam the book shut.

Suddenly a hand slides around my waist and a voice whispers in my ear, "How about that dance now, love?"

It's Bad Breath, now well drunk and reeking of wine. He pushes me from behind, into the open, and grabs my wrist tightly. As he tries to force me into a turn, I hiss, "I'll give you exactly three seconds to contemplate the mistake you're making before I break your—"

The man's eyes go wide, and his lips spread in a grimace as his free hand is twisted behind him—held tightly by a grim-faced Aladdin.

"Step away," Aladdin says softly, "and you might leave with your arm still attached to your body, you bastard."

The man moans, but he lets go of me and skulks off, muttering, "Why does this always happen to me?" to himself. Aladdin, pleased with himself, bows to me.

"Can *I* have a turn? Or do you only dance with cretins like Darian?"

Rolling my eyes, I drop Nessa's book into my pocket, then hold up my wrist. He meets it with his own, sweeping me into the midst of the other dancers. "I didn't need your help."

"A lady shouldn't have to get her hands dirty on a night like this."

"Oh, you are quite the prince. So did you sweep her off her feet?"

His expression changes then, shifting from smugness to misery. "She barely spoke ten words to me."

"I'm shocked." I smile, turning my back to him, our wrists meeting behind my head. "Did you try poetry?"

"You're not being helpful."

Turning to face him, I lean in and whisper, "Wish for her love, and I will deliver it to you."

He smiles grimly. "Then it wouldn't be love."

"And what do you know of love?"

"That it must be a choice."

"Oh, my naïve thief." I pause briefly to meet his gaze. "Love is rarely a choice."

The music slows, and most of the other dancers drift away to talk and drink. I start to follow, the need to find Zhian pulling at me, but Aladdin says softly, "Just a little longer. I think I'm starting to get the hang of this."

I glance up at him and find his gaze too warm to withstand. I resume dancing but keep my eyes lowered, fighting the knots twisting inside me.

Only two other couples are left: Nessa and Vigo, and Caspida and Darian. The prince and princess move with stiff formality, their steps rote. Darian seems frustrated at the princess's aloofness.

"She doesn't love him," I whisper to Aladdin. "With the right words, you'll win her over."

"If you have any ideas to share, I'm nothing but ears," he replies, his voice suddenly miserable.

My eyes narrow as I study his forlorn gaze. "Why, Prince Rahzad, are you starting to fall in love?"

He blinks, his eyes clearing, and then his gaze locks on mine. I spin away, then back to him, and his copper eyes don't waver.

"I'm not here to fall in love, am I? I'm here to avenge my parents."

"Don't the two work hand in hand?"

Abruptly, he stops dancing and steps away. He stares at me with eyes as deep as the night.

"No," he replies softly. "I'm not sure they do."

I stand still, bewildered, as he turns and melts into the crowd.

Chapter Sixteen

EXHAUSTED FROM DANCING, the people move into a grand courtyard beneath a starry sky and colorful lanterns swaying in a gentle breeze. They burn in the night like candle flames, bright and brilliant. I follow, only paying half attention to everyone around me, as I push my sixth sense far and wide and deep, probing for Zhian. I even send out tentative whispers in the silent jinn tongue: *Are you there? Brothers and sisters, is anyone there?* No reply comes trickling back.

Aladdin is at Caspida's side. They move in the midst of young lords and maidens, all laughing and flirting. The princess and my master are reticent, not looking at each other. Aladdin glances around, and then his eyes catch mine and hold. I stand apart from everyone else and, meeting his eye, nod pointedly at the princess. He stares a moment longer before turning back to Caspida and making a comment that draws a polite smile.

I find a quiet corner tucked in the tall hedges surrounding the courtyard and sit on the base of a tall statue hidden there. It is a marble sculpture of a gryphon with a face seemingly based on King Malek's, though this face is stronger and fuller, like the man Malek might have been had he not wasted himself over simmon.

Tipping my head back, the moon and I regard one another silently, like enemies facing off across a field of battle. It is the same moon that met me the night Aladdin brought me out of the vault beneath the desert: barely there at all, merely a sly wink in the deep dark sky.

Two days until it disappears completely.

I let my mind turn to the possibility of failure, something I haven't even dared consider until now. Shaza had warned that if I didn't release Zhian in the allotted month, Nardukha would rain death on me and Parthenia. It isn't hard to imagine what that means.

I still have Nessa's book in my pocket, and I pull it out and lay it on my lap, open to the first page, where an ink drawing depicts a sorrowful maiden looking down on a city being swallowed by waves.

I've seen him destroy cities with fire, with water, with the shaking of the earth. He destroyed Neruby with sand and wind. He destroyed Ghedda, the city in the drawing, by causing the mountain it was built on to erupt. He might have already destroyed Parthenia, if it wouldn't risk Zhian's life. It's a wonder the Shaitan has kept his notorious temper in check even this long. If I fail, he'll likely let Parthenia and all its people sink into the sea, then send his maarids to search the ruins for Zhian's bottle.

And Aladdin will die.

That thought hits me hardest. Lifting my eyes, I watch him laughing with the young lords, their faces turned to him like flowers to the sun. I have felt that same draw, that mysterious pull he has on me. I've been feeling it for weeks now, and it's getting harder and harder to resist. I think of him in the garden, lying on the grass, his hand brushing mine, and shudder at the pleasure this memory brings.

I slam the book shut and set it beside me. Enough sitting around, waiting for Zhian to show himself. Looking around, I spot Prince Darian lurking nearby, swirling a bottle of wine and watching Aladdin and Caspida stroll.

A plan unfurls in my mind, and I rise and walk to him.

"All alone on Fahradan? That's a shame."

He starts, spilling wine on his coat. He brushes at it with a look of annoyance. "Is that how you address your master? If I had a servant half so impertinent, I'd have her whipped and then cast out of the city for the ghuls to enjoy."

"You're drunk."

He shrugs as if that's to be taken for granted. "I've been thinking of ways to teach your master his place in my court."

"*Your* court? Forgive me, Majesty. I wasn't aware I was in the presence of a king." I eye Darian calculatingly as he glares at me, then gesture at a nearby bench in invitation. He sits beside me, a bit too close, his breath reeking of wine.

"Why is he *really* here?" asks Darian.

Grabbing his bottle, I take a deep swallow of wine before answering. "To gain the pleasure of your scintillating company."

With a curse, the prince suddenly grabs my wrist, his eyes fevered. "Tell me the truth, girl, or I'll have you both thrown out of this city."

Pulling my hand away with a scowl, I reply sharply, "You have no power over us. We are guests of the king."

"The king is an idiot and an invalid. Everyone knows my father is the real ruler of Parthenia."

I bite back a reply, forcing myself to focus on the real goal here, not petty sniping. Taking a moment to alter the course of my tongue, I smile coyly and reply in warmer tones, "Yes, the great Vizier Sulifer, commander of the Parthenian military. He is a great warrior, from what I hear."

Darian's chest swells. "He is. And everyone says I am very like him."

"I see." I slide closer to him and run one finger down his sleeve, my eyes lowered. "You must have killed many jinn."

"More than a few," he grunts, leaning in dangerously near. I lean back, out of reach of his questing lips.

"I don't believe you."

"What?" His face darkens.

Turning away, I shrug and run my fingers through my hair. "Anyone can *say* he has defeated many jinn, but a real warrior would prove it. Did you know in the mountains of Ursha, the tribesmen cut thumbs from their slain enemies and wear them on their belts as trophies?"

"That's barbaric."

"The men were allowed to take one wife for every thumb. Some of them had twenty or thirty thumbs." I glance at him sidelong. "How many jinn have you killed?"

Darian runs a lock of my hair through his fingers, and I resist the urge to pull away from his touch. His eyes burn intently as he stands. "I will show you."

My chest tightens with excitement, but I hesitate.

"Is it far?" I cast a worried look at Aladdin. I can't afford to get too far from him and be forced to shift in front of Darian.

The prince shrugs. "You won't miss anything here, believe me.

This festival's more boring than a tortoise race. It's just around the corner, anyway."

We slip out of the courtyard unseen, through a small door leading into the palace. Darian doesn't let go of my hand. His grip is sweaty and too tight, but I say nothing that will distract him. I want to see what he has to show me, and hope against hope I have gambled well and am not wasting more precious hours. Time is falling sand, and it streams through my fingers.

"This way," says Darian, leading me down a narrow, winding stair. I worry that "just around the corner" was an exaggeration, or that Aladdin might wander off and unwittingly summon me back to the lamp. But this chance at finding Zhian is too good to pass up. As we walk, I count my steps carefully.

... *64 ... 65 ...*

The sandstone walls echo with our passage as we descend, the darkness closing in and swallowing us up. The glimmer and light of Fahradan fade quickly, until the prince and I are alone in a dark subterranean world of black passages and dusty chambers. My sixth sense probes the emptiness of the palace's underbelly, but my reach is blunted, the clarity of my Ambadyan sight blurred. The walls here are lined with strips of iron, the metal interfering with my thoughts, and my sixth sense is repelled back at me. I blink furiously, hoping Darian doesn't notice my mental reeling.

One, two, three levels—the architects of Parthenia dug deep into the earth for these foundations. The farther we go, the farther we are from my lamp, and I feel the distance stretching like a tightening rope. I haven't explored this area before; we are far from Aladdin's rooms and well outside the perimeter that has held me captive every night till now. I thrum with excitement and nervousness. This is the closest I've come yet to finding Zhian and finally securing my freedom—now my every thought turns toward not ruining this chance.

. . . 101 . . . 102 . . .

My stomach tightens. Any moment, Aladdin could take a few steps one way while I take a few steps the other, and my leash will snap and I will turn to smoke. I wonder if Darian notices how tense I am. He still holds my hand, too tightly for me to pull away.

The walls are stone slabs, their faces etched with fading glyphs and symbols. Brass hooks hold burnt-out torches on the walls, but Darian manages to find one with a little oil left in it, and he lights it with a strike of the decorative knife on his belt against a bar of flint tied to the torch.

"The old crypt," says Darian, holding up the light. His hand tightens more around mine, and I stare at him curiously. Darian is afraid, of the dark, the deep, or the dead. As if sensing my glimpse of this vulnerability, he scowls and pulls me onward.

"The old kings and queens are buried here. Now we lay them in tombs above ground, in the hills to the north. But the walls here are lined with iron, which makes the crypt perfect for storing our . . . *special* prisoners."

The hair on my neck stands on end. This is it. This is really, truly it—the night I find Zhian.

And not a day too soon.

. . . 126 . . . 127 . . .

As everything in me screams to turn around and run back, I wonder if Aladdin has noticed me missing yet, then chide myself for even thinking of him right now. I need to focus fully on the mission at hand. I know that soon, perhaps even this very night, I will have to let Aladdin go forever. That is a thought I swallow for now, finding it too painful to touch.

"Prisoners?" I ask, keeping my voice high and frightened. "Are you sure—"

"You're safe with me," Darian assures me. "We're almost there."

. . . *138* . . . *139* . . . If I had a heart, it would be pounding like a drum.

He stops in front of a door made of iron, a massive thing he couldn't possibly open on his own. But, dropping my hand, he opens a wooden panel in the wall to reveal a clever system of gears. He pulls out a handle, fixes it to one of the gears, then hands me the torch so that he can grab the handle in both hands and throw his weight against it. Darian strains and curses, and slowly the gears begin to turn. The wall hums and clicks as levers begin to work, and the door slowly eases sideways, sliding into the wall.

When the door is open just enough for one person to fit through, Darian slides an iron bar into the gears to keep them from slipping, then turns to me with a grin.

"Now you'll see just how mighty we Amulen warriors are."

And not a moment too soon. I'm nearly sick with apprehension, the distance between me and the lamp seeming to hum dangerously. Just a few more steps. I can last that long. I *have* to.

He steps inside, and I follow, a sharp pounding in my chest like a phantom heart.

Inside the room, I can feel them all.

Hundreds of jinn, of every kind, are trapped in small bottles of clay and bronze, glass and porcelain, set on shelves that stretch wall to wall. The room is large and high-ceilinged, the floor bare save for a table holding a heavy scroll and several quills.

The jinn feel me enter, sense my true nature, and begin to clamor and cry out, their voices an overwhelming tidal wave. I sway, gasping a little at the impact of noise and desperation.

Darian of course can hear none of this, and he looks pleased at my reaction. "Yes, it's quite impressive. We've been bottling jinn for hundreds of years. There's no one better at it."

"You—you bottle them yourself?" I ask, putting out a hand against the wall to steady myself.

"Well . . . not *me*, personally. But I give orders to the Eristrati, who fight the jinn, and to the jinn charmers we imported from Tytoshi. Since I've been in command, we've bottled more than thirty jinn, just in a few years' time." He struts around the room, like a hunter displaying his trophies. "These are the maarids— water jinn. There are the fire ifreet, and the earth ghuls. We even have a few sila." He waves at some tall glass bottles on a high shelf. "Very hard to catch, because they're usually invisible."

Sister! Sister! Their cries ring in my thoughts like a storm. *Help us! Set us free!*

Some of them have been in here as long as three hundred years, I gather from their erratic shouting. I sift through the voices, trying to pick out Zhian's, but it's difficult to concentrate with Darian droning on about various jinn charmings he has witnessed.

". . . This one was hanging around near one of our fishing villages, so we waited all night until it appeared, and then I sent Vigo out with his flute . . ."

Be silent, all of you! I command, and the voices just clamor louder. My eyes scan the shelves, back and forth, searching. *Zhian! Zhian, are you here?*

". . . And *this* one," Darian is saying, "this one is our greatest prize. Not ghul or ifreet, not maarid or sila, but something else. Something bigger."

My eyes snap to his face, and I barely manage to keep myself from shifting into a tiger and pinning him to the floor until he speaks.

"Which one?" I ask, smiling demurely, hoping there isn't smoke streaming through my teeth.

Darian points to a clay jar above his head, with a fluted neck and a graceful handle. "There. We captured it two months ago. Thought it might be an ifreet, because of the fire it was throwing at us, but the way it changed form—from man to dragon to cloud of smoke—no ifreet can do that. Only ghuls can change form, and then only by eating the soul of a human or animal before taking its body. We've been debating what it might be. I think—"

"Can I hold it?" I ask.

Darian blinks, and then his eyes narrow. "Of course not. It's extremely dangerous. If you dropped it and it broke—"

"I only want to look!" I snap, my facade cracking, and at Darian's suspicious scowl I drop my eyes and whisper, "I'm sorry. It's just, I've never seen anything like this. You truly are a great warrior. The terror of the jinn!"

"Yes," he muses, his face relaxing. "Well, I've had a lot of practice."

Zhian, is that you? I focus the words on the clay jar above Darian.

The reply comes like a clap of thunder

GET ME OUT OF HERE!

I stumble at the force of his words, and Darian steps forward to catch me.

"Wine catching up to you?" he asks, grinning.

I just nod distractedly, stiffening a little when his hands slide up my arms.

Zhian, I'm here to help you.

GET ME OUT NOW!

Darian's hands are far too familiar, one on my back now, the other cupping my jaw. His touch is repulsive, his heartbeat erratic and too fast. I feel assaulted on all sides: by Zhian's shouting, by the jinn clamoring, by Darian's desire.

"You really are quite pretty," he says, his eyes dropping to my lips. "I've shown you something secret. Now what are you going to show me?"

Steeling myself, I grasp his coat and step forward, backing him into the shelves, and around him bottles shake dangerously.

"Easy," he cautions, but his eyes brighten greedily. Our faces are just inches apart, his eyes locked on mine. "You're a feisty one. I knew it the moment I saw you. No wonder Rahzad likes to keep you close."

"What about the princess?" I murmur, working a hand behind him as if to thread my fingers in his oiled hair.

"Caspida hardly appreciates the finer pleasures in life. I, on the other hand, have a king's appetite."

He kisses me forcefully, stepping away from the wall, and I'm barely able to grab Zhian's jar before it's out of reach. No bigger than my hand, it's simple to let it slip down my sleeve. The jinn prince rages inside, but I ignore him and focus on the human trying to force his tongue down my throat. I can feel myself hovering on the very edge of the lamp's boundary. Ripples of smoke race under my skin as I strain to keep from shifting, the effort bringing tears to my eyes.

I shove Darian hard, and he shouts as he slams into the wall of bottled jinn. A few topple from their shelves, and panic springs into his eyes as he struggles to catch them all.

"Bleeding gods, you whore!" he growls. "Are you mad?"

"My master is probably looking for me," I gasp. "I should go."

I turn and flee the room, letting out a soft, relieved cry as the lamp's pull on me slackens. Darian pursues too quickly for me to shift into a more speedy form. Zhian's jar rattling in my sleeve, I hurry through the dark crypt and up the stairs, the prince close on my heels.

"Stop!" he shouts. "Or I'll have you whipped!"

Sister! Zhian cries. *Set me free and I will devour the wretch!*

Shutting them both from my mind, I take the steps three at a time, barely keeping my feet as my skirts tangle around my legs.

When I reach the corridor on the main level, I put on a burst of speed, but Darian catches up to me. He grabs my arm, yanking me backward.

"Whore!" he snarls, slamming me into the wall so hard stars burst in my eyes. I hiss at him, the tiger in me threatening to emerge and rip out his throat, but a shout brings me back to myself.

"Zahra!"

I turn my head and see Aladdin running toward us. When he sees that it's Darian holding me roughly against the wall, his face twists into such rage that he seems unrecognizable.

He crashes into Darian before the prince has a chance to say anything. The two slam into the ground, Aladdin throwing a punch that cracks against Darian's jaw.

"Stop it!" I cry. "Prince Rahzad!"

The boys ignore me, rolling and thrashing like dogs.

Leave them! Zhian roars. *Let me out!*

"How dare you touch her?" Aladdin spits, grabbing Darian by

the hair and pressing the prince's face into the stone floor. "You bastard!"

"I didn't give her anything she didn't ask for," Darian hisses back. "Get off me or I'll have you executed!"

I start to step in, but a cold voice behind me makes all three of us freeze.

"Darian."

Turning, I see the vizier standing in the shadows, his face a mask of cold fury.

Aladdin lets go of the prince, who scrambles to his feet, his face reddening.

"Father, I—"

"My own son, scrapping in the halls like a dog over a bitch in heat? Disgusting."

Darian drops his head, shooting Aladdin a dark look.

"As for *you*, Rahzad," Sulifer says, his icy gaze sliding to Aladdin, "is this how the princes of Istarya behave in the houses that grant them hospitality?"

Aladdin, no fear in his eyes, spits on the floor before rising haughtily to his feet. "It's how we behave toward cowards who can't keep their hands to themselves."

Sulifer's gaze flickers to me disinterestedly. "Darian, straighten yourself up and come with me. Prince Rahzad, perhaps it is time you retire for the evening. I think our Amulen wine has proven too strong for your senses."

Darian smirks at that and gives us both threatening looks before joining his father. The two stride away, Darian slightly limping.

"You didn't need to interfere," I tell Aladdin.

He turns to me, still panting. "He had his hands all over you."

"Nothing I couldn't handle."

His eyes fall away, his hands clenching at his sides. "Is it true? Did you *ask* him to join you out here?"

Tell him yes, I think. With one word, I could sever whatever's between us. I could release Zhian and have no regrets behind me.

But . . . can I do that to Aladdin? Can I hurt him like that? And can I deny the truth growing inside me?

"Why are you here?" I say at last. "You're supposed to be with Caspida, offering your hand in marriage."

Aladdin's mouth opens, and he stares at me for a moment with hurt naked in his gaze.

"I just did," he mutters.

Then, his eyes clouding with anger, he storms past me and disappears around a corner before I can utter a word. I stare after him, my gut roiling with dismay and confusion.

You fool of a jinni! LET ME OUT!

Startled from my thoughts, I pull Zhian's jar from my sleeve and turn it over. I can easily imagine him swirling inside, a cloud of smoke and fury.

Be silent, Zhian. I'll decide when you're let out, and right now, you're not inspiring my merciful side.

He howls and hurls insults, which I try to ignore as I trail after Aladdin.

I have Zhian at last. At any moment I could break open the jar and free him, fulfilling my end of the bargain and claiming my freedom. But what happens next? The humiliation of being captured by the humans will have made Zhian furious. He's had two moons to feed his hatred of humans, and by now it is ravenous, destructive. If I let him out now, Parthenia will not stand a chance. He'll destroy the city from the inside out, regardless of my deal with his father.

I have to release him outside the city walls and trust that the wards will protect everyone inside from his inevitable wrath.

Aladdin heads back toward his rooms, and I follow at a distance, my chest feeling emptier than ever.

It's time to say goodbye.

Chapter Seventeen

I FIND HIM IN OUR ROOMS, standing in the courtyard. A few candles burn in colorful lanterns the palace staff has hung in the fig trees, lighting the grass with soft blues and reds. Aladdin leans against a pillar, his back to the door, and if he hears me enter, he does not show it. I pause only to drop Zhian's jar in my bedchamber; I can't bear to hear his threats and curses right now.

Aladdin doesn't flinch or even acknowledge me when I arrive at his side. His coat lies draped over the divan behind him, leaving him in a simple white kurta, the sleeves pushed up to his elbows. His turban lies rumpled on the ground.

His gaze troubles me. All night he has been bright as a flame, smiling, dancing, flirting. That boy is gone. The Aladdin before me looks haunted. His jaw is rigid, his hair messy, his hands clenched so tight the tendons in his forearms stand out like ropes.

"Aladdin . . ."

He tenses, not looking my way.

"What happened between you and Caspida?"

Now he looks at me, and the anger in his eyes catches me by surprise. "I told her all sorts of lies. That I have an army back in Istarya, and treasuries filled with gold, and that it would all be hers if she would marry me."

A servant has left a pot of tea and refreshments by the divan. I pour myself a cup and warm my hands wth it, trying to keep them from shaking. "What did she say?"

"That she would think about it." He laughs bitterly, then falls silent for a long moment. I wish I could read his thoughts, but his face is closed to me.

"When I saw you in the hall with Darian," he says at last, "I felt more angry than I've felt in a long time. I was angry and . . . and afraid, that you *wanted* to be there, that you wanted him touching you. In that one look, I felt more than I've ever felt with Caspida. Zahra, I think you're right—love isn't a choice. If I could choose to love Caspida, maybe this would all be going differently, but I don't think that's possible. Not anymore."

All the smoke inside me sinks as I stare at him. "What are you saying?"

He turns and meets my gaze squarely. As much I want to, I find it impossible to look away. The intensity of his copper gaze holds me entranced.

"I think you know," he says softly. "Or am I the only one who feels it?"

My skin and the roots of my hair tingle, as if the air around us is charged, a storm about to break.

"I don't know what you mean." The words are bitter on my tongue.

With a growl of frustration, Aladdin turns away and scrubs at his hair. "I can never tell when you're lying. It drives me insane. I'm a good liar, and I know a good lie when I hear it. But you . . . you're maddening!"

I smile a little, unhumorously, thinking how I could say much the same of him.

He continues, "Over and over I've imagined the day Caspida and I marry. I've envisioned sending Darian off to the ends of the earth and sentencing Sulifer to a life of scrubbing floors, finally avenging my parents. I've imagined these things all my life, but they no longer bring me the pleasure they once did."

He slips around the pillar, coming to stand behind me, and the pleading note in his voice cuts through all my defenses, leaving me breathless.

"The things that were once sweet to me are now bitter. The sun is not half so bright. The stars seem dimmer. All this wealth and luxury feels meaningless. All the world is in your shadow, Zahra. I cannot help but see you when I close my eyes."

His fingers brush tentatively through my hair. I stiffen, and his hand withdraws.

He moves in front of me, his eyes wild. "I know so little about you, and it eats at me night and day. Who are you? Why do you infect my mind?"

"Aladdin, stop. *Please.*" My voice shaking, I finally jolt into motion, stepping forward and holding up my hands. "Don't do this. Not now." *Not when I'm so close to my freedom.* I came here ready to part with him forever, but he played his opening move first, and now I find myself on the defensive, parrying and blocking the assault of his words. But too many blows strike home.

I've always been able to sense my masters, but with Aladdin it's different. When I close my eyes, he's there, grinning, laughing, daring me with those copper-brown eyes.

For the first time I think about what comes after I win my freedom. For so long that's been my single goal, but what happens next? Do I return to Ambadya, where they hate me? Do I stay in the human world, where they would destroy me if they knew what I was? I have nowhere to go to and no one to spend my freedom with, and for the first time I begin to wonder if that's really freedom at all, or if I'm exchanging one prison for another.

"I'm not *for* you," I say desperately. "We are so different. Our lives are a thousand and one worlds apart. It wouldn't work. And it's *dangerous*."

But his face only brightens. "Then you *do* feel the same."

"We are not the same—and that is the whole point! I am not human, Aladdin. Everything that was once human in me was destroyed, and I was forged into something entirely different. I'm not here to help you—I was never here to help you, or any of my masters."

He shakes his head. "I don't believe that."

"It doesn't matter what you believe," I say bitterly. "It is what it is, and it has nothing to do with what you *want*."

He walks around me, forcing me to face him. "You helped me get away from Darian in the desert. You got me into the palace when you could have let them find out who I really was. You taught me to dance, for sky's sake! You've had a hundred opportunities to trick me and betray me, but you don't. You've helped me when I didn't wish for it."

"A chicken doesn't fly like other birds, but it is still a bird."

"Zahra!" He spreads his hands, the wind ruffling his hair. "You *do* care. I see it when you think I'm not looking."

"Stop! I'm not what you think I am, Aladdin! I *will* betray you, and I *will* hurt you, because that is what I *am*. Why do you think Nardukha rips souls from the living and creates jinnis? Why do you think he sends us into the world? To make your miserable dreams come true? To bring you *happiness*?" I laugh sourly. "He gives you the thing you want most and uses it to destroy you. Look at yourself. You're a prince. You have money, power, privilege. The chance to avenge your parents. And you're miserable."

Aladdin stares at me, and in his eyes is pity. "I've been making myself miserable my whole life," he says softly. "I convinced myself long ago that if I could get revenge on Sulifer, I could finally *move on*. That I could erase the memory of the day my parents died, when I held their severed heads and watched their blood run in the gutters. But as you say, here I am, a step away from that vengeance—and it has soured on my tongue. I don't *want* it anymore."

He sighs and looks up at the sky, as if searching for words among the stars. "You don't make me miserable, Zahra. I do that to myself, because I'm too weak, too afraid to admit that it isn't Sulifer I'm angry at—it's *me*. My parents were killed because of *me*. The day before they were executed, I was caught by the guards for stealing an earring, and when they found out who I was, Sulifer had me whipped until I told him where my parents were. And after they were dead, he gave me back the earring as payment for turning my mother and father over to him." Lowering his gaze to meet mine, he brushes his fingers over the ring in his ear. "I've worn it every day since, to remind myself that nothing—*nothing*—is worth betraying someone you love."

Love?

The word hangs between us like forbidden fruit, ripe and sweet and oh, so deadly. I stare at him in dismay.

"Please," I whisper. "Stop."

"Zahra—"

"Don't you understand? It's forbidden, Aladdin! We jinn must abide by many rules, but first among them, most important of all, we must *never* fall in love with a human!"

He catches his breath, swallowing hard. "And do you always follow the rules?"

"I—" Casting my gaze skyward, I draw a deep breath, searching for words among the stars. "It's not about that. Do you know what kind of destruction we would cause? Have you not heard the story of your own people, how their city was destroyed, how thousands died? It was not hate that sparked the war between your people and mine, Aladdin. It was *love*. I held hands with Roshana the Wise and called her sister, and those words set our world on fire!"

There it is. My greatest shame, laid bare. The truth lies between us like broken glass. Surely now he sees what I truly am: a betrayer, a monster, an enemy. Aladdin stares at me, his face softening.

"That wasn't your fault," he says. "Loving someone is never wrong. And like you said, it's not a choice. It just happens, and we're all helpless in its power."

"That doesn't change the fact that the consequences are disastrous. As the poets say, shake hands with a jinni, and you shake hands with death."

"And what if you weren't a jinni? What if you were free from their rules?"

I stare at him. His jaw tightens, his eyes steely with determination that frightens me to my core. A cloud drifts across the face of the crescent moon, and the courtyard darkens. Here and there, the grass is still bent where Aladdin and I danced just hours earlier. I drop my gaze and glare at it, shaking from head to toe.

"Don't say it, Aladdin. Don't you even *think* it." Dread rises in me like a storm cloud, dark and menacing.

Aladdin moves closer. He takes my hands. His skin is warm and crackling with energy, setting me on fire.

"I have one wish left," he murmurs. "And this one is for you."

"*No*, Aladdin! Don't speak it. Don't make the Forbidden Wish. The cost—"

"Damn the cost. Zahra, I wish—"

I stop him with a kiss.

Because it is the first thing I think of to stop the terrible words. Because he fills me with light and hope and deep, deep fear. Because I have been longing to for days.

I feel shock splinter through him, his body going rigid. Then he relaxes, melting into me, stepping forward until I am caught between him and the wall, the torch crackling beside me. His hands slide down my back, over my hips and thighs, leaving a trail of fire. His heart beats fast enough for the both of us, its thunderous pulse echoing through me.

I bury my hands in his dark hair, fingers knotting around those thick locks. Desire pulls at my stomach, and I lean into him, lifting one leg and wrapping it around his waist. He lifts me, and my other leg coils around him, my skirts sliding up my thighs, my back pressed against the column.

His lips are soft and warm and gentle, underlined with barely restrained urgency. I cannot get enough of him. I pull his kurta over his head and let it fall on the floor. I press my hands against his bared chest, feel his heart against my palm, his lungs rising and falling. His shoulder is knotted with the scar from the arrow he took for me. He kisses me again, this time more strongly, and I run my hands down his jaw and neck, over his shoulders, the taut muscles of his back.

He turns, without letting me go or breaking our kiss, and we tumble onto the soft divan. Aladdin holds himself over me, his abdomen clenched and his hair hanging across his forehead. His lips wander downward, to my chin, to the curve of my jaw, to my neck.

My hands are ravenous, exploring the planes and angles of his body. His fingers find mine, and our hands knit together. He raises them over my head, pressing them into the pillow beneath my hair, as his kisses trace my collarbone, and then he sinks lower, parting the buttons of my dress and pressing his lips to my bare stomach.

I gasp and open my eyes wide, my borrowed body coursing with sensations I have never felt, never dared to feel, never thought I *could* feel.

"Aladdin," I murmur. "We shouldn't . . ."

"Sh." He silences me with a kiss, and I lift my chin to meet him. A warm wind rushes through my body, stirring embers and setting them aflame. I don't want to stop. I don't want to think about consequences. I only want Aladdin, everywhere.

I wish—

No. No, I can't wish. The cost is too high for both of us.

"Stop," I say, my voice laced with treacherous weakness.

He lifts his eyes to mine. "Why?"

"*Stop*," I say more firmly.

I shove him off me and sit up, my face in my hands, my hair a curtain to shield me. Aladdin doesn't move, just stares at me, still breathing heavily.

"Zahra? What's wrong?"

"Everything!" I lift my head and burst to my feet. "You don't understand. This can't happen!"

"I'm sorry." He rises to his knees, hands spread. "I'm so, so sorry. I don't know what came over me. Please—"

"Leave me alone!" I run through the door and slam it behind me, then sag against it, half panting, half sobbing, in the empty hallway. How did I let this happen? How could I have been so weak?

"Zahra?" He stands on the other side of the door, his voice muffled. "I'm sorry."

"It's not what you think it is," I tell him. "You don't feel anything for me. You're just drawn to my power, to the wishes I've granted you."

"No . . ." But his voice is uncertain.

Feeling the worst kind of traitor, I say, "I've been a fool to walk in this form around you. I'm not human, Aladdin. Nothing about me is right for you." I open the door and there he is, his hair mussed and his chest glistening with sweat, standing with that lamb-in-the-rain look that cuts through all my defenses. But I stand firm.

"This," I say, gesturing at myself, "this isn't me. This isn't what I look like. This body you see belonged to someone else, long, long ago, and like the monster I am, I stole it. It is a mask. A lie."

"I don't care what you look like."

"You say that, but you *do*. Would you have kissed me if I looked like this?" With a burst of smoke, I shift to a wrinkled crone. Aladdin swallows but doesn't look away. "Or like this?" I shift into a scarred, ugly man with warts on my face. Aladdin blanches.

Shifting back to my girl form, I sigh deeply and tug at my clothes. "This is just a shape. You're not seeing *me*."

"Then show yourself to me," he pleads. "I want to see you, Zahra. I want to know who you really are."

I stare at him, then, without a word, slowly shift into a whirling column of red smoke glowing with red light.

"I have no form," I say, my voice shifting and multiplying, a dozen voices speaking at once. "I have no name. I am the Slave of the Lamp, and your will is my will. Your wishes are my commands."

He shakes his head stubbornly but takes a step backward. I swell and advance, driving him deeper into the room, flashing from within like a thundercloud. I grow and fill the air, driving him choking and coughing to his knees. I press my smoky hands against the walls, curl around the columns, overwhelm him.

"Zahra, stop!" he cries. "Please!"

At once I shift and stand before him as a girl once more. Cautiously he looks up, his eyes wide with pain.

"Do you see now?" I ask tonelessly.

He's breathing heavily, his bare chest beaded with sweat. "Just answer me one question. Do you feel anything for me? Is there even a chance—"

"No." Gods, how the lie burns my tongue.

He hesitates, then nods once. His eyes flood with confusion and hurt, and he rises and turns away from me, his shoulders hunched.

Bowed beneath the weight of shame, I turn and go to the door. I pause before stepping through to say, "I never wanted it to come to this. I'm sorry."

Then I flee down the corridor, bumping into a smoldering brazier. It rocks precariously, lit embers raining to the floor and bursting around my feet like tiny exploding stars. I lean against the wall, my face in my hands, for several long minutes. I've never so felt out of control before, my body making decisions before my mind can catch up. I'm still shaking, and I breathe in and out through my mouth, trying to calm myself.

I shouldn't have kissed him, Habiba. But I didn't know what else to do. The words were there, rising in his throat, words of freedom, words of death. Better to kiss him and leave him than to let him make the Forbidden Wish.

I must find a way out of the city, to set Zhian free and then get as far from here as possible before I become any more entangled with this human boy.

Dimly, I realize someone nearby is shouting, and I pull myself out of my fog. Something is happening at the other end of the palace. A servant runs past me, laden with scrolls. I call to him, but he ignores me and hurries on. I follow swiftly, and the shouting grows louder. Then, over the sound, cuts a sharp and chilling wail.

"The king!" cries the voice. "The king is dying!"

Chapter Eighteen

"ZAHRA!"

I'm running through the palace when I hear Nessa's shout, and I turn to see her hurrying down the corridor. I wait for her to catch up. She's breathless and wild-eyed, her dreadlocks slipping free of the knot they'd been bound in.

"Did you hear?" she asks.

"Yes. Where's Princess Caspida?"

"With her father. I'm headed there now."

"I'll come with you."

Nessa and I race down the corridor. Word must be spreading of the king's bad turn, because people are beginning to emerge from their rooms, and the halls are filled with whispers.

We reach the king's chambers, which are near Caspida's and just inside the lamp's perimeter. A small crowd has already gathered, mostly nobles in their nightgowns, their hair and makeup still remaining from the night of revelry. A group of guards block the door, repelling any who try to enter.

"Nessa!"

Khavar and another handmaiden are standing nearby, and they wave us over.

"Any word?" asks Nessa.

Khavar shakes her head. "Caspida's inside, with Sulifer and the physicians. No one has come out."

"Excuse me," I say, backing away. "I should go back to Prince Rahzad."

The girls nod distractedly, not noticing that the corridor I take leads in the opposite direction of Aladdin's rooms. When I'm alone, I shift into a small sand-colored lizard and scurry back toward the king's chambers.

I weave through the feet of the nobles gathered outside the door, dart over one guard's boot, and slip beneath the door. Tongue flicking, I cross several opulent chambers before I reach the king's bed. The air here is thick with simmon smoke, and the people gathered around his bed all wear cloths tied over their mouths and noses. Caspida kneels by the bed, her hands wrapped around her father's. She is still wearing her Fahradan gown.

The physicians stand in a cluster on one side of the room, and judging by their grim expressions, they have given up. A group of women huddle at the foot of the bed, weeping. Sulifer and Darian stand over the bed, silent and pensive.

Malek's skin is yellow and crusty, his cheeks sunken, his eyes ringed with shadows so dark they're like smeared kohl. His breath comes ragged and uneven, his chest barely rising at all.

Caspida's eyes are dry and fixed on her father's face, burning with ferocity, as if she is trying to will him back to life. I crawl up the post of his bed and hang upside down from the ceiling, held in place by the sticky pads on my lizard toes. My round reptilian eyes enable me to see everyone at once.

Sulifer is holding a sheet of parchment and an inked quill, and he bends over his brother, speaking in a low voice.

"For the good of the people, Malek," he says, "you must ensure that this transition be as stable as possible."

"Leave him alone!" Caspida snaps. "He's *dying*, you vulture!"

Sulifer regards her with pity. "Even on his deathbed, a king has responsibilities. Take notice and learn, Princess."

She glares as he leans lower and puts the quill into Malek's hand, holding his brother's wrist so the king can press the tip to the parchment.

"Please, brother," Sulifer murmurs. "Your people will sing praises of your wisdom and foresight. With a king and queen to rule after you, they will feel safe, and your enemies will tremble. For who can stand against ones so well matched as my son and your daughter? Let your last act bless their happiness and ensure your legacy."

Malek's feverish eyes rove from Caspida to his brother, and he moans.

"Get away!" Caspida rises and throws a finger toward the door, her eyes burning at her uncle. "I will call the guards!"

"Stop acting like a spoiled child," Sulifer says patiently. "Your father is dying, and you insist on throwing tantrums."

"Baba, please," she says, taking her father's face in her hands. "I love you. Don't do this."

"It was he who arranged this match years ago," Sulifer says.

"Will you defy his wishes now, when he is a breath away from the eternal godlands?"

"He was led by the nose," she fires back. "This was *your* doing! You swayed him to your will when he was left weak by my mother's death!"

"You dare call the king weak?" Darian interjects hotly. "You dare question his will?"

"You dare to usurp him!" she cries. "And to manipulate a man at his weakest! I won't let you bully him into signing your stupid decree!"

Sulifer bares his teeth angrily. "Will you defy him until his last breath?"

She stares into her father's face, her eyes dazed. "Of course not. Baba, I will do whatever you tell me to. But please, let it be *your* will, and none else's."

Malek murmurs something.

"Baba?" Caspida bends over him. "What is it?"

"Best . . ." he groans. "Best . . . thing for you . . . Keep you safe."

"Baba?" Caspida's eyes fill with dismay.

Sulifer stares down his nose at her. "The king has spoken. Step aside, Princess, and let him make his dying will."

He brushes Caspida aside, holding up the parchment and supporting Malek's arm as the king signs. Caspida's face turns ashen, and Darian looks away, hiding a small smile.

"It is done," intones Sulifer. "The king's will is known. Signed and witnessed."

"The king's will is known," murmur the physicians. "We stand witness."

Darian takes Caspida's arm. "Even on this tragic night, we have cause to be glad. Your father has given us a great gift, Cas. Don't spoil it by being selfish."

Suddenly Malek gasps, his eyes growing wide, pupils constricting. The physicians rush over and fuss, but there is nothing they can do. Caspida throws herself to her knees beside the king.

"No, no, no," she murmurs, her eyes tearing up at last. "Baba, please!"

Malek's eyes find hers. He opens his mouth as if to say something, and she leans over in anticipation, but the only thing to come out of him is a long, thin breath that trails off, until his lungs are empty and do not rise again.

"My brother has departed to the godlands," intones Sulifer. "Sweet may he rest."

"Sweet may he rest," echo the physicians.

The women begin wailing and tearing their clothes. One holds a jar of ashes and begins throwing them in the air. As the physicians hasten to begin performing the death rites that will send Malek's soul into eternity, Caspida stands and slips out of the room.

Unsticking my toes, I follow her.

She runs out of the king's chambers, bursts through the nobles standing around, and ignores her handmaidens when they call to her. Her gown flapping around her legs, she runs up and down the palace corridors, losing the few people who try to follow her. I have to drop to the floor and shift to a cat to keep up, my paws silent on the stone. Caspida weeps as she runs, leaving a trail of dark spots on the stones where her tears fall.

Eventually she stops in front of Aladdin's rooms. There she stands for a moment, leaning against the wall with her arms wrapped around herself as she struggles to control her breathing. She stops sobbing and scrubs her face with the hem of her gown.

Then she takes a deep breath, squares her shoulders, and knocks on Aladdin's door.

It opens at once.

"Zahra, I'm so—" He freezes. "Princess Caspida."

"Prince Rahzad. Can I come in?" she asks.

Aladdin glances up and down the hall, then nods and stands back. Caspida slips inside, and just before he shuts the door, I dart through. Aladdin notices and watches me warily. I sit in the corner, my tail curled around my paws, watching impassively.

Caspida stands in the grass courtyard, looking small and lost. Her loose hair is tangled from running, and her feet are bare. Aladdin approaches her slowly, his face etched with concern.

"Are you all right?" he asks.

"My father has died," says Caspida flatly.

Aladdin stops and shuts his eyes, exhaling softly. "I'm so sorry."

She shrugs and looks away, her jaw tight.

Hesitantly, Aladdin walks to her. "Is there . . . anything I can do?"

She blinks rapidly, holding back more tears. Her body is rigid and tight, as if she's poised to flee. "I came to accept."

"Accept?"

"Your offer of marriage."

Aladdin's mouth opens and shuts. He blinks at her, stunned.

"Well?" she snaps. "Are you going to gape, or are you going to say something?"

"Um. I don't think . . . I'm not sure you're in a frame of mind to really make a decision like that. Your father just died. You should be mourning him, not—"

"Sulifer made my father sign a decree just moments before he—he passed. It says that I must marry within two days, before I am crowned, or I must abdicate."

Aladdin's lips form a perfect circle. "And . . . you've come to marry me instead of Darian."

"The decree doesn't mention Darian by name—only that I must marry a prince."

Aladdin chews his lip, his eyes creasing. "Are you sure you want to do this?"

"You said you wanted to help me! Well, this is it. This is me asking for help!"

"Okay, okay," he says, holding up his hands. "Of course I'll help you. I just want you to be sure this is what you want."

"I want you to marry me," she says firmly. "And then I want you to summon your army."

Aladdin's face goes still. "My army."

"You *have* an army, right?" Her gaze darkens dangerously.

"Uh . . . sure. I mean, of course."

"Well. How soon can they be here?"

"Um. I don't know. A month, maybe?" Aladdin glances anxiously at me, and I look down at my paws.

She nods. "Good. We must begin drawing up battle plans."

"Battle plans," he echoes tonelessly.

"My scouts report that there are jinn gathering in the hills— more than we have ever seen."

I straighten, my cat's ears alert.

"Something is brewing out there," Caspida continues. "And it can be nothing good if there are jinn involved. We fear they are going to launch an attack, and we must be ready. Your men can help, can't they?"

"Of course." Aladdin glances at me in a silent plea for help. I remain right where I am, sitting on one of the cushions he'd kissed me on just minutes earlier.

"Princess, perhaps I should walk you back to your chambers. Your friends might be better able to comfort you." He hesitates, then adds, "I'm really sorry about your father. I lost mine when I was twelve. I know what it's like."

"Do you know what it's like to feel an entire kingdom suddenly fall on your shoulders?" she asks sharply, and then she squeezes her eyes shut. "I'm sorry. That was rude. You must think I'm pathetic, running in here like this."

Aladdin gently catches her hands and lifts them. "You're not pathetic. And you're right. I don't know what it's like. But I do know that you can bear it. I know that you are strong enough and that you are surrounded by people who will stand by you through every moment. You aren't alone, Princess."

Her eyebrows pinch together, and she draws a steadying breath. "I should go back. My father . . . I must make arrangements."

Aladdin nods. "Let me help."

"Later," she says. "Tonight I must keep the death watch."

Suddenly she rises on her toes and brushes her lips against his, awkward and hesitant. His brows lift in surprise, and his eyes dart briefly to me. Envy flares in me, but I stamp it down ruthlessly.

All I wanted was for Caspida to accept the marriage proposal, and here she is, not a moment too soon. Usually I am the first to dismiss the idea of destiny, but perhaps in this case I would make an exception. Aladdin got his princess after all. Perhaps this once, a wish won't end in misery and loss—at least, not for the humans. The prospect should make me glad. But I am a selfish spirit, and it doesn't.

Caspida rushes away as quickly as she'd arrived, leaving Aladdin dazed in the grass. He stands there for a moment, his shoulders drawn tight as a bow. Then he walks inside, takes a clay jug from behind a pillow, and drinks long and deep. When he lowers the jug, he totters toward me and collapses on the cushions.

"Well." He lifts the jug to his lips, his eyes wide and unfocused. "I guess I win after all."

With a ripple of smoke, I shift and am human once more. I sit by him and stare at the floor, trying to feel a sense of relief.

"Congratulations," I say.

"So now what?" He drinks again, hurtling toward intoxication. "I wish for an army?"

"It would seem so."

Maybe I should just tell Aladdin the truth about Zhian and the deal I made with the jinn. But can I bear the disappointment in his eyes when I confess that I've been manipulating him all along, tricking him into a marriage he doesn't want, just to serve my own ends?

"Zahra, what happens to you when I make my last wish?"

"When your third wish is granted, you will cease to be my master. You may possess the lamp, but you cannot call me. I will return to it and await the next Lampholder."

Abruptly he stands and walks across the room. When he reaches the wall, he turns and stares down at me. "So to win my revenge, I must lose you."

"It would seem so." And I *must* find a way to free Zhian before that happens, or we will all be lost. Nardukha is watching closely, and my time shrinks with the moon. There are jinn gathering in the hills.

"Zahra!" In three steps he runs to me, grabs my shoulders, and searches my eyes. "Don't just stare like that! Say something!"

"What do you want me to say? What do you want me to do,

Aladdin? Beg you not to make a wish? Insist that there is another way? There isn't."

He turns away. His shoulders are drawn up, stiff with tension. He is like a caged lion, pacing back and forth, brooding.

"Stop it," I snap. "I always knew it would end like this. It always does. There's no point in fighting it, Aladdin. It is simply the way of things."

"I can't accept that."

"You *must*."

"How can you just give up? How can you *say* that?" His eyes light up, and he takes the lamp from his sash and grips it so tightly his knuckles whiten. "Earlier, before you kissed me, I was about to wish for your freedom."

I leap to my feet. "Aladdin, you *must not do that*. You must never even think it!"

"Why is that so bad? You'd be *free*."

"It's called the Forbidden Wish for a reason!"

"By *whom*? Nardukha? Let him come. I have a few things I'd like to say to *him*."

"*I* forbid it. Aladdin. If anything we have done together means anything to you, please, *please* trust me now. Don't make that wish. It is the worst wish you can make. It is—it will break my heart."

"What is it?" he asks softly. "What is it you're not telling me? What happens if I wish for your freedom?"

I stand trembling, the words clawing at my throat, until I can hold them back no more.

"Like all wishes, the Forbidden Wish comes at a price. My freedom must be bought with a death, a life paid in sacrifice. And I will not let you make that sacrifice, not for me."

I shut my eyes, unable to bear the shock and pain in his expression. He sits in silence for a long while, staring at nothing. Then at last he rises and goes to his bedchamber.

I spend the rest of the night hunched in a corner, thinking of you, Habiba, and that moment on the mountaintop when you saw that all was lost, that we were defeated. You turned to me and said you wanted to make the Forbidden Wish, that you wanted to offer your life for mine. I remember so sharply the horror I felt . . . and to my eternal shame, the flicker of hope. Hope that I would at last be free of the lamp. Even now I flush with self-loathing. But despite that hope, I couldn't let you give yourself for me. Though as it turned out, I didn't have to stop you.

Nardukha did.

I am filled with horror that Aladdin nearly did the same, without even knowing what he was doing. Well, now he knows the price of my freedom. Now he knows how hopeless it truly is.

The only way I can save us both is by carrying out my deal with Nardukha. I'll be free, and Aladdin will be alive. Then I'll go as far from this city as I possibly can, because only a fool would return. Even free from my lamp, I'm not free to love Aladdin. That rule still stands for all jinn. Loving a human is the worst thing I could do, and it's not a mistake I want to make twice. I'll go somewhere so distant that no mortal will ever see me again—the far, far north, where the world is white and covered with ice. I'll be alone, but I'll be *free*.

Isn't that the most important thing?

I spend the rest of the night trying to think of ways to free Zhian, but my thoughts rebel, continually returning to the look in Aladdin's eyes when I finally told him what my freedom would cost him.

Dawn brings mourning and wailing that echoes eerily through the palace, coupled with the unceasing blast of horns on the outer ramparts, announcing to the city that the king has died. Khavar and Ensi arrive at our door, cloaked and hooded, and I wake Aladdin. The girls have brought trays of hot tea and fruit, bread, and cheese, but most of it goes untouched as they sit with us and tell us they have come at Caspida's behest.

"The next few days will be crucial," says Ensi. "Sulifer controls the army and most of the court, and this announcement of Caspida's engagement to Rahzad will be met with much resistance."

"We are here to protect you, Prince Rahzad," says Khavar, stroking her snake.

Aladdin looks a bit skeptically at the two slim girls. "I think I can take care of myself, but thanks for the offer."

"We're not going anywhere, so get used to us."

Ensi leans forward. "We're going to announce the betrothal immediately following the king's burial. According to the decree Malek signed before he died, Caspida is to marry Darian tomorrow. Instead, she will marry *you*."

I suck in a breath. The king's burial . . . Darian told me the kings are buried in the hills north of the city. That could be my chance to set Zhian free, safely outside the city gates.

Khavar glares at Aladdin. "Let me make one thing clear. Any one of us would die for Caspida. Any one of us would kill for her." She raises her arm, and her snake slithers out of her sleeve and raises its head to stare at Aladdin. "You hurt her just once, and it's the last thing you'll do. You won't see us coming. You won't get a second chance."

Aladdin swallows and leans back, looking to Ensi. The other girl meets his eyes steadily.

"How fortunate she is," he says evenly, "to have friends like you."

The girls seem to accept this and exchange looks before Khavar says, "The funeral procession is leaving soon. We are all expected to be in attendance. We will wait here while you change, and accompany you outside."

Aladdin nods and looks relieved to get away, disappearing into his bedchamber. Ensi slips a knife from her sleeve and picks at her nails. I clear away the breakfast dishes, listening to the girls' hushed conversation.

"I like him," Ensi says.

"I don't," Khavar replies.

"You don't like anyone."

For a moment, I imagine what it would be like to truly be Aladdin's servant. To become part of this household, perhaps even join the Watchmaidens in guarding the royal family. But with a shudder, I turn my thoughts away.

I have been among these people too long, and their human problems and drama have ensnared me too deeply. I remind myself how fleeting they are. I blink, and they will be gone. Time has a different meaning for me, and these events that seem so monumental in the moment will one day be nothing more than a line in a scroll. These humans are but letters to be inked into history. A hundred years from now, I will be free. I will have forgotten their names and faces, and the struggles they have will not matter. Time has a way of burying things, shifting like the desert and swallowing entire civilizations, erasing them from map and memory. Always, in the end, everything returns to dust.

There is no point in pretending I am anything other than what I am. It is time to move on.

It is time to claim my freedom.

Chapter Nineteen

THE PARTHENIAN MONARCHS lie buried in massive stone vaults built into the side of a steep cliff north of the city. Many of the tombs are weathered and chipped, the elaborate friezes carved on them worn away to vague forms. The tomb of Malek is still only partially constructed, and stone chips and unfinished friezes attest to the ongoing work. A great slab is fixed in place over the tomb's entrance, and Caspida stands before it, looking lonely even in the midst of the crowd. She stands a little apart, dressed in black robes that flutter in the wind.

The day is hot and the air heavy. Clouds roil over the sea, advancing slowly toward us. Seabirds wheel overhead, crying out warning of the oncoming storm. Nobles stand fanning themselves under the shade of cypresses and oaks studding the hillside, and wailers stand in front of the tomb, crying out in ululating tones. They are surrounded by black-cloaked Eristrati, who watch for jinn, and I spot Vigo and Nessa roaming the perimeter, their flutes trilling softly to enchant any jinn that might try to sneak into the humans' midst. I have conjured a silk scarf tight around my head and ears to block the music; though they cannot bottle me because of my bond with the lamp, their melodies can nonetheless put me into a trance, exposing my true nature. The jinn keep their distance; I cannot sense a single one among the trees and rocks. They're waiting, I'm sure, until tonight, when my time runs out and Nardukha orders them to attack the city.

We stop a short distance from the tomb. Aladdin watches Caspida, his face unreadable. He's dressed head to toe in black, his head uncovered. His hair, combed neatly this morning, has been tousled by the driving wind. Khavar and Ensi stand by, rigid and alert. Ensi's eyes water, but she blinks her tears away.

I hang back until the crowd is focused on the burial ceremony, then slip into the brush and make my way across the hill. Zhian's jar rattles under my skirt, his endless stream of demands prying at my thoughts.

Set me free! What are you waiting for, you stupid creature!

"You!" cries a sharp voice. "Where are you going?"

I turn and see a veiled Eristrati glowering at me, his grip tightening on his spear.

"Oh, um . . ." I wince and point at the bushes. "I'll just be a minute. Please. I can't hold it any longer."

The man coughs uncomfortably, then nods and mutters something gruff along the lines of "Make it fast."

Don't worry. I intend to.

I find a small grassy clearing, not far from the river where I bathed Aladdin's wound that first, wild night, exactly 142 steps from the lamp. It's a pretty spot, overlooking the city and the sea beyond, the trees ripe with olives. I'm out of hearing of the jinn charmers, so I lower the silk from my head and let the wind tangle my hair.

Drawing a deep breath, I pull Zhian's jar from a satchel conjured beneath my skirt. Letting the satchel disintegrate into smoke, I hold the jar in both hands as excitement pounds through me, almost like a heartbeat.

Do it, Zhian urges. *Let me out, Zahra. Let me out.*

Listen to me first, I demand. *There are jinn charmers out here— did you hear them? They are playing, filling the hills with their charms. You must not go near the humans, or we will both end up right back where we started.*

We could take them together, he replies. *You and I—working as a team. We would be unstoppable!*

To that, I only send him an image of the lamp, and he curses. I quickly relay to him the deal I made with Nardukha. Zhian stews in his jar, his impatience hammering through my thoughts.

When I finish, he spits, *So do it! Let me out!*

I glance around, making sure we're alone, then lift the jar high before dashing it against a rock. The pottery shatters, as does the charm that held Zhian captive inside.

A burst of smoke fills the air, red and angry. It swells and thunders.

"Quiet!" I hiss. "They'll come!"

I do not fear mortals!

"Then you're an idiot. If it weren't for me, they'd still have you bottled up in their crypts."

My father would not allow it! Zhian swirls around me, his wind pulling at my hair and my black cloak. Dragon heads materialize in the smoke, snapping and hissing dangerously close to my face.

He would burn their city for my sake! He would sink their ships and wreck their walls!

"Well, he didn't, did he? He sent *me*. Settle down, because I have one more thing to say."

Zhian rages about a bit longer, cracking trees and whipping up whirlwinds of dust. Then, at last, he assembles himself, taking the form of an enormous, human-like figure, nine feet tall with hooves and horns. It's one of his favorite forms, modeled closely after his father. He wears only a leopard-skin loincloth, and his chest swells with muscle and pride. In his hands is a long chain, from which dangles a spiked morning star.

Curl-of-the-Tiger's-Tail, he purrs, his black eyes glittering. *Smoke-on-the-Wind. Girl-Who-Gives-the-Stars-Away. You have chosen a beautiful form. Subtle, but desirable.*

Rolling my eyes, I reach out and grab the chain between his hands, pulling him close. "Your father is waiting, so fly up that mountain and through the alomb. Find Nardukha and tell him I have upheld my end of the bargain. Now it is his turn."

He stares at me, a dangerous light in his eye, and then his gaze travels beyond me, in the direction of the funeral. My hand moves to his muscled forearm, and I squeeze it hard.

"No."

He sneers, his hand moving quickly to catch mine. He yanks me close, his head bending to look down at me.

"Zahra," he murmurs, his voice like falling rocks. "Why do you care for these humans? For thousands of years they have enslaved you, forced you to bend and bow to their silly whims. They have mistreated you, abused you, and yet you defend them still?" He drops his morning star to cradle my head in his other hand, and he licks his lips. His fangs flash. "Come with me to Ambadya. Be my bride, as you were always meant to be."

Revulsion choking my throat, I pull away, slapping him hard across the jaw, but he barely registers the blow. "I'm not anything to you, Zhian. I never will be. You should have abandoned that notion long ago."

"I did not bargain for your life so that you could play servant to these mortals! My father would have killed you thousands of years ago, like all the other Shaitan, if I hadn't intervened!"

"I never asked you to."

He roars, and I clap my hands over my ears at the terrible sound. Somewhere behind me, a horn blasts twice.

"They heard you, you fool!" I snap. "The Eristrati are coming, and their charmers will bottle you up again! Go, *go*!"

He snarls, his hand grabbing for me, but I shift into a tiger and snarl back at him, my hackles on end.

Get out of here, Zhian! Go find Nardukha and tell him I have set you free! Now he must free me.

The horn blasts again. At last Zhian comes to his senses, and he pulls back, scowling.

I'll be back for you, he promises. *And you and I will be joined at last, the jinn prince and his princess, unstoppable and undisputed!*

Shifting back into a girl, I wave at him furiously, and at last he goes, his monstrous form shifting into gray smoke and gliding uphill toward the distant Mount Tissia.

Then I turn and run back the way I came, shifting into a songbird. I flit through the trees, over the heads of the Eristrati running toward the clearing.

I alight on a rock near the funeral and shift back into my

human form, taking a moment to compose myself before slipping back through the crowd to Aladdin's side.

"Zahra!" he hisses. "Where have you been?"

"What do you mean?" I murmur, my eyes on the mountain above.

He frowns, but doesn't press the issue.

I continue gazing at the mountain, wondering how long it will take Nardukha to fulfill his promise, and how it will happen. What will I feel? Will he come himself to do it? I don't see any sign of Zhian, so I can only hope he is on his way to the alomb, if not already through it.

After the funeral ends, Caspida leads the procession back to the palace. She walks alone, with Sulifer and Darian a few steps behind. The wind picks up until it's nearly howling, and everyone must cover their noses and mouths against the dust whipping up. An ominous rumble sounds in the distance, over the choppy gray sea.

Aladdin, anticipating the wards on the city gates, offers me his arm to lean on, and with a mighty effort I keep my pain hidden as the Eskarr symbols glare down at me. We hurry through, Aladdin acting casual while I simply do my best not to pass out. These gates are smaller than the ones through which we first entered the city, and the wards release me sooner, but it is several minutes before my vision clears and I can breathe again.

The court convenes in the throne room, where Caspida stands before her father's great seat, facing the crowd. Four guards are positioned at each corner of the dais, and a row of scribes sit behind her, poised to record everything that happens on long scrolls of creamy parchment, their sleeves rolled back and ink pots at their elbows.

Sulifer and Darian stand at the foot of the throne, wearing

identical expressions of solemnity. Opposite them stand Raz and Nessa, deceptively demure in their funereal black, but their eyes miss nothing.

The crowd whispers and rustles, looking drab and almost indistinguishable from the gray-clad servants who line the walls. High above, through the openings of the domes, the storm clouds roll and rumble, making the hall echo with thunder. Large clay urns have been set directly beneath the holes in the roof, in case rain should begin to fall.

Once everyone has gathered in the hall and the great teak doors are shut with a series of heavy booms, Caspida stands. Everyone falls quiet, and faces turned toward her display a range of expectations: curiosity, hope, pity, and hunger.

In a loud, clear voice that rings across the hall she cries, "My father, Malek son of Anoushan son of Arhab son of Oshur, King of Kings, King of Parthenia, Chosen by Imohel, King of the Amulens, is dead."

"The king is dead," murmurs the crowd in response.

"I am Caspida, daughter of Malek and Parisandra, Princess of Parthenia, Chosen by Imohel, Princess of the Amulens. By the right of my birth, I claim this throne."

"The king is dead," the crowd says again. "Long live the queen."

Beside me, Khavar and Ensi's faces shine, their eyes flooding with pride as Caspida sits on the throne, her chin high and eyes bright. Already she fills the massive seat better than her ill father did.

The proceedings are making me edgy, and I find it hard to focus on my surroundings. I wait, tense and impatient for Nardukha to uphold his end of the deal. I watch the openings in the domes above, as if the Lord of the Jinn himself might come swooping down.

A crier takes position behind the throne. "Look on your queen,

Amulens, the one on whom Imohel's favor rests, the daughter of kings. Caspida the First, who has been found worthy."

"Worthy is she, and favored," replies the crowd.

Silence falls as Caspida raises a hand.

"Before my father's death, he made a final decree," she states.

Ensi leans to Aladdin and whispers, "This is our cue."

Slowly, she and Khavar take up position in front of and behind Aladdin and begin escorting him toward the throne. There is some distance to cover, and the nobles throw angry looks as we press through the crowd. But in the vastness of the hall, our movement is barely noticed.

Caspida continues, "To ensure the future of the kingdom, King Malek wished that I, heir apparent, be joined in marriage before taking the crown."

The crowd murmurs appreciatively. Sulifer's hand closes on Darian's shoulder, and Darian's face glows. He looks up at his father, his eyes shining, and Sulifer gives him a small smile.

"Go, go," urges Ensi under her breath, prodding Aladdin.

"In keeping with my father's will," says Caspida, "I shall take a husband tomorrow at dawn."

My attention snaps to the queen, the faces around me sharpening into focus.

All eyes turn to Darian, most of them smiling. He can't hold back a grin any longer, and he tugs his coat straight, preparing to ascend the dais.

"And so, I am pleased to announce my betrothal to the man who will rule at my side and usher Parthenia and its people into a new era."

Darian clasps hands with his father, then turns and sets a foot on the first stair, looking up at Caspida with passion burning in his eyes.

Without looking at him, Caspida swings a hand wide and announces, "Prince Rahzad rai Asnam of Istarya!"

The crowd gasps as one.

Darian falters, confusion twisting his features, while Sulifer's chest swells and his eyes darken. Heads swivel our way as Aladdin reaches the dais and climbs the stairs. Caspida holds a hand out to him in welcome, while mere paces away, Darian turns scarlet.

"No!" he bursts out. Everyone holds their breaths as he moves to intercept Aladdin. "This is a lie! *I* am the one who will marry the queen! Our betrothal was sealed years ago!" He turns to his father. "Father, tell them!"

Sulifer is surrounded by officials, whispering and gesturing angrily. Caspida steps in before her uncle can say anything.

"Step down, Darian." Her voice is rigid and commanding. "My father's decree was that I should marry. He did not state that I should marry *you*."

Darian stammers and looks from her to Sulifer. The vizier finally makes a move, climbing the dais and looming over Caspida. Aladdin starts forward, but Caspida holds up a hand, and he pauses.

"Princess," says Sulifer in a low voice, "this is childish and irresponsible. You cannot break troth, not even as a queen—which, let me remind you, you are not yet."

"I cannot break a promise I did not make myself," Caspida replies calmly. "And no promises will be made on my behalf. From now on, no voice will command my future but my own. Step aside, Uncle. I will keep my father's decree, but on my terms and not yours." She draws herself up, unflinching. "Leave our presence."

Sulifer stares at her with a blank expression, but his eyes are dark with anger. He turns to Darian. "Come."

Without looking back, Sulifer descends and strides through the crowd. Darian hesitates, his face scarlet.

"You heard the queen," says Aladdin coolly.

After giving Aladdin a furious look, Darian runs to catch up to his father. The astonished people part wide, none wanting to be caught in Sulifer's path. The vizier and his son leave through the central door, letting it slam behind them.

Only then does Caspida turn back to Aladdin and hold out a hand. He takes it, his face pale, and together they face the court.

"Let the wedding preparations commence," says Caspida.

Then she sits on the throne, Aladdin standing beside her, their hands still joined. The crier, brought forward by a flick of Caspida's free hand, dismisses the nobles. They are slow to leave, and long, calculating looks are cast at the couple on the dais. Guards speed up the process, ushering them all out, until at last the room is empty save for the few guards, Caspida and Aladdin, and the Watchmaidens and me.

The princess exhales deeply and bends over, her face in her hands. Her girls flock to her, brushing Aladdin aside and kneeling before their princess.

Aladdin stands by quietly. I move to his side, and he meets my gaze. The look he gives me is longing and uncertain, and soon I must avert my eyes, unable to withstand it.

It is for the best, my thief.

Caspida says, "Sulifer won't give up this easily. Even now, he is regrouping with his followers. We must move quickly. The Eristrati are loyal to me, at least, as are a few of the ministers."

Khavar takes over, assigning tasks to the others in preparation for the sudden nuptials. Within minutes, the girls have planned the entire ceremony, with special attention paid to security.

"Find Captain Pasha," says Caspida, who sits with her knees drawn up on the throne, her face creased with thought. "He is loyal to me. Tell him to gather the Eristrati and every guard he trusts and bring them here."

Nessa's eyes grow round. "You think Sulifer will attack?"

"We've known this moment was coming for years. Sulifer will try to control me the way he did my father. If I give him any ground, even for a day, he will inextricably insinuate himself into my reign. These next hours are crucial. I must establish myself independently of him and prove to my people that I will not be ruled. I want to speak to my council of ministers, to discuss the coronation."

Aladdin speaks up, startling the girls a bit. "Then what are we waiting for? Why don't we throw him into the dungeons now?"

Caspida frowns. "It's not that simple, Rahzad. The vizier has the loyalty of the army as well as much of the court. Locking him up will only turn them against us."

"But you're the *queen*. Can't you do whatever you want?"

"I don't know how your Istaryan kings and queens behave," she returns, a bit sharply, "but in Parthenia, our power relies on the good will of the aristocracy and military. If I did 'whatever I wanted,' I'd have riots breaking out on every corner."

Aladdin gives me a frustrated glance, but there is nothing I can do. He must learn that Caspida is right. His vengeance will have to wait a while yet.

"Rahzad, I do not mean to be sharp with you," Caspida says more softly. "How patient you have been, while I have dragged you about like a goat on a leash. I wish we had time to do this properly. To send gifts to one another's kingdoms, to discuss terms of our alliance. I have not met your family, and I know so little of your people."

Aladdin winces. "There's really not much to know."

"When this is over, we will retrace our steps and begin anew. I cannot leave my city until the jinn have been dealt with, but when the time is right, I will journey with you to Istarya and see your land for myself."

He smiles a bit weakly and glances at me, his eyes bright with panic. I feel a bit ill as I return his look, knowing I won't be around to help him. Knowing it's my fault he's in this mess. The consequences of my recent actions seem to be piling up, and I feel like a spider that has spun too thin a web.

Caspida makes us wait until Captain Pasha arrives with a contingent of Eristrati before leaving with her handmaidens. Aladdin and I, surrounded by a dozen guards, exit after her.

Back at Aladdin's rooms, he insists the guards wait outside, which they do only after thoroughly searching the chambers for assassins, poison, or other plots.

Alone at last, Aladdin slumps onto the cushions and lets out a long, groaning sigh. Outside, the storm winds rip at the silk curtains hung between the arches, and rain patters on the courtyard. Though it is midday, it is dark enough to be midnight.

"It's all happening so fast," he says. "I didn't think . . . I'm marrying the princess in a matter of *hours*."

"And yet you look as if you've swallowed broken glass."

He slowly runs his hand through his hair, his eyes fixed on the floor. "She doesn't love me."

I go stand in one of the arches and let the rain dampen my face as the curtains billow around me. The smoke roiling and pulsing inside me echoes the wildness of the storm. I watch the sky for any sign of jinn, the bond with my lamp chafing like a rope around my core. Where is Zhian? Where is Nardukha? Why do they delay? I long to fly away from here, to outrun Aladdin's gaze and hide myself in the clouds.

"Love is a path lined with roses," I say bitterly. "But it leads to a cliff's edge, and all who follow it tumble to their doom. You will not find your happiness there."

"Then what *does* bring happiness, Zahra?" he asks harshly, rising to his feet. "Tell me. In four thousand years, have you unlocked that secret?"

There is a challenge in his tone that makes me flinch. Drawing my eyes from the sky, I turn to him. "No. I have not. Which can mean only one thing: There *is* no secret to happiness. Because happiness itself is a mythical construct, a dream you humans tell yourselves to get you through each day. It is the moon, and you, like the sun, pursue it relentlessly, chasing it around and around, getting nowhere. And yet it never occurs to you that your quest is in vain. Why?" I step forward, eyes intent. "Tell me, Aladdin—*why*? What drives you into this insanity?"

His eyes thoughtfully stare into the rain, and he says, "Faith."

At that, I laugh sourly. "In what? Imohel? The undergods?"

"Maybe," he says. "For some. For others, faith in ourselves. Faith in the ones we love. Faith in tomorrow."

"You sound like a bad poet."

His eyes settle on me probingly. "What would it take to make you believe, Zahra?"

"I have lived too long to believe in happiness."

"You've been in that lamp too long. It's curdled your heart. I think you do believe. I think you just don't want to get hurt. You're afraid."

I clench my hands into fists, turning my back to him and facing the storm.

He stands and walks to my side, firm in the wind that blows around him, ruffling his hair and making his black cloak lift and swirl. "You loved before, and she was taken from you. Ever since, you've been afraid to love again. You insist you're a monster because you're afraid of being *human*."

I stand before him speechless, defenseless. What good is it, Habiba, to deny the truth? Your friendship woke something in me all those centuries ago, some dormant humanity that had lingered through the years, and after you died, it recoiled and hid again.

But Aladdin has woken it once more. With his sun-bright smile and his laughing eyes and his way of asking the hardest kind of questions. After you, I swore never to love again.

But I love him.

And so I must let him go.

Chapter Twenty

I TELL MYSELF TO BE PATIENT. It has only been a few hours since I released Zhian, and Ambadya is a vast world. It will take him some time to cross the red wastes and jagged mountains to Nardukha's stronghold, where the Shaitan holds court. And who can say how long Nardukha will take to grant my freedom, or what manner in which he will do it. Time moves more slowly for the ageless; he may pass days as humans pass hours, and I could be stuck here for a while yet.

Strangely, the thought brings some comfort. As much as I long to be rid of Aladdin and the feelings he stirs in me, I also want never to leave his side. As soon as I do, he will be alone in this vipers' nest of a court.

There is much to do in the hours before dawn, when the wedding will take place. Generally Amulen weddings take a week of preparation, with each day carefully parceled out into ceremony.

But tradition must be sacrificed for speed, and so we tackle the bare minimum.

Most important, Aladdin needs a bath.

The ceremonial bathing the day before the wedding is one of the more sacred traditions. And so Aladdin, accompanied by a half dozen soldiers, is escorted to the palace baths. I follow in the form of a sparrow, flitting from here to there down the hall, a few steps behind. Before leaving his room, Aladdin made me promise to wait outside, but I perch on the top of the last guard's peaked helmet and pass unnoticed inside the baths.

The room is dark except for thin rods of light that beam through small holes dotting the dome above. Six large, round pools are spaced evenly in a white tiled floor. White lotus and rose petals drift tranquilly on the turquoise water. The room is empty when we arrive, and Aladdin turns to the guards.

"You, um, wouldn't mind waiting outside, would you?"

"We are under strict orders not to take our eyes off you," replies a stoic man.

Aladdin rubs his face. "Yes, I know that. But look, I'm the only one here. If I need you, I'll yell or something."

The man simply stares blankly back at him.

With a groan of frustration, Aladdin adds, "You do realize that after tomorrow, I'll be your *king*?"

The guards exchange uncertain looks, then acquiesce begrudgingly, streaming out through the door. I flit away and land on a ledge along the wall.

Aladdin sighs and disrobes down to a white cloth around his waist, careful not to set down the lamp. This he strings onto a chain around his neck, and then he sinks into the first pool. He vanishes beneath the surface, bubbles streaming around him, and does not emerge for several long seconds. I begin to worry that he won't come back up at all, that he will go the same route as so many of my masters who came to regret their wishes—but then he bursts upward, shaking his head and sending water spraying. He glides across the pool and sits on the opposite side in a shaft of sunlight, stretching his arms along the tiled rim. His head falls back, and he shuts his eyes.

"I know you're there," he says. "You might as well come down."

I fly to the edge of the pool and shift to human, dressed in a thin white kurta that comes to my knees. I dangle my legs in the water.

"For some kind of all-powerful jinni from the dawn of time," says Aladdin, his eyes opening a crack to peer at me, "you're damn predictable."

I lift one foot from the water, splashing him. "You might want to dunk again. You still smell like you sleep with goats."

He swipes a hand across the water, dousing me, and I shriek and tumble into the water, where I drench him with a series of splashes. He sputters and holds up his hands defensively, then with a roar, launches off the side of the pool and catches me around the waist, dragging me under the surface.

For a moment we are weightless, eyes open and locked underwater, flowers drawn down with us, swirling around us in a current of white bubbles. My hair floats around us both like black silk. His hands are still around my waist, mine pressed against his bare chest. My lamp drifts between us.

Aladdin plants his feet against the bottom of the pool and kicks off, pushing us upward to burst through the surface. He gasps in air and shakes the wet hair from his eyes. Without pulling away, we float in silence, and I cannot take my gaze from him. Water runs down his cheeks and lips, dripping from his jaw. A lock of his hair is stuck to his forehead, and I gently lift it away, curling it around my finger before letting it go.

"What are we doing?" he whispers, pulling me closer.

I cannot reply. I don't trust my own voice. He brings his forehead down to rest against mine, and everything outside this pool and this moment ceases to exist. All that matters is the gentle sound of our breathing, our reflections on the water, the feel of his hands around me.

He is the sun, and I am the moon. We must stay apart or the world will be thrown out of balance. But what I must admit is that I *do* understand the insanity that drives humans to chase happiness they will never grasp. Because I feel it too, Habiba. Every time I try to pull away, I find myself drawn back to him. Even now, on the eve of his wedding, I cannot let go, no matter how many times I tell myself that I must.

It will all be over tomorrow, I think. *He will marry Caspida, and surely by then, Nardukha will have set me free.*

I rest my head on his shoulder, feeling his heart beating against me. I wish I could gather time around us, slowing the minutes, making them last a lifetime.

"I was born on the island kingdom of Ghedda," I whisper. This is a story I never told even to you, Habiba. I tell it now only because I cannot bear to leave him without the truth, knowing only half of me. I raise my head and meet his eyes. "That was more than four thousand years ago. I was the eldest daughter of a wise and generous king."

Aladdin stares at me, his eyes soft and curious, encouraging me to go on.

"When I was seventeen, I became queen of Ghedda. In those days, the jinn were greater in number, and the Shaitan held greater sway over the realms of men. He demanded we offer him twenty maidens and twenty warriors in sacrifice, in return for fair seas and lucrative trade. I was young and proud and desired, above all else, to be a fair ruler. I would not bow to his wishes, so he shook our island until it began to fall into the sea."

I shudder, and Aladdin draws me closer.

"I climbed to the alomb at the top of the Mountain of Tongues, and there offered myself to the Shaitan, if he would only save my city from the sea." My voice falls to a whisper, little more than a ripple on the water. "So he took me and made me jinn and put me in the lamp. And then he caused the Mountain of Tongues to erupt, and Ghedda was lost to fire. For he had sworn only to save my people from the sea, not from flame."

Falling silent, I wait to see what Aladdin will do. Call me naïve for trusting the word of the Shaitan? Tell me I should have bowed to Nardukha's wishes in the first place?

But Aladdin says nothing.

Instead, he lowers his face and softly kisses the side of my neck, his mouth trailing up to the skin behind my ear. Goose bumps break across my skin, and I turn my face to meet his lips with mine. This kiss is gentler than our last, long and slow and restrained. It is a kiss of longing. A kiss of farewell. His hands tighten around my waist, pulling me against him. We drift in a slow circle, sending out ripples that make the floating flowers bob and dip.

"You keep so many secrets," he murmurs. "I could spend the rest of my life discovering you." He tucks my hair behind my ear, his eyes devouring my face. "Of course you were a queen. Of course you sacrificed yourself for your people. You did all you could, Zahra. You can't blame yourself for what the Shaitan did. He would have done it anyway."

"I should have died with my people."

"If you had, I would have never met you." He kisses me again, more deeply, his hands twining in my hair. I let his touch wash away the past.

It is Aladdin who pulls away first, with a soft, husky laugh.

"This is crazy. I'm getting married tomorrow," he says.

I nod and lay my head on his shoulder.

"It's not too late," he says. "Zahra, I—"

"Sh." I lay a finger across his lips. "Don't say it. You will marry Caspida, and you will learn to love each other. You will live a happy life, long after my lamp has passed to new hands."

"I won't make my third wish," he says. "That's the answer! If I don't make the wish, you can stay here in the palace for as long as you want. You'll never have to go back to your lamp. We can fight off anyone who tries to take you from me."

"Even if that were true, you would grow old and die. Or more likely, someone would discover my existence and kill you for my lamp. Or most likely, Caspida would learn that you're a fake and that I am one of the jinn she so deeply hates, and she would destroy you and me both."

"She'd understand."

"Would she?"

He winces. "Fine. I won't marry her."

"And what of your vengeance? Will you let Sulifer win that easily?"

He lowers his gaze. "Everything I've lived for will have been in vain. Sulifer will win. He will force Caspida to marry Darian.

She'll become their puppet, if they even let her live long at all. And no one will be left to oppose him. He'll get away with everything."

I nod. "It would be our fault."

He looks up, his forehead creasing. "Why do you care what happens to her? I thought we humans were vapors to you, here today and gone tomorrow."

"Caspida is . . . different. She reminds me of someone, someone I'd give my life for if I could."

"The queen?" he asks. "The one who died?"

"Roshana. My dear Ro." My voice is soft as a ripple on the water. "She once ruled the Amulens, and Caspida is her descendant. She has Roshana's strength of spirit, and I cannot look at her without thinking of my old friend. If she were to come to harm on my account . . . I could not bear that through the centuries." I already carry a mountain of shame, a constant reminder of that day on Mount Tissia.

Aladdin lifts a hand and brushes the hair back from my face. "You truly are remarkable, Zahra of the Lamp."

"Don't," I say, pushing his hand aside. I swim away to the edge of the pool. "You understand why you must go through with this marriage."

"You say you couldn't live with yourself if anything happened to Caspida. Yet you ask *me* to live with myself, knowing I sentenced you to *this*!" He holds up the lamp. "What's the difference?"

I look away angrily. "The difference is that this is my choice, Aladdin."

"Well, it's a stupid choice!"

I stand up. "Promise me you'll go through with it."

He shuts his eyes.

"Promise me! *Please!*"

He opens his eyes then, and they are filled with pain. But he nods.

"I have to hear you say it."

"I promise."

Refusing to look at me, he sinks under the water again, until he is just a shadowy blur below. I go sit against the wall, curled up, and try to still the emotions roiling inside. What was I thinking, kissing him again? Am I doomed to make the same mistakes over and over? Falling for humans, getting too close, too involved, watching as they destroy themselves for me.

I taste salt and realize I'm crying. Angrily I rub my eyes. Soon I will get what I always wanted: my freedom. And none of this will matter. Didn't I tell myself a month ago, when this all began, that I would do anything for freedom? Losing Aladdin may be the hardest thing I have to do, but I must do it.

A door opens and shuts at the far end of the room, and I look up, startled.

It is Darian, and four boys are with him.

I shift at once, before they can see me, into airy smoke. I drift upward and hover on the ceiling, barely visible.

The boys circle around the bath and stare down at Aladdin, who is just coming up for air. His eyes are shut, and he wipes his hair back and runs his hands down his face before opening them and seeing Darian standing over him.

Aladdin goes still.

"Prince Rahzad," says Darian.

"I appreciate the thought," says Aladdin, watching him warily. "But wedding gifts can be left at my rooms."

"This one must be delivered in person."

"How did you get past my guards?"

"They're not *all* your guards. At least, not anymore." He smirks. "It's amazing what a few gold coins can buy, and the three guarding the back door happen to be greedier than most."

Darian begins peeling off his clothes. The other boys do the same. Aladdin stays in the center of the pool, floating nonchalantly, but his eyes are alert to every movement. He lazily turns until he's facing me, and his eyes explore until he spots me, hovering against the ceiling.

The lamp.

Terror strikes me like lightning on a cloudless day. Aladdin has the lamp around his neck. If the boys see it . . . I catch sight of Aladdin's hands beneath the water, moving the lamp so that it's hidden behind his back.

Darian cases into the water. His body is lean, not powerful like Aladdin's, but lithe and muscular. The other boys are more solidly built, and they slide into the pool around Aladdin, hemming him in. Aladdin treads water, and the muscles in his shoulders and neck grow tense.

"If you think this game you and Cas are playing is going to work," says Darian calmly, "then you're an even bigger idiot than I thought."

"Careful," says Aladdin. "I'd hate to have to uninvite you to the wedding."

"She is *mine*, and has been since the day she was born. We were meant for each other."

"Funny, she doesn't seem convinced of that."

"Her mind has been poisoned. She spends too much time reading false histories of mythical queens and fancies herself one of them. Her arrogance and delusions are regrettable, but nothing the firm hand of a husband can't fix."

"You *animal*," says Aladdin, dropping all pretense of amicability. "You speak as if she were your property. As if she were a horse or a dog to be trained."

Darian shrugs one shoulder. "Horses. Dogs. Women. They all have their place, and when they try to upset the order, things fall into chaos. If we let queens rule the world, we'd all stay holed up in our palaces embroidering and gossiping."

Aladdin raises a brow. "And . . . running around beheading people is somehow more civilized?"

"If Parthenia is going to become the power it once was, we need a strong leader. Someone the people look up to. Someone they've admired and respected for years. Not some weak prince from some far-off kingdom nobody has even heard of. These people will never follow you."

"I don't need anyone to follow me. They will follow *her*."

"You don't get it!" Darian snarls. He moves forward, until only an arm's length separates him and Aladdin. "She belongs to *me*! She is my birthright!"

"The only birthright you have is your bloated arrogance," says Aladdin. "At least *that* your father could rightfully give you."

"Don't you *dare* insult my father."

"Your father," says Aladdin, smiling and swimming closer, "is a self-important, conniving bag of pus."

Darian turns red. "My father is the bravest man in Parthenia. While the king wasted away over a simmon pipe, my father has held the jinn at bay."

"Your *father*," Aladdin continues, "murders the innocent. He beheads anyone who disagrees with him. Tell me, Prince, how did the king really die? I wonder if he wasn't pushed into the godlands."

With a snarl, Darian lunges forward, tackling Aladdin and thrusting him under the water. Aladdin thrashes, plunging upward again and gasping in air, but the other boys join in, grabbing his shoulders and head and pushing him under. He struggles, legs kicking, making the bath froth and overspill. Darian's face is grim, his lips curled in a tight smile, and he doesn't flinch.

I shift into wind and gust across the room, forcefully blowing open the door behind which the still-loyal guards are stationed. They look in, see the struggle, and shout out. Darian looks up, his face twisting with rage, and he and his cohorts scramble out and grab their clothes. They run from the room, pursued by the guards.

In the corridor outside, I shift to a girl and run into the baths, jumping into the pool and grabbing Aladdin, who has sunk to the bottom. I drag him up and onto the tile, the lamp clanging on the floor.

"He's not breathing!" I cry, but there is no one to hear. The guards have chased Darian and the others and are too far away. I begin pumping Aladdin's chest with my palms.

"Come on, come on," I say. I should have done something sooner. I was too worried they would find the lamp. I should have changed into a lion and devoured them all.

Aladdin coughs, water spilling from his mouth. I lift him up and turn him on his side so he can empty his lungs.

His eyes, wide and panicked, find me, and he tries to speak.

"Shush," I say. "You're fine. You're fine. Just breathe."

He gasps in and out, a raspy, watery sound, and coughs up more water. His hand pushes the lamp beneath him, hiding it from view.

The guards return now, looking stricken. I toss Aladdin's shirt over the lamp.

"Did you catch him?" I ask.

They shake their heads.

I turn back to Aladdin, who is beginning to breathe more evenly. He covers the lamp further with his arm, hiding it from the guards' view.

"I could have taken them," he says hoarsely. "I was getting around to it."

I long to hold his head to my chest, so relieved am I that he is alive. But I can't, not with the guards looking on. So I let him go and stand up, then hand him his clothes. He refuses help from the guards and rises to his feet, taking care to cover the lamp, but doesn't argue when they insist on returning to his rooms. Two of the guards want to tell Captain Pasha and Caspida what happened, but Aladdin convinces them to let it lie.

"We can deal with him later," he says. "He isn't worth hunting down."

When we are alone again, Aladdin is quiet, and I can tell he's holding back his anger at being attacked.

I, however, let mine run freely, and I rage around the room in the form of a tiger, snarling and clawing at the floor, my hackles raised.

"Would you stop that?" he says sharply. "You're setting me on edge."

"You're not already on edge?" I growl. "He tried to *kill* you!"

"He's done it before," says Aladdin. "And I have a way of staying alive."

"Because I'm there to save your skin!"

"Exactly!" He grins sunnily. "Which is why I can't lose you. Who else will watch my back?"

With a snarl I shift into human, my gown patterned with tiger stripes. "Aladdin, you *promised*."

His smile drops. "I know, I know."

"You promised."

"What do you want me to do? Swear on my mother's soul? Cut my hand open and sign my name in blood?"

"It wouldn't hurt," I mutter.

Aladdin sighs and starts to reply, but a knock at the door interrupts. I open it to find a tailor and his two apprentices standing there with bolts of cloth and sewing boxes.

"We're here to fit the prince for his wedding clothes," says the tailor. He's a small, clean-shaven man with a turban wound high to make up for his height.

I tell him to return in five minutes, which gives Aladdin time to hide the lamp in his room. I reluctantly return to it, loath to leave him unguarded for even an hour. I reach out with my sixth sense throughout the fitting, wary as a caged cat, but all goes smoothly, and once the tailor and his assistants are gone, Aladdin quickly releases me again. There follows an endless procession of servants knocking at the door, bearing food, wine, gifts from Caspida—all the traditional items that should have been parceled out over a series of days, now crammed into the few hours left.

It is well after midnight when Aladdin, exhausted, tumbles into bed. I sit in the midst of his gifts: daggers and gold, clothing and carved chests, mirrors and candlesticks. It reminds me of your first betrothed, Habiba: handsome and bold Elikum of Miniivos, and of the elaborate preparations we made for your wedding. Of course, your wedding week ended with the groom being poisoned by a traitor on the eve of the ceremony. We held a funeral instead, and you did not weep until three weeks later. You always claimed you did not love him, but I never believed you.

I can only hope this wedding will end on a better note. To be sure, I stay on watch all night, guarding Aladdin's door as if the whole host of Ambadya might try to storm in.

Two hours before dawn, I wake him with a soft knock. He stumbles out, his eyes red from lack of sleep.

"Already?" he groans.

"You should go change," I say. "You're to be wed in less than an hour, and you can't meet your bride looking like you just rolled out of bed."

He draws a breath as if about to speak, but then sighs wearily and returns to his chamber.

I change my garments, swirling and rearranging them into festive blue and gold silk, my hair loose and long. I watch as artful brown curlicues and flowers coil down my arms and over the backs of my hands. The henna is meant for a bride, not a jinni, and with a sigh I let it fade away.

Aladdin emerges minutes later. He wears the rich set of clothes the tailor made for him the night before: a close-fitting coat of muted gold and beige that opens in a split in the front and back, over loose red leggings, and a red cape that hangs over his right shoulder and brushes the floor in front and behind.

"Wait," I say. I motion for him to sit, then rake my fingers through his hair, conjuring a comb of jade with a tiger handle that I use to part his hair and sweep it into a neat wave high over his forehead. So rich and dark, that hair; I long to bury my fingers in it and kiss his forehead.

"There," I say. "Let's have a look at you."

He cuts a striking figure and will make a handsome groom. I ignore the pang in my stomach the sight of him causes. *Let him go*, I tell myself. At any moment my bond with the lamp could break, and my feelings for him must break with it. But my heart is a treacherous star, refusing to dim when the sun rises.

"How do I look?" he asks, and he strikes a ridiculous pose, watching to see if he can elicit a laugh.

"Like a fool." I shake my head. "But a princely one."

He takes a step toward me, a hand reaching out. "Zahra, I . . ."

"Don't speak." I look down, fussing with my gown. "We should go."

"Of course. You're right." His reply is so soft I nearly don't catch it.

"Just one more thing . . ." I look around the room, spot a gold spoon on the tray of tea Khavar and Nessa brought, and pick it up. I hold it in the coals of the brazier, which are still hot from the night before. In minutes, the gold is cool enough to shape. With a few quick movements, I peel away most of the gold and use the rest to form a ring. As the metal cools, the outside is impressed with the prints of your fingers, Habiba, which I wear like gloves. It seems fitting, given that the bride is of your blood. Before the metal cools completely, I use my nail to impress Eskarr glyphs into the inside of the band, representing undying love. The ancient symbols, which carry a magic of their own, glow white before fading into the ring.

"Here," I say. "It's all right, the metal has cooled."

Aladdin takes the ring and turns it over. "Zahra, you're a wonder."

"It's not much, but it's better than nothing."

He swallows and nods, then hands it back. "You must carry it for me."

"I can't." I back away, lifting my hands in refusal. The ring bearer must be the groom's closest friend, one who symbolically carries his deepest trust and affection. Usually that person is his brother or oldest friend.

"I want you to," he says. "After all, this was all your idea. Please, Zahra?"

His gaze is earnest, and my eyes fall to the ring on his palm. Mouth dry, I nod and take it, closing my fingers over it protectively, feeling small and unworthy.

"We should go," I say gruffly. "You've got a wedding to catch."

Chapter Twenty-One

THE NOBLES FLOW IN WAVES toward the palace temple, watching and whispering like a flock of doves, and they part for Aladdin, who walks ringed by his guards. The crowd wears a strange blend of dark funeral clothes, in keeping with the traditional twenty days of morning for a king, and bright festive colors for the wedding.

We reach the temple to find it overflowing with people. We are barely able to squeeze in, and the looks that follow us are malevolent. There is little love for Aladdin among this court, which until an hour ago had been expecting their own beloved prince to be the one standing at the princess's side today. But I do spy a few smiling faces among those nobles Aladdin managed to charm in his short time at the palace, and I doubt it will take him long to win over the rest—so long as his true identity goes undiscovered.

Six drummers stand in front of the temple, beating a wedding tattoo that echoes throughout the palace, announcing the arrival of the bride and groom. Around the edges of the room, acolytes swing incense on chains, filling the air with the sweet scent of jasmine and moonflower. Each door is guarded by a priest bearing a prayer staff in one hand and a scroll of holy verse in the other, to ward off evil spirits and discourage jinn from entering. Their efforts are more symbolic than anything, and I pass by without incident.

We are met by Captain Pasha, who escorts Aladdin to a dais in front of the temple, beneath a four-story statue of Amystra, the goddess of warriors and judges. Her stone wings curve around the dais, enclosing it on three sides, while her arms stretch high above her upturned face, holding aloft a sword.

Aladdin stands at the foot of the stair leading up to the dais. He tugs at his collar, his eyes roaming the crowd. Those officials loyal to Caspida stand behind him, while scribes record everything at small wooden desks set to one side of the dais. Little girls strew rose and jasmine blossoms around the temple while singing a soft, sweet melody.

With Aladdin in place, Caspida enters from the left. The princess wears a long, trailing gown of white, embroidered from neck to hem with tiny white roses, with one arm bare and the other draped with sheer silk. Her hands and wrists are covered with red henna that stands out in contrast to her olive skin. Gathered into braids beneath a simple silver band, her hair is studded with the same tiny white blossoms that are also sprinkled on the dais and down the stairs. Caspida's handmaidens follow her, dressed in shades of green, like the leaves of a rosebush with Caspida as the flower.

Two priests step forward to officiate. One carries a pot of burning embers, and the other a sprig of an olive branch. He taps Aladdin's shoulders and forehead with the branch, symbolically purifying him, and then casts it into the bowl, where it burns in seconds. Then the priests scatter rice around Aladdin and Caspida's

feet, a symbol of good luck and fortune to come. At last two acolytes take a length of red silk and hold it over the couple's heads,
and the priests begin intoning the words of binding, their sentences
interspersed with lines sung by a young acolyte boy with a voice as
sweet as honey.

Aladdin is as edgy as a beggar in a guardhouse. He watches
Caspida sidelong and tries to mimic her actions. I'm half afraid
he'll run. Caspida, on the other hand, is serene as a swan, her face
composed and regal. She doesn't meet Aladdin's eyes.

I try to be happy for them, Habiba. Truly I do. And a part of
me *is* happy for them—I have grown fond of them both, and to see
them joined makes me believe some stories do end happily. Here is
one wish I didn't twist. Two lives I didn't ruin.

And yet . . .

Part of me feels shriveled and rejected. I am the weed cast out
of the rose garden. I am the crow chased out of the dovecote. I am
where I belong, and shouldn't that be enough? Doesn't that merit
some sense of happiness or, at the least, fulfillment? Haven't I won
the more important prize—freedom?

Then why, Habiba, do I feel as if I have lost something instead?

I force the question out of my mind. There are more important
things to focus on, such as the prolonged absence of Darian and
Sulifer, which has not gone unnoticed by the gathered nobles. The
vizier and the prince leave a hole in the assembly, and it seems I
am not the only one this worries. Caspida's handmaidens are also
alert and watchful, keeping an eye on the crowd. A clumsy murder attempt in the baths cannot be their only plan, so what are
they waiting for? My eyes sweep the rooftops, looking for a hidden
archer, but I see nothing suspicious. Still, something pulls at me,
something that isn't quite right.

Aladdin and Caspida repeat the words given to them by the priests, speaking vows of troth, fidelity, and love that neither truly feels. A few more minutes, and they will be wed in truth. Instead of feeling relief, I feel as if I'm about to be hanged, waiting for the floor to drop and my neck to break. My unease grows like a swelling wave, rushing inexorably to shore.

Maybe it won't come. Maybe after his failed attempt to drown Aladdin, Darian cut his losses and ran. Maybe Sulifer decided he'd much rather spend the rest of his life fishing on the coast of Qopta than scheming of ways to manipulate this court.

Tense with unease, I turn back to the ceremony, which is moving to a close. An acolyte brings out a beautiful jade tea set. Once Aladdin and Caspida exchange rings and serve each other a cup, they will be officially wed in the sight of gods and men.

"In the presence of Imohel and these witnesses," says one of the priests, "this man and this woman have come forth to bind their fates together. What token do you bring as a seal of this union?"

Aladdin turns to me, and I open my fingers to reveal the ring. He stares at it, his hand hovering over mine.

"Take it," I whisper.

He swallows and picks up the ring, turning it over slowly, light flashing off the symbols carved into the metal. Then his eyes lift and meet mine.

"Zahra . . ." He closes his hand over the ring. "I can't do it."

My mind freezes. I open my mouth but cannot even form a thought to speak.

Aladdin turns around and draws a deep breath, lifting his chin. "I'm sorry, Princess. But this has to stop."

The crowd breaks out into whispers, while Aladdin and the

princess stare at one another with equal regret and relief. The priests exchange baffled looks.

"Your Highness, what is the meaning of this?" one asks.

Aladdin draws himself up bracingly. "Princess Caspida, I have nothing but respect and admiration for you. Truly you will be the queen this city needs. But I can't marry you."

The princess stands still as stone, her face unreadable. "Why not, Prince Rahzad?"

"I am sorry," he replies. "The truth is, I am in love, but not with you."

He turns to me, and my spirit takes flight like a flock of doves, startled and erratic. I cannot move, cannot speak, as he takes my hands in his and looks me earnestly in the eye. He presses the ring into my palm, and the gold feels as if it burns my skin.

"This belongs to you, and you alone. I've been so blind, Zahra. So caught up in the past that I've failed to see what's happening in front of me. I've been such an idiot, I don't know how I can expect anything from you. But I have to try. I have to tell the truth, and the truth is . . . I love *you*."

"No," I whisper. "You *can't*."

"I don't care if you're a . . ."—he pauses to clear his throat—"a servant. You're beautiful and wild and kind, and I can't stop thinking about you." A sunny, foolish smile breaks across his face. "It's wrong and stupid and wonderful, Zahra. I didn't mean for it to happen, but here I am. I love you."

Silence settles like a chill across the room, and we are surrounded by a sea of astonished faces. A few priests whisper to each other, looking panicked. Someone slips out the back door, perhaps to find Sulifer and tell him what has happened. Captain Pasha and his men grip their weapons and look from the princess to my master as if unsure whether they should arrest him or not.

Aladdin seems to notice none of this. He stares at me deeply, imploringly, waiting for me to speak. But I can't. I am rigid with shock and fear and . . . if I am entirely honest, a tiny flicker of hope. My hand closes over the ring.

"Far be it from me," says Caspida in a frosty tone, breaking the silence at last, "to stand in the way of such love. This wedding is over." She turns to the crowd. "There will still be a feast later and dancing through the night. Priests, thank you for your service, but I believe we're done here."

She seems indifferent as the moon. But I can see deeper than the skin and sense she is bewildered and embarrassed, eager to get away. Her Watchmaidens flock to her, pulling her aside with murmurs of concern.

Aladdin watches only me. "I know you must think I'm an idiot," he whispers, "but will you give me a chance? Will you let me start over?"

I back away, pulling my hands from his.

"Zahra, what's wrong?"

"I am *poison.*"

His brow creases. "I don't believe that."

I back up until I'm on the edge of the dais, feeling like a cornered animal. He doesn't understand, just like you didn't understand, Habiba. Why do you humans insist upon courting destruction? Aladdin's eyes are hurt, waiting for me to respond, but my voice sticks in my throat.

"Zahra," he says softly, "do you love me?"

"I—" I shouldn't. It's wrong, it's dangerous, it's forbidden.

He stares pleadingly, waiting. "Zahra?"

"What of your vengeance?" I whisper, my words unheard in the noise rising from the crowd. "What of your parents? All your life you have lived for this moment."

He shakes his head. "I'm tired of living for the dead. I want to live for *you*."

"Aladdin, we *can't*. You must not say such things!" I look around wildly, wondering who can hear us. If Nardukha heard these forbidden words, the price would be catastrophic. "The risk—"

"You are worth *every* risk. I know what I want, Zahra. Do you?"

"I—"

Suddenly a loud, brassy trumpet sounds across the temple. My skin turns to ice, and I almost expect the Shaitan himself to come roaring in. But it is Sulifer who appears, dressed in a black military coat with a sweeping cape, his dark turban adding to his already considerable height. His beard has been trimmed short, enhancing the streaks of gray that run down his chin. Behind him march two dozen soldiers, all wearing armor and helmets, bearing lances and swords. Darian slips in beside them, his face unreadable.

The vizier pauses a moment, taking in Caspida's icy expression and my and Aladdin's clasped hands. Then, with a grunt of dismissal, he strides down the length of the temple yard, and the ring of his and the soldiers' boots is the only sound to be heard. He doesn't speak or change his expression until he reaches the foot of the dais.

There he stops, his eyes fixed on Aladdin.

"Guards," he says. "Seize this man. He is not who he claims to be."

Chapter Twenty-Two

In the silence that falls, I release a long, slow breath, my eyes falling shut for a moment. My spirit plummets, and I can feel everything around me start to unravel. What gave us away? Did Darian see the lamp after all?

"Use your wish," I whisper to Aladdin, opening my eyes. *"Please."*

"If I do," he replies softly, "I'll lose you."

Caspida has pulled herself together; whatever emotions she's reeling with after being humiliated at her own wedding, she hides them well.

"Uncle, stand down," she says. "You are my kin, but I will have you banished or imprisoned if you continue this charade."

Sulifer doesn't even blink. "This man stands accused of murder, sorcery, and communion with jinn."

The blood drains from Aladdin's face, and an audible gasp sweeps around the room.

"That is ridiculous!" says Caspida. "How dare you—"

"Let him speak for himself," says Sulifer calmly. "And let him tell us if he is innocent."

"Of course I am!" Aladdin replies. Dropping my hands, he steps around Caspida and faces the vizier. "You're mad."

"Am I?" Sulifer turns to Darian and gestures him forward.

"Enough of this insanity," says Caspida. "Guards, remove my cousin and uncle from this place!"

Her guards hesitate, but Captain Pasha steps boldly forward. With a wave of his hand, Sulifer brings his own soldiers forward. They lower their lances at the captain, who falters and looks back at the princess. Sulifer and Darian don't even flinch. They have the power of numbers, and they know it. The audience shrinks away, pressing against either side of the temple, well clear of the bared weapons.

The light in Caspida's eyes is dangerous. Without breaking eye contact with her uncle, she motions for Pasha to stand down.

"Is it to be war between us?" she asks in a soft voice.

Sulifer raises a hand, palm up. "Let the boy prove his innocence, and I will leave this city today and never return."

Caspida's eyes narrow suspiciously. "And how do you propose he do that?"

"Let him be searched," replies Sulifer calmly. "Surely you cannot object to that, for if he has nothing to hide, I shall be proven wrong in front of this entire court."

"Very well," says Caspida after a short silence. "Let him be searched."

The blood drains from Aladdin's face.

Sulifer bows, a bit too shallow to be genuine. "Thank you, Princess."

Darian eagerly ascends the dais and steps toward Aladdin, drawing a knife as he seizes my master by the shoulder.

"You can't seem to keep your hands off me, can you?" says Aladdin. "First in the baths, and now this. I'm flattered, truly, but my heart belongs to another."

Darian just grins and wrenches Aladdin's collar aside, exposing the scar on his bare shoulder. He presses the dagger's edge against it, until Aladdin winces and blood trickles from beneath the blade.

"I knew who you were the moment I saw this in the baths," the prince whispers in Aladdin's ear. "I can't believe I didn't see it sooner, but it doesn't matter now. You're finished, *thief.* You'll be wishing for death before I'm done with you." He slides a hand down Aladdin's coat, until he reaches the lump on his hip.

Aladdin swallows.

With a laugh of triumph, Darian pulls Aladdin's sash, and the lamp comes swinging into plain sight. Curious murmurs rustle through the crowd; they aren't sure what it is he's discovered, but they know it must be important by the way Darian shouts excitedly. Aladdin grabs the lamp's handle, trying to tug it away from the prince. I feel nauseated as once, twice, thrice I am nearly sucked into the lamp, only for Aladdin to regain possession of it.

"Sorcerer!" Darian cries. "Jinn-worshipper!"

The crowd picks up his cry, and the words echo across the room. Caspida angrily intervenes, grabbing Darian and pulling him away. The lamp, still bound to Aladdin, is torn from his grasp, and Aladdin catches it.

"What is this?" she asks, but by the dread in her voice, I think she already knows.

"Yes, thief, what is this?" asks Darian, smirking.

"It's a custom of my people," says Aladdin hoarsely. His face is drained of color, but still he tries to maintain his cover. "You know. Symbolizing light and . . . good fortune . . . All Istaryan grooms carry a lamp to their wedding." He stares challengingly at Darian, daring the prince to announce that Aladdin had stolen the lamp from *him*, thus condemning them both.

"Liar," snarls Darian. "You conspired with the jinn to pass yourself off as a prince, when you are nothing but a criminal. And with the jinn's help, you murdered the king!" Darian pulls a vial from his pocket and holds it up. "This was found in his rooms—a deadly poison called Serpent's Bite, the selfsame potion that took the life of our king!" He throws a finger toward Aladdin. "Murderer! King-killer!"

Aladdin's jaw drops open. "The king? I didn't—"

"Every word this man speaks is a lie!" Darian declares. "He is no prince. This man is a fraud and a criminal! His own parents were traitors, beheaded by my father for stirring up rebellion. He is not Rahzad, prince of Istarya, but Aladdin, a common thief who has plagued our city for years!"

And with that declaration, my glamour hiding Aladdin's true face shatters and dissipates, revealing his true image. Recognition flares in Caspida's eyes, and with it, dark anger.

"*Aladdin*," she whispers, raising a hand to her temple. She blinks hard, as if unable to understand what she's seeing. "Can it be?"

He steps forward, a hand raised. "Princess, I can explain—"

"Be silent," she orders coldly, her gaze icing over. Then, stepping closer, she whispers angrily, "I have never been so humiliated in my life. You have ruined me and killed my father! I thought . . . I thought you a friend. *Both* of you." She blinks away a tear, her eyes burning into Aladdin's. "May you carry the weight of this betrayal to your grave."

Aladdin shakes his head furiously. "I may be a thief and a liar, but I'm no murderer! I swear it—I did not kill the king! Caspida, please believe me!"

She doesn't look at him. Defeated, Aladdin turns to me, and I can only smile sadly.

Darian turns and scans the room, his eyes probing, searching. And then they fall on me. His eyes grow wide.

"Of course," he murmurs. "The pretty servant girl."

Without another word he turns, drawing a dagger from his belt. He slices through the sash and grabs the lamp. The world seems to spin around me as my bond with Aladdin, which had grown so familiar to me it was like another limb, snaps like a twig. A new bond forms between me and Darian, strong and absolute, threads weaving together and coiling around us both, until our wills are knit into one. He turns to me, his eyes hungry.

"Monster!" he cries, pointing. "Reveal yourself!"

No point in hiding anymore. If it's a monster they want, then a monster they shall have.

Every eye in the temple suddenly turns to me as I begin to shift, hair, clothes, and even the ring in my hand turning vaporous. It feels almost good to finally shed my human form and burn with all my power before them. Red smoke roils around my feet, growing and swelling to surround me. My eyes are locked with Aladdin's, and he watches wretchedly as I am unbound, thread by thread. The court gasps and recoils, and Caspida and her handmaidens regard me with repugnance.

Here I am, mortals. Look and tremble, for I am the jinni of the lamp, the daughter of Ambadya, the monster in your midst.

Up I rise, borne on a cloud of scarlet smoke. I burn with fury and channel my anger through my shape-shifting magic, red lights flashing in my smoke, my eyes glowing like coals, my skin turning translucent to reveal the fire raging inside me. I am a creature of nightmare and shadow.

Shouts of fear ring out, and the nobles stumble over one another to escape the temple. Sulifer calls for his soldiers.

"Seize him!"

The soldiers run to Aladdin, as Pasha and his men fall aside to create a protective perimeter around Caspida, who already stands surrounded by her handmaidens. The girls look up at me with rage and disgust, and brightest of all is Caspida's quiet, controlled anger, her eyes wounded by betrayal. And it seems it is not Caspida at all who stands before me, but you, Habiba, on the mountaintop, as your death came to swallow you. Their gazes all pierce deeper than they can know, and I realize how stupid I was to ever think them friends. I should have known better than to open myself to such inevitable pain. When did I forget to stay aloof and unattached? When did I let my armor soften, leaving me vulnerable? This is what I get for playing human.

The soldiers approach Aladdin warily, their lances down and angled at his chest. The thief stands still, his gaze still on me, his shoulders slumped in defeat.

"I'm sorry," he whispers, his voice lost amid the screams and shouts, unheard by all but me. He alone can meet my eyes without disgust or fear. He alone still sees the girl inside the monster. But it is not enough.

I hurl myself at the soldiers, whirling around him in a long coil of red smoke, driving the soldiers back. Darian stands gaping, half afraid, half delighted with my display.

"Run!" I say to Aladdin, my voice like the wind, rushing around him, tugging at his cloak. "Go *now*!"

He bursts into motion but runs toward the soldiers instead of away from them. He reaches Darian, catching him in a wild tackle. Both boys roll down the stairs and land roughly, each with a hand on my lamp. They struggle to wrench it free, Aladdin pinning Darian down and getting in one solid punch to the prince's face before the soldiers are on him. They drag him off, and Darian scrambles away, the lamp clutched in his hands. Still Aladdin fights on, wrenching a lance away and wielding it with sharp efficiency, driving the butt into one man's stomach, using the tip to sweep another's feet out from under him. But their numbers overwhelm him, and when his lance breaks, they pounce, twisting his arms behind him and forcing him to his knees.

Furiously I condense into half tiger, half smoke and fling myself at Darian, claws and fangs bared and glinting, but he holds up the lamp, grinning madly.

"Jinni!" he cries. "I command you to return to your vessel!"

Like a dog that has reached the end of its tether, I am halted in the air as the lamp takes control and pulls me toward itself. Helpless, I shift entirely to smoke and pour inside, as Aladdin calls my name.

I rage inside the lamp, throwing myself against the walls, shifting in a blinding flurry from smoke to water to sand to fire. It's pointless. Outside the lamp, I sense Aladdin's pain as the soldiers beat him with the butts of their lances. I sense Caspida's raging fury at being betrayed. I sense Darian's elation through the drumbeat of the pulse in his fingers, the lamp ringing out in time with his heart.

"Take him below," Sulifer commands. "He will die a traitor's death at dawn."

No! Horror washes over me like a wave. I hear Aladdin grunt as he's hauled to his feet, and push my senses as far as they will go, feeling Caspida's steps as she descends from the dais.

"Caspida," Aladdin croaks. "I can explain—"

"Silence," she says coldly.

I follow Aladdin for as long as I can, but too soon he is dragged beyond my senses and lost to me. Despair churns inside me like nausea, and I curl into smoke on the floor of the lamp. Where is Nardukha now, when I need my freedom most? Why has he not come? Have I been played for a fool? I knew I should not have taken his deal. I knew he couldn't be trusted.

"I must withdraw for a while," says Caspida, her voice starting to break. "I have much to think about."

She and her Watchmaidens turn to go, heading for the back door of the temple, but Sulifer's voice stops them short.

"I'm afraid I cannot let you go, Your Highness," he says.

Caspida turns. I can hear the astonishment in her voice. "What did you say?"

"Guards," says Sulifer softly, "arrest the princess."

"What is the meaning of this?" Caspida cries.

Sulifer's voice is hard as steel. "Princess Caspida, you stand accused of complicity with sorcery and communion with demons."

"This is absurd!"

"Did you not receive the jinni Zahra to your chambers several weeks ago?"

"That proves nothing." I can hear Caspida's composure fracturing like ice beneath a hammer. "I did not know her true nature. I knew nothing of—"

"That will be determined by the judges."

"The judges!" She laughs acidly. "The judges are your leashed dogs, trained to tear apart whomever you point out."

"Imprison her," says Sulifer. "And her handmaidens too."

I sense the soldiers moving toward the girls, but they never reach them. Nessa and Khavar slice through their midst like a sharp and deadly breeze, while Ensi flings poisoned powder in a glittering arc. Soldiers fall, clutching their throats and chests, as the girls' attack parts them like a scythe through dry grass. Caspida spins free of the soldiers holding her, felling them both with a series of strikes, her bare hands slipping past their defenses to decimate their nerve points, leaving them twitching on the ground. Before Sulifer, Darian, or the remaining guards can make a move, the girls vanish, running from the temple and disappearing into the palace.

"After them," Sulifer says to Darian in a low voice. "Bring that girl to me, whatever it takes! Wait—give it to me first."

I can feel Darian's hesitation, but he slowly gives the lamp over to his father. Sulifer's will replaces Darian's, clamping down on my mind like an iron cage.

The prince calls the soldiers to himself, and they run from the temple.

Just like that, all comes undone.

Chapter Twenty-Three

THE DAY PASSES IN A BLUR.

Sulifer meets with members of the council. There are many hushed conversations in the shadows of the corridors. I don't listen. I withdraw utterly into myself, cowering in my lamp, the darkness around me filled with whispers.

This is your fault.

You failed him.

You've killed him.

I don't try to block out the words, because I know they are true. This is the price of Aladdin's second wish, the wish *I* convinced him to make. The price of every lie is that the truth will always come out. I knew that, I knew it, and yet I still led him into it. And for what? Where is Zhian? Where is my freedom? Why am I still bound to my lamp? Like a smith with a lump of twisted metal, I begin forging my fear into anger. Sooner or later, Sulifer will have to call me from the lamp. When he does, I don't know what I'll do,

Habiba. But I have to do *something*. I can't just let them execute Aladdin.

Later that night, when Sulifer is alone in his rooms, poring over a map on his desk, a knock sounds at the door, and Darian enters. I stir from my black fog to listen.

"Well?" Sulifer rises from his desk. "Where is Caspida?"

Darian hesitates a moment, then says softly, "She's gone. We scoured the palace, but there wasn't a sign of her or her girls. We believe they fled into the lower city, and the guards will be searching all night."

Without a word, Sulifer steps forward and backhands him, sending Darian reeling into the wall. He freezes there, his back to his father, clutching the stones as if trying to melt into them.

"*Failure*," hisses the vizier. His entire being transforms, as if he has shed his mask of composure to reveal the true man beneath. "I give you every chance in the world to make something of yourself, and you bring me failure!"

"I found the lamp!" says Darian defensively, turning around.

Sulifer grabs the front of his coat and backhands him repeatedly. "Do not talk back to me, boy! You failed to bring the lamp to me the first time. You failed to wed the princess. You failed to bring her to me." With each statement his blows grow harder, until blood spurts from Darian's nose. Only then does his father release him, and Darian stumbles away, holding his sleeve to his face.

"Well?" Sulifer snarls.

A bit dazed, Darian drops to his knees and lowers his head. "Thank you, Father," he says miserably.

"Thank you for *what*?"

"For disciplining me in my youth. I hear and receive your admonishment." The words are rote, flat. He has said them many times, I suspect, and the feeling has long been sucked out of them.

"Get up," says Sulifer in disgust. "I can't stand to look at you, groveling like a peasant."

Darian rises silently, wiping his nose, as his father draws out the lamp. I cower inside, pulling in my senses, letting the room go dark. I want no part of this. I wish I were back in the cave. I wish Sulifer would call me forth and make his wishes and be done with me. What is he waiting for?

"Where is the thief?" Sulifer growls.

"In the dungeon, like you asked," replies Darian softly.

"Good," Sulifer grunts, his fingers drumming the side of the lamp. The sound is deafening, reverberating through me. "The boy shows more initiative and strength than you ever have."

"Let me have an hour with him. We'll see how his *strength* holds out," says Darian bitterly.

"Don't be base. We do not act out of such petty pursuits as revenge, as if we were common rabble. Now leave me and go search for Caspida. Look everywhere—she's a sly one, like her mother was. Do *not* fail me again."

"But—"

"Leave." The vizier's voice sinks to a sibilant whisper, and Darian slinks away.

Once his son is gone, Sulifer devotes his full attention to the lamp. He leans against a pillar and turns it over, like a man flirting before going in for a kiss, desire and triumph rolling off him in stifling waves.

"I have you at last," he sighs. "Let us meet face to face."

He rubs the lamp, slow and measured. I have no choice but to respond.

I pour from the lamp in a thin stream, spiraling and coiling my way to the floor, where I gather like a fine mist. I shift to cobra and rise, eyes glowering, until I am high as his waist, and then I shift again to girl, scales turning to skin, tail into legs, hood into hair. Black silk studded with diamond flecks drapes over my form, and I feel a weight on my hip, where Aladdin's ring rests in a hidden pocket. I dress myself with the night and stare at him with eyes as dark and hollow as the spaces between the stars.

"I am the jinni of the lamp," I intone. "Tell me your wishes three, that I may grant them and be rid of you."

His eyes feast on me. He takes his time replying, circling me while I stand rigid. As if to prove that I am real, he reaches out and strokes my hair, then trails his fingers down my cheek. I resist the urge to shudder, and when his fingers stray too close, I snap at them with tiger fangs, my teeth closing on empty air.

Quick as a striking snake he slaps me.

The pain is sharp but fades quickly. I shift at once to a black leopard, snarling and crouched. I cannot hurt him, but I spring anyway, all rage and fangs.

I am thrown back at once, before I ever touch him, skidding away across the floor to land in a heap against the wall. I lose my form, shifting to smoke in an effort to shed the pain that comes from the magical rebuff.

"I have read of your kind," says Sulifer, watching me pitilessly. "I know all about your vile tricks and treachery. Fiend of fire, hear me well: *I rule you*. Attempt to cross me and you will suffer for it."

"And I know of you." Re-forming into a girl, I narrow my eyes at him. "I know what you want. You dream of raising up the great Amulen Empire from the ashes of the past, when your people ruled all the lands from the east to the west. You want to be conqueror and emperor." I walk to his desk and spread my hands on his map, the parchment crinkling beneath my palms. Sulifer moves to stand behind me, watching with silent intensity.

"When Roshana ruled from the great city of Neruby," I say, "it was said no man could reach the edge of her dominion if he rode for a year and never stopped. There were more cities in her empire than there are stars in the sky." I turn to him. "I can give you anything in this world, Vizier. I can deliver you the nations. And I will do it gladly . . . if you'll only stop Aladdin's execution."

He laughs, a small, contained sound, but coming from him it seems the height of hilarity. "You'll help me whether you like it or not. I believe that's the whole *point* of you."

Bristling, I snatch the map and rip it in two, letting the pieces drift to the floor. "Then you're a fool! Say your wishes, and let's see how well they work out for you! I've destroyed smarter men than you with their own words."

His face hardens, put on guard by my threat.

"But if you free Aladdin," I say more gently, "I will not twist your wishes. I will serve you in both deed and spirit."

He pulls the chair from the desk and sits, his fingers strumming thoughtfully on his knee as he watches me. I stand, hands spread, waiting for his reply like the condemned awaiting her sentence.

"No," he says, and he gives me a small smile.

My hands curl into fists, and I grow as heavy as if I were made of marble, rooted to the ground. I can see no mercy, no room for bargaining in his eyes. I have known a thousand and one men like this, Habiba, and I know that he takes pleasure in my pain.

"Then make your wish," I say in a flat tone, my eyes half lidded.

He leans forward, his gaze fervent. "I wish for all the jinn to bow to me, calling me lord and obeying my every command."

Holding his breath, he waits, eyes glowing.

I almost want to laugh, but my spirit is still too heavy, so I simply sigh. "I told you I can give you anything in *this* world. The jinn are not of this world, and so they are not in my power to give."

Sulifer's face transforms. He is again the man who beat his son, who watched his niece defy him from her father's throne. His fury is a swelling wave, dark and deep, rushing like a juggernaut to shore. I can see it getting larger and nearer in his eyes.

And then the wave breaks.

He bursts from his chair, face red. He raises a hand to strike me, but I dance away, shifting to smoke and rendering him powerless to touch me. So instead, he grabs an inkwell from his desk and hurls it against the wall. Black, oily liquid splatters everywhere.

"You cannot subjugate the jinn," I say, re-forming behind him. "Do you think Nardukha would be so stupid as to let such things happen? You're hardly the first human to try it, and you won't be the last."

I get some small satisfaction from seeing his frustration. Sulifer sits back in his chair to stroke his beard. The wave of anger recedes, falling back into the sea, until once again he is still and cool.

"No matter," he says, a tremor still in his voice like an angry tic. "There are other ways."

He falls silent for a moment, his fingers tapping and his gaze distant as he thinks. Then he picks up the lamp and slams it onto the desk.

"Back inside, jinni. I need to think."

I am almost glad to return to my lamp. There I can sink into a fugue, trying to numb myself to the guilt and terror poisoning my spirit. He sits for some time by the light of a single candle, staring into the shadows and thinking hard.

Then, at last, he calls me out again. I hover before him, little more than a shadow myself, and wait.

"I wish to possess an army," he begins, "more numerous than the stars, invincible to any and all forces either of Ambadya or of this world, able to overcome any enemy, requiring no sleep, food, or water, and obedient to my every command."

Slowly my form solidifies, until I'm a girl in black robes, and I breathe in the magic of Sulifer's wish. His will is like water, patient and persistent, dark and cool. It fills me up until I am leaking with it.

His eyes glitter in the candlelight as I walk past him, toward the balcony adjoining his rooms. It looks out to the palace gardens and the dark hills to the north. This night is blacker than most, with no moon to grace the sky. But the stars are visible, perhaps brighter for the deepened darkness.

The vizier follows me out, watching closely, as if suspicious I will betray him. He need not worry. I will grant his wish, every word of it.

"There is only one thing more numerous than the stars," I say, looking up to the heavens. "And that is the darkness that holds them."

I open my hands, palms up, and let the magic flow through me. It spreads and grows and thickens, dark and quiet as oil flowing across glass. In the gardens, in the hills, on the walls around the palace, shapes take form. Shadows with the aspect of men, a hundred, a thousand, a million, more. They grow and then stand, staring around with eyes inky black. Wherever there is darkness, there stands a shadow man, gripping a shadow spear and a shadow shield. They are barely visible at all, for they are the night itself.

A guard patrolling the northern wall stops, blinking at the gloom, uncertain if his eyes are playing tricks on him. He waves the torch he carries, but the shadows only slip behind him.

Sulifer is watching him.

"I give you an army of shadows, O Master," I say to the vizier. Exhausted from the effort, I lean on the balcony rail. "And here is how you will call them. Once to summon, twice to dismiss."

I hold out a hand, and on it forms a black ram's horn hung on a strap of leather. Sulifer takes it, almost reverently. He runs his hands along its curling length, then puts the smaller end to his lips and blows. A deep, rich note sounds across the palace grounds, and the guards on the wall look around in confusion. At the call, all the shadow men turn and stare up at Sulifer, waiting.

"Give them a command," I say.

He licks his lips, then starts when a shadow man appears at his elbow. The vizier looks the soldier up and down and cannot help but smile.

"Kill that guard," he says, pointing at the man on the wall.

The shadow vanishes, and in less than a moment, a scream goes up below. The guard howls as a black spear cores him, then disappears, and he drops to his knees. His scream cuts off then, and he falls heavily.

Sulifer laughs.

"This is perfect!" he says. "This is—this is even better than the jinn!"

He turns to me, triumph bright in his eyes. "This is a force to conquer the world."

"Yes, O Master," I reply.

He turns back to the waiting shadows and blows his horn twice, and the shadow men vanish, sinking back into the darkness from which they were born. Twice more Sulifer summons and dismisses the shadow army, until he is satisfied no trickery is afoot.

"Well done, jinni," he says at last. I can see he is more pleased with himself than with me. He spent hours thinking of that wish, checking it for any cracks or loopholes.

I'll admit, it's a fairly solid wish, as wishes go.

Sulifer turns to go inside, and I linger, looking around at the shadows that wait to spring to the vizier's bidding.

When he commands me back to my lamp, I go with a bitter smile.

It is one hour before dawn and Aladdin's execution.

Sulifer is fast asleep, the lamp resting beside his pillow. I drift smokily inside it, indistinct, unhappy fog, until I suddenly hear footsteps in the room. Four guards stand at the entrance to his chambers, but these steps come from the direction of the window, below which is a three-story drop.

Curious, I stir and slide against the walls of the lamp, feeling for the intruder. The footsteps draw closer, soft and slow, and a thrill runs through me when I recognize Caspida. Perhaps all is not lost.

I let my sixth sense wash over her. Her hands are still decorated with her wedding henna, but she looks far from bridal. Her black waistcoat and leggings hug her athletic form, and there are blades of every size and shape tucked into her belt, shoes, and even her tight braid.

Moving carefully, she lifts the lamp. When the bond forms between us, I am stunned at how remarkably familiar it feels—so much like being bonded to you, Habiba. Caspida hovers a moment longer over her sleeping uncle, her free hand straying to a knife at her belt.

But then there is a knock at the door, and she freezes.

"Lord Vizier?" calls a voice. "It is nearly dawn, my lord."

She ghosts across the room, tucking herself behind the door as it slowly swings open. A guard pokes his head inside, and Caspida springs on him. She hooks an arm around his neck, plunging his head down to meet her rising knee. He drops, unconscious, and she drags him into the room. Sulifer stirs but does not wake.

Two more guards stand watch, and before they can shout out, Caspida drops one with a kick to his groin and a blow to his head, and the other with a blade across his throat. He sinks, blood running down his chest, and she steps over him, wiping scarlet specks from her cheek with a shaking hand.

Breathing a little harder, Caspida wraps the lamp in her cloak, ties the ends together, and slings it across her shoulders before heading out into the hall. She sets off, drawing her knife from her belt.

Faster and faster she moves, until she's running through the halls, making for the nearest exit. But then the creak of an opening door stops her short, and she sucks in a breath when Darian steps into the hall. He stiffens at the sight of the princess, and he looks around, his hand moving to his sheathed sword.

"Cas?"

"Hello, Darian."

"What are you doing here? I've orders to throw you in the dungeon. Cas, they're going to *execute* you!"

Caspida's forehead wrinkles. "Cousin, surely you don't believe these ridiculous accusations. I was fooled by Aladdin as much as anyone. More so, in fact. I agreed to *marry* the bastard. You think I don't want his head as much as you?"

He bites his lip as he studies her, his gaze conflicted. "Ever since we were kids, Cas, it was supposed to be you and me."

"I know," she groans, rubbing her temples. "I've been such an idiot. My first duty has always been to our people, Darian, and I thought I was fulfilling that." She lifts her eyes to meet his, and tears dangle from her kohl-lined lashes. "I can't expect you to forgive me, but I must beg it of you anyway. I've been monstrous to you."

"Cas..." He opens his arms and she runs to him, her body shaking. He embraces her tightly, one hand around her waist, the other caressing her hair. "Cas, it's all right. Look, I believe you. I know Father will too, once we have a chance to talk about it. Everything just happened so fast today, we panicked. And you *ran*. Why did you run? It only made things worse for you."

"Like you said, it all happened so fast." She lifts her face to look at him. "I panicked too."

"Oh, Cas." He wraps her in his arms and kisses her hair. "This is why you need me. Ruling is difficult enough for a man—a girl like you can't expect to carry this burden on your own."

"You're right," she says softly. Her hands run down his back, gentle and inviting. "I've been such a child. So naïve. No wonder I fell for the thief's lies."

"Marry me, Cas. Forget him."

She tenses. "You . . . you'd take me back? After everything I've done?"

He smiles and lifts her chin. "It wasn't your fault, love. He manipulated you. You were alone and afraid, and he offered you strength. Naturally you were drawn to that. But he was a lie, and I am the truth. Let *me* be your strength. Let *me* help you see through the deceptions. I can protect you, Cas."

He bends his neck and presses his lips against hers. Her eyes slide shut, and she melts into him.

"I love you, Cas," he whispers.

"I know," she says. "I'm sorry."

He pulls away, his brows drawing together. "What?"

"Oh, cousin." She cups his face in her hands, her eyes filled with pity. "You want so desperately to be loved. If you'd stop being an ass for five minutes, maybe someone could."

He begins coughing, and his legs weaken. He topples forward, and Caspida supports him.

"You *whore . . .*" he gasps.

"Sh. It'll go easier if you don't talk."

Darian's lips and fingernails are turning bluer by the second, and he fights to breathe. Caspida gently lowers him to the floor, stroking his hair and murmuring consolingly as he gags and twitches. She pulls a handkerchief from his pocket and wipes the rest of the creamy red crimsonleaf poultice from her lips. His eyes fix on her, wild and frightened.

"You'll pass out, then wake in an hour," she murmurs. "You'll have a terrible headache for days, but you'll live. I could have killed you, Darian. But we were friends once, you and I, so I'll give you this one chance." She kisses his forehead, then bolts upright when shouting breaks out down the corridor, from Sulifer's rooms. Dropping Darian, she flees.

Footsteps pound after her, and Sulifer's angry shouts ring out. Torchlight begins bouncing wildly on the walls behind and ahead. Caspida is trapped.

The princess skids to a halt, her braid whipping as she looks back and forth between the guards sprinting toward her. Then she runs to a window, kicking out the carved trellis covering the opening. She gets one leg over the casement as Sulifer, flanked by guards, runs into view and calls out, "Stop her!"

Caspida throws herself out the window.

Chapter Twenty-Four

WE'RE ON THE SECOND STORY, and her landing is painful. She hits the ground and rolls, but still the impact knocks the wind out of her and wrenches her ankle. Sucking in the pain, she is up and running by the time the guards reach the window.

Arrows slam into the ground around her. Caspida ducks and runs faster, hopping on her wounded ankle.

"Kill her if you must!" Sulifer yells. "She is a traitor!"

The palace grounds are extensive, thick with night guards and with little cover to shelter Caspida as she flees across the wide stretch of grass in front of the palace. A storm of shouts fills the air, and torches flare up along the outer wall, toward which she is sprinting. The lamp bounces on her back until I am quite dizzied.

Two guards intercept her, and the princess doesn't hesitate. She swings the cloak with the lamp inside, clouting one on the head—and sending sparks of pain dancing through me—while she uses the momentum of the swing to whirl into a kick. Her foot strikes the second guard's jaw and sends him reeling. Without waiting to finish him off, Caspida dashes the rest of the way, grimacing with pain.

When she reaches the wall, she clenches the cloak in her teeth and begins climbing, finding footholds in the eroded mortar between the bricks. Arrows stud the wall around her, striking sparks as they clash with the stone, before falling away. The walls are nearly as high as the palace, and her climb is perilous, but she continues doggedly on.

"Hand!" cries a voice from above. Khavar and Nessa are leaning over the top of the parapet, and they grab Caspida's hands and pull her up.

"Looks like it went smoothly," says Nessa, frowning at the oncoming wave of soldiers.

The guards posted on this section of the wall lie senseless, hands bound with their own belts. But farther down the walls, to the right and left, others are now charging our way.

"Cas, you all right?" asks Nessa.

"Let's just keep moving," says the princess stonily.

Khavar already has a rope tied around the rampart, and she throws it wide. Without waiting to check if it's secure, Caspida wraps the end of the cloak around her hands, grabs the rope, and slides down, planting her feet against the wall to slow her descent. The other girls follow.

Ensi and Raz are waiting below, furiously fending off a handful of guards. The air glitters with crimsonleaf powder, which Ensi slings in wide arcs. The quarters too close for Raz to use her bow, she makes do with a small curved scimitar.

"Hurry!" Ensi cries. "I'm running out!"

Caspida, Khavar, and Nessa drop to the ground in quick

succession, just as the one remaining guard reaches Ensi and raises his sword, poised to take off her head with one strike.

Moving in a blur, Caspida whips out a knife and throws it. The blade sinks into the man's shoulder with such force that he drops the sword and stumbles backward, screaming.

"Let's *go!*" Caspida yells.

The girls cut right and race along the outer wall. When guards take position above and begin firing arrows, they dive behind an abandoned cart of cabbages.

"What now?" cries Ensi.

"We have to go south, through the city," says Caspida.

"This is a disaster," moans Khavar. "Poor Gao is so stressed." She strokes the head of her snake, which emerges from her collar.

"Your *snake* is stressed?" hisses Nessa.

"Everyone quiet!" Caspida orders. "Get this cart moving. Stay low, and it'll block their shots."

The girls, still crouched, grab the side of the cart and begin rolling it forward. Arrows pound into the other side and sink into the cabbages with a wet sound very much like flesh. Bits of leafy greens rain down on their heads.

"Ugh," says Ensi. "I *hate* cabbage."

Caspida hazards a look over the cart, ducking swiftly when an arrow drives into the wall above her head. "Not much farther."

I have a sickening sense of where we are going, and trapped as I am, there is no way to plead my case, to make her see the truth. Panic begins pulsing through me. I swirl around and around, curling and twisting with dread. *Stop, please, let's talk, let's think this through, I can help you . . .*

The girls reach the wall separating the palace district from the common one and hurtle over it like a troupe of acrobats, dropping to the other side, oblivious to my cries.

Caspida glances up and down the wall. "They'll not stop here."

The city is waking as the girls hurry through the streets. Though the sun is still hidden, the sky is turning faintly lighter, and the smells of baking bread and brewing tea waft through the air. The girls are forced to slow their pace, to blend in to the early crowd of yawning commoners on their way to set up stalls in the market. Caspida leads the way, moving with familiarity along the alleys and side streets that bend crookedly between the looming buildings. The others keep a sharp eye out, all of them walking in a tight knot, still hidden in the predawn gloom by their dark clothing. Caspida ties the lamp to her belt so she can draw her cloak around herself, her hood low over her face.

"Guards to the left," murmurs Khavar. "Don't look, but they're coming this way."

"Have they seen us?" asks Caspida.

"Not yet. We should split up. They're looking for a group of girls. Separately we'd have a better chance."

But it's too late. The guards catch sight of them, shouting out and drawing their weapons. The Watchmaidens peel away in all directions, and the princess bolts into an alley. She ducks into a doorway, swiping aside the curtain covering it and overturning a stack of pots behind it, bursting in on a startled family sharing a loaf of stale bread. A baby in the room begins to cry. Caspida holds a finger to her lips, slipping into their midst, drawing her cloak tightly around herself and covering the lamp.

"Please," she whispers, dropping her hood. "Don't say anything."

The peasants stare at her, then cry out in alarm when a guard storms through the door. He looks around, and the people recoil, faces averted. Caspida lets her hair hang over her face, hiding her features. The guard lifts a lip as he looks around, then wordlessly steps out again.

Caspida stands and pulls her hood back over her face. "Thank you," she says. "I . . ."

She stares at the meager meal they are sharing, at the crying baby and the four skinny, half-starved children. "I'm so sorry. I will not forget you. I swear it."

She slips out the door and dashes back the way she'd come, wandering at random up and down streets, all the while gradually heading south. She is shaken and afraid, her breathing fast, her pulse racing. I can sense the clamminess of her skin.

Eventually she reaches the southern city gates, only to find the traffic going out has been reduced to a trickle as the guards question every person attempting to leave. Caspida stands uncertainly, tucked out of sight between a stall selling fig jam and a pair of men arguing over the price of a cart filled with fish.

After a short deliberation, the princess starts forward. The square in front of the gate is growing crowded with murky forms that seem to swim in the gloomy light. Several people carry torches, flickering beacons that circulate through the darkness. Voices, still hushed and yawning, murmur like a flowing current, into which Caspida dips and flows like a minnow. When she reaches the gate, she sidles up to a man holding the reins of a half dozen camels, waiting his turn to exit the city.

"What's going on?" she asks the drover.

He shrugs and scratches a sore on his cheek. "They're looking for someone, I'd guess."

She nods absently, then suddenly lashes out, cutting through the camels' ropes with a blade that she seems to conjure out of the air. As the drover cries out indignantly, she grabs a torch out of the hand of a startled spice vendor and waves it in the camels' faces. The animals bray in alarm and bolt, kicking and tossing their heads. Screams break out as people and stalls are knocked over, and the guards at the gate are distracted just long enough for Caspida to slip past them.

Outside the city, the princess breaks into a run. She barrels down the dusty street, dodging the incoming fishermen bringing up their first catches of the day, as shouting and cursing break out around the gate, where the spooked camels are causing a panic that spreads to the other animals in the area.

The road takes a sharp downward turn, zigzagging across the face of the cliffs to the beaches below, which glitter with the fires of the fishermen and their huts. Farther out, ships rest quietly in the bay, rocking back and forth on the incoming tide. Everything is still and quiet outside the city walls, waiting for dawn.

Caspida leaves the road and crosses the wide crest of land until she comes to where the cliff drops away, her boots and trousers turning damp from dew in the tall grass. She walks along the cliff's edge until the beach below dwindles and she is standing on the farthest point of land, staring out at the wide, wide sea. To her left, the horizon burns red, where the gods light their hearths in preparation for the day.

It is nearly dawn.

Aladdin is minutes from death.

My mind is filled with the last image I have of Aladdin: being dragged away to his death. Despair closes on me like the jaws of some great beast. Is he dead already? Would I feel it if he were? Even if he's still alive, even if there are a few minutes remaining to him, his last and only hope is standing on the edge of this cliff, too far away to do him any good, on the verge of destroying the one thing that could save him.

Perhaps I'd have a chance if I were free, but Nardukha is either taking his time or not coming at all. Even if he does fulfill his end of the bargain, it will be too late for Aladdin.

Caspida draws out the lamp, letting her hood fall back. A salty breeze rustles her hair. Far, far below, the black sea froths at the cliffs. I recoil inside the lamp, immobilized with dread.

Please, please just let me out. Let me speak, oh, just let me have one last chance!

If Caspida lets the sea take me, I will sink to its depths and likely rest there until the end of days. I have spent five hundred years sleeping in darkness. Five hundred more, and I will crack. I will split into a thousand pieces, and I will go mad.

I have known mad jinn. They are worse than monsters.

I begin to rage inside my lamp, throwing myself against the brass walls with the force of a stampeding bull. It will not make a difference to her. I could be a feather, I could be a lump of stone—the lamp would feel no lighter, no heavier. I could crash into one wall with all my force, but she would notice nothing. The interior of my prison is a pocket in the fabric of the universe. When I am in it, I am like a man with one foot on sand and one foot in water—neither here nor there, neither in this world nor out of it.

I have one hope.

Rub the lamp, I urge the princess. *Rub the lamp, rub the lamp, give me just one chance—*

The feel of the sea is stronger now; she must be holding me over the cliff, dangling me over the water. Any moment now and her fingers will release the lamp and I will fall and the waves and darkness and eternity and madness will suck me down, down, down—

All I need is a brush of finger on brass, the caress of palm . . .

Then I feel it: Caspida pulls back and rubs the lamp vigorously, her hands shaking.

I plunge out of the spout and pour downward. Below me is the dark sea and the white froth and the sharp rocks, crashing like a storm, hungry like a beast.

I quickly reverse direction and stream, scarlet smoke, over Caspida's hands and wrists. As I rise, my airy tendrils coalesce into hard, sleek scales, until I am a white snake with blue eyes coiling up her arm, fast as lightning. I slither over her shoulder and around her neck and, as I intended, she stumbles backward in horror, away from the edge.

I shift to a less threatening form: a soft gray kitten the size of her hand. I perch on her shoulder and mewl in her ear, so pitifully that the Blood King of Danien himself would have melted for a moment.

Caspida is tense as stone. She freezes, but her eyes watch me sidelong, her breath shallow. It seems she has been struck dumb by my escape.

"Zahra." A tremor weakens her voice.

Shifting again, this time to my usual human form, dressed in ethereal white silk that flutters in the ocean wind, I stand in front of her and meet her gaze.

"I am the Slave of the Lamp," I whisper. "The mighty Jinni of Ambadya. I hold the power to grant your desires thrice." She stares, eyes as cold as the northern sky, as the required ancient words fall from my lips. I feel the edge of the cliff beneath my heel; a few clumps of dirt come loose and tumble down. "Princess, why did you let me out? Why did you not drop the lamp?"

"I had to know." Her eyes harden. "You're *her*, aren't you? The monster who betrayed Roshana. You're what the ring led to, and the thief had you all along."

I look aside, at the eastern horizon, where the fires of dawn leap ever higher. Not much time. I envision a sword falling on Aladdin's neck, and I shudder.

"I was there when Roshana died, it is true." My voice is hard and clipped. There is no time for secrets, no time to pretend that the past does not have its hands locked around my throat. Aladdin will die if I cannot convince this princess to set aside five hundred years of hatred and fear.

"You killed her."

"I loved Roshana," I whisper. Unable to meet her gaze any longer—there is far too much of you in her, Habiba—I turn away and face the sea. "She was dearer to me than a sister. After more than three thousand years of slavery to cruel and selfish masters, I met your ancestress, the great Amulen queen. Not only clever and diplomatic but a fierce warrioress. Very like you, in fact. And unlike those countless masters who came before, she was *kind* to me. She saw not an enemy, not a monster, but a . . . a girl."

"Then tell me why you did it."

Bowing my head in submission, I draw a deep breath. "I had no choice. I didn't want to. When the king of the jinn learned how close Roshana and I had become, he came to punish us. We had broken the cardinal rule of Ambadya: that no jinni may love a human. There, on the summit of Mount Tissia, he commanded me to kill her—to strike down my dearest friend. I had no choice, for his power over me is absolute. I destroyed her, and then Nardukha sent his jinn to ravish the city of Neruby as a warning to all humans that his laws must be obeyed. But make no mistake: I can offer no excuses for what happened that day, for it was at my hand that Roshana met her fate. My love was her destruction."

Caspida stares at me, the lamp gripped tightly in her hands. It is then that I realize it's not Roshana's death she is trying to understand, but her mother's. I may not have killed her myself, but to Caspida, I may as well have.

"For five hundred years my sisterhood has passed down a sacred vow," says Caspida coldly, "to destroy the one who destroyed our queen. You know this, and you speak these words only to deceive me as you deceived her. You would have me believe that you are capable of love."

"Believe me when I say I wish that I were not!" Angrily I round on her. "I do not tell you this for myself! Aladdin will die any moment, and the only way to save him is if *you* make a wish! Please, Caspida—they will kill him at dawn!" I point at the horizon, where the sun is minutes away from rising. "Let me save him, I beg you!"

I drop to my knees before her, doing what I never thought I could: grovel before a human. My pride unravels into smoke, carried away on the wind. Always I have thought myself above these mortals—I, immortal, powerful, able to shift from this form to that. But I let all of that go now, and I beg as I have never begged before. "Do what you like with me after that, but just let me *save him*!" I dig my fingers into the earth, my eyes damp with tears. My voice falls to a cracked whisper. "Please."

"Why?"

I raise my face, finding her gaze unyielding. "Because it was my idea. Him wishing to be made a prince. Courting you. Lying all these weeks. I manipulated him and used him, and now they will kill him for it."

"Why would you lead him into the palace knowing that eventually the truth would come out and he would have to pay the price?"

"Because . . ." I grind my teeth together, wishing the earth would swallow me up. "Because I was trying to win my freedom. Your people had captured the prince of the jinn—Nardukha's own son. The Shaitan sent me to free him, and in turn, he would free me from my lamp. If I failed, he planned to sink your city into the sea. I had to get into the palace. Aladdin was my only way in."

"So you don't deny that you're a monster. You used him for your own ends."

I drop my head. "I know what I am. I know nothing can excuse what I did to Roshana, or to Aladdin, or to you. I've wronged so many, and there is so much I wish I could take back. I can't save Roshana. But please—I beg of you—let me save *him*."

Caspida lowers to her knees and studies me. I meet her gaze, humbled utterly.

"You want me to believe that you love him," she whispers.

"Yes." The word is but a breath, a stir of air in my treacherous lungs. "We're running out of time. I cannot reverse death or the hours. Time is the strongest magic, and no jinni—not even the Shaitan—can rewrite the past. Once Aladdin is gone, he is gone. Let me save him, and I can help you win your city."

She stares at me long and hard before shaking her head. "No," she says at last. "If I must rely on the magic of the jinn to deliver my people to me, then I don't deserve to rule them. I will not be the latest fool you trick."

She rises, her eyes hard, and I know nothing I can say will sway her. I plummet into despair, unable to move or think or breathe. This is it. Aladdin will die. I've killed him as surely I killed you, Habiba.

Caspida walks to the edge of the cliff, the lamp held in front of her. Her face is solemn, almost sorrowful, and I wonder if she has any regret for what she is about to do. I don't have the will or energy to stop her. I can only stare blankly at the grass as my spirit drains from me.

"Goodbye, Zahra," says the princess, and she pulls her arm back, preparing to throw the lamp.

"Do it, Princess," says a voice, "and I will tear your head from your shoulders."

Chapter Twenty-Five

I'M ON MY FEET IN A TRICE, throwing an arm out protectively across the princess, who lowers the lamp and stares.

Zhian stands just feet away, deceptively calm and well disguised in a human form, tall and darkly handsome, dressed in brilliant red robes that fade to black at the hems. They swirl around him, likely more his own doing than the wind's. Zhian has always been fond of dramatic entrances.

"Who are you?" Caspida demands, and I can sense the effort she puts into making her voice remain strong.

Without taking my eyes from him, I whisper over my shoulder, "It's Zhian. The jinn prince."

She inhales sharply, but doesn't flinch.

"Why are you here?" I ask Zhian.

He spreads his hands. "I bring good news, Zahra. I have been to Ambadya and back, and am here to tell you that my father is well pleased with you."

Catching my breath, I feel Caspida's eyes on me, narrow with suspicion. This isn't helping my case, to have the King of the Jinn bestowing his favor on me in front of her.

"Well?" I ask softly.

Zhian's mouth splits into a draconian smile. "He has agreed to grant you your freedom."

My spirit leaps. I take a half step forward, hardly believing the words. There may be a chance to save Aladdin yet.

"You're to come with me," Zhian continues. "Back to Ambadya. You'll receive your freedom before Nardukha's throne."

"No. It has to be here. It has to be *now*." I look to the horizon, where a brilliant line of gold burns ever brighter. We have minutes left, maybe seconds, before Aladdin's sentence is carried out.

"Don't be ungrateful," he growls. "Or you might inspire the Shaitan to have a change of heart."

"He has no heart," I spit. "Zhian, *you* must do it, this moment."

"You know I can't. You're being invited *home*, to freedom and to me!" He scowls, his eyes darkening.

I am pulled in two directions, my soul quailing in the face of the choice in front of me. How long have I waited for this moment, these words? Freedom is mine for the taking—but if I take it, I will lose Aladdin forever.

"I—I can't go yet. I have business to finish here."

His gaze flickers to the princess. "With *her*?"

I know then that he didn't overhear our conversation and that he still doesn't know about Aladdin. I turn slightly to whisper to Caspida, "Princess, I know you don't trust me, but you *must* believe me when I tell you this jinni will kill you. You have to make a wish. It's the only way I can protect you. Take us back to the palace before—"

"What's wrong with you?" interrupts Zhian, baring his teeth. He steps closer. "Zahra, this is the moment you've been waiting for. If you won't come willingly, I'll *make* you come. Give me the lamp, human!"

He makes a move toward Caspida, and the princess sucks in a breath and steps back, drawing her small blade. This only makes Zhian grin.

"And what will you do with that?" he says. "Prick me? I will crunch your bones and cast you to the ghuls for their sport."

"No," I murmur, stepping between them. "You won't touch her, or the lamp."

Zhian stiffens, his eyes flashing angrily. He looks from me to the princess, calculating, until at last a dark fury descends on his features.

"The boy," he murmurs. "The boy who had the lamp, the boy you argued with the night you found me in that jar."

He rushes forward suddenly and grabs my wrist, twisting my arm savagely. I grit my teeth and hiss at him but don't cry out. "Didn't you learn your lesson? Or will my father have to make you kill this one too?"

He wraps a hand around my jaw, lowering his face until his breath is hot on my cheeks. "You little fool. You could have been free, you could have been with me, but instead you betray your own nature for another human. How many of them will you destroy with these whims of yours? How many cities must burn? I recall the last human you thought to call friend, and I recall how my father had you strike her down." I feel Caspida gasp beside me as Zhian continues. "Yet you would commit the same crime *again*?"

I shift to smoke, and his hand closes on nothing, as I swirl around him and take shape again when I am out of reach. He turns away from Caspida. She still holds the lamp, and I throw her a pleading look. *Come on, Caspida. You must make a wish!*

"Do you realize what you'll lose," Zhian says, "if you do this?"

"Yes," I whisper.

Zhian holds out a hand, suddenly quiet. "Forget this boy, Zahra, and come with me. All will be made right. This doesn't have to end like last time."

Swallowing, I shut my eyes, my skin clammy. A part of me yearns to take his hand, to give in to him, to finally, *finally* seize my freedom. I can almost picture it, the greatest prize, the deepest desire of my phantom heart. It tempts me more than anything ever could.

I think of all the places I could go, the things I could do, with no one to command me. No one to shut me up in my lamp. What it would feel like to finally be in control of my own power.

To grant my *own* wishes.

"Would you really trade an eternity of freedom," Zhian says, and I open my eyes to meet his, "for a moment with this boy?"

If I choose Aladdin, the consequences will be disastrous. I've been down this road before. I haunted the ruins of your city, Habiba, for five hundred years, with the ghosts of those I condemned to die—all because I was stupid enough, arrogant enough, to believe I could love. Perhaps it would be better to go with Zhian now, for the sake of everyone in Parthenia.

The horizon burns like molten gold, and somewhere, Aladdin is being dragged from a cell. What must he be thinking? That I have abandoned him? And suddenly I realize: I never told him I love him. He must have said it to me a dozen times, but I was always too afraid to speak the words. I feared the consequences, wanted to postpone the inevitable—but now the moment has come, and I must choose. *Love or freedom?* A month ago I would have laughed to think I would feel such agony at the choice. But that was before Aladdin. That was before I knew the kind of freedom I felt just being with him.

"If you're not free to love," I whisper, "you're not free at all."

And suddenly I know.

I've known for days. Since I kissed Aladdin. Since we danced, our breaths held and our eyes locked. Since we lay in the grass, laughing in the sunlight at my miserable attempts at thievery. Every glance, every touch, every whisper between us has been a pebble added to the scales, tipping me toward a new direction. I don't know the exact moment I fell in love with Aladdin, but I know I am still falling.

And I never want to stop.

"I'm not going to Ambadya with you, Zhian," I say. "I'm staying here."

Zhian lets out a long, slow breath, his pupils dilating until his eyes are entirely black. His form changes, growing and sharpening, horns sprouting from his head and his feet hardening into hooves. His skin takes on a reddish tint, and smoke gathers around him. He is part man, part bull, part smoke.

Caspida gasps, and the sound catches Zhian's ear. He turns toward her, his eyes settling on the lamp.

"If you won't come by choice, sister," he growls, "then you will be dragged to the Shaitan's feet!"

"No!" I shout, springing and shifting all at once. With my abilities limited by the lamp, I can't take a shape to match his in strength, but I have to do something. I take tiger form, bounding across the grass and leaping to intercept him before he can strike Caspida. The princess bravely holds up her blade, ready to meet him, but it will hardly save her. Zhian is twice her size now and much, much deadlier.

I strike him in the chest, just enough to throw him off balance and block his blow.

"Caspida!" I growl. "I can't hold him off much longer!"

Zhian clouts me hard in the ribs, and I fly through the air and land hard on the grass, digging in my claws to spring back at him. Dirt flies everywhere as I bound toward the jinni, a snarl baring my fangs. He's ready when I spring, and he steps aside, batting me hard into the earth. I roll wildly toward the cliff's edge, barely saving myself from toppling over it. Zhian holds out a hand, a flame flickering to life above his palm. In moments, the flame swells into a writhing knot of fire.

This he hurls at me, and I throw myself wide as the flames explode where I'd been standing.

"*Caspida!*" I cry, shifting again, back into my human form. This time, I'm dressed in leather leggings and a cropped bandeau, my hands each gripping a long, curved sword. I run toward Zhian, and when he swings at me, I drop to my knees, skidding across the grass as I slice at his legs. He roars when one of the blades cuts his thigh. Smoke pours from the wound, which closes immediately.

He manifests a sword of his own, and I stagger in the attempt to block his strike. I parry once, twice, thrice, before his superior strength knocks both my swords from my hands and they dissolve into smoke. He lets his own evaporate, and he lunges for me, wrapping a massive hand around my throat and lifting me high, my feet dangling.

"All those years ago," he growls, "when my father was purging the Shaitan, eliminating all his rivals, I begged for your life. You would have been killed like all the others, but I told him you were different. I saved you, and this is how you repay me?"

I can't reply. He's crushing my throat. I start to shift, but he shakes me hard, making my head ring until I can't even think what to shift to. My vision turns dark, and I realize he isn't going to stop. He intends to kill me here and now.

But then a sudden prickle of energy races across my skin, and words penetrate the raging pain in my head, like soft feathers drifting through a storm.

"I wish for my Watchmaidens to be brought safely to me."

Caspida has made a wish. Not the wish I'd wanted to hear, but it's enough to grant me a thousand and one times more strength than I have on my own. I burst into smoke, swelling in a plume above Zhian's head. He snarls and whirls to Caspida, but she is not alone. Raz, Ensi, Nessa, and Khavar all stand around her, staggering a bit, their eyes wide with confusion and horror at the sight of the jinn prince. I pour onto the grass, back into human shape, and run to Caspida.

"What's going on?" cries Ensi, her hands in her powder pouches. "What by Imohel is *that*?"

Zhian draws himself up, his dark gaze fixed on me. "You know what happens next."

I nod.

"I will tell Nardukha of your treachery, and he will come. He will rouse from the depths of Ambadya and bring with him all his jinn, and we will destroy you, this boy, *and* this entire city."

"Go, then," says Caspida suddenly, stepping forward. She spits at the jinn prince. "Damn you, and damn all your kind. I am Queen Caspida of the Amulens, and I do not fear you. Bring your worst, because I will be waiting."

I touch her arm. "Princess, you don't have to—"

She shrugs me away and raises her sword toward Zhian. "This

war between our people has gone on far too long. Let it end today. Aladdin and Zahra are *my* citizens, and I will defend them to my last breath."

He snarls, tensing as if to spring at us, but Caspida whirls and cries, "Now, Nessa!"

As Zhian lunges, the jinn charmer pulls out her flute and begins to play, the music stopping him dead. I conjure a thick turban for myself, covering my ears and blocking the sound. Her music holds Zhian enthralled, his mouth slack and his eyes dull. Her hands tremble, but she doesn't miss a note.

"Caspida, dawn will break at any moment," I say.

She tears her eyes from Zhian and stares at me as if she hasn't heard.

"They'll kill Aladdin. *Please*—"

"All right," she mouths, her words muffled through my turban. "I believe you, Zahra. You aren't responsible for Roshana's death. The Shaitan is. And you truly love the thief. You would even surrender your freedom for his sake."

"Don't let it be in vain," I plead.

She nods and looks around at her girls, who still look shocked at their sudden change in circumstances. But they meet her gaze solemnly, staunchly loyal.

Turning back to me, Caspida reaches out and grasps my hand, as if the monstrous son of the Shaitan were not looming over us, his mind enchanted by the notes coiling around us. The princess's eyes catch and hold the fires of dawn as she speaks.

"I wish to save Aladdin's life."

Chapter Twenty-Six

THE SIX OF US VANISH from the cliffs in a swirl of smoke, and Nessa's playing ceases. I just have time to glimpse Zhian shifting to smoke and racing toward Mount Tissia and the alomb atop it, to return to Ambadya.

We do not have much time.

The crest of the sun rises from the sea just as the girls and I appear on the steps leading up to the palace. At the top, Aladdin is on his knees, struggling against the guards who are shoving his head down, one of them lifting a sword. The sight sends a spasm of horror racketing through me, and as Caspida and the Watchmaidens stumble, disoriented, I spring into motion. The power of the princess's wish still courses through me, silver-bright as the moon, and I shape it instinctively. I stride quickly up the steps toward the executioners, throwing out a hand.

Tigers of smoke and wind materialize behind the soldiers around Aladdin. The men cry out in shock and terror as the phantom beasts spring, tackling them to the ground and dragging them away from the thief. Swords and lances clatter on the stones. When their job is done, the tigers evaporate into the air. With a snap, I release the rest of the remaining magic, and thick vines burst from the ground and tether the soldiers down, pinning their arms at their sides.

There is no longer any point in hiding what I am. And so I ascend the stair in a gown of red smoke and silk, long and fluttering and coiling, driven by a singleness of purpose and a clarity of thought that I have not felt in a very long time. I have lost my last and only chance at freedom, and I regret nothing. The ring I made for Aladdin disappears from my pocket and reforms on my finger, glinting in the dawn.

Aladdin rises, using a fallen sword to cut the rope binding his wrists. His eyes widen, and when I reach him, I don't hesitate.

I throw my arms around him and kiss him deeply, pouring all the fear, despair, and hope of the last day into that touch. He responds at once, one hand on my back, pressing me to him, the other in my hair. His lips are urgent and intense, and I feel his own fear and relief, the adrenaline coursing through him.

When we break apart, he rests his forehead against mine and laughs hoarsely.

"If I am dead," he murmurs, "then let them kill me a thousand times, just so I can be greeted like that on the other side."

"I thought I'd lost you."

"Thought I'd lost me too. But you came."

"I had help." Pulling reluctantly away, I look to Caspida and the Watchmaidens, who are running up the steps.

"Trouble!" Ensi warns, pointing behind us, and we turn to see more soldiers gathering outside the palace.

Caspida curses. "They know we're here."

The soldiers are getting closer, their spears flashing in the dawn light. The Watchmaidens brace themselves, looking small and delicate in the wave of men rushing toward them, until a barrage of arrows is suddenly loosed from a row of archers to the left. We retreat down the steps and behind a low stone wall as the arrows clatter on the stair where we'd been standing. The sound of shouting and clanging weapons gets louder as the men draw nearer. Raz leans around the wall, firing arrows and holding the soldiers at bay for a few moments.

"Sulifer has the entire army and the Eristrati under his control," says Nessa. "We won't even make it to the doors!"

"Wish for the city," I say urgently, "and I will deliver it to you! Caspida, you *must* see that this is the only way!"

"I can't!" she shouts, her composure cracking as she meets my eyes. "Don't you understand? If I use jinn magic to fight Sulifer, then I'm no better than he is! Then I'm no queen at all!"

"But we have no army," says Nessa gently.

"Your Highness," says Aladdin suddenly, "you don't *need* an army."

She gives him a questioning look, and he turns and waves a hand at the city spread below.

"You have the *people*. They've been waiting for months for the Phoenix to give the signal. They will follow you anywhere!"

Caspida's eyes brighten a little, but then she shakes her head. "I can't ask them to fight my battle for me, not against armed and trained men."

"This isn't just your battle," Aladdin replies. "This has been our fight for years. It's our families Sulifer has been tearing apart, our lives he has crushed. We've only been waiting for the right person to lead us, and here you are. They wear your colors, paint your sigil on the walls. Maybe you didn't set out to create a revolution, but the revolution has been waiting for years for the right spark. Let us fight, and we will all take back our city together."

Caspida looks around at her girls, and they all nod. To Aladdin, she opens a hand in assent. "Go, then. May Imohel grant you speed."

His eyes burn with purpose, and he begins slipping away, squeezing my hand before letting go.

"I'll bring help," he says. "Hold them off as long as you can."

And then he's gone, dashing down the stair and dodging the few arrows fired after him. I stare in disbelief, unable to bear seeing him disappear after only just getting him back. But Caspida still holds the lamp, and I cannot follow.

"I'm out," says Raz, throwing down her bow and dropping her empty quiver. "They're coming."

"Watchmaidens," says the princess, looking at each of her girls in turn, her gaze finally settling on me. "Are you with me?"

Khavar, her snake coiled tightly on her forearm, draws a short dagger and licks the blade, her eyes glinting with a feral light. "In victory or death, I will be at your side, sister."

"And I," the others echo.

"And I," I murmur, and they glance at me, surprised. I lock gazes with Caspida. "If you won't wish for the city, then let me fight with you." Slowly, my silk robes harden into shining battle armor, and twin swords appear behind my shoulders.

Caspida secures the lamp on her belt and nods. She grasps my hand, her pulse pounding through me like a battle drum. "In victory or death, jinni."

With that, she stands, and we rise behind her.

There are about twenty soldiers marching toward us, all lancers.

They are too near us now for the archers to continue firing without hitting their own men.

Caspida leaps onto the low wall and cries out, "Men of Parthenia! I am your true queen! Stand down, or be found guilty of treason!"

The men exchange glances but don't stop advancing.

With a heavy sigh, the princess twirls her knives, then nods to us. We charge from behind the wall, the Watchmaidens calling out in ululating tones like the wild mountain warriors of old.

Ensi takes the lead, laughing madly, and the Watchmaidens draw their veils over their faces as she slings the first handful of blue powder. It hits three soldiers, blinding them, and they scream and drop their weapons to claw at their eyes. Ensi launches herself off the ground, flipping over their fallen forms to sling more powder at the next row of men.

Then the rest of us clash with the soldiers, steel ringing against steel. I stand back-to-back with Nessa, my ears roaring with the sound of battle. We fall into a rhythm, parrying, slashing, dodging lances. I keep glancing at the steps, hoping to see Aladdin leading in reinforcements, until the soldiers close in on us and I'm forced to focus on fighting.

The Watchmaidens are cunning, and they draw the soldiers apart. Any one of the girls is the match of two soldiers, but we are outnumbered nearly four to one, and more soldiers will doubtless arrive any moment once Sulifer learns we are here.

A man swipes at my legs with his spear, trying to trip me, and I leap over it and spin, my sword catching his arm and forcing him to drop the weapon. He lands on his knees, white with pain, and I knock him unconscious with the hilt of my sword. With a moment to breathe, I look around and see we are being pressed back, their numbers proving too strong. More soldiers come running in from our left, and I hear Sulifer shouting above them:

"Kill the traitor queen! Bring me the lamp!"

I drop my hands and shut my eyes, letting myself dissolve into the wind, scarlet smoke. I swell and expand, filling the wide avenue and obscuring the soldiers' vision. The new arrivals skid to a halt, confused and disoriented, slashing blindly in the fog.

"Fall back!" Caspida cries. "To me!"

The Watchmaidens follow the sound of her voice, and I cover them as they retreat behind the wall. While the girls catch their breath, the soldiers advance from the palace, their ranks swelling with black-clad Eristrati. They press on slowly, blinded by my smoke but driven onward by Sulifer's commands. I withdraw to join the princess, shifting back into my human form.

"They are nearly upon us," I say. "Thirty, forty, perhaps fifty of them, and more coming. We won't last five minutes."

Above us, the sky is growing darker despite the sun rising. Black clouds gather near the summit of Mount Tissia, and I know that Zhian has reached Nardukha, and that our time grows thin. I watch the mountain anxiously, knowing the real battle waits at its peak.

"We have no choice," murmurs the princess, drawing me back to the battle at hand. "Sisters, I am sorry I have led you to this."

"We would have it no other way," says Nessa, and the others nod and grasp hands.

"If we're to die," says Raz, "let us die fighting."

At that moment, a shout turns our heads.

"For the Phoenix Queen!" the cry goes up. "For the people!"

Aladdin appears, running down the street, carrying a sword he got from who knows where. Behind him, a horde of people are racing, gripping knives and scythes, staves and camel whips.

Butchers, carpet sellers, fishmongers, housewives, Parthenians of every age, size, and trade, men and women both, raise up a mighty shout.

"For the Phoenix Queen!"

"For the people!"

And even a few scattered cries of "For the Tailor's Son!"

They all wear red armbands, and someone waves a huge banner with a phoenix sigil on it, likely stolen from a temple to Nykora, the phoenix goddess. Aladdin whoops and cheers them on and whistles when he catches sight of us. He's flanked by Dal and Balak, the girl and the doorman from the Rings.

Behind us, the soldiers falter, realizing their numbers are not so great, not when faced with the people they've oppressed, cheated, and enslaved for years.

Somewhere toward the palace, Sulifer is screaming, "Fight, you fools! They're only peasants with sticks!"

But many of those sticks are sharpened or on fire, and someone hurls a flaming brand at the soldiers. It lands harmlessly in front of them, scattering embers, but it breaks the courage of the armed men. They retreat, but not quickly enough.

Aladdin reaches me just as the fighting breaks out. He is laughing wildly, throwing his head back and crowing. Leaping up onto the wall, he pulls me after him, waving his sword like a madman.

"As soon as I told them who the Phoenix really was, that she needed our help, they dropped everything!" he says. "Look at them! They're fantastic!"

"And look at you," I reply, smiling. "The revolution of one. Whatever happened to not fighting for lost causes?"

"I guess I found a cause worth fighting for," he murmurs, leaning in for a kiss, but then his eyes fix on something behind me, and his face hardens. I turn to see Caspida standing near the palace below a second-story balcony, her sword upraised and her Watchmaidens surrounding her. Above her, Sulifer leans over the railing, his eyes furious.

"He won't even come down and fight," Aladdin growls. "The coward."

"Come on." Grabbing Aladdin's hand, I plunge through the battle, dodging spear and sword, until we reach Caspida's side.

"Come down, Uncle!" the princess calls. "It is finished!"

"You think some rabble with kitchen knives makes you a queen?" he returns.

Caspida glances back at the people, fighting tooth and nail against the better-equipped soldiers. To her uncle she replies, "They're *exactly* what makes me a queen."

"Then let's see how they fare against my *real* army." He pulls from his cloak the black ram's horn I made for him last night. Caspida frowns uneasily.

"What is he doing?" she asks.

"Just watch," I murmur.

Sulifer raises the horn to his lips and sounds the call. It rings across the grounds as the vizier lowers the horn and its blast echoes away. Caspida is very still, her hand clenching the hilt of her dagger.

Behind us, the men and women continue fighting, the peasants moving in packs like wolves. More of them flood in from the city, until the noise is deafening. Sulifer sounds another blast, but it is nearly drowned out by the fight. He lowers the horn, his eyes settling on me, demanding an explanation.

I lift my chin and stare defiantly at him. "Even the darkest shadow may not stand before the light of the sun," I shout. "Every child knows this."

"You have broken the rules!" he shouts. "I said, 'invincible to any and all forces either of Ambadya or of this world'!"

"The sun is not of this world. It belongs to the heavens and to the gods. Your shadow men will not come, not until night."

"Surrender, Uncle!" Caspida calls. "Let no more die today! We can talk and settle this between us!"

He only snarls in reply and turns to disappear inside the palace. Caspida starts toward the doors, intending to pursue him, but I catch her arm.

"Princess, we have a bigger problem."

"What?"

I point to Mount Tissia. Above its summit, dark clouds swirl and thunder, heralding the coming jinn. They give the mountain the appearance of an erupting volcano. "The Shaitan will be here any moment."

Caspida pales. "I thought we had more time."

"You have your fight here," I say. "Let me handle Nardukha. Use your last wish to send me and Aladdin to Mount Tissia. It's us he wants. If we don't meet him there, he will come down on this city with the full force of Ambadya, and nothing will stop him then."

"I can come with you."

I shake my head. "This is where you belong, with your people."

She looks around at the chaos, the housewives and butchers, fishermen and beggars, many armed with nothing but bare fists against the organized Eristrati and palace guard. Caspida's eyes flood with pride and sorrow.

"You're right," she says, meeting my gaze. "But Zahra, you *must* stop him. We cannot become another Neruby."

I nod grimly and take Aladdin's hand. He smiles, but I see the worry in his eyes. My skin flushes with shame. If only there were some way to keep him out of this, to face Nardukha on my own. But the Shaitan would tear Parthenia apart stone by stone to find the thief. The least we can hope for is that he will spare the city and its people.

"I'm sorry," I whisper. "Aladdin, I don't know what will happen on that mountain. I don't know if we can—"

"Have faith, Smoky," he says softly, cupping my face in his palm, "This isn't over yet. Whatever happens, we'll be together."

Caspida takes the lamp from her belt, as her Watchmaidens tighten their perimeter around us. The soldiers are regrouping, and half a dozen of them come charging toward the princess. Anxious knots twist in my stomach as they clash with the Watchmaidens, who barely hold their ground against the larger, stronger men.

"Hurry, Caspida!" I urge.

She nods and holds the lamp between us, her eyes meeting mine.

"I wish for you, Zahra of the Lamp, and you, Aladdin of Parthenia, to go with all speed to the summit of Mount Tissia, and there defend us all from the Shaitan and his jinn."

At that moment the soldiers break through the Watchmaidens' defense. Caspida whirls, drawing her sword, and throws the lamp toward Aladdin. He catches it, and the familiar bond forms between us once more.

I am filled with Caspida's wish, golden swirls of glittering magic racing along my skin. But still I hesitate, looking around at the soldiers closing in on Caspida and her girls. They fight wildly, hair flying, steel glinting, Ensi's poisoned powders shimmering in the sunlight. An Eristrati, wielding an Eskarr scimitar, makes a dash for me, his blade lifted. Aladdin moves like lightning, throwing himself in front of me and tackling the man, heedless of the weapon. He punches the man once in the jaw before the Eristrati throws him wide and leaps to his feet, his scimitar falling toward Aladdin's neck. But the man freezes, gasping, when Caspida's blade drives through his back.

"Go!" she shouts, blood streaked across her face, as she helps Aladdin to his feet. "This is our fight! Yours is on that mountain—so get out of here!"

She shoves Aladdin toward me, and he grabs my hand. I ache with magic, no longer able to resist the pull of Caspida's third wish. Leaving her to her battle, I pull Aladdin close and draw a screen of red smoke around us. Our clothes fluttering, we hold tight to one another and lock eyes as the world spins around us.

The chaotic roar of the fight fades away, replaced by a deafening rush of wind. Aladdin crushes me against his chest, his arms wrapped tightly around me, and he presses his lips to my forehead.

"Together," he whispers. "No matter what."

I cling to him with all my strength, sighing a little as the last of the magic drains away.

Everything stops. The smoke falls away and dissipates. I let him hold me a moment longer before I pull away and draw a deep breath.

Here I stand once more, right where everything began, on the stony, chilly peak of Mount Tissia. Around us, the summit stretches wide before dropping away, the ground a series of stony plateaus. No plants or animals are to be found here, where the wind is sharp as knives, gusting around us with an eerie howl. Swirling clouds gather above and below the peak, obscuring the lands in every direction, until it seems we stand utterly apart from the world.

The alomb rises ahead, a massive structure built in the days when the gods walked the earth. Four corner pillars support a vaulting roof of black stone coursed with glowing blue veins, an ancient magic far more powerful than I could ever wield. It was quarried from the rock that once supported the great isle of Phaex, where the gods feasted every summer solstice, and which sank into the sea many ages ago. Once a doorway to either the godlands or Ambadya, now only the jinn use it, for the path to the gods has long been lost.

In the center of the alomb stands the doorway itself, a perfectly round, seamless ring of stone. There are twelve such doorways in the world, each named for a different god. This one is known as the Eye of Jaal. Two massive buttresses carved in the likenesses of kneeling men frame either side, the sides of the ring supported on their backs.

Usually the doorway sits empty and silent, but now a tunnel of fire swirls and flashes inside, creating a path to the world of the jinn. Blue and red and green the fires burn, hotter than any mortal flame, enough to turn a man from flesh to ashes in a heartbeat. From the Eye wafts the scent of sulfur and smoke.

And then there are the jinn. They crouch all around us, hover in the air, some seen, some unseen. Ghuls and maarids, ifreet and sila. They are silent as death, watching with golden eyes. Many bare their teeth, silently hissing, making their hatred for me quite clear. To them, I am the ultimate traitor.

Aladdin puts an arm around me, as if to guard me against the horde of jinn.

"You know we don't stand a chance," I whisper.

Aladdin looks down at me, his hand squeezing my arm. "We're still alive, aren't we? Come on, Smoky. Where's your sense of adventure?"

But his attempt to lighten the mood falls short, and he tightens his grip on the lamp.

When a figure appears in the tunnel of fire, my breath stops. A rustle passes through the jinn, and they shift and whisper as the figure steps through, planting a foot on the stone.

It is Zhian, half man, half beast. He wears black robes, his head horned and his arms scaled armor, as if in anticipation of battle. His gaze rakes over us, lingering a bit on Aladdin, all fury and fire.

"You're just in time," he says, deceptively calm.

He turns slowly to face the Eye, giving us a view of his muscled back and his long black braid. He lifts his arms and clenches his fists, the veins in his arms standing rigid.

Around us, the jinn begin slowly pounding the stone, a slow, measured beat that echoes through the alomb. It sends a chill up my spine. Their whispers come next, a voice with a thousand and one tongues.

He is coming!

He is coming!

Aladdin gathers me into his arms, and I shrink into him, sick with dread. The pounding of the jinn begins to grow faster and louder, and the wind generated by the sila whips around us, tugging and pushing.

He is coming!

He is coming!

Zhian drops to his knees, stretching his hands out in front of him. All eyes are fixed on the doorway, on that hypnotizing tunnel of flame that seems to stretch into infinity. The heat intensifies. I can feel Aladdin's pulse racing through our clasped hands, but he doesn't waver.

Soon the jinn's pounding becomes deafening, and then—all at once—everything stops. The noise. The wind.

Then we are thrown flat by a massive ripple of air that pulses outward from the doorway, rolling like thunder. A hot, sulfuric wind with the strength of a tidal wave pours from the Eye, pressing us down.

In the flames a shadow appears, tall as three men, horn and darkness, fire and smoke. Two eyes like coals flicker and form, centered on pupils of utter black. I sit up slowly and fight the wind, working my way to my feet and drawing Aladdin up with me.

The figure steps through the fire, plants one massive foot on the floor of the alomb. Then he lets out a soft, rumbling laugh, a sound that is all breath and wind, yet somehow manages to be deafening. That laugh sends a cold chill crackling down my spine.

Nardukha has come.

Three: The Jinni

At last, when the dust settled, the Queen and the Jinni stood on the mountaintop and looked down on the battlefield and the bodies spread like leaves across the desert. The Queen fell to her knees, wearied and wounded, and her sword dropped from her hand. Before her, the doorway to Ambadya burned with fires of every color.

"All I wanted," said the Queen, "was peace between our peoples. But I see now that this is not possible, for my people are ruled by a dreamer, and the jinn are ruled by a monster. My only consolation is that thou art by my side, my Jinni. I would die in the company of a friend, and give thee my final breath. For I have one wish remaining, and it is for thy freedom, yea, even at the cost of mine own life."

At this the Jinni shook her head, replying, "Nay, my queen. The time for wishing is passed. For here is the Shaitan, Lord of all Jinn and King of Ambadya."

And even as she spoke, the fires in the doorway rose higher, and through them stepped Nardukha the Shaitan, terrible to behold.

"O impudent woman," said the Shaitan, looking down at the Queen. "Wouldst thou dare make the Forbidden Wish?"

"I would," she replied. "For I fear thee not."

"Then thou art a fool."

As the Queen's heart turned to ashes, realizing her doom was upon her, the Shaitan turned to the Jinni and said, "Dost thou recall the first rule of thy kinsmen, Jinni?"

And the Jinni replied, "Love no human."

"And hast thou kept this commandment?"

"Lord, I have." And up she rose, as the Queen cried out in dismay.

"Are not we like sisters?" asked the Queen. "Of one heart and one spirit?"

And the Jinni replied, "Nay, for I am a creature of Ambadya, and thus is my nature deceitful and treacherous. My Lord has come at last, and I would do all that he commands."

The Shaitan, looking on with approval, said to the Jinni, "This human girl is proud and foolish, thinking she could rule both men and jinn. I am well pleased with thee, my servant, who hast brought her to me. Slay the queen and prove thy loyalty to thy king."

And the Jinni grinned, and in her eyes rose a fire. "With pleasure, my Lord."

Then, with a wicked laugh, she struck down the good and

noble Queen, the mightiest and wisest of all the Amulen monarchs, whose only mistake was that she had dared to love a Jinni.

—From the *Song of the Fall of Roshana,*
Last Queen of Neruby
by Parys zai Moura,
Watchmaiden and Scribe to Queen Roshana

Chapter Twenty-Seven

HAND IN HAND, Aladdin and I stand before the Shaitan. Beneath Nardukha's primal gaze, all I want to do is cower and flee, but I focus instead on Aladdin's pulse in my palm.

"Nardukha." I lift my chin, meeting his black eyes.

The Shaitan is old, older even than the race of men. He was one of the first creatures ever formed by the gods, long ago when Ambadya was lush and beautiful. Looking in his gaze now, I find nothing remotely human. No emotion, no pity. He is more a force of nature than a living being, like a walking volcano. Rarely does he set foot in this world at all—and never do his visits result in anything other than catastrophe.

He looks down slowly, his eyes shifting from me to Aladdin. Then, with a sound like thunder, a black pillar of smoke envelops him. When it falls away, Nardukha stands not much taller than us, vaguely human in form. His skin is black and charred, cracking at the joints to reveal lava-red muscle beneath. His robes are smoke and silk, and instead of hair he has two curling horns protruding from his elongated skull.

He is a walking nightmare.

"The-Girl-Who-Gives-the-Stars-Away," he murmurs. His voice is soft and beautiful, clear as a crystal and sweet as honey. I guard myself against the dangerous allure in that voice. "Curl-of-the-Tiger's-Tail. What have you done?"

"I freed Zhian," I say, drawing his attention back to me. "I kept my part of the deal. But you were never going to grant me freedom, were you? It was all a lie."

"You were to be freed from your lamp, just like he promised," Zhian cuts in, rising to face us. Fury rages in his eyes.

"And then what?" I snap, my gaze still locked on Nardukha's. "Be killed?"

"Be joined to me," says Zhian. "As you were always meant to be."

I know what he means, the ceremony the jinn perform like some kind of perverted wedding. I would have been bound to Zhian in every way, unable to disobey his commands. It is similar to the bond Nardukha holds over all jinn, and the thought of being made slave to Zhian in this way is repulsive. Once more, another of Nardukha's "deals" has turned out to be nothing but a trick. Last time, Ghedda paid the price of my foolish hopes. Now it will be Aladdin who suffers.

"I would rather be bound to my lamp than be bound to you," I snarl.

Zhian opens his mouth to reply but falls silent at a look from the Shaitan. Nardukha circles me and Aladdin, his train of smoke coiling around us.

"My beautiful jinni," he murmurs. His voice is wind on hot coals, sparking and sighing. "More powerful than any other, made of fire and water, of earth and air. Why have you defied me?"

The horde of jinn raise a chatter, like the hissing and clicking of cockroaches, that rustles through the air. Nardukha silences them with a single uplifted hand.

"Why does it matter so much to you?" I ask. "What are you so afraid of?"

But even as I say it, the answer hits me like a dash of icy water. Nardukha fears the Forbidden Wish.

It is the one wish he cannot stop from happening, because the magic behind it is older, older even than he. It is a power far greater than any the Shaitan could wield. And love, love makes people do stupid things, like sacrifice themselves for one another. Nardukha fears love because he fears it will lead to the Forbidden Wish and my freedom.

For the first time, I realize I might be strong enough to defeat him.

If I were to let Aladdin make the wish, giving his life in exchange for mine, perhaps I *could* defeat Nardukha then.

But I already know I won't let that happen. The price is not one I am willing to pay.

"You have broken the first rule of the jinn," rumbles the Shaitan, his voice dangerously low. He stops in front of me. "And you must be punished."

Before I can say another word, his hand wraps around my arm.

"Let her go!" shouts Aladdin, grabbing Nardukha's arm and hissing when the Shaitan's skin burns his hand. Zhian steps forward and easily knocks Aladdin to the ground, and Aladdin's head strikes the stone hard. Smirking, Zhian pulls the lamp away from the thief. The bond between Aladdin and me unravels, and I'm left suspended, neither confined to my lamp nor bonded to a new master, for my wish-granting power is meant only for humans, not jinn. At least that's something to be grateful for. I don't have to feel Zhian's will invading my own.

"Zahra is *mine*, boy," Nardukha says. "I created her. And in my benevolence, I allow you dismal creatures to borrow her. But as always, you grow greedy."

"She doesn't belong to you," Aladdin declares, rising to his feet, his temple bleeding. "She belongs to no one."

"You think you love her? You can't even *comprehend* her." Nardukha's voice turns me cold. He eyes me, snakelike, his hand searing my skin. I dread the calculation in his black stare. Looking at him, I realize how futile any struggle is. He will win. He will *always* win. Against him, I have nothing more to wield than empty defiance. I will die today, and Aladdin will die with me. I have loved him to his death, just as I did you, Habiba. This has been the great lesson of my long life: To love is to destroy.

With a look of disgust, the Shaitan throws me down, and I land hard on my knees. I can tell Nardukha is growing bored. He is not one for long conversations. His punishment is always swift and absolute. I turn to Aladdin, my body going numb, my chest emptier than ever.

"I'm sorry," I whisper.

He takes my face in his hands. "I'm not. I'm not sorry I met you. I'm not sorry I fell in love with you. I have no regrets, Zahra, and neither should you. I love you."

A blast of pain cuts through me, and suddenly Aladdin and I

are ripped apart and thrown wide by a burst of angry power from the Shaitan. He steps between us, bristling, and hauls me upright with a hand around my throat.

"Enough," he growls, his honeyed voice turning to stone. "Before I rip you apart, I will in my mercy allow you to repent. You will show me your allegiance, and you will beg for forgiveness."

His words begin to swell with power as he draws magic to himself, leaching it from stone and sky, from fire and flesh. Energy streams from the world and coils about him, and I tremble as he releases me, my hand going to my aching throat. I know what comes next. I have seen him draw in power like this before. I know what words he will speak even before he says them, but still they strike like a battle-axe, relentless and final.

"Kill the boy."

With the words he unleashes the power he has knitted around himself, and the force of it washes over me in a wave. I sway on my feet, gasping out, "*No.*"

"*Kill. Him.*" Each word is a hammer against my temple, pounding me into submission, compelling me to obey. The compulsion is stronger even than a wish, for it is a different kind of magic, pulling on the bond between jinni and maker.

I whirl to Aladdin, eyes wide, my heart of smoke bursting into sharp fragments. Nardukha's command drags at my every fiber. It whispers through my thoughts, muddling my mind.

Kill him.

Yes, that is what I want.

No! It's not! You love him!

But I want to kill him.

No, you don't! Get control of yourself, Zahra!

My name isn't Zahra. I am Smoke-on-the-Wind, Curl-of-the-Tiger's-Tail, Girl-Who-Gives-the-Stars-Away.

He loves you!

He is just a mortal. Just a boy, a moment in time that will soon pass.

His name is Aladdin.

I have known a thousand and one like him. I will know a thousand and one more. He is nothing.

He is everything.

"Zahra?"

My legs shift to smoke. My eyes turn to fire. I rise, hands held out, fingers crackling with lightning. It sizzles up my arms, singeing my false skin. I am no human. I am jinni, the most powerful of all Nardukha's children, exalted above all the hosts of Ambadya.

"Tremble, mortal," I intone in a thousand and one voices. "I am the Slave of the Lamp."

"No!" The boy's hair whips around his face as the wind of my breath swirls around him. "Your name is Zahra!"

Above the alomb, clouds roll and multiply, flashing with lightning. A hot, sticky wind howls through the columns, and in the wind are the jinn, and the jinn are laughing.

"Zahra!" The boy holds up a hand, trying to block the sand that stings his eyes. "I know you can hear me! Stop this! You're stronger than this!"

I shift my eyes to my master, who stands glorious and shining as a god. He smiles at me, and I bask in his approval.

Kill him.

"I love you," whispers the boy, his words reaching me improbably through the howling wind and the crackling fire. "I love you. Do you hear me? I love you. No matter what."

Kill him.

I stretch my hands toward him, preparing to launch the lightning that sizzles across my fingers, biting me like a thousand and one angry snakes.

KILL HIM.

I draw a breath, and my palms burn white, blindingly white, as the lightning bunches and readies.

Then something glints on my hand, drawing my eye, just for a moment.

A ring.

The ring I forged for the thief to give to the princess, which he gave to me instead, and with it, his heart. The symbols I myself pressed into the gold seem to shine at me: *love, undying, infinite, unity.* Symbols of power, symbols of truth. They burn into my ears, sear themselves into my soul.

Time slows.

The clouds overhead roll backward.

My thoughts stumble and reverse.

Kill him.

Kill him?

But I love him.

The moment is but a heartbeat. There is no time. With the next breath Nardukha's command will overwhelm my heart. I *will* kill him. I don't have a choice. I never had a choice.

No.

I do have a choice.

What was it Aladdin said to me, so long ago? *You can't choose what happens to you, but you can choose who you become because of it.*

I can't stop Nardukha from killing us both, but I can choose to not be the monster he wants.

Zhian still stands by the Eye, holding my lamp with one finger curled through the handle, dangling at his side.

Not trusting myself to think it through, not daring to take another precious fraction of a second, I shoot the lightning from my hands—toward Zhian. The jinn prince dodges, but not fast enough. The searing energy strikes him in the chest, doing little harm but throwing him off balance. He may hold the lamp, but he is jinn and cannot command me, so its power doesn't protect him from my attack. Before he can recover, I am upon him, driving toward him in a funnel of smoke. My arms wrap around him, and I propel us both forward, toward the great Eye of Jaal and the fiery tunnel within. As we cross the threshold, Zhian cries out and lets go of the lamp, but too late.

Time rushes forward.

The clouds overhead coil and burst with lightning.

Zhian is sucked away into the tunnel and lost to sight, screaming in fury. I begin to pour into my lamp as it hurtles toward the hungry flames. Nardukha reacts, reaching—but not fast enough.

The lamp falls

falls

falls

falls into Ambadyan fire, the only force in this world or the next capable of destroying it.

I have time only to smile, my face momentarily forming through the smoke, and to whisper to Aladdin before the bronze walls close in on me and start to melt in the flames.

"I love you."

Chapter Twenty-Eight

FORMLESS, I DRIFT.

Where do jinn go when they die? Humans are said to be destined for the godlands, where they will either dwell in ease or toil for the gods, depending on their deeds in life.

But jinn are cursed, and many believe they have no souls at all. When they die, they simply cease.

But I am still here—wherever *here* is.

Slowly I come to, my consciousness reluctant to wake. I am smoke, airy and thin, spread wide across a dark sky.

With much effort, I am able to assemble myself, finding that I am all in one piece. Instinctively I reach for my lamp, but I cannot sense it. Then I remember—it is gone. I saw it melt in the fires of Ambadya, felt the searing flames on my own skin.

My fate is tied to the lamp.

But I'm not dead.

The thought sends a jolt through me, and I take stock of my

surroundings. The sky above is dark, but there are no stars, no moon, and no clouds to obscure it. Below I see only sand, sweeping toward every black horizon.

I sink and take my human form, turning a full circle. And then I see it: the only thing to be seen for leagues about.

A door, half sunk in sand.

A door I know at once.

I open it, because I know that is what I'm meant to do. Certainty settles in that I am not in Ambadya, nor the godlands, nor the human world. Where I am, I cannot say, though my best guess is that I am still burning with my lamp, and this is some fevered hallucination. All I can do is follow the path before me.

The steps behind the door are not broken and covered in sand, as they were when Aladdin set foot here—or in the real version of *here*. Despite being sunken beneath the desert, the room looks the same it did the day I first created it, when you said you wished for a garden that would never fade, Habiba, more beautiful than any in the world.

The jeweled trees refract the light of the glowing diamonds above, scattering red, green, and blue flecks of light like dancing fireflies. Water babbles through the brook lined with rocks of silver and gold. A wind from nowhere softly shakes the emerald grass, filling the air with a musical tinkling.

I walk through the garden, feeling unattached to my own body. Ahead, I can see where I'm meant to go. The lamp sits on the throne, waiting for me. It's as if my mind is rewriting the day Aladdin and I met.

When I reach the throne, I stare at the lamp for a long moment, my eyes tracing the familiar contours with a blend of hatred and love. I've been bound to it for so long, despising it, cursing it, but it has been the only constant in my long, lonely life. It is, in a twisted way, home.

I reach out and have the strange sensation of being inside the lamp at the same time, looking out at myself, feeling myself getting closer.

But before my hands can touch it, the bronze melts, bubbling and oozing, dripping onto the floor. I jump back, my stomach wrenching, as I imagine what it would be like to be inside it when that happened. *Did* happen. May still be happening.

"What is going on?" I murmur. "What is this place? And why am I not dead?"

"Of course, you already know."

I spin and suck in a breath.

You stand before me, Habiba, dressed in the same armor and leather you wore the day you died. Your hair is long and loose, with little braids behind your ears. You shine like a goddess, but your flesh bears wounds and bruises from battle.

"A life as sacrifice," you intone, "will set you free. And isn't that what the Shaitan fears most? A jinni with the power to grant her own wishes?"

"I can't grant my own wishes."

"What do you do best but turn wishes into reality? You wished to die that the boy might live, and you made that wish come true. You opened a door to a magic long lost, far more powerful than any the Shaitan wields. A sacrifice for freedom—that is the Forbidden Wish. You made the sacrifice, now accept the consequence. Freedom bears great responsibility."

I stare at you, my mind a flurry of questions, but I can articulate none of them. With a smile, you step closer and press your lips to my forehead.

"Live, my old friend," you say. "And remember: Time is the strongest magic."

You vanish as the room begins to shake, just as it did the day Aladdin stole me away. I break into a sprint, dodging chunks of stone that fall from the ceiling. Sand pours in waterfalls all around, burying the glinting jewels. I reach the stairs and bound up them, throwing open the door—to find not a desert but a void.

The universe spins around me, stars glaring bright, galaxies pulsing bursts of color. Looking back, I see the garden collapsing into itself, getting smaller and smaller. Flame rushes toward me, and without another thought, I jump.

I fall backward and upward, feel the wind rush around me, and I lose all sense of weight and direction.

The universe unfolds around me in a dazzling dance of light and color, opening circle by circle, each curling into elaborate patterns: sun and rose, starfish and pupil, tiger's mouth and elephant's ear. I fall through their center.

Stars are born, grow old, and burst apart into new stars. Galaxies blossom like flowers, shooting out tendrils of light, teeming with life. Spinning planets circle a million bright suns, and I see it all.

I have spun out of time. I stand on the edge of eternity, looking in at all the brilliant worlds. They are strung on invisible threads in a vast tapestry, each pulling the others, everything connected by the finest of lines. As I watch, the threads quiver and hum. The universe sings a deep, eternal song, sound in waves, in deep sighs, in whispers, in swirling chords and rising, falling tones. The music of the worlds, weaving in a pattern that is both chaos and order, both beauty and terror, without beginning, without end. Tears run down my face, and I dare not blink.

I lift my eyes, above it all, and see the one weaving the stars.

Imohel, the God of Gods. He smiles and pauses briefly to touch a finger to the center of my forehead, and at his touch, I fall.

Fall through the stars.

Through time.

Through light and wind and fire.

Through smoke and a sky gray like ashes.

Nardukha stands in the same spot, staring furiously at the fiery doorway. Less than a moment has passed since I threw myself into the fire, determined that I would not repeat the past, would not strike down Aladdin as I struck you down, Habiba. Determined that this, at the end, would be *my* choice. And somehow, it worked.

Somehow, I am still here.

It takes me a moment to find myself, to determine that I am standing in the doorway, in both worlds and neither. I turn around and see flames behind me. I myself am smokeless fire that burns red and blue, indistinguishable from the blaze that separates the mortal world from the immortal.

Turning back to the human world, I see Nardukha look down at Aladdin, who stares in disbelief at the doorway, unable to see me amid the flames, believing, no doubt, that I am dead. He doesn't even struggle when Nardukha wraps a hand about his throat and lifts him into the air. But his eyes begin to widen, and he gasps with pain.

At once I step through the doorway, a girl of fire and fury, taking human form in a gown of black smoke that curls and trails behind me. Never have I burned so hot. Never have I felt so powerful, not even when granting the most incredible wishes. A new power rages through me now, something completely wild and untrammeled, and I realize what is missing: the invisible tether that bound me to my lamp. The bond has been broken.

Whether it was really you I saw, Habiba, or a ghost conjured by my mind, I know the words you spoke were true: In sacrificing my own life for Aladdin, I unwittingly triggered the Forbidden Wish. The bond between lamp and jinni is severed.

I am alive.

And I am *free*.

Chapter Twenty-Nine

"*Stop*," I say.

Nardukha drops Aladdin, who crumples to the ground. I run toward the thief, dropping to my knees at his side. He groans and blinks.

"Who are you?" he whispers.

"It's me," I reply. "Lie still. You're hurt."

"Zahra?" He seems bewildered, and suddenly I understand why. I put my hands to my face and suck in a breath, for it is not the face of Roshana I wear.

It is the face of a young Gheddan queen. *My* face. It is rounder and softer, my hair thick with brown curls and my skin a shade darker. How strange it is to wear it again, after so many years disguising myself in other forms.

"*You*," Nardukha rumbles, and I whirl to face him. There is a wariness in him that I have never seen before.

I realize I have lost something else in my strange journey

through the Eye and back: my fear of him. For four thousand years even the thought of him made my soul tremble. Now I look at him, and it's as if I see him for the first time and find him . . . lacking. What did I fear in him before? By what power did he enthrall me? Whatever it was, it is gone now, and I will never cower before him again.

"All this time," I say, rising to my feet to stand between him and Aladdin, "you've been so desperate to keep me—to keep any of your jinn—from loving a human. You knew what could happen if a jinni ever loved a human, loved one enough to *die* for them. That's why you went to war with Roshana—not because Roshana sought to make peace with the jinn, but because I loved her enough that I would have died for her. You couldn't let that happen because you knew what I would become. You knew the Forbidden Wish could work both ways."

"What you *are*," he breathes, "is an abomination. A jinni without a master, without ties to Ambadya or the gods. The order exists for a reason. I do not love chaos for chaos's sake. All things are held in balance, and you are a loose thread in the fabric of the universe. One wrong move and you could unravel everything."

"I have seen the threads of the universe, and they are stronger than you know."

Squaring his shoulders, his eyes flaring red, Nardukha exhales streams of black smoke. "It is called the Forbidden Wish for a reason, girl. I was not the one who named it so—creatures like you have been forbidden since the dawn of time."

Wings flare from his shoulders, spreading the length of the alomb. Claws sprout from his fingers and fangs from his lips. His skin shifts to smoke, his clothes to flames. He is shadow wrapped in fire, and he leaps forward, set on destroying me.

I meet the Shaitan in midair, drawing conjured blades. I raise my swords, clashing with his claws in a shower of sparks.

"You can't defeat me," he hisses, all trace of human form gone. He thrusts his head over my crossed blades, fangs snapping.

I roll aside, clear of his teeth. This fight is not going to be determined by swords and stances. Nardukha's attacks are primal and powerful, not to be overcome by human tactics.

I draw him away from Aladdin, who is struggling to his feet amid a crowd of creeping, hissing jinn. He draws a short knife from his boot and holds it up, a paltry defense against the claws of a ghul or the teeth of an ifreet.

"Leave him," the Shaitan snarls, and the jinn back away.

Then he pauses a moment, his eyes intent on me. Once, I would have cowered to be the center of his terrible attention. Now, I want only to finish this. Live or die, this is a fight I cannot abandon.

I draw a deep breath and relax, my conjured blades evaporating. I reach for my magic.

And for the first time in my long, strange life, it answers *my* call.

With a gasp, I sway and nearly topple, but gritting my teeth, I stand my ground and let it swell. Always the magic has come from a human, siphoned off them and into me.

This time, the power is born at *my* center. It is an entirely different feeling. It's dizzying and terrifying and wholly exhilarating. It spreads like white fire through my body, filling my limbs, my head, even my hair.

I can do anything. The Shaitan formed me into the most powerful of his jinn, and now I truly know what that means.

Nardukha acts first. He sends a funnel of fire shooting toward me. The blast of heat hits me first, blowing my hair back. I react instinctively, throwing up a wall of smoke to break the flames.

By then he is already on me, striking me hard in my stomach and flinging me through the alomb. I let the momentum of his blow carry me out into the open, over the side of the mountain, where I shift to smoke from the waist down and hover in midair.

The Shaitan doesn't immediately follow. Instead, he stands at the edge of the alomb and waves a hand. The clouds around the summit part, affording a view of Parthenia below. He looks at me, then at the city, and the moment I catch on, I throw myself at him.

"No!"

But he sends me reeling with a shake of his arm. Before I can recover, he directs a finger toward the summit, and the ground splinters with a succession of deafening cracks, which begin to glow red with swelling lava. The shaking of the ground knocks Aladdin to his knees, and he retreats farther into the alomb as the mountain rumbles.

"Aladdin!" I shout. "Stay down!"

Horrified, I try to dive past Nardukha to help, but he grabs me and hurls me outward. Without pausing, he issues a command to the jinn, and they rise and begin winging toward Parthenia.

"This is the price of your treachery!" he spits out. "This is the cost of your pride!"

He will destroy Parthenia, just as he destroyed Neruby and Ghedda, all to punish me.

But this time, I can fight back.

I fly away from the mountain, which begins to spew black smoke from the cracks opening in its sides. Nardukha follows, his enormous wings of shadow fully unfurled. He rolls onto his back and brushes a hand through the air, causing the stones of the mountain to break apart and rise up, igniting one by one. These he sends arcing toward me like comets.

I dodge his flaming stones while flying farther out. The sky is filled with falling fire and trails of black smoke. I blaze through them, then turn and fling my hands wide, sending a powerful wind gusting toward him. At my thought, the wind hardens into icy fangs that whistle as they speed through the air.

Nardukha crosses his arms in front of himself, breaking the icicles. I am already moving, heady from the power that pours through me in boundless amounts. Usually there is a limit to my magic, proportionate to my master's wish, and I must wield it judiciously. Now with a mere thought I release floodgates inside, fueled by my desires, hampered only by the limits of my own imagination. And after four thousand years of granting wishes, my imagination is the most powerful muscle I possess.

I conjure at a rate that dazzles even me. Fire, wind, water, stone: All the elements bend themselves to my command. I send glittering eagles of flame screaming toward Nardukha. They claw at his eyes until he dashes them into a shower of sparks.

With a snap of my fingers, a pair of dragons appear in the sky above him, one of ice, one of fire. They roar and dive, spiraling around one another, their jaws gaping to swallow Nardukha. He turns and catches each by its muzzle, and with a growl, he reduces them to tiny harmless sparrows.

Enraged now, he goes on the offensive, slinging fire and rock in a crude but effective barrage. I dissolve into smoke and race through the air, flying over Parthenia, streaking toward the cliffs. Below me, the city is in chaos, as the people catch sight of the mountain erupting above them. The fighting around the palace begins to die down as they realize a greater threat is upon them. The earth beneath the city cracks and splinters, and when the walls begin to break apart, the wards protecting the people are broken. Jinn pour into the city.

My spirit aches, longing to fly down and defend them, but I can barely hold off Nardukha.

The Shaitan is close on my tail, his massive wings beating with a sound like enormous drums, whipping up powerful gales with each stroke.

I re-form into human shape on the spot where Caspida nearly dropped me from the cliff not long ago, my back to the sea. Nardukha lands in front of me and conjures a pack of shadow wolves. They snarl and snap and salivate, and I shudder. Of all animals on the earth, wolves I hate most, as all jinn do. Wolves thirst for our flesh and take particular savage joy in hunting us. How Nardukha can even conjure them I do not know.

Nardukha's wolves leap forward at an impossible speed, fangs bared and eyes glowing. Fear courses through me, immobilizing me. Nardukha's eyes flash with triumph. I can't look away. Can't think. Can't—

No. I am a slave to fear no more.

I spread my feet and hands and call to the one thing I fear more than wolves: the sea. For a moment, nothing happens.

The wolves are a breath away. They jump high, stretching their jaws wide, revealing far more teeth than any wolf should have. Their eyes burn red in their black shadow forms, and my body seizes as I turn my face away, eyes squeezing shut, knowing this is the end.

And then the sea answers.

It rises behind me in a mighty wave, deep gray coursed with rippling veins of blue, frothing and foaming, blocking out the sun. The wolves drop to the earth and cringe, tails between their legs. I stand, arms uplifted, holding up the sea. Then, thrusting my hands forward, I send the wall of water gushing over my head, dashing the wolves away. They dissolve into puffs of smoke as the wave washes over the cliff top and pours back down, leaving several fish and one green turtle floundering on the grass. I lift them with a thought and gently drop them back into the water.

Breathing hard, Nardukha and I stare at each other for a moment. He is drenched with seawater, but it turns quickly to steam on his hot skin. His wings droop to the ground, leaving him standing tall as two humans, more coal than fire after the drenching I gave him.

"You are not the first jinni to break free of my rule. Do you wonder why you have never heard of the free jinn? Because none of them survived more than a few days. I will not allow it."

I want to reply, but I can only pant, sore and exhausted.

His wings and hands begin to glow red. He pauses, just for a moment, to say, "You could have been a queen of Ambadya. Now look at you. I will finish you, jinni. I will crush you by crushing that damnable boy."

With that, he rises and streams toward the mountain, and I race to catch up.

Sacrificing subterfuge for speed, I rise high into the sky before driving northward at a blinding pace. The sky is dark despite its being afternoon, and it is impossible to tell jinn from clouds. But they are there, flying to and fro, dropping into the city like hawks hunting mice. I dodge columns of black smoke rising from the city and race up the lava bubbling down the mountainside, its heat stifling. It has reached the city and begun to engulf the palace's north wall. As I fly, I conjure a rash of frost across the slope, and at its touch, the lava begins to cool and harden.

Nardukha has almost reached the alomb when I catch up to him. I spring on him from above, bringing us both crashing onto the obsidian floor by the Eye and nearly on top of Aladdin, who scrambles out of the way.

At once I leap up, conjuring a torrent of sand, then spread my hands wide. My sand separates and hardens into a line of shining glass warriors who advance on the Shaitan, brandishing glittering spears. Light refracts through their crystalline forms, making them seem to glow. Caught off guard by their sudden appearance, Nardukha shifts to smoke to avoid being impaled.

While Nardukha is distracted, I shift to sand and stream across the floor, re-forming behind him, conjuring a trio of tigers, one of light, one of water, one of sand.

Nardukha, snarling, is driven back by my barrage of conjurations. He is stronger than me, and I know that if I give him one moment to think, he will destroy me—for good, this time. So I don't let up. I whirl and weave, teeth gritted, hair flying, crafting creatures of sand and fire, air and water, in a dizzyingly endless barrage. Scarlet and blue tigers, flaming eagles, a massive stone bear, warriors of water and smoke. They throw themselves at Nardukha, who furiously defends himself, shredding my weaves as quickly as I can conjure them.

He may be stronger, but I am more imaginative.

And after four thousand years of practice, I am *fast*.

I gather the elements and shape them in a blur, until the air in the alomb is thick with magic, flowing in ribbons of light and curls of smoke. I conjure as I have never conjured before, throwing everything I have at him. And he is losing ground. Framed by the fiery doorway, Nardukha is a dark shadow, wings spread, fangs bared.

Light flashes off the ring on my hand as I weave, and I glance at it.

My mind stumbles.

The symbols on the ring have been obliterated, probably by the fire blast that knocked me into the sea. I realize then that I've seen this scorched ring before, before even I forged it for Aladdin.

My eyes grow wide as the weight of this crashes over me like a tidal wave, but I hesitate too long.

The Shaitan tears through my last conjuration, a glittering dragon of glass and water. With a shriek it bursts into a thousand and one tiny flashing pieces, which fall like rain around the Shaitan.

And in that moment he attacks, throwing two powerful beams of blinding lightning—but I am not the target.

Aladdin is.

I move without thinking. I spin, a trick to gather as much magic as I can hold. The lightning is so close to Aladdin that his hair crackles with it, his eyes wide.

I reach deep, deep, deep, guided by instinct, guided by the memory of my strange journey back from death. I reach through the elements, through the unseen fabric that binds the world together. I reach farther and deeper than I have ever gone before, to those threads of the element I have only seen once, when I stood on the edge of the universe—the threads of time itself.

Time is the strongest magic, your voice whispers in my thoughts.

Wrapping my fingers tight around the seconds and minutes, I twist the strands. The effort leaves me gasping, as if I've grabbed hold of a comet's tail, but I do not let go. Unlike the four main elements with which I usually work my magic, these threads are *alive* and moving. Manipulating them is like trying to change the direction of a river. And yet I stand firm, bracing myself against the flow of the hours. The tide pulls at me, courses *through* me, beginning to separate my fibers. If I hold on much longer, I will dissolve once and for all and be lost in that eternal current. Easier it would be to hold back the sea with one's hand.

But I will not let him kill Aladdin.

He took you, Roshana. He took the Gheddans. He took me, for four thousand years.

No more.

With a deep cry that wells from the bottom of my lungs, I twist the threads of time. Around me, events pause and reverse, Aladdin falling to his feet, the fragments of my sand and water dragon reforming into their original shape, the mountain sucking in bright streams of lava. Faster and faster the events unwind, flowing like a river running uphill. Deeper and deeper I dive, until the current begins pulling at me, and I must brace myself against it like an anchor dragging through the sand. When we stop, a thousand and one moments all happening and unhappening around us, only Nardukha and I stand outside it all, staring at each other as the time threads flow and pulse around us.

"How are you doing this?" breathes the Shaitan.

"I fell outside time," I reply. "I saw the gods weaving the universe."

Nardukha looks around, but I can tell by his gaze that he cannot see the threads I've twisted around him, trapping him in a single moment. He has never journeyed to death and back, as I have. He has not stood on the edge of the universe and seen the turn of the hours. And if he cannot see it, he cannot manipulate it. Finally his gaze returns to me, thoughtful, even a bit awed.

And then the fury flashes in his eyes. Nardukha opens his mouth in a wordless roar, his throat a cavern of flames, and he lunges—

I close my hands, and time collapses around him. His roar is cut off as he is washed away like a twig in a flood. The minutes swallow him up, pull him beneath the current, until he is simply *gone*.

With the last of my strength, I pull from my finger the ring I forged for Aladdin and let it fall into the current. It is swept away, lost into the flow of the hours, to land by the side of a fallen queen, to be found by her handmaidens, to wait five hundred years for the right person to put it on. With it I send a whispered prayer.

"Find me, my thief."

Then, with a soft cry, I release the threads. Something inside me snaps, and, gasping, I pitch forward into darkness.

Chapter Thirty

"ZAHRA."

My eyes open, and Aladdin is there, peering anxiously at me. He brushes the hair from my face.

"Are you all right?" he asks.

I sit up. My thoughts swim languidly through still waters. Everything is blurred and unfamiliar. Instinctively I reach out for my lamp, finding nothing but a vague tingle, as if I am missing an arm.

"I was unconscious?" I ask.

"Yes." He cradles my head in one hand. The other holds my arm. "Zahra, what did you do? What happened?"

My head aches as if it's been beaten with rocks. I groan and wrap my arms around it, trying to quell the pain. Aladdin holds me for several moments, stroking my hair, while I whimper and cringe.

"Are you all right?" he whispers. "Zahra?"

"I'm okay," I say through my teeth, pulling back a little. "What about you?"

He grins tiredly. "Alive, so I'm not complaining. Where's the Shaitan?"

I lift my head and blink rapidly, and the world reluctantly takes shape. I'm still in the alomb. Only seconds have passed, it seems, but much has changed. The sky is clear and blue, except for the tattered remnants of clouds drifting northward. The Eye of Jaal lies in two pieces, cracked straight down the center, the fiery tunnel to Ambadya vanished. All around me, massive cracks splinter the stone and the massive columns, as if a god has struck the alomb with a celestial hammer. The sight chills me; I realize that I caused it, that the magic I drew upon to trap Nardukha is greater and more dangerous than I know.

"He's gone." I ache to my core, my limbs leaden with fatigue. "Held prisoner by time. He only exists in a single moment, and he can never touch us again."

Aladdin blinks, then asks, "Will he come back?"

"No." He couldn't even see the threads that ensnared him. What must it be like to be imprisoned in a moment, to not even see the walls that trap you?

"And the jinn?"

I cross to the doorway and run my hands down its sides, then step through experimentally. Nothing happens. Walking to the edge of the alomb, I look down on Parthenia. Smoke rises from the city, but no jinn soar above it.

"They must have fled back to Ambadya. They felt the loss of their king and panicked. For ten thousand and one years the Shaitan has been the only force that joined them together. They will fracture into their ancient tribes, and they will not return for a long, long time."

"How do you know?"

Grimly, I turn and meet his gaze. "Because they know that I am here, and they know I defeated their king."

"So it's over."

I nod, a bit stunned. The world has taken on a dreamlike softness, not quite real.

"Zahra . . . what happened to you? I saw you go through the doorway, and I thought . . . I thought you were gone. Where's the lamp?"

I tell him about the jeweled garden, and the vision of you I saw. But when I reach the point where I fell through time and stars, my words fail me, and tears spring to my eyes. The beauty and purity of those moments still overwhelms me, and I wonder if I will ever truly understand all that I saw.

"I came back," I conclude. "And for the first time, my magic was my own. I'll never spend another moment in that horrible lamp."

"I still can't believe it's really you," he murmurs, running his fingers down my cheek. "This face . . . it's *yours*, isn't it?"

"The one I was born with," I admit, heat rising under my skin as I feel a surge of shyness. I look down at my hands. "Do you . . . like it?"

"Zahra."

I can't help but lift my gaze at the warmth in his tone. His eyes are shining, his lips slanted in a small smile.

"You're beautiful," he says. "I mean, you were beautiful before, of course, but knowing that this is the real you . . . I didn't think I could love you more, but I do."

I grin. "You're just glad I didn't turn out to be an old hag after all."

He laughs. "There is that," he admits.

"We should return to the city," I sigh, thinking of the fight at the palace. "Caspida needs our help."

"Can't you just magic us there?" He waves his fingers as if casting a spell, and I laugh a little and nod.

Such a small thing, moving us from here to there, but less than an hour ago it would have been impossible without a wish. I draw in a long breath, reaching for my magic.

But nothing happens.

No tingle. No rush of magic.

Because there *is* no magic. Or if there is, I cannot find it. Panicking, I reach deeper, shutting my eyes, trying to probe with my sixth sense—only to find that it, too, is cut off.

With a gasp, I open my eyes and lean against the doorway, staring without seeing.

"Zahra, what's wrong?"

"It's gone," I gasp.

"What is?" He looks me up and down. "Are you hurt?"

"I..." Thinking back to the moment when I trapped Nardukha, I remember the snap I felt deep, deep within. "I stretched too far," I whisper. "I have heard of this happening before, when a jinni goes too deep, attempts magic too big. Something breaks."

He looks alarmed. "But ... you'll get better?"

I keep reaching inward, trying everything I can, but already I know the truth. I'm still jinn, but manipulating time drained every drop of magic in me. Even my shapeshifting is gone, I realize with a sinking spirit. What am I now? Less than jinn, more than human. Still a creature of smoke and fire, but that fire is smaller now. Without magic to sustain me, I'm practically mortal. In Ambadya, I would be an outcast, ridiculed and despised, turned into a worthless slave. But here in the human world, I'm almost . . . normal.

"Zahra . . ."

"No, it's all right." I manage a smile and grasp his hand. "I'm here, I'm alive. I'm *free.*" If losing my magic is the price for saving Aladdin, then I would lose it a thousand and one times.

I rise onto my toes and kiss him, and he responds at once, pulling me closer, his hands pressing against my back. Around us, ashes flutter like rose petals, covering the ground and our hair. I barely notice. Never has he felt so real, so warm, so possible. The emptiness inside me, where magic once welled and sparked, now floods with all the hope I never dared to hope before. Always, I've held a part of me back, afraid to fully trust myself.

But now, for the first time, I do.

My magic is gone, but this seems to leave room for everything else to deepen: the taste of his lips, the texture of his cloak, the feel of my own true face. This is the first time I have kissed him with my own lips and held him with my own hands. I could go on like this forever.

But time is no longer at my command, and I reluctantly pull away. Aladdin tries to find my lips again, but I laugh softly and press my fingers to his.

"We have a long way to walk," I say. "And who knows what we will find when we reach the city?"

He groans a little, but nods. "Are you sure you're up for it?"

I want to shift into a hawk and show him just how up for it I am, but of course nothing happens. "Just you try to keep up," I say instead.

The battle is over by the time we reach the palace, hours later. Priestesses move among the wounded, and soldiers sit in little defeated groups, watched over by angry citizens. But the fight seems to have gone out of everyone. The jinn attack was brief but disastrous, and I see signs of the Ambadyan horde all over: scorch marks, smashed buildings, ripples of magic still curling through the air.

We find Caspida and the Watchmaidens at the top of the steps leading to the palace's main doors. The princess looks exhausted, and she wears a bandage around her shoulder, her clothes ripped and bloody. The other girls look no better.

"Aladdin!" She rises stiffly to greet us. "And . . ." She stares at me, uncertain.

"I'm still Zahra," I assure her. "Just with a new face. It's a . . . jinn thing."

She doesn't look entirely convinced, but she shrugs wearily. "What happened?"

"We met the Shaitan, and he fell."

She spreads her hands. "Is that all? We had jinn dropping from the sky! The wards are broken, and the Eristrati are under guard until they swear allegiance to me, so we can't possibly—"

"They are gone," I cut in. "And the alomb is destroyed. They will have to use one of the others to enter this world, but it will be many years before that happens. Princess, it is over. We won."

She stares at me for a long moment, as if afraid to believe it, but then she shuts her eyes and lets out a sigh.

"Gods be praised," she whispers. "It is over."

"What about Sulifer?" asks Aladdin. "And Darian?"

"Darian is imprisoned until we can hold a proper trial. And my uncle . . ." She winces and glances behind us.

We turn and see a stake driven into the ground, a severed head atop it. My stomach turns over, and I look away.

"He should have been tried as well," Caspida says. "But the people got to him first."

"So it really is over," Aladdin murmurs. He seems tired rather than pleased to see his lifelong enemy dead. I take his hand and squeeze it, and he gives me a little smile.

"What do we do now?" asks Ensi, looking around at the destruction.

"We mourn what has been lost," Caspida replies. "And tomorrow, we rise."

Chapter Thirty-One

I SENSE THE BOY the moment he sets foot in the garden.

I am lying on the fresh grass, holding a rose to my face and inhaling its sweet scent, and at the sound of his footsteps on the gravel path, I sit up.

"Zahra?" He looks around, his eyes brightening when he sees me. He walks over and sits, removing his turban and setting it beside him. "It's almost time for the coronation. What are you doing out here by yourself?"

"Hiding from Caspida's tailors. You're looking princely," I say, smiling at Aladdin and reaching out to run my hand along his fine red coat.

He grins and pulls me closer, into a deep kiss. In the weeks since the Invasion, as the Parthenians have come to call their clash with the jinn, we have hardly been out of each other's sight. Though no one regards him as a prince anymore, Aladdin is a regular visitor to the palace, where he has been named Queen's Liaison to the Southern District. He helps with the rebuilding efforts, which have paradoxically included a good deal of destroying as well as building, since the walls between the districts have been brought down for good in an attempt to unify the people.

I lay on my back, and Aladdin leans over me, his lips exploring the line of my jaw. I shut my eyes, wishing we could stay out here all afternoon, while the garden is deliciously deserted. But Caspida wants us both standing by her during the coronation, and we promised to be there.

"We should go," I murmur.

"Just a few more minutes. I feel like we're never alone anymore. There's always the queen or someone from the palace or . . ." His voice trails off, and he bites my earlobe playfully.

Laughing, I shove him away and sit up. "We *promised*."

He groans and drops his turban over his face.

"Aladdin." Pushing the turban aside, I run my fingers through his hair and lightly kiss his forehead.

"Have I told you I love you?" he whispers.

I smile. "Not since this morning."

"Unforgivable. I will tell you every hour of every day."

"Do not the poets say, the man who catches a fish every time he casts his line will soon tire of fishing? Now get *up*."

I stand and pull him to his feet. He comes reluctantly, wrapping an arm around my waist. We stroll into the palace to find a panicking Nessa.

"There you are!" She rushes toward us. "I've been looking everywhere!" Stopping short, she takes in our flushed faces and rolls her eyes. "You've been kissing in the bushes again."

Aladdin plucks a book from the satchel over her shoulder. "And you've been reading again. We all have our vices, Nessa."

She snatches the book back. "Hurry! They're about to start!"

It's well past midnight when I'm summoned to the queen's side. Aladdin is asleep in his old chambers, which are kept for him as a part of his new office, and when he stays at the palace I often join him. But though many of my jinn attributes are gone, I still do not sleep. Often I wander, through the palace and the city, marveling at how far I can go without worrying about the lamp pulling me back. Tonight, though, when Khavar comes to tell me Caspida wants to talk, I am sitting against one of the columns by the courtyard, feeding bits of bread to a stray goose that wandered into the yard a week ago and has since lain eggs beneath one of the fig trees.

Khavar is quiet as we walk through the palace, which has finally gone to bed after a long night of feasting in celebration of Caspida's coronation—a ceremony long overdue, but in which she refused to indulge until the city's restoration was complete. "What precedent does it set for my reign," she had put it, "if I put my desire for the crown before the needs of my people?" So though she became a queen in everyone's minds the day of the Invasion, tonight it was official, and the name of Caspida the First was inked into the great annals of the Amulen monarchy, the same annals where your name was written so long ago, Habiba.

The queen kept her old rooms. Whatever Malek's chambers are now used for, I don't know. Perhaps she auctioned them off to the clamoring nobles. Perhaps they were sealed off, as Sulifer's rooms were. A search of the former vizier's chambers brought to light many secrets into his dark magic, including various symbols of power carved into the walls and floor. He was greedy for magic, exploring dangerous arts that should never be touched, even attempting to summon jinn. Caspida, after a brief look, had ordered the entire set of rooms walled off completely. Darian's rooms were spared and given to a new occupant, since the prince left the city weeks ago, after choosing exile over imprisonment. Where he went, no one knows, but few regretted his departure.

Khavar steps out again after I am inside the queen's chamber. A single lantern burns by the bed, but the queen is nowhere to be seen. I walk through the rooms until I come to the courtyard, and she is where I expected her to be: on the grassy island at the center of the shallow pool, standing beside your statue, Habiba, where we first talked weeks ago.

Leaving my shoes behind, I wade through the water and onto the grass. The queen watches me approach, one hand resting on the base of the statue. When I stand in front of it, one stone wing blocks the full moon, making the sculpture seem to glow around the edges.

"Your Majesty." I bow. "What can I do for you?"

"Good evening, Zahra." Caspida looks up at the statue and runs a finger down your stone foot. "You know, Aladdin told me who you were, before you were turned into a jinni." She turns and regards me with a hint of fascination in her eyes. "You ruled one of the greatest cities in history. A queen in your own right."

I meet her gaze steadily and say nothing; that part of my past will always hold a measure of pain.

"I will be brief. I know the hour is late, but I won't put this off any longer." She looks at me directly. "I've asked you here because I want to invite you to join the Watchmaidens. I want you at my side. I want your counsel as you counseled Roshana. You have seen so much of the world, lived through so much history—I need you."

"No," I reply. "You don't."

She blinks. "What?"

"Caspida, you don't need me. You were ready to marry Aladdin to secure your throne. You probably would have married Darian for the same reason. All your life, people have told you that you can't do it on your own, that you need this person or that person to support you. But I have seen you rule. I have seen you battle for your people and rebuild their homes." I take her hands in mine and look her in the eye. "You don't need anyone to give you permission. Stop thinking like a princess and *be* a queen."

She stares for a long moment, and even without my sixth sense, I can see something giving way in her eyes.

"Thank you, Zahra," she whispers, embracing me. "You are truly a friend." She pulls away and clears her throat. "Well, I'm glad we understand one another. But you *will* be one of my Watchmaidens? I talked it over with the other girls, and they all want you. Even Khavar."

"Even Khavar?" I suppress a laugh. "Thank you, Caspida, but no. For four thousand years, my existence has revolved around granting the wishes of my masters. My identity has always been built on the desires of others."

She smiles and accedes with a nod. "And now you want to grant your own wishes."

I shrug. "I've got a lot of catching up to do."

"Then I will not try to persuade you further. You've earned it, Habiba."

Startled, I suck in air sharply. "What did you call me?"

Her brow wrinkles. "Habiba. It's an old word that means dear friend."

"I—I know. Sorry, I just . . . Anyway. Yes, I'd like to make a few wishes of my own."

"Starting with?" She leans in curiously.

"I want . . . it's silly."

"I promise I won't laugh."

I sigh. "I want to go to the vineyards in Ashori and eat grapes."

"Oh." She squints a bit. "Well, that sounds nice."

"There's nothing in the world sweeter than an Ashori grape. If the vineyards are still there. If *Ashori* is still there. It might have sunk into the sea or been burned by pirates or—"

"Zahra." Caspida puts her hands on my shoulders and smiles. "Go to Ashori. Take Aladdin with you. Gods know he hates being a bureaucrat. He's been getting twitchy in the meetings, making everyone edgy."

I nod slowly. "I will."

"I'll give you everything you need for your journey. You have my blessing and my thanks. Oh, and I nearly forgot." She fishes in her pocket a moment, then pulls something out. "We found this when we cleaned out Sulifer's rooms. I think you should have it."

It's the ring, the one Aladdin used to find me in the cave. I take it and gaze silently at the scorch marks on the surface, and the symbols blurred by time and fire. A ring forged with love and Ambadyan flame, impressed with symbols forever uniting two souls, no matter what centuries came between them. I wonder who found it on that mountaintop, lying beside your cold body, and placed it in the Watchmaidens' vault, where it sat five hundred years, waiting for a certain thief.

"Nardukha told Sulifer that the ring would lead to me," I say. "But how did the Shaitan know?"

Caspida raises her eyebrows. "The ring has its own legend, you know. The Amulen scholars studied it and found that it was imbued with jinn magic. The Watchmaidens took it into safekeeping, trying to hide its existence, but stories of the ring leaked out. Some believed it was the handle of the lamp, that it had broken off during the battle. Others believed Roshana had it made for the jinni, or vice versa. Through the centuries, the ring has always been linked to the queen's jinni—to *you*, I should say. But no one knew how it worked."

I slide the ring onto my finger, and it fits as perfectly as it ever did. Half-truths and lies guided it through the years, somehow bringing Aladdin to me. It is not just jinn magic that hums in the gold, but something deeper and older.

"Thank you, Caspida."

She nods. "You will always be welcome here, Zahra of the Lamp. Imohel guide you."

"And you, O Queen." I turn to go, but Caspida stops me with a brush of her fingers. When I turn back, her eyes are solemn.

"You've ruled before," she says. "So tell me, does it get easier?"

"No," I reply. "But you get stronger."

"I'm so happy," says Aladdin, "I could *kiss* you. In fact, I think I will."

"Not now, you fool, the queen is waving."

He sighs and genially leans over the ship rail to wave. The crowd is small, but everyone there matters: Caspida and the Watchmaidens, Captain Pasha and several Eristrati, and various nobles and bureaucrats. Even Dal and a few of Aladdin's old friends from the Rings.

It isn't long before we pull around the head of the cliffs and into the open sea, leaving them all behind in the misty morning gloom. The salty sea spray and pitching of the deck make me uneasy, and I hold tightly to Aladdin.

He's laughing, of course. "It's just like our old voyaging days, eh?"

"I'm surprised you remember much of them," I reply. "You spent most of the time leaning over the rail."

"*I* did? Ha. You're hilarious. Come and kiss me."

I do, and the now-familiar warmth of his lips steadies me. He tastes of salt and the wine we shared with the others at our small farewell party.

Aladdin pulls away first and lifts one of my hands to his lips, kissing the delicate henna patterns on my skin, then turning my arm over to kiss the inside of my wrist. The ship's crew makes themselves busy on the other side of the ship, giving us privacy.

"You're the most beautiful girl in the world," Aladdin murmurs. "Have I ever told you that?"

"Enough to make me wonder if your father was a parrot."

He laughs. "Look, we can see the sunrise from the stern."

Taking my hand tightly in his, he leads me at a run across the deck, both of us wobbling and stumbling from the roll of the waves. We are laughing and out of breath when we reach the stern, just as the sun begins to peek over the far horizon. The mist on the water catches the light and begins to glow soft and gold, until it seems we are sailing across a sea of clouds.

"My lady," says Aladdin, extending an arm toward the sun, "I give you gold as a token of my love."

"All I want is you," I reply. I turn and kiss him, pulling him against me, feeling the warmth of the dawn in my hair. Then I rest my head on his shoulder, simply feeling his arms around me, his heart beating against me.

"Are you cold?" asks Aladdin. "You're shivering."

"A little."

"I'll go get a blanket. And breakfast. If I can find the kitchen."

"Galley, love. It's called a galley."

"Right. Galley. Got it. I'll ask the captain. What was his name?"

"Sinbad, I think?"

"I'll be right back."

But I catch his hand. "I'm all right. Don't go yet."

He stays with me, and together we watch the sun stain the sea and sky a thousand and one shades of gold. My thumb rubs the ring on my finger, its dents and contours as familiar to me now as my hand.

So this is what it feels like to have all your wishes come true.

The End

Acknowledgments

ZAHRA'S STORY has been calling to me for years, but without a wildly talented team alongside me, this book would never have been possible. I owe a mountain of gratitude to the team at Razorbill and Penguin Random House: Jessica Almon, my peerless editor, thank you for believing in me and in Zahra, and for your critical insight as this story took shape. Working with you has been such a wonderful experience, and I'm so lucky to have your guidance! Thanks to Ben Schrank, who has believed in me since the beginning. Phyllis DeBlanche, for combing this book line by line and making sure all the i's were dotted and the t's crossed. Thanks to Theresa Evangelista for your gorgeous cover art. Tara Shanahan, Anna Jarzab, and the tireless team of marketers and publicists who helped Zahra find her audience: many thanks!

Lucy Carson, you've encouraged, guided, and inspired me all the way, and I don't know where I'd be without you. You're part agent, part jinni, part warrioress, and if I had three wishes to give, they'd all be yours!

Like Caspida and her Watchmaidens, no writer could get far without the support and encouragement of friends, and I have many to whom I owe special thanks: Lauren Miller, Tamara Ireland Stone, Beth Revis, and Megan Miranda, you were some of the very first people I told this story idea to, and without your encouragement I might never have mustered the courage to write it. Morgan Matson, Marie Lu, Jen Johansson, Brodi Ashton, Jennifer Bosworth: You were there at every stage, whether it was encouraging me early on to write it, helping me hash out the first draft with fierce word battles, or brainstorming titles around the pool. I couldn't ask for a more inspiring group of women to have around. A very special thanks goes out to Jessica Brody, without whom I'm not sure this book would have ever seen the light of day. Thank you for being my plotting guru, and for lending me your late-night brainstorming superpowers, your willingness to read, chat, or advise at any moment, and your friendship.

Certain family members were vital to the creation of Zahra and her world: my sister Katharine, the real-life Habiba, who helped with Arabic translation. My husband Ben, always there to support and encourage beyond everything I could ask for. You're my rock, my heart, my best friend. And finally, Papa. For years you asked me to write a book inspired by your homeland, and at last I can say I've done it! I'm so lucky to have the greatest grandfather in the world, and this book is, of course, all for you.